Praise for the Flavia Albia novels

'Enter the feisty, savvy and attractive Flavia Albia ... Davis continues her wonderful portrayal of the city and its inhabitants, and the delightful Flavia Alba adds an important element – the complicated status of working women.'   *The Times*

'Lindsey Davis's many fans will have been made anxious by the news that she is embarking on a news series with a new sleuth. They need not worry. Marcus Didius Falco's adopted daughter, Flavia Albia, is a wonderful creation, rendered with a surprising tenderness ... Just as closely researched and yet light-hearted as the Falco novels, *The Ides of April* is more touching.'   *Bookoxygen*

'As Flavia Albia takes over from Falco, the twisting plot mixes high politics and low life with all her classical aplomb.'   *Independent*

'Davis conjures up this teeming, vigorous era with such verve that the trip in time she offers is irresistible.'   *Express*

ENEMIES AT HOME

Lindsey Davis

HODDER

First published in Great Britain in 2014
by Hodder & Stoughton
An Hachette UK company

First published in paperback in 2014

I

Copyright © Lindsey Davis 2014

Maps by Rodney Paull

A CIP catalogue record for this title is
available from the British Library

ISBN 978 1 444 76660 8

Typeset by Palimpsest Book Production Ltd, Falkirk, Stirlingshire
Printed and bound by CPI Group (UK) Ltd, Croydon, CR0 4YY

Hodder & Stoughton policy is to use papers that are natural, renewable and
recyclable products and made from wood grown in sustainable
forests. The logging and manufacturing processes are expected to conform to
the environmental regulations of the country of origin.

Hodder & Stoughton Ltd
338 Euston Road
London NW1 3BH

www.hodder.co.uk

ENEMIES AT HOME

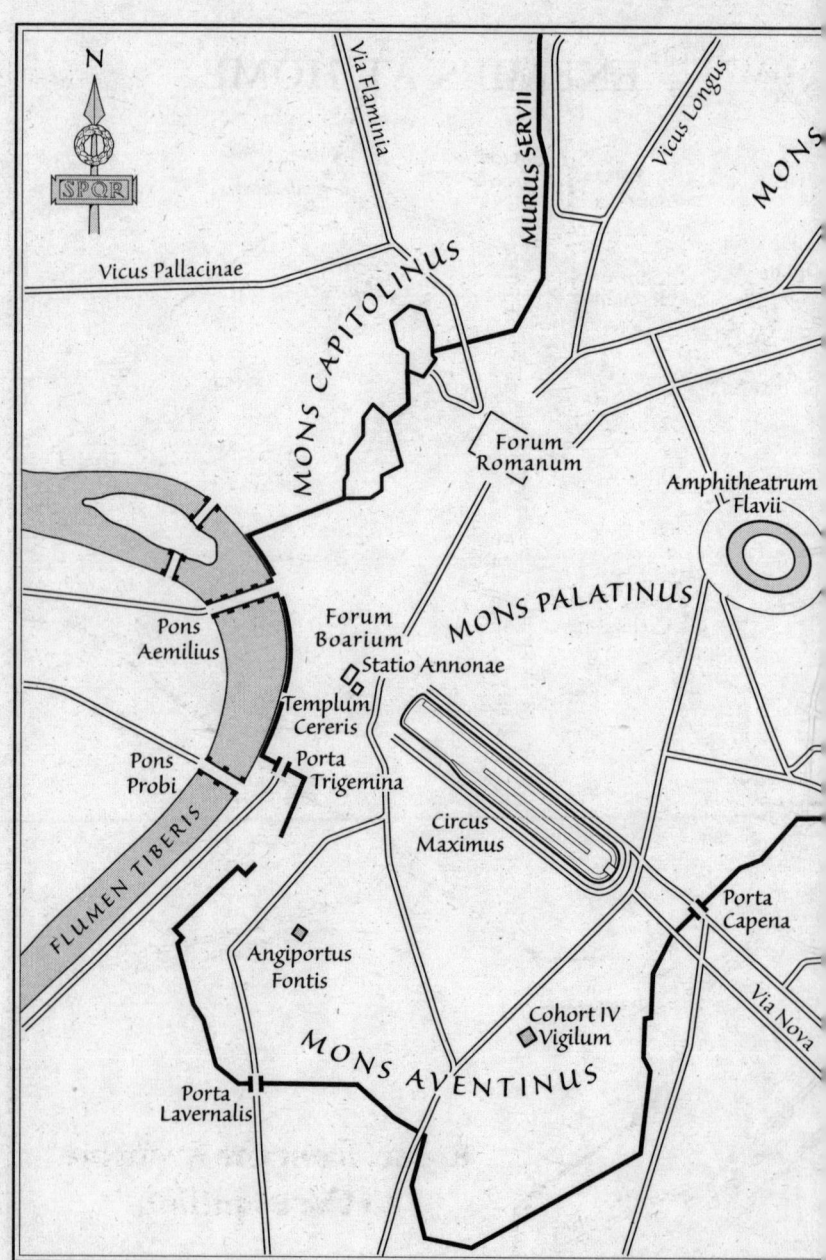

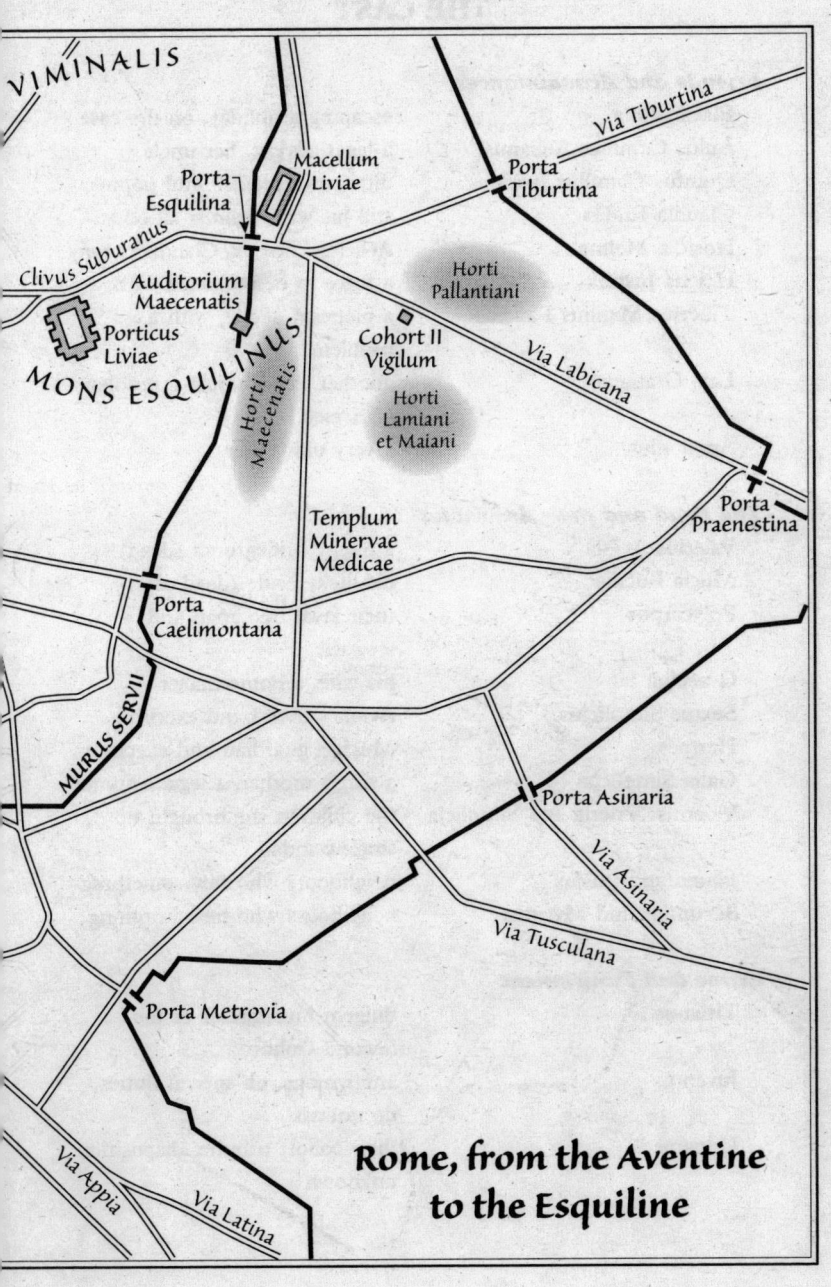

Rome, from the Aventine to the Esquiline

THE CAST

Friends and Acquaintances

Flavia Albia	escaping a holiday, on the case
Aulus Camillus Aelianus	a legal adviser, her uncle
Quintus Camillus Justinus	ditto, more raffish and popular
Claudia Rufina	still his wife, against all odds
Hosidia Meline	Aelianus' first ex, Claudia's crony
Helena Justina	a force to be reckoned with
Tiberius Manlius Faustus	a plebeian aedile, with a problem
Laia Gratiana	another ex-wife, just a problem to herself
Apollonius	a very old waiter

The Dead and their Associates

Valerius Aviola	a happy bridegroom (dead)
Mucia Lucilia	his lucky bride (dead also)
Polycarpus	their loyal freedman and steward
Graecina	his wife, a home-maker
Sextus Simplicius	Aviola's friend and executor
Hermes	Mucia's guardian and executor
Galla Simplicia	a single mother, a legacy-hunter
Valerius, Valeria and Simplicia	the children she brought up single-handed
Fauna and Lusius	neighbours who saw something
Secundus and Myrinus	neighbours who heard nothing

Crime and Punishment

Titianus	diligent investigator of the Second Cohort
Juventus	anonymous, on special duties, do not ask
Unnamed	their cohort tribune, disposition unknown

Cassius Scaurus	caring tribune of the Fourth Cohort
Fundanus	on contract for torture and burials
Old Rabirius	a shadowy capo
Young Roscius	a coming threat
Gallo	fixer and trusty, do not trust him
A prisoner	a dead man

Slaves, various

Dromo, Gratus, Libycus, Amethystus, Diomedes, Daphnus, Phaedrus, Nicostratus (not for long), Chrysodorus, Melander, Amaranta, Olympe, Myla (and a baby), Gratus, Onesimus (off the scene), Cosmus

Pets

Puff	a spoiled lapdog, a bad girl
Panther	itching for trouble, a good boy

ROME, the Esquiline Hill:

June AD89

I

Even before I started, I knew I should say no.

There are rules for private informers accepting a new case. Never take on clients who cannot pay you. Never do favours for friends. Don't work with relatives. Think carefully about legal work. If, like me, you are a woman, keep clear of men you find attractive.

The Aviola inquiry broke every one of those rules, not least because the clients had no money, yet I took it on. Will I never learn?

One warm, starry June night in the city of Rome, burglars invaded a ground-floor apartment on the Esquiline Hill. A large quantity of fine domestic silverware was taken, which people assumed was the primary target. The middle-aged couple who rented the fashionable suite had married only recently, which made what happened to them more poignant. After the robbers left, their bodies were found on the marital bed, amid signs of violent struggle. Both had been strangled.

The dead couple were wealthy enough to merit an investigation, a privilege that was generally thought too good for the poor, though it was normally available to victims who had left behind influential friends, as was the case here. Enquiries were first assigned to a vigiles officer, Titianus of the Second Cohort. In fairness, Titianus was no more inept than most vigiles. He knew that two plus two made four – unless he happened to be preoccupied with watching a good cockfight, when he might inadvertently say five. But he had a decent record of arresting pickpockets in the Market of Livia. For about two hours he even thought that trying to solve a double murder was exciting. Then reality set in.

Titianus found it impossible to identify the thief or thieves. After asking around a bit, he turned his attention to the household, declaring that this must be an inside job. Inevitably his gaze fell on the owners' freedmen and slaves. The freedmen were mature, articulate and well organised; that was how they had managed to gain their liberty and how they now bamboozled Titianus. The slaves were more vulnerable: younger and naive, or else older and plain dim. Nobody ever said any of them had threatened their master and mistress, but to a law officer in Rome any culprits were better than none and with slaves no real proof was necessary. They could be accused, tortured, prosecuted and executed on simple probability. Titianus put on a clean tunic to look good, then went and announced to his cohort tribune that he had the answer. The slaves did it.

The slaves got wind of their plight. They knew the notorious Roman law when a head of household was murdered at home. By instinct the authorities went after the wife, but that was no use if she was dead too. So unless the dead man had another obvious enemy, his slaves fell under suspicion. Whether guilty or not, they were put to death. All of them.

The good thing about such systematic capital punishment, occurring in public of course, was that it helped make other slaves, of whom there were hundreds of thousands in Rome, more well behaved. The proportion of masters to slaves was

4

very small so nobody wanted this big slave population to get the idea of staging a rebellion. In our city it had been decided not to dress slaves in any distinguishing way, because then they might realise the power of their own numbers.

Many owners lived in constant fear of slaves turning against them. You cannot batter loyalty into a sullen, captive foreigner and neither can you even guarantee that kindly treatment will gain their gratitude. In Rome, executing slaves who betrayed their masters was extremely popular therefore. At least it was among the slave-owning classes.

Terrified, and with good reason, some of the accused slaves bolted from the elegant Esquiline house and took refuge a distance away at the Temple of Ceres. By tradition, this monument on the Aventine Hill offered a haven for refugees. They could claim sanctuary, be kept safe and even hope to be fed.

In theory, the authorities fostered the great temple's famous role as a focus of liberty and protector of the desperate. However, nobody wants to take fine ideals too far.

In a swift, panic-stricken meeting just after dawn, the issue of how to get rid of the fugitives was handed to a magistrate whose duties gave him close connections to the temple. His name was Manlius Faustus, one of that year's plebeian aediles, and I knew him. I liked his methods. He always stayed calm.

Charged with solving the problem, Faustus solemnly agreed with the Temple of Ceres authorities that it was important to take the correct action. This situation could easily turn ugly. They wanted to avoid censure. The public were shouting for a solution, preferably bloody. The *Daily Gazette* had already asked for a quotable comment and was about to feature the story in its scandal section; publication would fire lurid Forum gossip. The unseen eye of the emperor was probably on the Temple. Faustus had been handed a rather hot platter here.

As this dutiful man tried to come up with ideas, he walked to a bar called the Stargazer. There, while he pondered the meagre choice for breakfast, he ran into me.

2

I had seen the aedile coming – always a good idea with magistrates who can impose large fines. Anyone who runs a market stall, anyone with a pavement outside their premises, anyone whose profession is heavily regulated (any prostitute, for instance), loathes aediles. Informers like me avoid them. My relatives who ran the Stargazer would not thank him for eating there, given that part of his job was the regulation of bars. They would not thank me either. They would think he had chosen it because he knew it was my local.

I had first met Faustus a few weeks before, working jointly on an investigation and sometimes putting our heads together in this very caupona. I had known him to go about in disguise, though not today. He was a solid man in his mid-thirties, who came down the drab street with a steady tread. He had no flashy train of attendants, relying on his purple-striped tunic to deter trouble-makers. Aediles were not given bodyguards. They were sacrosanct, protected by religious laws. Besides, he was obviously tough; even when he was preoccupied, Faustus looked as if he punched his weight. That was assuming people even noticed him; he was not the kind of official who made a lot of noise wherever he went.

He cannot have expected to see me sitting at a table. He

thought I was with my family at our villa on the coast, though I had recently come back to Rome because I was tired of sun, sand and fishing expeditions. Before anyone wonders, I was not hankering for Faustus. I might be a fancy-free widow, but a magistrate was way out of my league.

'Flavia Albia!'

'Manlius Faustus.'

Formal name terms. After he ordered a bread roll with Lucanian sausage, the Stargazer's only deal that morning (or any morning), he took a seat at my table, though he asked permission first.

'Mind if I join you?'

'Always a pleasure.'

'Good to see you.'

'You too, aedile.'

Play acting. We were both unsure. The last time we met, I made embarrassing advances, which Faustus sensibly rejected. Despite my gaffe, the aedile had expressed a hope we might work together again. Being polite, I thought. Still, here he was in my aunt's horrible bar.

Manlius Faustus had responsibilities for neighbourhood law and order – fair trading, clean streets, quiet baths and decorous brothels. I knew he was currently advising magistrates in other districts too, as they tackled a rash of random street killings that were happening throughout Rome. We lived in troubled times. The Vesuvius calamity, a decade ago but still vivid in the memory, had shaken people. We now had a paranoid emperor, who at just short of forty was still young enough to inflict many years of dread upon us. Our empire's borders regularly came under attack from barbarians, so there was constant unsettling military talk. The city was also full of bitter satirists, outlawed philosophers and pouting poets who had failed to win prizes. In this climate all kinds of madness flourished.

As for me, I was a private investigator. Don't point out it's an unusual job for a woman; after twelve years, I had heard that enough times. I was hired by clients who wanted help when life went wrong – or sometimes before it happened: parents checking out gold-diggers their silly daughters had fallen for; small traders whose rivals were stealing business; litigants searching for witnesses to back them up in court; executors of wills who feared they were inheriting large debts. Many of my enquiries led to divorce. Most clients were sad people: either hopeless idiots who had caused their own predicament or well-meaning innocents who had been targeted by fraudsters.

Faustus glumly tapped his bread roll, which was definitely yesterday's. He looked around. The Stargazer stood on a corner, with the usual arrangement of crazy-patterned marble counters at right angles where, come lunchtime, big pots of unappetising broths would attract more flies than customers. Inside, a wonky shelf had been nailed to a wall, using too-short nails. Beakers in various sizes were perched on it, ready to crash off when the fixings gave way. A faded sign on one wall offered varieties of wine, with illegible notes of their prices. Falernian was permanently listed, though always 'sold out' if you asked for it. Mostly the bar was visited by local labourers in search of cheap scoff. They would stand in the street, snatching a bite and a drink. Sit-down diners were rare.

Old Apollonius, who called himself the head waiter, leaned on one counter and stared into space. My aunt or my cousin would come in later; Aunt Junia was an abrasive character

9

who should never have been running a bar, but her son, Junillus, made the best of this sad place.

A stray dog snuck in for a sniff around; she didn't like it and left quickly. The second table indoors was empty, which was all too normal.

Making conversation, I described to Faustus my boredom with sun and seaside stuff. He patiently listened, then told me about the double murder on the Esquiline and needing to remove the fugitive slaves from the temple. He never gave much away, but I could tell he felt despondent.

He was sturdy, in the way of plebeian Romans, though taller than many and not bandy-legged. He had that way of implying he thought himself affable, while in fact remaining reticent. His eyes were grey, which does happen; mine were too, though his had no blue tint but were entirely pale, like the mist that comes off the Tiber at dawn. His dark hair was not yet tinged with grey, though gave the impression it might be soon. When he bothered to shave and spruce up, he was a fine-looking man. He had bothered today.

Faustus speared his sausage slice on the point of his own pocket-knife then gingerly tasted it. Even the Stargazer could do little damage to a bought-in Lucanian, so he cheered up. I reached over and pinched a gherkin that Apollonius had plonked on as a garnish. Faustus let me do it but quickly nipped up the other gherkin himself. We were easy together, for some reason that I never troubled to analyse.

He started complaining that the Esquiline, where the Aviola couple were murdered, was not his patch. When a group of new aediles began their year in office, they divided up Rome, each hoping to get areas that produced high revenues. They couldn't take the income home (well, not legally), but public service is all about 'my record is shinier than yours'. Each wanted to win the fines challenge. Success would attract votes if ever they stood for election again, or at least they might be rewarded with some minor priesthood.

Faustus had managed to get jurisdiction of the Aventine, home ground for both of us and a busy hive of wrongdoers. The Esquiline was one of the other Seven Hills, lying beyond the Circus Maximus and the Forum. It was not an area I knew well and Faustus seemed to think little of it.

'I need to find out what really happened in the apartment that night, Albia. If the slaves are exonerated, they can go home. We are stuck with them until then.'

'You're even stuck with them if they are guilty – they have sought asylum.'

'Don't I know it! I have to prove somebody else is guilty.' As Faustus leaned back in his seat and considered me, I saw where he was heading: 'I don't have the time; I need an agent.'

'What about the vigiles?'

Succinctly, Faustus described Titianus of the Second Cohort.

'Well, I can't help you,' I warned, getting in first. 'I welcome new work, but not an exhausting trek over there every day.'

Faustus smiled sweetly. I was too experienced to fall for that. 'I could organise some accommodation nearby,' he offered. 'And for assisting the Temple of Ceres, your fee would be worth having.' I was tempted. I was short of work after my holiday. The temple could afford to pay well, since it benefited directly from all the fines the aediles slapped on people. 'Go on,' he urged. 'It's fascinating, Albiola. You know you want it.' It always disturbed me when he used that diminutive, which he had invented.

I outlined for him why no informer would do this: the

11

impossibility of tracking down the burglars now Titianus had muddied the trail, the difficulties of making slaves give reliable answers, the need for speed, the risks of any inquiry that was conducted in the public eye . . .

'You are exactly the woman. Discreet, shrewd and no-nonsense,' Faustus flattered me.

'Damn you, Tiberius.' I was not being over-familiar; he used his first name when working incognito, as he had been when I first met him.

'I am delighted you accept. Do you need a written contract?'

'I believe I do,' I answered coldly. 'Let me draft it; then I can specify draconian terms.'

Faustus grinned as he ordered up more breakfast. He could afford to be cheerful. His troubles were over. Mine were just beginning.

At least he told Apollonius to bring Lucanian sausage for me too. 'Make that with big Colymbadian olives on the side and double gherkins!' I growled, exploiting my new employer, who agreed it with a look of resignation.

To be honest, I fancied working with him. He was an interesting character.

I was already planning where to start. I told Faustus that the first thing the Temple of Ceres must pay for was decent legal advice. I happened to know two lawyers who were no more devious than normal and who, for the kind of money a religious body paid, would certainly oblige.

My uncles. Yes, I know what I said about never working with relatives, but the Camillus brothers were always so skint they would welcome this.

3

I sent a message to warn them. The aedile provided an errand boy. Even though Faustus was nominally alone, any man of affairs has an attendant, who tags along then sits on the kerb outside, waiting for orders. They squat there unnoticed among all the other slaves who are kicking their heels while their masters lurk in bars. At night, some streets are lined with rows of cute little boys asleep on their lanterns; in the day, pavements are clogged with liveried flunkeys, playing board games in the dust. High numbers make their owners look swanky. Faustus genuinely did not care about that, but had a lad with him for convenience.

Later that morning I took the aedile to meet my mother's younger brothers. They occupied a pair of houses at the Capena Gate, which sits in the old Servian Wall, just past the end of the Circus Maximus. Faustus and I walked down from the Aventine together in silence, but as we ducked under the dripping arches of the notoriously leaky Claudian Aqueduct, trying to cover our heads, I briefed him.

'They are Aulus Camillus Aelianus, senior of the two, and Quintus Camillus Justinus. We'll go in first to see Justinus then we'll probably adjourn to Aelianus' house.' Faustus failed to ask why I preferred to start with Justinus. That saved me having to tell him. 'Justinus is very much a family man; no one gets much quiet thinking done where he lives. His brother's house is the opposite, as dead as an old tomb in a necropolis. He is on his third wife, but the marriage is failing.'

'That's sad,' Faustus observed conventionally, steering me around some of the beggars who lurked under the aqueduct. 'Children?'

'Fortunately no.' Aelianus, an awkward character, would probably have been a high-handed father. 'Both my uncles are in the Senate, although it was a big financial struggle. I don't know all the details, except that my father contributed.'

'Generous.'

'He had worked with both. Still does. You know how Roman families operate.'

Faustus nodded. He himself lived with an uncle; they shared business interests and perhaps other sins. 'The Camilli are now a partnership?'

'Yes, but on sometimes spiky terms.' The pair had matured slightly when they hit their late twenties and came good as court prosecutors, which is almost a respectable career. But they were temperamentally different and Justinus had once eloped with Claudia Rufina, a Baetican heiress who had really come to Rome to marry his brother. Years later, it still rankled. The brothers were thirty-nine and forty now. Old enough to be consuls, though for them it would never happen. They lacked the right political friends. My father reckoned that was what made them decent and likeable.

'Are they good, or just your uncles?'

'They are good.' They really were. He gave me a look. 'Honestly, Faustus.'

'And you work with them?'

'Sometimes a case benefits from a woman's touch.'

Yes, and sometimes those two casual lads were just too lazy to do the legwork themselves.

Camillus Justinus' house looked half-painted; I could not remember any maintenance being done since my grand-parents' time. We were admitted by an age-old Janus who had rudely forgotten my name even though I had cursed him a hundred times before. A desultory housekeeper showed us to a salon where a sleepy serving boy just stared at us. Faustus and I exchanged glances; we were both thinking about slaves and their habits today.

Claudia, my aunt, popped her impressive nose around a door, rattled an armoury of bangles, evaluated Faustus, and disappeared. She was well-groomed and jewelled up (Spanish olive oil money) but she flapped about the house with the long-suffering air of a mother of six whose husband was more loyal to her bank-boxes than to her.

My uncles turned up together. They looked furtive, as if they had been gossiping about how I came to know an aedile. A slew of young children tumbled into the room with them; Justinus rounded up his offspring and shooed them out again, arms wide, like a farmer penning heifers, yet he somehow projected gravitas. Aelianus looked as if he had indigestion, which was understandable in a man who had just sworn that his third marriage was absolutely the last, and who was brooding on how he would have to hand back yet another dowry. Despite having already spent it.

I performed light-hearted introductions: 'Aulus Camillus Aelianus: trained in Athens and Alexandria, past son-in-law to the eminent law professor and legendary social drinker, Minas of Karystos.' Aelianus scowled, not because he was ashamed of being taught by that great Greek symposium boozer, but at my allusion to his first wife. The rest of us once viewed Hosidia Meline as an interloper, but her father had shamelessly divorced her from Aelianus in order to marry her to someone richer; insultingly, it was a mere six months after Aelianus wed her. But that was long enough for Hosidia to form a warm friendship with her fellow foreigner, Quintus' wife, and now she was never out of their house. This deeply irritated Aelianus.

'Quintus Camillus Justinus: trained in Rome and at what he calls the University of Struggle. At least it has cheap fees.' Lovely Uncle Quintus, the better-looking younger one. Affable, talented, everyone adored him, even his put-upon wife. That was how the rascal got away with being rascally.

'Tiberius Manlius Faustus: plebeian aedile.' Faustus nodded and said nothing, though I knew he was not shy.

Just outside the doors, rioting children ended their game in ear-splitting wails as one fell over and pretended he had hurt himself. We hastily migrated to Aelianus' house through a communicating door.

Our new location was peaceful and neat, with swept floors and up-to-date wall frescos, but it always had a cold, unscented emptiness. If I had lived there, I would have filled it with puppies, fed birds in the garden, and hired a lyre player. Then I would have evicted Aelianus and had an affair with a furnace-stoker.

Let us not discuss my tragic history with Aulus Camillus Aelianus.

While Faustus outlined the Aviola murders and the slaves' flight to the temple, I scooted to the kitchen where I organised tisanes and what Father calls nicknackeroony comports. In my relatives' homes, the wise seek out their own refreshments.

Only my mother is a thoughtful hostess. In the Aelianus ménage everything was there if you hunted for it, not just dates and miniature pastries but a perfectly willing little tray carrier. Three hauls of wedding presents had made Aelianus the owner of many matching fancy bowls. His wives tended to abandon the pottery and carry off his cash, insofar as cash existed.

He could have set up a food bowl stall, but lacked the charisma to be a successful salesman. Besides, for a senator, involving himself in retail would be breaking the rules.

I arrived back at the conference just as Faustus finished: 'So my task will be identifying who really committed the murders, so the slaves can be evicted from the temple without offending the goddess. The Esquiline is not my jurisdiction, but I have been given a free hand.'

'Oh, you mean *I* find the killers for you, then you sponge me out of the picture,' I grumbled, asserting myself in the conversation.

Faustus replied quietly, 'You know I give you credit.'

My uncles observed this exchange shrewdly.

We reclined on couches as we talked. Aelianus ignored the refreshments. Justinus ploughed into his brother's snacks as if he had eaten no breakfast. Of course he had. In homes full of children, breakfasts go on for most of the morning chaotically.

He mumbled through a mouthful of pastry, 'We need to remember what Seneca said: "Every slave is an enemy." Most owners are paranoid that their staff are plotting against them.'

'So often true!' Aelianus had gone to another room, returning with his muscular arms full of legal scrolls. He now found his way around the documents by means of papyrus slips that he must have inserted earlier while preparing for this meeting.

Both my layabout uncles enjoyed taking an instruction. They emphasised that until I had seen the location and interviewed those involved, all they could tell us was general law.

'Today we are just setting out the principles. I hate these cases,' Justinus complained. 'The traditional approach was to condemn all the slaves who were in the house. More recently, that kind of mass cull became unpopular and I would argue to have this dealt with liberally. Single out the culpable, but ignore the rest. If this couple were wealthy, are we talking about substantial numbers?'

'No.' Faustus shook his head. 'After their wedding, they had planned to go to a villa that Valerius Aviola owned in Campania. Almost all the household had been sent on ahead. There was some delay, I don't know what, so the couple were slumming it in Rome overnight with a skeleton staff.'

The small list of suspects had been a sweetener for making me take the job. I would not have agreed if there were big squads to investigate.

Aelianus' advice was practical and focussed: 'Start by asking specifically who was in the bedroom. Were any attendants present when the thieves rushed in? If so, they absolutely ought to have defended their master, regardless of risk to themselves. Identify any who failed to help, and any who did try to defend their master but were unsuccessful.'

'Not forgetting,' argued Justinus, who never entirely agreed with his brother, 'those elsewhere who *might* have assisted, but who were unaware an assault was happening.' He told me to list the Aviola household and draw a plan of the apartment, plotting people's whereabouts. Well, obviously I would do that. 'Albia, check who was within earshot. Was it night? Had the whole household gone to bed? Were the newly-weds . . .?' He tailed off demurely.

'At it?' I suggested, looking helpful.

'Enjoying a full marriage . . .'

Most couples in Rome made love with half the household listening in. Often with servants right there in the room. 'If they were wrestling conjugally,' I teased, 'any cries for help might have been mistaken for joyous sound effects.'

Faustus shot me a prudish look, but Justinus simply carried on. 'If they liked privacy and were alone together, it's critical whether any slaves nearby could hear calls for help. You might even ask how loudly could the murdered couple shout? What about slaves who were hard of hearing and have an excuse? You see what I mean.'

Aelianus must be growing long-sighted. He leaned back and squinted down his nose at a scroll as he put in his thoughts: 'The law is usually interpreted as saying that any slaves in the house had a duty to come running. But does "in the house" mean in other rooms or corridors, or does it include the garden or grounds, or even the street outside, if shouts and screams might reach that far? Think about that as you negotiate the apartment.'

I had a vision of conducting aural experiments. Standing in different places and yelling 'Help!' while an assistant checked off results on a list . . .

'You sound as if you would like to put these questions to a court.' Faustus looked nervous. He must be hoping the Temple of Ceres would not have to pay for litigation, simply to fund my crazy uncles' professional curiosity. With slaves, the authorities had probably thought there would be no trial.

'Good advocates try to avoid lawsuits,' returned Justinus, smiling.

'Too expensive?'

'Too prone to uncertain outcomes.'

'You distrust juries?'

'Seen too many.'

'You said silverware went missing. What about the burglars?' demanded Aelianus, changing tack.

'Persons of interest – serious interest, clearly,' said Faustus.

'But persons unknown? Aedile, do not involve Flavia Albia in tracing them.'

Before I could flare up, Justinus stressed the point. 'My niece is special to us, Faustus. My brother and I stand *in loco parentis* when necessary.'

'Nuts!' I shrieked. 'Your brother and you aren't fit to be *in loco* to a worm!' I realised the idiots must have talked over the dangers to me before Faustus and I arrived. I had to steer them all off this subject. No informer should allow a bunch of men to quibble about how she conducts her enquiries. 'Uncle Quintus, you know perfectly well Didius Falco has nominated an old Bithynian freedman as his daughters' guardian.' Turning to Faustus, I joked, 'My father holds the traditional view that any woman without a father or husband should be placed in the care of a lecherous fraud with his filthy eyes on her money – as if my sisters and I couldn't fritter away our property for ourselves.'

'I thought Falco chose Nothokleptes, that disaster of a banker he uses,' grinned Justinus, happily sidetracked. 'That way, the cash can just be reassigned in a ledger and won't even need to be physically moved.'

'He told me he had found a degenerate priest.' Even

Aelianus played the game. 'One who likes pretending he's the Pontifex Maximus and beating naughty girls on their bottoms with rods.'

'I imagine Flavia Albia can run rings around the guardian system.' Faustus was rubbing a scar on his hand where I had stabbed him with a meat skewer once; he was subtly reminding me how I had once over-reacted to something he said. There was no need to explain that to the uncles.

Aelianus returned to his original caveat. 'The point is, aedile, we cannot sanction sending our dear niece among violent criminals.'

'Not an issue,' replied Faustus, stiffening up. 'I admire Flavia Albia's work, and I have witnessed her personal courage, but my intention is to use other means to follow up the burglary.'

He probably just that moment decided. Until the Camilli acted up, Manlius Faustus, the fast-thinking plebeian rich boy, had seen me as a tough, street-savvy worker he could send anywhere. He would have been right. I would have done whatever was necessary. Now, half the inquiry had been whipped away from me.

They agreed that the more tiresome task – detailed interviews with members of the Aviola household – was suitable for me. I groaned at the prospect of mumbling pot-scourers, shrine-tidiers and clothes-attendants, but I let the men enjoy the thought that they could snooze in their studies, overlooked by busts of poets, while I wasted note tablets on domestic minutiae.

In the end they would claim the credit for whatever I learned. Yes, I had been a female informer for a long time. I knew all the disadvantages.

'It should be simple,' Uncle Quintus assured me. 'Remember the proverbial answer: *the cup bearer did it.*'

4

M arry in June. May is a month of ill-omen, but once it is over the goddess Juno presides kindly over couples who unite in her festival period, slathering them with good prospects, including fertility for those who can abide babies.

Camillus Justinus and Claudia Rufina had married in May, though that was in North Africa where different gods preside. I was adopted into the family after that, but relatives who pursued the eloping couple were still shocked that during their trip they had to watch another uncle of mine being killed by an arena lion. Even in my family, this counts as an unusual day out. They were all thankful for a bridal bash to take their minds off the screams, despite Claudia's visible qualms about marrying Quintus. Still, weddings should be traditional and nothing beats watching a young bride riven by huge doubts, does it?

Marcus Valerius Aviola and Mucia Lucilia were a mature couple, so presumably knew what they were doing. They can never have had much anxiety, except in their last frightful moments. Theirs was a perfectly conventional wedding, properly in June. They died on their second night together. I arrived at their apartment a week later. Their funerals had already taken place and unfortunately the apartment had been tidied. I like to inspect a crime scene with any blood or tangled bedsheets still *in situ*.

Manlius Faustus accompanied me to the Esquiline, still intent on finding accommodation for me. My idea was a room above a bar: anonymous, local, quiet by day when I wanted to review my notes, handy for eats, safely full of people at night. My headstrong employer had other ideas. He seemed to think I would drink cheap wine and pick up men. Well, those were traditional male Roman fears about women, and he hadn't known me very long. I assured him that I like to be sober when I'm man-hunting.

He then came up with a gem: I should stay in the Aviolas' guest room, at the heart of the inquiry. 'Rent-free to the temple? What misers! Oh Faustus. You really think it's wise for me to live where a violent murder was committed?'

'Dromo will sleep on a mat outside your door each night.'

'Oh spare me that, aedile!'

Dromo was the slave Faustus took about with him. I knew Faustus' uncle normally purchased better specimens, so I guessed this loon had turned out badly and been dumped on the aedile, who seemed an oddly docile nephew.

The boy was about sixteen, podgy, sullen, and he smelt. In a city where baths were so plentiful, with many free even for slaves, Dromo must pong on purpose. He certainly didn't copy his horrible hygiene from his master. Up close, Faustus was sweet and fresh, I happened to know. 'You can use him as a messenger, Albia. Somebody has to bring me your daily action notes.'

'Who says I am sending you notes?'

'I do.'

In our one previous case together, we had both enjoyed

the way the magistrate tried to play the stern monitor and I kicked against it. Now I stared him in the eye until eventually he ducked his head like a submissive dog, allowing himself a tight smile.

I told him he ought to smile more often. 'It makes you look rather appetising.' He tried to ignore that, though he came close to blushing. The man was fun to tease, although I suspected no one else ever did it. He had been unmarried for years and from the little I knew about the uncle he lived with, his only visible family, Tullius was not the type.

Of course he was entitled to progress reports. It was a routine part of my service. 'Daily' might be pushing it, but I was not foolish; until we apprehended the killer, I wanted somebody else to be aware of my movements. Faustus knew it would not give him supervision rights.

Or maybe he thought it did. He would soon learn.

The long stroll over from the Aventine confirmed that Rome really is built on Seven Hills, and they are highly inconvenient. Three, the Quirinal, Viminal and Esquiline, are steep ridges that run down in parallel and dominate the northern part of the city, getting in your way whenever you try moving about. Most easterly is the Esquiline, which lies mainly outside an ancient fortification, the so-called Servian Walls; the rampart overlooks an area that was once unhealthy and full of graveyards, though now some parts have been reclaimed and fancied up. People who think themselves quite grand nestle alongside workshops with unneighbourly trades and the destitute.

On the city side of the old embankment lurks Nero's Golden House, a madman's playground that once covered the Forum and beyond. Down at the bottom of the Esquiline stands the

Temple of Minerva Medica. Up at the top is the Market of Livia, named after the Empress who also built an elegant Porticus in this region, full of fountains and an enormous vine that covered all the walls. Livia's Market is by the Esquiline Gate, where the main road that runs under the arch arrives from the once-rough district called the Subura.

On this road, the Clivus Suburanus, Faustus and I found the Aviola apartment. It took us several tries, asking where Aviola lived, so he was not well-known in the district. Faustus played things unobtrusively but when I despaired of his approach, I walked into a bar and mentioned the robbery and deaths; all the gossipy waiters rushed to point out the crime scene.

It was a discreet house with several shops fronting its pavement, between which staircases led to upper levels. As was common in Rome, a substantial building had been divided internally then leased out in as many lucrative units as possible. The best suite occupied most of the ground floor, including an enclosed courtyard. This had been rented for some years by Valerius Aviola, I guessed expensively. Here he had brought his new bride after their wedding. Here they had died, before passion or economic rationale had had any chance to grow jaded.

Our first contact was the household steward, a freedman called Polycarpus. He looked as if his geographical origins were somewhere eastern, with chin stubble up to his cheekbones as if he came fresh from the desert. Even so, he spoke adequate Latin and had absorbed all the Roman myths about masculine superiority. He ignored me, but was perfectly pleasant when Faustus explained his official interest; the freedman readily agreed I could lodge there temporarily.

He showed Faustus the room. It was in a good position, just to the right of the main entrance area. Over the aedile's shoulder I could see that it had fancy frescos and a geometric mosaic floor, but was barely furnished. Only a bed with a footstool alongside and an empty cupboard. I don't ask for flower garlands, but a chamberpot would have been handy.

'Our guests are people of status who tend to bring their own home comforts,' Polycarpus explained, still addressing all remarks to Faustus. 'Shall I find a few bits for the lady . . .?'

'Don't bother,' I snapped.

I was not ready to interview the freedman, well, not while Faustus was lingering. I said I would see Polycarpus first thing next morning, to discuss what precisely had happened and who had been in the apartment when the murder took place. I shooed Faustus away as soon as I could, then set about familiarising myself with my surroundings.

Even before Faustus took his leave, their apartment seemed extremely quiet. Once he had gone, it was sepulchral.

Very pleasant.

I settled down on my bed to read a list of the refugee slaves, which had been given me by Faustus. Ink on papyrus. Nice lettering. Only later would I realise that even though he came from a home packed with staff, and could also call on the publicly employed secretaries in the aediles' office, he wrote this himself. Charming. I do like a man who pays attention to my personal needs.

He listed those who took sanctuary at the Temple of Ceres by name, age, sex and occupation.

Amethystus, approx. 50, general work in house
Daphnus, 18, tray carrier/table attendant
Phaedrus, 24, litter bearer/door porter
Nicostratus, 28, litter bearer/door porter
Chrysodorus, approx. 40, philosopher
Melander, 20, scribe
Olympe, 15, musician
Diomedes, 47, gardener
Amaranta, 29, attendant/adorner to Mucia Lucilia
Libycus, 36, body slave/dresser to Valerius Aviola

No cup bearer. Still, I prefer the other proverb. *The flute girl did it.*

I wondered if Olympe, 15, wore ankle chains and had wanton eyes? My father reckons castanets are always suspect – but most Roman men get excited when talking about foreign female entertainers. My mother points out that it is not necessary to have a big bosom to play the lyre well; in fact the opposite. Too much anatomy gets in the way.

Polycarpus turned up again while I was still pondering. He was clearly drawn by curiosity though he said he needed to explain arrangements for my meals: there were no kitchen staff, so trays would be brought in for my lunch and dinner from a thermopolium. I told him not to bother about lunch as I could never be sure where I would be; for example, one day I would certainly have to go over to the Temple of Ceres to interrogate the runaway slaves. Polycarpus said I could eat dinner in my room, or in the garden if I preferred.

Why no staff? Valerius Aviola had sent the chefs and pot-washers to Campania, ready to look after him in the holiday villa; he borrowed slaves from a friend while he and his bride remained in Rome – a normal kind of favour among the property-owning set. The slaves on loan had gone home that night, so I could assume they were not involved in the murders, though they could have passed details of the silverware to thieves.

'You definitely saw the borrowed slaves leave?'

'I counted them out every one. You cannot be too careful.'

Quite. On the same basis, I took a good look at Polycarpus, letting him see me do it. He was the usual – thought himself special, but he was overestimating. Rome was packed with freedmen, some of whom were genuinely talented. Others, like this one, just had big ideas.

He was trying to assess me. I had been introduced by Faustus as 'a professional investigator who regularly assisted him'. I normally stress my independence, but I had accepted this. I needed validity, the right to give people instructions.

What Polycarpus was seeing was a nearly thirty-year-old woman of spare build and inscrutable expression. I could tell he judged everyone solely by appearance. So many people make that mistake. I look beyond, which is why I am a good informer.

I was quietly dressed, though with coloured hems on my gown and stole. I wore a wedding ring, plus everyday earrings. In working mode, I came with nothing on my belt where leisured matrons carried their manicure sets and keys, but a neat satchel slung across my body, in which I kept a note tablet, small change and a very sharp knife. Dark hair, simply knotted at the nape of my neck. Laced shoes I could walk in. Businesslike, but nothing to attract notice on the street.

'No attendants?' asked the freedman. He meant females;

for chaperone purposes Dromo didn't count. Polycarpus had judged me as not quite respectable – theoretically correct. I watched him wonder if it was an invitation for groping.

'Touch me and you're dead!' I mentioned quietly. He extinguished the hope without remorse; he would give me no trouble, well, probably not much. This was Rome. He was a man. He had to dance the dance. 'Let's get one question out of the way, Polycarpus. Where were you when the attack happened?'

He pretended affront at the question (again as a matter of principle) then confidently declared: 'I left after dinner for my own home.'

'Which is where?'

'A small apartment upstairs in this building.'

'I may need to see your accommodation . . . Who can vouch for you leaving?'

'My people, and everyone here.' His alibi was unsound, since everyone he mentioned would be biased, and moreover he could have bribed them. I made no comment. I would return to the subject later, if I had to.

'As a freedman, you still worked for your original master?'

'Aviola found me indispensable. I continued with my old duties as his steward.'

'How long?'

'Past five years.'

'Paid?'

'Enough to live on. I moved out; I have rooms, with a wife and family. I come in on a daily basis.'

Separate living quarters were now his entitlement. He was a citizen, though he could not stand for office; however, any descendants would hold full civic rights. He managed not to sound too proud of it, just letting me know he had a normal life, able to come and go. His own place, his woman, his freeborn offspring.

'Are there other freedmen associated with this household?'

'Yes, but all gone away to run the master's country estates.'

Time to tackle the crimes. 'So! When and how did you learn of the tragedy, Polycarpus?'

'I don't know why, I just had a strange feeling that night, so I came back.'

'No one fetched you?'

'Oh, they would have done. But in fact I walked in during the hubbub straight afterwards.'

'Had the thieves left?'

'No sign of them. It was me who called the vigiles.' Polycarpus wanted me to know that. Since suspicion had fallen so quickly on the household, he was anxious to seem law-abiding.

'Did you go to fetch the vigiles yourself?'

'I stayed here to supervise, to make sure no one touched anything . . .' He had the subdued look of a man remembering horrors. I reckoned it was genuine, but I kept an open mind. 'A slave went.'

I asked which one, but he still seemed too affected by shock to answer. I could ask them directly. I gestured to my list. 'I have these details of the slaves in the temple. Did the whole household flee? Are any left in the apartment?'

'Myla,' said Polycarpus. 'Heavily pregnant at the time. Too unwieldy to run. She popped a child out three days ago. Anyway, she seems to think her condition will rule her out as a suspect.'

'I think I'll run that idea past our legal advisers!'

Polycarpus caught my sceptical tone. 'Not a defence?'

'In Roman law? Probably no,' I told him cynically. 'Roman

law probably says that the foetus should have broken out of the womb to defend Aviola and his wife, whose property it was . . . What is her role here?'

'Oh, she's just Myla. Been with us for years. She does whatever is needed. You're bound to see her pottering around. Feel free to ask her for anything.'

'What – even though she just gave birth?'

'I had her back on duty straightaway. She knows what is expected. She was *verna* – born in the house.'

'As her child will be,' I commented. 'Boy or girl?' The freedman looked blank. 'What is this baby Myla has produced?' He shrugged; he had no idea. 'Don't you have to list it as a new possession?'

'A scribe's job,' Polycarpus reproached me huffily. 'I run the home. I never touch anything secretarial.'

Melander, 20, scribe, was in the Temple of Ceres.

The steward must have seen my face so he decided to elaborate. 'I have to know manpower numbers, yes, and their capabilities. We use them young, carrying the odd towel or basket, but I don't want any disturbance, no little wobbler going arse-over-tip. So I'm not interested in a babe-in-arms that will probably die in the next few years anyway. It's no use to me until it's decently walking.'

I said that was fully understandable.

Polycarpus was not to know that I had once been a small child in a house where I was expected to fetch and carry for people who viewed me as a commodity. I tried not to dislike him for this conversation – though I did not try hard.

5

As afternoon subtly became twilight, the youth Dromo reappeared. He had been taken away by Faustus, but came whistling back with a high-piled handcart. The aedile must feel guilty about my bare room, so his slave produced various items to improve my comfort: writing materials; a set of bowls, beakers, spoons and scoops, all on a tray; two cushions and a bolster, with embroidered covers; a couple of floor-mats; a small side-table with curved legs; three lamps, oil to put in them and a lighting flint (a thoughtful man); even a comfortable lightweight wicker chair. And a cudgel.

'*What?*'

'That's for me to use,' protested Dromo, grabbing it as I tried its weight.

'For protecting me?'

He sniggered. 'No! For protecting all this stuff of my master's. I bet I know what they are like here. He's asking to have everything pinched. Don't you go looking at that handcart; I've got to take it back.'

I smiled at his presumption that I would snaffle a hand-cart for personal use. Mind you . . . 'You can take it tomorrow when I send you over to Faustus with a report.'

'You think I'll forget it!'

I knew he would. Dromo regarded himself as the archetypal clever slave, but really he was much less clever.

He slouched off into the colonnade outside my room, where he started making himself a nest, laying out the best of the mats, then arranging his choice of crockery around it with the cudgel as a phallic centrepiece. I pottered indoors, doing what I knew he would consider suitable women's work like positioning cushions. I soon grew tired of that.

I marched out and was about to begin investigating the apartment's floor-plan when someone arrived with my supper. Dromo snatched it from the take-out waiter (who would be annoyed because he lost his tip). I was ushered back to my room. Dromo disapproved of where I had put the side-table, so he moved it, plonked the tray down, relocated my chair too, rattled me up a bowl and spoon, then produced a napkin grudgingly.

I lifted covers and found two kinds of cold bar food, one beaten-up bread roll, a wilting side salad and some spotty fruit.

'I expect I have to make do with your leftovers,' said Dromo, fixing me with a glare.

'What if there aren't any?' I asked mildly.

'Better be, or I'll starve.'

Gods, this was hard work. I remembered why I did not own slaves myself.

I soon gave up on my unpalatable dinner, so took what I didn't want to Dromo then set off to explore.

The apartment was unsymmetrical due to the street-plan outside. The front row of street shops meant there was a very long entrance corridor through them, after which came a decorative space that would have been an atrium, except that upper storey apartments overhead prevented it having an open roof. Where a collecting pool for rainwater might have been stood only a marble table: rectangular, heavy supports at each end, nothing on it. Unexciting. I would have kicked it out and got a rude statue.

Beyond the roofed hallway and overlooked from above was an open courtyard; looking across it should have given a fine view to impress important visitors. Not impressive, in this case. Too small and bare, with no flowers, and scruffy colonnades where the cheap pillars had chipped. Again, statues would have helped. If they existed, they had been taken away to Campania (low plinths remained, so this was likely).

The room allocated to me and other good guest bedrooms lay to right and left of the entrance suite, facing onto the courtyard. There were three or four, all handsome.

On the left were summer and winter dining rooms. Since they both faced the same way, the distinction was pointless. They had folding door-leaves that could be opened for air and a garden vista, had there been one – I made a mental note to ask 'Diomedes, 47, gardener' how exactly he spent his time, since he cannot have been tending topiary.

Over on the far side of the courtyard lay a service area, fairly well disguised. More prominently, the best feature of this apartment was a large, double height saloon. There I discovered the kind of domestic basilica that is supposed to give people of status somewhere to hold banquets or semi-public meetings – judicial hearings by minor magistrates or local government gatherings, when they are convened in a big man's private house. Inside, it had two rows of columns dividing the space into a nave and side-aisles, although as this was a modest property not the elite home it wanted to be, the ceiling height, even in the domed centre, was too low. The only light came through high square windows, so the interior was as gloomy as tenements back in Fountain Court, where I lived. And I can tell you that Manlius Faustus and his uncle were important in their community, but I had been in their house, which was bigger than this, yet they did not bother to have a Corinthian oecus, as I knew such saloons are called.

I was acquiring a feel for the Aviola residence and its owners. Comfortably off – or in well-hidden debt. Outwardly ambitious, but trying harder than funds allowed. An absolutely typical Roman family, in fact.

I wondered what the man had done in life. Then I wondered how much dowry the new wife had brought in. I would have to ask.

Either side of the oecus stood the best bedrooms. One was completely empty. In homes where the husband and wife wanted their own rooms, they would snaffle one each of these, separated by their prized Corinthian saloon. With the newly-weds, decisions may not yet have been taken. Following their wedding, while desire was warm, the couple had shared the second bedroom, the one closest to the courtyard corner. The freedman Polycarpus had identified it when talking to Faustus and me. He had also mentioned that the scene had been tidied up, but since I knew what had taken place there, I braced myself before I went in.

It was a pleasant room. A good size. Frescos with flower garlands and mythological plaques, on a white ground. Black and white mosaic on the floor, with slightly lopsided panels depicting the four seasons. A bed with high ends and back, against the right hand wall. Someone had remade the bed,

35

plumping its pillows, smoothing and tightly tucking in the corners of its undersheet and carefully arranging the colourful coverlet so it hung down evenly.

There were cupboards and clothes chests. A long footstool, probably repositioned neatly after the fracas, stood by the open side of the bed.

The bed was a noble size, not some scrimped single cot, but plenty of room for two people to sleep, or do whatever else they chose. They cannot have envisaged violently dying in it together.

I propped myself against the opposite wall, moving to one side to avoid squashing Perseus making a manly approach to a monster. It might be a painting, but the gritty Greek hero had a very big spear and he wasn't going to get ideas about my resting posterior.

Although no sign remained of the crime that took place here, I tried to imagine it, to hear the sudden onslaught of noise and confusion, to feel panic giving way to outright terror, to envisage the dead couple as they had been discovered afterwards, lying on that bed.

Were they cowering together? Out-flung? Curled up foetally? I wondered if they had been awake, or if they woke when their room was invaded, or were they killed before they understood what was happening? With two to be despatched, it was likely that one did realise what happened first to the other. Was it dark? Were there lamps? Did the criminals bring lights of their own? From what I knew so far, neither Aviola nor his wife had time to make any escape attempt. Neither managed to scramble off the bed. Their killer or killers would have dealt with the nearest victim, then leaned across the warm corpse to kill the other. I guessed that Mucia Lucilia, the weaker victim, was second.

She may have shrunk against the backboard in terror while she heard Valerius Aviola being choked. Then came her turn. She, poor woman, would have known what was coming.

When I married years ago, I deliberately chose a marriage bed that was not designed with one solid side like the back of a couch. Otherwise, one of you is always having to climb out over the other person. It is so much more convenient to give both partners free exit on their own side of the bed, much more convenient during marital tiffs. Besides, it saves a feisty woman having to spell out for her beloved that she is not allowing him the access side. Which will come as a big shock to him, and inevitably leads to one of those tiffs I mentioned.

Then, too, when someone thinks they have heard a noise at night, the wife who stays in bed does not want to be crushed by enormous feet while her ridiculous husband insists on going to investigate. Or again when he comes crashing back, after he has found nothing.

But what about when the suspicious noise turns out to be a real emergency?

What if you don't hear intruders until they burst in, rush at you and tighten a rope around your throat?

Did the robbers bring rope? That would show premeditation. Spur of the moment strangulations tend to be carried out with belts or other items of clothing, anything to hand that can be snatched up in fury.

Another question for tomorrow.

While I was musing at the murder scene, it had grown really dark. No lights had been set out anywhere. I found my way back to my room, stepped over Dromo who was snoring on his mat, and fetched one of my lamps. Thank the gods I am a woman who can strike a spark with a flint for herself.

The entire apartment seemed deserted. Although the slave Myla was supposed to be here, I had not seen her and never once heard a baby crying. Perhaps that was common in a home like this. Slaves would be instructed to keep their infants out of sight and silent. Indeed in some houses, the slaves themselves would be expected to remain invisible.

I was working my way into back corridors in the service suite where I might come across the new mother. But it struck me that as I moved around with my single lamp, anyone up to no good in the unlit spaces would be able to track my progress. There was no indication I was being watched, but I felt uncomfortable. I gave up and went to bed.

Needless to say, the guest bed had high ends and a boarded side. Since I was sleeping alone, I could live with that. If anyone tried to break in, I would hear them coming. To make sure, I had fastened my belt around the handles of the double doors, and stood the side-table right against them.

6

I started awake.

Furniture was being scraped across the mosaic floor. The doors were being forced inwards.

I had slept longer than I thought; there was sufficient daylight for me to interpret this and woozily decide to put a stop to it. Bloody Dromo. He had worked his matted head through the crack between the doors, ignoring any risk to his brain. Not wanting to desecrate my favourite knife, I threw a pillow at him.

'Can I go out for my breakfast?'

'For one happy moment, Dromo, I thought you were bringing me some.'

'I'm a messenger, that's not my job.'

'What happens normally about your breakfast?'

'I get it in our kitchen of course. Our house is proper. That's if I don't have to drag out after my master and get thrown an old crust at that horrible place he hangs around with you.'

'It's the Stargazer. And your master does not "hang around", he drops in for business occasionally.'

'I thought the pair of you were smooching.'

'I do not smooch magistrates; I have more class. And you ought to know the aedile better.' I wondered if Dromo had ever seen Faustus dally with women. I couldn't imagine it, but men who seem moral can be a disappointment. In fact, from experience I would say they generally are. 'Go on then. Use the bar directly opposite the house; don't wander off.'

'I haven't got any money.'

What a whiner. Still, it was not his fault. Slaves have to be trusted first; I could see why Faustus would avoid giving this back-chatting boy any petty cash. I answered mildly, though won no thanks for it. I told Dromo to go ahead and I would come to fix up a daily tab for him.

Faustus could pay. I would eat separately at a better-looking bar further down the street, then Faustus could pay for that too.

Service was slow on the Clivus Suburanus. Eating was slow too, since even the apparently superior bar served very hard bread. Lucky for them that I had grown up in the hopeless backstreets of Londinium. I had known far worse.

By the time I returned to the apartment, the freedman Polycarpus was tapping his foot, delighted to look down on me because I had kept him waiting.

Whatever he thought, I know my job. I became impressively businesslike. I marched him to a pair of seats that I had already put out in the courtyard. I had clean waxed tablets ready. I had planned my questions. I drew out the background information I wanted, giving Polycarpus no chance to bluster that he had to keep confidences.

Valerius Aviola had been in his early forties. His money came from land; he owned productive country villas, which either brought in rent from tenants or he ran them himself and took all the profits. Mucia Lucilia, the new trophy wife, was fifteen years younger; she came with attractive inherited wealth. They had known one another socially, an acquaintance that matured naturally into a convenient marriage. They shared friends, who were delighted for them.

I nearly asked if they had previously been lovers, but it seemed irrelevant and I chose a different question. 'Did you think they would be happy?'

'Yes,' said Polycarpus.

The wedding ceremony took place where Mucia had lived on the Quirinal Hill, then Aviola brought his bride home for their first night. A feast for friends was held here the following evening. It ended at a reasonable hour, because the couple were planning to travel to Campania early next morning. They retired to bed. Polycarpus saw the borrowed kitchen staff off the premises, then checked everything was in order before going home. The slaves were well behaved, he told me, and not given to rioting; so he assumed the household would settle down quietly when he left.

The intruders battered their way in through the front doors. They surprised and severely beat the duty night porter, who was Nicostratus (now at the Temple of Ceres); he was discovered lying bloody and unconscious by his colleague Phaedrus (ditto). Phaedrus raised the alarm. At first it was thought only that a display of fine silver had gone missing. Then Amaranta, Mucia's attendant, went in to wake her mistress and tell her what had happened. She discovered the bodies.

The stolen silver, a wine service, was itemised for me by Polycarpus at my request. He dictated a list, which I wrote down, wondering if he was illiterate. I had expected him to bring a written inventory.

He described four sets of double-handled drinking goblets, two to each set, in different sizes; four patterned beakers in two sizes; two trays; eight small round drinks coasters with little tripod goats' feet; assorted jugs, two with hinged lids; a large and a small strainer, pointed and pierced; two ladles; a very large wine-mixing bowl.

The items had been collected over time, but were all of high quality and fine design. This bullion had stood on a display cabinet in the summer dining room; it had remained here to be used in the wedding feast, or it would have been safely parcelled up and sent away for the couple's intended summer in Campania.

'Were any other valuables in the house?'

'Not really. All the sculpture and vases had been sent to the villa. Our mistress had her jewellery in the bedroom. That was not taken.'

'Did they even look at it?'

'No, the casket appeared untouched.'

'What have you done with it?'

'Given for safe keeping to the executors.'

'I shall need to be introduced to them.'

It seemed the robbers knew exactly what they were looking for – the silver – and where it would be. They may also have gone to the bedroom in order to find the jewellery, only giving up that idea in panic after the murders. 'So, let me just get this straight,' I said, not looking up from my note tablet. 'You were intending to send the silverware to the summer villa after your master and mistress left? First the cups and jugs were used at the feast, after which things were presumably washed up in the kitchen . . . so, Polycarpus, why was this silverware replaced on the display shelf, rather than packed up ready to go?'

'The hour was too late. I felt whacked; we were all exhausted after the wedding.' Polycarpus spoke defensively, looking as if he was unused to having his actions queried. 'I had it taken out of the kitchen because the staff were on loan and I wasn't prepared to trust them. Then the most discreet thing to do at that time of night was quietly store it as normal. The master and mistress were to go by litter to the city gates at first light and pick up wheeled transport there. I myself would come in to pack any final items, then we had a cart ordered for drive time.'

In Rome, apart from some exceptions, carts are banned in the day in order to ease congestion. What Polycarpus said sounded reasonable.

'Were you going to Campania?'

'Er, no. There is another steward at the villa. I would have the summer to myself.' Was there a flicker of feeling when he said that?

'And the slaves who had stayed here after the wedding – were they meant to travel south?'

'They were expecting to go with the last baggage cart.' Polycarpus seemed to hesitate, though he carried on. 'Then I was to close up the house.'

'What about Myla, who was on the verge of producing?'

'Not her. Arrangements had been made.'

'So the house would be locked up during the summer. And if these thieves knew about the silver, they may have realised that night was their last chance to grab it for a long time?'

Polycarpus sighed. 'Presumably . . . And before you ask, no, I was never aware of any of our staff talking to outsiders about our valuables. Nor had I seen anyone suspicious watching the house.'

'The vigiles asked you those questions?' It was their usual approach. As an approach it often works, though as any vigiles enquirer would know, the weaknesses are that none

43

of the staff would admit to Polycarpus that they had loose tongues, and most professional burglars are unobtrusive when they case a joint. 'The vigiles like to believe items like this stolen silver may reappear and help identify the thieves,' I mused. 'But I am not hopeful.'

The steward continued, 'The man who came to investigate, Titianus, said the collection must have been stolen to order. He thought it was taken for someone who had been here as a guest, saw it and liked it. But surely, the point of owning treasure is to display it? This supposed guest would never be able to show it off or people would know he stole it. So why bother?'

I agreed. 'From your description, this stuff is also too distinctive to show up at auction. I know people in that business. Questions would be asked.'

'Titianus assured me a list would be circulated to jewellers and auctioneers.'

'I am sure he will do that. Sadly, Polycarpus, the likelihood is that the items will be melted down for the value of the metal – in which case that has happened already.'

'It seems a terrible waste of such beautiful things.'

'Criminals have limited choices. Occasionally,' I told him, 'a well organised professional gang will hide their loot, then keep it as long as they have to, until the heat dies down. Then they may eventually sell it for its artistic value. But even if these robbers use such long-term planning, people died here. Murder attracts attention. What was stolen may stick in the public's mind. Selling it will be too risky.'

Mentioning the deaths was my cue to move on.

After the attack, Polycarpus had gone into the bedroom and had seen the bodies. He confirmed what I had suspected:

Aviola was lying nearest the front edge of the bed, with his wife behind him. Mucia was found close against her husband and had one arm stretched across his body, a defensive, protesting position, as if the new bride was trying to fend off her groom's attacker.

'That doesn't sound as if the killers turned violent because the master and mistress came out and disturbed them. Aviola and Mucia were still in bed. Perhaps the thieves went to see what was in the bedroom, then their victims woke and tried to raise an alarm . . . They were strangled, I'm told. What with?'

'A piece of rope.' So it must have been pre-planned.

'What happened to the rope afterwards?'

'Perhaps the vigiles officer took it away.'

'I shall ask him. Do you remember anything about it, Polycarpus? What kind of rope? Not very thick, I imagine. Thick rope is too stiff to twist around necks with enough torsion to kill someone.'

The steward shrugged. Assessing rope was not for him. There were so many boundaries in household management, I was surprised anything ever got done.

I asked him to show me the apartment's layout, not mentioning that I had already explored. We took a walk-through. There were no surprises in the main rooms. Now I saw more of the offices. They had a two-oven kitchen, plus the usual pantries and store rooms. I glanced into the latrine. It was decent, though its cleanliness would not have satisfied either of my grandmothers, both women who would walk through Rome for an hour with a screaming toddler, rather than let any of us use a lavatory from which we might catch something.

'Where do you get your water?'

'The apartment came with its own well, but when my master first took the lease we found the water is too bad to use. I have to organise a carrier to bring in fresh buckets daily.' Polycarpus indicated the disused well, in a corner of the courtyard. It had wooden boarding at ground level, over which a stone urn had been placed to deter people from opening it.

'One thing I notice,' I said thoughtfully, 'is that you have little obvious accommodation for your slaves.'

'What we provide is normal.' Polycarpus obviously despised me for not knowing how staffed houses work. He showed me a couple of small cells on the service corridor. Numbers of slaves slept there, layered on pallets in wall niches, in much the same way as crockery was stacked on shelves elsewhere in walk-in cupboards. These slaves would have no time to relax at leisure, no personal possessions and absolutely no privacy. One such cell was crammed with mattresses and mats; these could be used on the floor anywhere. 'Normally the house is full of people looking after the master. They all find space for themselves where they can – the kitchen, corridors, the garden. But they are the master's *familia* and we make our accommodation versatile, Flavia Albia. When we have no guests, the best slaves may sleep in greater comfort in unused bedrooms.'

'Well, that raises a question, Polycarpus: did any of the guests at the feast stay overnight?'

'None. They all live locally and were taken home as soon as the meal ended.'

'So, let's go back to the attack. I need details of who was where at that point. What do you know about where the fugitive slaves were sleeping – if that is what they were doing – when the thieves broke in?'

All Polycarpus could say was that Nicostratus, the porter

on duty, was by the front door. We went to look. Off the entrance corridor was a tiny cubbyhole, but Polycarpus said neither of the porters liked it, finding it too stuffy and enclosed; they tended to sleep on a mat in the corridor. That was where the wounded Nicostratus had been found.

Otherwise, Polycarpus reckoned that the gardener, Diomedes, generally curled up in the garden or one of the cloisters around it. Then the steward remembered giving permission for the two females, Mucia's personal attendant and her young musician, to sleep in one of the decent rooms at the front of the apartment. He suspected that Chrysodorus, the philosopher, would have taken it upon himself to sleep in another, probably the one I was now using.

'Your master had a tame philosopher?' I kept my expression neutral.

'My new mistress liked refinements,' answered the steward stiffly. This was the first hint that there might have been friction between him and the householders, but it was only a hint.

'Stoic, Cynic or Epicurean? What variety is he?'

'A bone idle one.'

'I see. Perhaps he would say he has successfully cultivated an untroubled inner life.'

'Possibly, Flavia Albia. My feeling is that somebody should give him a kick up his untroubled arse.'

I noticed Polycarpus letting himself express something less bland than normal. It made me think I might enjoy meeting Chrysodorus. It was also a clue to explore relations between the master's established staff and new people brought by Mucia Lucilia. When I asked, Polycarpus assured me they all got on perfectly together, but he was bound to say that.

★　★　★

We were coming to the end of my meeting with the steward, except that I did mention my unhappiness with the eating arrangements. I instructed him to buy in food for me and Dromo, which I would prepare. If he provided salad and meats, little work would be necessary. He agreed, so we went back to the kitchen where he showed me equipment, crockery and cutlery.

A fire was kept in for hot water. Myla had that job. We found her there, adding firewood in a desultory way. She was the first of the household slaves I met, and I did not take to her. She was a slow drudge with a dreamy manner who accepted my presence in her domain, received instructions to look after me, but said nothing.

The newborn babe lay quiet in a basket. I was curious to ask who its father was, but kept that for another time. Polycarpus was still with us and from what I knew of freedmen with power in a house, he might be a candidate.

The steward treated Myla offhandedly. I had the impression he had given up trying to impose discipline. Myla seemed to be one of those slaves who lived in her own world, and somehow persuaded everyone else to go along with that. Clearly she did the minimum necessary to avoid notice or criticism.

I did not blame her. If I was a slave, I would have behaved the same way.

7

I took advantage of the steward believing our talk had gone well. Soon I would finish my initial enquiries, where I maintained a neutral attitude on purpose while I assessed the scene and familiarised myself with the witnesses. Once I began applying pressure, Polycarpus would realise he had failed to ingratiate himself, but for the moment I played grateful.

I fetched a stole and asked him to show me where to find Aviola's executors; on the way there we could see what the local shops and stalls had to offer and I would point out the kind of provisions I liked.

Out in the streets it was immediately clear that around here Polycarpus had made himself a man of account. Everybody knew who he was. People bustled up to greet him. Whenever we paused at a greengrocer, salami seller or fruiterer, the proprietor dropped what he was doing to attend to us personally. If we failed to stop, traders left their stalls and shops and actually followed us for some distance, offering Polycarpus deals, treats, pleas and samples of their goods. I lost count of the times I was told what a wonderful fellow my companion was. Had he not been a freedman he could have stood as a local tribune and beaten all comers.

It was based on favours, naturally. He must have steadily built relationships along the Clivus Suburanus and nearby, using his importance as controller of Aviola's domestic budget; in return he could depend on these suppliers, making himself look good at home by miraculously providing whatever his master wanted, even at short notice. He probably had equally smooth dealings with building contractors and so forth.

I saw no coins changing hands; it would all be done on account, with creditors no doubt having to beg for payment weeks in arrears in the classic Roman way. Nor did they yet seem too afraid that with the master dead the account might be closed, though one or two did enquire what would happen now. Polycarpus claimed not to know, implying that if it was left to him transactions would continue as usual.

I was convinced little bonuses passed to him regularly. I don't criticise. He was a really good steward. Whether I would want someone exercising that kind of influence in my household is another matter.

'*What household is that supposed to be, Albia?*' my family would roar. They thought I lived like a vagrant.

The main executor was called Sextus Simplicius and had an apartment in a block three streets from Aviola's. A door porter let us in; then we saw a polite functionary much like Polycarpus. He told us his master was out on business and made an appointment for me the next day. Polycarpus took the lead in our conversation, of course, though at the end I intervened and mentioned that when I came back I would like to see the will. Eyebrows were raised. I remained calm, simply letting the two stewards know I expected my request to be taken seriously and passed on to the executor.

I could always call on Manlius Faustus to help me obtain sight of the document, though I preferred not to. Who wants to look incompetent?

If Aviola and Mucia really had been murdered by strangers, knowing the contents of the will ought to be routine, simply covering all angles. On the other hand, if the slaves were implicated as the vigiles argued, anything Aviola had had to say about their disposal might be helpful. Which did he trust and value?

I would have liked to know this before my next move but decisions were urgent for Faustus. I was now ready to go over to the Aventine and visit the group in sanctuary.

Polycarpus seemed to think it one of his duties to attend these interviews. You guessed: I refused. I marched him back to the apartment, where instead I picked up Dromo.

'Why've I got to haul myself all that way with you? You can report to Faustus yourself.'

'Any more backchat. Dromo, and I'll say he dumped a useless dropout on me, who needs to be reassigned as a dung-shoveller.'

'Can't I ask a simple question?'

'Questions are my job. And if you don't get a move on, I won't have time to ask any at the Temple.'

I told him to bring his cudgel in case it was late when we came back. That went down badly. Dromo was afraid of being out in the dark.

I took it to mean my client Faustus rarely went to late-night parties. Intriguing!

My parents owned a few slaves, most of them pitiful purchases with two left feet and ten grades of insolence, so I knew what to expect. Walking with Dromo was tedious. He dragged along, he moaned about how far it was, and I had to keep stopping to make sure he was still there behind me.

Eventually we made it. Back in my home district I cheered

up, and when I had a bowl of chickpea broth at a bar counter by the Circus Maximus, I fed Dromo too, which at least made him temporarily stop whingeing.

The Temple of Ceres is on a corner of the Aventine, not far above the corn-dole station. (Pay attention. Ceres is the grain goddess.) Hers is a mighty great shrine with ancient Greek styling, its interior containing three magnificent cult statues funded by fines raised by the aediles. As a centre of plebeian power, this big temple sends a message of defiance over to the aristocratic gods who live on the Capitol. It is presided over by an important Roman priest, the Flamen Cerialis, but it also has a group of female devotees.

Head of the cult was a very old priestess who had been brought to Rome specially from Neapolis because of Campania's Greek connections. (The rites of Ceres are said to be Greek, though unlike most Romans I have been to Greece and I say that's pigswill.) Cosying up to the priestess was a dreary bunch of stuck-up local matrons who carried out good works. One of these shrine-nuisances was a bugbear of mine. Just my luck: I ran into her.

An attendant had already told me that the slaves were now at the aediles' office. To move them out of the religious areas, some dispensation had been arranged, no doubt by the sensible Manlius Faustus. I was heading off to his office when, too late, I ran into the bossiest of Ceres' cult women. She was a skinny blonde madame who always looked at me as if I was something smelly she had picked up on her expensive sandal. This woman and her brother had inherited a fortune, and if she could have walked around with a placard saying how superior that made her, she would have done it.

'Laia Gratiana!' In a previous case of mine, this Laia had

made herself thoroughly obnoxious. Neither of us had forgotten. One day I would be compelled to knock her down and jump on her. I could tell you it would be for her own good, but the truth is it would be for my personal pleasure.

'What are you doing here?'

I explained my business quietly.

'You had better get on with it then.'

'Well, thanks for your permission, Laia. I shall do that!'

I left the temple, seething inwardly but trying not to look riled.

'Cor,' muttered Dromo, admiringly. 'You really got up that one's nose! What have you done to her?'

'I have no idea.' I knew perfectly.

'I bet she's jealous of you, being so sweet with my master.' Dromo became excited, thinking he knew a secret. 'I bet you don't know who she is, Albia?'

'I know who she *was*.'

She was Faustus' ex-wife. Laia Gratiana left him because he had an affair (I had not been surreptitiously delving; Faustus told me himself). It happened ten years ago, but the embittered divorcee still harboured a grudge. I supposed it was subconscious, but she looked highly annoyed to find me assisting Faustus. It would suit her best to see him fail in his task.

Well, that made up my mind. If I had anything to do with this, Manlius Faustus would not fail.

8

The aediles' office was close to the temple. I had been there before. It held unhappy memories, about a man I should never have tangled with. (Let's face it, all my bad memories concern men in that category.) Luckily, the offender no longer worked there. I could revisit the scene with indifference.

I learned Manlius Faustus was out but expected back, once he finished working the streets to monitor the public. Pity the public; he was a stickler.

The slaves were loafing in the courtyard, looking relaxed; that was typical of slaves. There was nothing they could do about their predicament; other people owned their lives and would decide their fate. The threat of death had stopped worrying them, at least for the time being.

Although the aediles were given no personal guards, their building contained strongboxes full of fines from the many who broke regulations (well, those who were spotted) so the place had protection. Its guards were temporarily keeping an eye on the Aviola slaves.

'We lost one this morning.'

'Careless! Someone run away?'

'Died on us. The porter who was beaten up. He's still on the premises if you want to have a look at him.'

'I may as well.'

★　★　★

Nicostratus lay dead on a pallet, covered with a cloth, which did little to allay the stink of his rotted wounds. I could learn little about him from his corpse, except that he had been short, dark and hairy – and cruelly treated. The battery was pointless; why would thieves stop and beat up a porter so badly, when a couple of well-aimed blows is usually enough to have such a man whimpering in a corner? Or couldn't they just have slipped him a few coins to lose himself for half an hour?

Were these robbers in love with violence? And had the porter's beating fired them up, so they went on to attack Aviola and his bride too? But that would mean the murders were unplanned.

'Someone knocked all hell out of this one! Did anyone try to look after him when he arrived here?' The guard pulled a face. Fairly neat bandaging had been carried out on the dead man and one of his legs had a splint. 'Manlius Faustus let him be seen by a doctor?'

'But of course! Faustus insists we treat them all tenderly. We want them in good condition for the arena beasts, don't we? There's no fun if convicts are submissive and limp.'

I did not suppose having the man fit for the lions was Faustus' motive.

'Will someone ask the doctor to come and have a word with me? Dromo can take a message, if you give him directions. The patient may have said something, while he was being treated.'

Dromo did go, only to return bitterly complaining that the doctor was a bad-tempered Greek who had been horrible to him. That did not surprise me. I sympathised with the doc.

The man sent me a verbal message that he had better things to do than attend the dead. However, to satisfy

Manlius Faustus, there was also a written report. The doctor described Nicostratus' injuries, including a broken leg, a hole in his skull, and various traumatic wounds that appeared to have been inflicted by a blunt flat-faced weapon, such as a plank. Splinters of wood were in the wounds.

In the doctor's expert opinion (his phrase), the savagery used on Nicostratus differed significantly from the controlled force required to strangle the other two victims.

In answer to my query, the patient gave up the struggle after a week of drifting in and out of consciousness, during which he never said anything about the attack.

Thank you, Hippocrates.

By the time Dromo brought me this, I was interviewing the slaves one by one, in the room Faustus used as his office. Afterwards, those I had seen were kept separate from those I had yet to see, so they could not confer.

Some owners acquire slaves who are all of a type. Not these. The nine survivors were a mixed bunch, all heights, colouring and weights. I reckoned they varied too in their levels of intelligence, skill and willingness. The young men had hair to their shoulders, normal practice, and all wore simple patched tunics in neutral colours. They looked fit and tidy, products of a decent home. In conversation none of them really told me much about Aviola or Mucia, though they spoke well of both.

Before we started, I reminded the group that the law said slaves had to give evidence under torture. I would not be doing that. '– Not at this stage.' They knew what I meant.

I saw Phaedrus first, the other door porter. He was a sturdy, fair-haired young man with north European origins, a Gaul or German. He had an open face and honest manner – which generally signals a lying witness. According to him, although I had been told Nicostratus was the night porter, it was the other way around. Phaedrus was to have been on late duty but had stayed in the kitchen, having his supper first; it was when he went to relieve his colleague that he found Nicostratus and raised the alarm.

'So were you in the kitchen throughout the robbery and murders?'

'Yes, but I heard nothing.'

'Phaedrus, I have been in that kitchen. I know the layout. Are you sure you never heard the intruders breaking in and attacking Nicostratus?'

'No. They must have put him out cold with the first blow.'

'Then they continued knocking him about? Unlikely! You heard no one come across the courtyard?'

'They must have tiptoed through the columns on the opposite side.'

I agreed that fitted with them going over to the dining room to take the silver. 'Would you have run to help if you heard a commotion?'

'Of course I would have! Sorting trouble is my job.'

'You don't shy from a rumpus?'

'I would have been straight in.'

'So what made you deaf? Was anybody else with you?' The blond belligerent looked shifty but said no. 'Oh, come on, Phaedrus. You can do better than this. What was taking up so much of your attention that you missed all the racket? Were you playing around with somebody?'

Phaedrus had no answer, or none he would give me.

I asked about working with Nicostratus. Apparently they hardly knew each other, but got on well. It was routine for a house to have two porters, since one could not stay alert both day and night. (*'Alert'*? In my family, we reckon door porters are dopey at all times.) Phaedrus let slip that he himself was an incomer from Mucia's household.

'Really? It's common on marriage for staffs to merge,' I mused. 'Sometimes they don't gel, and that causes upsets.'

'Oh, not us!' maintained Phaedrus, looking innocent. Maybe the young men bonded. They were both in their twenties, Nicostratus slightly older. They could have palled up, talked about gladiators, discussed women (shared one?). A woman could well explain why Phaedrus was oblivious to noise that night.

'So were you very upset when you discovered Nicostratus so terribly hurt? How do you feel about him dying today?'

His face changed then, showing true distress.

I let him go.

Who next? I chose the gardener.

Diomedes was short, lumpy in the body, big-eared and almost bald. He readily agreed that he was not over-taxed in his duties, though he claimed to hanker for the wider acreage of the country villa in Campania. At the Rome apartment he was a general handyman. He supplemented the water carrier, fetching extra buckets from the local fountain. He nailed things and cleared gullies. He went up ladders to wash shutters – which presumably meant he looked in through windows and saw room contents. He would have known the silver existed.

I told him Polycarpus had said Diomedes was asleep in the garden. 'The robbers went through to the dining room, then the bedroom. So you are the person most likely to have seen them. What do you say?'

Diomedes said shamelessly that there had been wine at the feast, to which he and Amethystus helped themselves. So yes, they were slumped in a corner of the peristyle, but he bragged that both were completely 'crocked'. They would not have woken if the robbers had trampled all over them and left boot-prints on their heads.

I bought the story. He was clearly a sloppy workman, yet I found him free of guile.

How trusting, Albia! You ought to know how that works: the 'honest' suspect makes a small confession – to hide a bigger one.

Amethystus obviously came next. Taller and leaner, he carried his years better than Diomedes. It could have been because he had lighter work indoors, although I noticed he had more scars from punishment beatings. As he told it, his life was hard. He not only mopped marble and swept up detritus, he was constantly moving furniture, fetching and carrying, and being sent on errands outside the home, usually for heavy goods that, poor thing, he had to transport unaided.

He confirmed Diomedes' story. These two were old cronies who often got at amphorae while they were standing unattended outside dining rooms; this pair had even been known to raid the stores, if they thought they could get away with it. On the night in question, in the free and easy atmosphere that followed the wedding, these unreformed winestealers had cheerfully managed to make themselves paralytic. Amethystus heard nothing. His only memory was of waking woozily to find everyone else running around in panic, with the master dead. Had they been sober, according to him, he and Diomedes would have given the intruders a good thumping.

I would have to ask my uncles about this: what penalty pinching fine wines carried for these slaves – and would their blind intoxication exonerate the drunks from their obligation to protect their master's life?

Next I sent for Daphnus, to see whether as server at the feast he knew about amphorae being raided. Unsurprisingly, he did. I wondered if he had a tipple himself.

This tall young man was snappy and smart, the only one who had somehow obtained an ornament (a cheap amulet, hung on a thong) and better shoes than the general issue (probably his master's cast-offs; they looked too big for him). He had oiled hair and he oozed ambition.

He was the first to check my role. 'Are you the one who is going to get us off?'

'That depends on your story, Daphnus, and whether I believe it. Even if I do, I shall need to pin the deaths of your master and mistress on somebody else before you can be reprieved.'

He looked crestfallen.

His work consisted of delivering refreshments to the family and visitors, and serving formally at table; when the chef was absent (the chef was among the staff sent to Campania), Daphnus even carved the meats, a task in which he considered himself an expert. He must have been indoors doing that when the two others siphoned off half an amphora, he maintained.

'Would you have reported them, if you saw them do it?'

'Oh yes,' he assured me, unconvincingly.

He told me he wanted to make something of himself, gain his freedom, start a small business. If Polycarpus could manage that, Daphnus reckoned anybody could.

'What do you think of Polycarpus?'

'Complete crook. He came from nowhere, has no aptitude or skills. It's all a big bluff. He gets other people to run around and do the business, then takes all the credit.'

'Isn't that what his job requires?'

'Fair enough.' Daphnus shrugged, as if there was no real animosity between him and the steward, only envy.

'But he got on well with your master.'

I thought I detected a slight delay, before Daphnus agreed Polycarpus was held in good regard by Aviola.

Daphnus had 'worked his rocks off' at the feast, he said, so he claimed he knew nothing about the burglary because he had passed out from exhaustion in one of the slaves' cells, with the door closed. The scribe, Melander, was with him. They only woke when Phaedrus hammered on the door and yelled that someone had killed the master.

'Is Melander your special friend?'

'He's an idiot. But he's my brother.' Daphnus executed a big theatrical start, jumping back with his hands in the air. 'Oh! Flavia Albia, I do hope you didn't think me and my beloved bro was in there *bum-fiddling?*'

'That's a new word for it . . . No,' I replied, smiling. 'I'd put you down as a ladies' man.'

'Yes, but fat chance! We are not supposed to mingle with the women – and anyway who was available? Olympe's a child; I like them when their busts have grown. Myla was the size of a granary, and I ask you! I wasn't that desperate.'

'Then I take it you are not the father?' Daphnus acted out a look of indignation and disgust, so I suggested, 'I wondered if Myla was the household donkey – ridden by everyone?' Many homes have one of those, but Daphnus would not comment on who slept with Myla.

I pointed out that of the potential conquests for the lad-about-the-colonnades, he had not mentioned Amaranta, Mucia Lucilia's maid. 'Nice!' he agreed. 'Old enough, a looker, tantalising hints of past experience – and, sadly, taken.'

I laid down my stylus on my waxed note tablet. 'By? . . .'

'Onesimus.'

Not a name on my list. 'And he is?'

'Came from the other household. Lucilia's pet steward. Sent off to Campania. But he reckons he is in with the ornamental ornamenter.'

'To which she says?'

'Nothing! Very discreet woman.'

'And you like her?'

'Lots of people like Amaranta. If you want to know who *she* likes, you will have to ask her.' Daphnus, an unashamed chancer, admitted, 'I was biding my time. I like to play the game, but I reckon there were other people in the queue ahead of me.'

'Care to say which people?'

He shook his head – then the cheeky chap gave *me* a speculative, flirty once-over, to which I returned my standard get-lost glare. This young man would try it on with anyone, though he gave up easily. As young men go, he was typical.

'So tell me, Daphnus: would you have been willing to defend your master?'

'I certainly would. Saving him would have been ideal for me. He would show he was grateful. I could have got my freedom and a nice little pension out of that.'

'Good point! What about your brother, Melander?'

'He would have joined in with anything I did.'

'Are you close?'

'No, but he's a bit slow and I look after him. My master

was ready to sell him, but kept him on as a favour to me.'

Daphnus thought a lot of his own worth – though I could believe he was useful to Valerius Aviola, so his confidence might be justified.

'Are you to be freed by your master's will, Daphnus?'

His eyes widened. 'Never thought of that!'

'Don't get excited. If you are executed for murdering the man, it will never happen.'

When Melander shambled in, I could see the fraternal likeness, along with differences. He had a similar long face, mostly nose, but much less intelligence in his dark eyes. He told me they were twins, clearly not identical. They were born in the household; their mother was now dead. My notes gave them different ages, but that was wrong; Melander said they were both twenty.

He was a contrast to his lively brother. I wondered if he had been starved in the womb, as I believe can happen with twins, or if he suffered in a long birth process. Though not literally an idiot as Daphnus had called him, he lacked personality. He said he could write, but only if he was told what to put.

Other people amaze me. I would have made this one the tray carrier and trained up his sharper brother to do secretarial work, not the other way around.

Maybe Aviola did not care about correspondence and record-keeping. Not my family's style. Some of mine are literary by nature, while even the rest keep tight control of their accounts because they are constantly being creative with their taxes. You have to get everything right when you're fixing your declaration. Not that I ever would. Fortunately, as a woman I don't have to.

Melander gave the impression his brother had rehearsed him. Both twins would go on swearing they had been oblivious to the intruders. I kicked the scribe out.

Hoping to refresh my spirits, I had the philosopher fetched.

Big mistake. His principle was that life is a turd we have stepped in, then we die. I could not tell which school of thought he belonged to, though it must be a gloomy one.

He had been bought by Mucia Lucilia on a whim at the slave market two years ago, merely as a fashionable accessory. He described her as a nice enough woman, but she made no intellectual demands of him, nor indeed of herself. Once she had boasted to all her friends that she owned a philosopher, Chrysodorus was simply forced to look after her very old, sick, smelly lapdoggie, a pampered thing called Puff.

He had been sleeping in a store room.

'Alone?'

'I can never be alone, dear. My duties are ceaseless. I shared the space with Puff.'

'Because you love her really?'

'No. Because no one else will have her near them.'

'No hope of her sleeping on the end of her doting *domina*'s bed?'

'Not after the mistress married. Aviola put his foot down.'

'Pity. She might have nipped the intruders.'

'I doubt it. If thieves burst in, Puff would run away.'

'And would you have done the same?'

He was enough of a philosopher to know this was a critical question. He sighed. 'I would defend life, wretched though it is. One needs to be civilised – though god knows what for.'

'To avoid crucifixion or being eaten by a lion, Chryso-dorus . . . There must have been noise. Didn't the dog waken?'

'The dog is stone deaf.'

'And you?'

'I sleep the heavy sleep of doomed humanity. In explan-ation: since the dog snores atrociously, I have prevailed upon a medicine-man to give me a sleeping draught. He prescribes for the dog officially, but slips me a potion too.'

'This doctor is on the staff?'

'Aviola's.'

'Sent to Campania?'

'Correct. Fortunately he left me supplies. Puff had been fed unsuitable titbits at the feast, so she was farting like a furnace-stoker. That became a night when I needed a sleeping draught merely to continue to exist.'

I tried to look sorry for him, though I am fond of dogs. 'I have not seen a pooch at the apartment. What happened to her?'

'Puff has been brought to me. My earthly suffering never ends.'

'What will happen to Puff now your mistress has passed away?'

'A vicious rumour whispers I am to be freed in Mucia Lucilia's will – but legally compelled to take care of the dog. So, believe me, Flavia Albia, I gained no advantage from killing my mistress! The one joy I will take from being led into an arena is that I may feed bloody Puff to a wild beast as an appetiser.'

'Then you can die happy?'

'Happiness is an overrated concept.'

I would have liked to dispute that, but Chrysodorus

seemed too glum to enjoy theoretical argument. Which may be overrated, I accept – though it's better entertainment than listening to a string of people lying to you.

Well, they were slaves. You know the saying: I blame the owners.

I went and inspected Puff. She was the kind of dog you see in cities that are full of small apartments: a tiny, fragile-boned ratty thing, which seemed to be parts glued together from different varieties, none of them pretty. A woman's lapdog – for a woman with no sense.

I did not pat or speak to Puff. She was no use to me. Dogs, like women, do not possess legal capacity and cannot bear witness in a Roman law court.

To change the script from masculine blather, I called Olympe as my next interviewee. I had heard her singing, in a low, unmistakably Lusitanian style. No one appeared to be listening.

She was scared, tiny and pretty. She looked her age, around fifteen, though she had more bust than Daphnus had suggested; she held herself in with a band. Her main instrument was the lyre, though she told me she could play the double flute passably. Mucia Lucilia had once heard her performing among a band of travelling entertainers, Olympe's relatives, and offered to buy her. She had not been a slave before, but was sold into bondage by her family. It happens. I had once lived among people who were planning to do that to me.

Olympe had convinced herself that one day her relatives would be in funds and come to look for her. So she was dimmer than she looked, because I guessed they never would.

'Don't bank on it. You have a marketable skill, girl. Use that to make something of your life.'

Like Chrysodorus she was an exotic acquisition, though unlike him her mistress did frequently call on her skills. Olympe had played and sung at the feast. Afterwards she was tired, she claimed. She closeted herself with Amaranta in one of the good bedrooms. She heard nothing, though if she had, she would not have known what to do.

'You could have yelled, Olympe. Called for other people to help.'

'But I never knew I needed to.'

The robbers must have passed right outside the room where Olympe and Amaranta were asleep; that thought reduced her to helpless trembling. Olympe was the first of the accused slaves to show fear. She cried. She rushed across the room and clung to me. She begged me to help. She was terrified of facing trial (such as it would be; I didn't disillusion her) and of the fate that a conviction would bring.

I was calming her when Manlius Faustus put his head around the door. He signalled that he would not disturb me; I mimed back that I had nearly finished. It had been a long session. He must have seen I was tiring; he sent in some basic refreshments.

What I liked about this aedile was that, having commissioned me, he made no attempt to muscle in on my interviews but left me to continue in my own style.

I next saw Amaranta, a neat, sad girl with many plaits and ribbons. Like Olympe, she was conscious of the threatening situation, though bore it with quiet resignation. I would not have classed her as a beauty, but she had enough vivacity to appeal to lustful male slaves. She possessed the manner of a very clever waiting-maid, and I reckoned she could deal with men.

I called her a girl because of her status; she was about my own age really, and said her mistress was the same. She had served Mucia Lucilia for ten years, helping her wash, dress, arrange her hair, put on jewellery. It was an intimate relationship. She tweezed Mucia's eyebrows, cut her nails, made arrangements for sanitary cloths during her monthly periods. She had learned her moods, her hopes of making a good marriage, her annoyance that the trip to Campania had had to be delayed.

'Yes, tell me: what caused this delay?'

'We were not told.' She paused slightly, and I wondered.

That night she must have been the last person other than Aviola to see Mucia alive. She had helped her mistress undress. She locked up the jewellery in its casket. Then, as I had been told by Olympe, the maid retired to one of the good bedrooms on the far side of the courtyard, in company with the young musician. They had the door closed, which Olympe had not explained, though Amaranta admitted it was to deter male slaves from wandering in.

'Do you get much trouble?'

'Nothing I can't handle.' I believed that.

I asked about her hopes for the future; did she want to marry and have a family?

Amaranta was non-committal about who she might share her life with, but readily said that she was on good terms with Mucia Lucilia, who had promised to free her as soon as she reached her thirtieth birthday. That was close enough for her to look forward to it patiently, but Amaranta was now frightened that Mucia's death meant she would be sent to a slave market instead. Assuming she escaped the murder charge.

'You don't know what was in her will?'

'No. What are our chances, Flavia Albia?'

'Slim,' I said honestly. 'A judge is likely to say all of you should have rushed to help your master and mistress. I shall conduct experiments, but any prosecutor will claim you should have heard their cries.'

Amaranta had been giving this thought. 'What if they never called for help? – I don't believe they did.'

'We would need to explain why not – though, without being indelicate, it could be they were so involved with each other they were slow to realise intruders had come into their room. Do you know – were they passionate?'

'They liked it,' replied Amaranta matter-of-factly. I waited. 'Quite a lot, from what she told me. After the wedding, she was a happy woman next morning, looking forward to more.'

'Had they been to bed together before?'

'A few squeezes and fumbles. Not the full thing. So it was only their second bout of proper play. And they would not have been expecting anyone to interrupt. We were all told to keep away.'

'I imagine they had the bedroom doors closed too – or didn't they care who heard them?'

'My mistress was modest. I shut the doors for them. If the room became too airless, they could always be opened afterwards.'

Slave-owners barely climbed out of bed to pee in the pot. Their attendants put them to bed, where they generally stayed until the attendants got them up next morning. 'Your master or mistress would call out for someone, if they wanted the doors to be opened?'

Amaranta had nodded before she saw the implication. 'Libycus!' She cheerily landed the master's attendant in trouble. 'He was supposed to stay within earshot, in case anything was wanted during the night.'

I dismissed her, and called in Libycus.

His black skin said he had been named for his country of origin, though he must have come here as a child or been born here because, like all the Aviola slaves, he was thoroughly Romanised.

Libycus had been as close to his master as Amaranta to her mistress, turning out Aviola smartly each day, having first listened to the man's mental anxieties and washed his bodily crevices. He chose clothes. He acted as barber. He wielded the ear-wax scoop and toothpick, and applied pile ointment between the buttocks.

Yes, he was supposed to remain close, always on call. He, more than anybody else, should have been in a position to intervene when Aviola was attacked. He did not want to tell me why he had not done so. In the end, I squeezed it out of him.

'I wasn't there.'

'Not nearby?'

'Not in the house.'

'*What?* Are you allowed to leave the house during the night?'

'No.'

He hung his head while I absorbed this. Then Libycus mumbled his confession: thinking Aviola was unlikely to want anything, he had gone to one of the shops on the apartment's street-side, where he sometimes met with friends. It was his last chance to socialise before he was taken to Campania for an indefinite period. He and two other men spent some time drinking, chatting and playing dice. When he came back, everything was over.

'Did Nicostratus open the door for you to go out?'

'Yes, he let me out, then he or Phaedrus was going to let me back in.' Libycus pleaded, 'I don't suppose being somewhere else will get me off?'

'You know the answer. Quite the opposite, Libycus. You had abandoned your master, against orders.'

I felt sorry for him. But the fact was, he was even more likely to be convicted than the others.

9

When I emerged into the courtyard, stiff limbed and boggle-eyed, I noticed that the slaves were being fettered and taken indoors, to stop them running away in the night.

Faustus was talking to Dromo. (No chance *he* might abscond.) I was so tired I lost my discretion and snapped, 'Do you have a serious sinus condition, Manlius Faustus, so you can't notice smells? Why don't you send your messenger for a bath sometimes?'

Dromo looked shifty. Faustus sniffed and winced, then looked guilty too. 'As far as I know, Flavia Albia, all our household receive bath house money.' He fixed Dromo. 'What do you have to say for yourself, boy?' Slaves are called 'boy' even if they are seventy years old. I had never heard Faustus do it before, but he wanted to indicate annoyance.

Squirming, the messenger admitted he was regularly given the necessary *quadrans*. I asked what he did with it. Dromo whimpered that he saved up until he had enough money for a cake.

Faustus looked angry, though I think he was also trying not to laugh. 'Let's not be harsh,' I intervened. 'While you are working for me, Dromo, use the money properly, then each time you clean off, I will buy you a cake myself.' Some baths have their own pastry shops, or at least a hawker with a sweetmeat tray.

Dromo had no idea when to keep quiet. 'Can I choose my own?'

Faustus rolled his eyes, but I agreed.

Faustus and I sat down for a review of the evidence.

'You're going soft,' he said as we arranged ourselves, nodding towards Dromo who loafed at a distance.

'Not as soft as you, putting up with him. I have a brother and cohorts of cousins. I know boys.' It was men who got the better of me – sometimes. I shuffled my note tablets, so Faustus would not read that thought.

My report took time. Halfway through, one of the aediles' public slaves appeared, bringing a tripod table and a supper that Faustus must have pre-ordered. A change of scene would have been welcome to me after such a long set of interviews, but if we had walked out to eat in a public place we might have been overheard.

It was pleasant enough in the courtyard. As part of a magistrates' office, it was there for display; in order to show the benefits of well-run government under our benign and wondrous emperor, its garden was better kept than that at the Aviola apartment. With food, drink and a sympathetic listener, I relaxed. For me, coming from a very different climate, one great joy of Rome was how you could sit with friends and family out of doors late into the evening.

Once I had reported, I was happy to sit quiet. Manlius Faustus was famously taciturn; he seemed in no hurry to be off home, so he sat on with me. The slave who had served our food came to take away empty bowls, bringing us a beaker of wine each and a jug to water it to taste.

Faustus raised his cup in a good-mannered salute, to which I responded.

'I suppose time is still of the essence, Tiberius?'

'Take all the time you need. Let's get it right.'

Faustus was capable of fending off the authorities. That was good, because today's interviews had given me some unease about this case. 'Don't book the arena lions quite yet – but you may have to.'

Faustus turned to me, on the alert. 'Something bothering you, Albia?'

'Perhaps.'

'Talk it through.'

'Well . . . interviews need absorbing. You tend to take people's first answers literally; you concentrate on whether their stories are probable . . . To be honest, I am not used to talking to slaves, except a few I know well at home.' My parents were liberal owners; their staff were outspoken to a fault. 'I'm sure I have not been told the whole story by these suspects. But they are slaves and I'm a stranger. They are bound to hold things back.'

'Being under threat of death would make anyone anxious,' Faustus mused.

'They need me to help them – so why be quite so wary?' I mentioned something I found particularly odd. 'Start with this – did you see Nicostratus, the porter who died? I agree with the doctor: the beating he took was excessive. I'd like to show you, if you haven't seen.'

'No longer here. The rules say any dead slave must be removed within two hours.'

'From your office?'

'From anywhere. It must derive from an assumption that slaves are polluted by their condition, not normal human beings.'

'Do you think that?'

'No. I believe slavery is an accident of fate. All people are born the same. Some are enslaved, the rest of us are lucky . . . What do you think?' I made no reply. Even though we were easy together, I had no intention of telling him that I had nearly been sold into slavery once. Faustus did not press it. 'I did see Nicostratus when he was still alive,' he said. 'I agree; the violence used on him needs to be explained.'

I had a theory. 'Nicostratus had let Libycus out of the house to socialise with friends.' Faustus listened. 'The story is that the robbers "broke in" – but is that true? There is no sign of damage on the front doors. I shall double-check tomorrow for repairs, but I don't expect to see any.' Faustus nodded. 'So I wonder if Nicostratus accidentally let in the thieves, thinking it was Libycus returning. When the porter saw his mistake, he probably started yelling – and that's why they turned rough.'

'Sounds right . . . This is your only anxiety?'

'No. I am sure the survivors are hiding more, Tiberius. I can't tell – yet – if it is a conspiracy, or whether each slave has their own secret.'

'I trust your intuition,' Faustus answered. 'Take time to dig deeper.'

'If you approve . . . Won't we just hate it, if the vigiles are right and the slaves did it?'

That would leave Faustus stuck with them in sanctuary – though I guessed if we proved they committed murder, the temple authorities would take a hard line. 'You hired me to show the slaves were innocent. But it begins to look as if they must all have ignored the fracas – and that makes them guilty.'

10

I went back to the Esquiline in a carrying chair. Faustus
paid the fare in advance. Expenses up front? That was
civilised, for a client of mine.

He kept Dromo, saying he would send him over tomorrow
with a Stargazer breakfast and other supplies. A take-out
from the Stargazer had many drawbacks, but the street-food
I knew was still better than what I had found so far anywhere
around the Clivus Suburanus.

Arriving at the Aviola building, the carriers bunked off
smartly, leaving me in the street. Now I had a quandary.
The apartment doors were closed and locked. One door
porter was dead, the other in sanctuary. Thank you, gods!

Knocking failed to induce the girl Myla to let me in; I
suspected the dozy lump would not have responded even
if she heard me. Hades, I was thinking like an owner: blaming
a slave simply because she lacked vivacity.

I tried that trick with a hairpin, which never works. I had
a go with my paring knife. I even walked around the block,
looking for the usual weak point, a back entrance. No luck.

I stayed calm. A lock-out could easily have happened at
home in Fountain Court, where the ridiculous porter Rodan
often fastened up, vanished and went deaf even to tenants
and legitimate callers.

It was evening, but not so late that I felt anxious, even

though I was alone and very tired. At least this helped me envisage how the robbers must have faced their break-in: the apartment's narrow entrance through the street-front shops meant only these double doors would give access, and they were strong. They were designed to look formidable; the lock was a serious one, needing a good key. A sliding spyhole would allow a porter to look out at visitors, but although it was wooden (some doors have a metal grille) it was so small there was nothing to gain by smashing it.

I would have done if it would do any good. Every girl should be ready to find a stray brick – and to use it.

I knew the steward lived somewhere up above. However, I might not need to go knocking at the other apartments to find him. Three of the shops were closed up now, but one showed light. When I approached and called out, there was a pause, then two men of North African appearance pulled open their shutter a crack and looked out cautiously.

I guessed these were Libycus' cronies. When I mentioned him, they let me in and sat me down politely on a stool that they brushed clean. They realised he was in big trouble. I made sure they knew that if he was innocent I might help him, so it would be good to assist me.

They were leatherworkers. Not tanners; the smell of hides in preparation is outlawed from city centre neighbourhoods. Leather was supplied to them. These men cut out and put together purses, belts and other fancy goods, punching them with patterns and creating tassels. They had this typical workroom unit, from which they could also make sales. Finished goods hung on strings all around. At the back, steps led up to a mezzanine level where they slept.

I had not expected to continue my enquiries at this time of night, but you take what fate offers. So I learned that with a background in common, Secundus and Myrinus had made friends with Libycus at the baths; knowing these premises were empty and suitable for their business, he passed on a tip. Since they moved in, if ever Aviola didn't want him, Libycus popped along to see them. They confirmed his story of visiting their shop on the night of the murders.

'When he left you, was that only because the hour was late – or had you heard a disturbance?' They said Libycus left because he was nervous in case his master wanted him. Worn out, Secundus and Myrinus then fell into a dead sleep. According to them, they knew nothing about the tragedy until next morning.

Well, that was possible.

Myrinus went up to fetch Polycarpus for me. When the steward came down and let me into the apartment, he was perfectly respectful, went ahead and set out lamps. I suggested he ought to supply a key; he promised to attend to it next day.

'Do you know those leatherworkers?'

'They seem a couple of good boys.'

Polycarpus asked how I had got on with the fugitive slaves. I confined myself to saying 'we held useful discussions'. The slaves were not the only people who could be tight-lipped.

I was pretty sure Polycarpus believed himself capable of winkling more out of me, but he was professional enough to drop the subject. Maybe he guessed that if he didn't, *I* was professional enough to thump him. Also, if he showed too much curiosity, it might look significant.

'Do you feel any great loyalty to the fugitive slaves, Polycarpus?'

'Yes, I feel responsible for them, as their supervisor. We all belong to the same household – one where I was a slave myself once. It counts, Flavia Albia.'

As Aviola's freedman, he was supposed to feel *more* loyalty to his master, but was that really the case? If the slaves were in trouble, how far would Polycarpus go to protect them? Would there ever be a situation where he took their part against his master?

Something to ponder as the inquiry proceeded.

After I was sure Polycarpus had left, and before I went to bed, I made further checks. As I had thought: there was no damage on the front doors or their fancy frame.

Something else failed to fit too: as far as I could tell by the tiny light of an oil lamp, there were no bloodstains on the corridor floor. It was black and white mosaic, with extremely small tesserae, neatly laid. Given the blood Nicostratus must have shed, I would expect to see indelible marks in the grouting, even if the floor had been deep-cleaned. I must double-check tomorrow in the light. Maybe Nicostratus managed to struggle away from his attackers and into the apartment – yet Phaedrus had definitely told me he found his colleague lying unconscious in the entrance corridor.

I was unsure whether this was good news or bad, but I had now identified the first inconsistencies.

11

Next morning I was busy. Fortunately Faustus sent Dromo quite early. He seemed subdued and biddable. I wondered whether he had been ticked off.

Breakfast in hand, I set about close inspection of floors. I felt like a picky housewife, looking for a reason to beat somebody. Someone else here must be equally meticulous, because what I was looking for proved very hard to spot. Eventually I did make out a patch in the hall, where something that might be blood had been cleaned as successfully as possible, though darkened mortar remained between the tiny marble pieces. Back in the narrow entrance corridor I still found no marks.

Further exploration led me to a store room used for collecting rubbish, where someone had dumped a bloody mattress of the thin, lumpy type the slaves used. This must have been Nicostratus' bed, where he was put after he was attacked. I gave it a tug, but recoiled. I was trained to be inquisitive, but some jobs are too disgusting.

A thought struck me. If the porter was that badly hurt, however had he travelled to the Temple of Ceres? Faustus could help me out on that. I would write a report this evening, setting some homework: Faustus must ask the slaves how they escaped and reached the Aventine (on foot, presumably) – then specifically, how did the semi-conscious

Nicostratus manage to cross half Rome with them? Maybe they carried him, but it was a long way.

Given that Nicostratus was the only suspect with an excuse – he was too physically hurt to help his master and mistress – why did he want to go?

I spent much of the morning diligently carrying out the experiments the Camillus brothers had suggested. I stood Dromo in the best bedroom, beside the bed where the murders occurred. I then went to each place where a slave had claimed to be asleep or drunk during the attack. I signalled when I was ready: 'Now, Dromo!' At which, if he was paying attention, Dromo yelled back, 'Help! Help!'

Each time his cries were audible. Of course Dromo had already heard me calling his name in the other direction . . . Still, a good informer double-checks.

I had not replicated the effects of drink or sleeping medicine, which some suspects claimed to have taken, but the kind of lawyers who might be defending the slaves (assuming slaves are given lawyers, which I doubted) were unlikely to query that. Drink or drugs put them at fault anyway.

While I went through this probably pointless exercise, I noticed someone looking down from a small window in one of the upper apartments. A woman poked her head out wondering at the shouting. I called up and made contact, then once I had finished my checks I found the way via the stairs from the outside street and interviewed this neighbour.

Her name was Fauna. She was a worn-looking party of thirty or forty, wife of a vegetable porter at the nearby Market of Livia. 'That's where he is now, of course – unless the bum has given them the slip and slunk off somewhere.'

Fauna had a wrinkled tunic and bare feet, at least at home, with a whole armful of tacky bangles that implied her husband brought one for her out of guilt every time he visited a brothel. Or perhaps he just had little money and appalling taste. Surely if he did frequent brothels, he must have seen better jewellery even on the worst whores?

I hate this aspect of my work – glimpsing other people's lives and becoming angry about it. I have never managed to teach myself that if people choose to be stupid, it's their affair. I wanted to yell at Fauna to sort her bastard husband out.

As soon as she let me in I realised there was not much chance this couple upstairs had seen anything below on the night of the attack. They rented a cramped two-room apartment lit only by small high windows, so when she heard me experimenting Fauna had had to stand on a stool and crane out. For the tenants at ground level this was good, because it meant their courtyard was not really overlooked. For me it was a disappointment.

Fauna said the dinner party itself had been sedate, but later on they had been bothered by a lot of noise, until Lusius, her husband, actually got out of bed to look. Lusius peered out first, then Fauna shoved him off the stool and took a turn. In the dark, they could not really see what was going on.

'I glimpsed figures running to and fro with lamps. About the time we had a peek, it all quietened down anyway.'

'Could that have been when the steward turned up?' I wondered. 'Polycarpus – he would have sorted out the chaos . . . Do you know him, Fauna?'

'They live on this level, but the other side of the building, above the street. I know her slightly.'

'His wife?'

'If that's what she calls herself. He's had her salted away there for years.'

'Ah!' So Polycarpus had not waited to gain his freedom before he started his own household. 'He says he just happened to go back that night and then discovered the crime.'

Fauna shrugged. 'I don't know. While I was looking, people were still talking, but in very low voices. We went back to bed. We never even realised the vigiles had been until next morning. Some fellow came up to see if we heard anything. He didn't really want to know, in case it meant he had to do something useful.'

'Never mind him then, can you describe the disturbance for me?'

'Yelling to start with. Bumps and shunts later. When it first kicked off someone was really angry.'

'How many voices?'

'Well, it must have been several. They say a gang of robbers came—'

'No, no; don't tell me what you *suppose* you heard. I need what you really did hear.' She looked baffled by my distinction. 'All right. Let me ask something else, Fauna. This is important. Did you at any time hear Aviola or his wife calling out for help?'

'Well, someone wanted the world to know he was upset. A man's voice, bellowing furiously. That was what really worried us first and made Lusius go to look . . . He's dog tired in the evening after work; it takes a lot to get him out of bed. The bawler must have been Aviola, mustn't it?'

'Could well be . . .' Or anyone. 'You don't remember hearing a woman?'

'No.' This time she was certain. 'No, I never heard a peep from her. You know, Albia, we couldn't tell what in Hades was happening; we never thought it was as serious as it turned out. To be honest, there had been such a lot of bother to do with the wedding, Lusius and me just thought it was more of the same. That lot, they had grown to be a menace lately – there was always something going on.'

'What kind of thing?'

'People having a go.'

'At each other?'

'Right.' Fauna thought about it. 'There always seemed to be someone sounding off, and then somebody else telling them to shut it.'

'Not just the staff clattering and throwing their voices too loudly? Some don't see the point of going about their work quietly. Houses can be lively places.'

'Ha! My father was a roofer. Nobody beats roofers and scaffolders for shouting . . . There was a lot more commotion lately than there used to be. We knew they was all going away for the summer, and we was looking forward to that, I can tell you. Lusius keeps saying he'll go down and complain, but he's too bone idle to do it.'

'Probably not much point now,' I murmured.

'No, I suppose not. Someone new will move in. I hope we get a quiet family . . . What's going to happen to them slaves?'

I shook my head resignedly.

'Aviola didn't seem to get a grip,' complained Fauna. 'Once, a couple of the men was having a pottery fight, it sounded. But he just asked them to stop, really mildly. I blame him. He ought to have sorted them out properly.' It was indeed a householder's duty to control and prevent quarrels. 'Still,' Fauna giggled. 'When you get married, if you are given any presents, people seem to choose horrible things – then you get stuck with them for years because you can't upset your hubby's awful auntie if you chuck 'em out. Perhaps Aviola was glad to see one or two of his wedding presents broken.'

'I bet he was,' I smiled in return. ' – Remembering some of mine!'

But playing the sympathetic wife and widow failed to squeeze anything more useful out of her.

12

It often happens on a case: the first story you hear seems straightforward, yet it soon starts to show cracks. First the tale of what happened to the door porter did not add up. Now, despite Polycarpus assuring me all was harmonious among the workforce, here was contradictory news of disturbances and pottery fights. Back at the apartment, I poked around in the rubbish store but found no smashed dinnerware. It might already have been carted off to a tip.

I was due to see Aviola's executor, but had time to prepare lunch; a snack stopped Dromo muttering. He was worse to look after than my young brother.

In the kitchen I found Myla feeding her baby, so I took my time and had a closer look at her. As slaves go, she was fairly clean and tidy, with features that suggested she came from an eastern province like Syria or Judaea. I had seen very beautiful Syrian women, with wide-set eyes and straight noses down which they looked with imperious awareness of their own stunning looks. Myla had a heavier face; in another ten years she would be jowly. Even so, she had the imperious expression; for no obvious reason she appeared full of self-belief.

Polycarpus had bought in some basics for me, a loaf, plus boring hard-boiled eggs and salad leaves, though among the stuff Manlius Faustus had sent over were treasures: a crock of good honey, squids in brine and another stone jar of best

87

quality olives. I created a warm drink with the honey and some wine vinegar I found on a shelf. While I stirred it over the fire, I was able to tackle Myla.

When she finished nursing and laid the child in its basket, I dutifully viewed the wrinkled, milky creature. The poor little thing was a girl. I said how sweet she was. This failed to impress the mother.

'So, Myla, are you going to tell me who her father is?'

The mother hunched up at the question, looking as if she had not heard, or more likely did not even know the answer.

'Is this your first?'

'No.'

'How many have you had?'

'Some.'

'What happened to the others?'

'Gone.'

I couldn't tell if that meant dead, sold, or sent to Campania. A slave's children would all be slaves too, of course. Myla had no rights over her babies.

I tried asking her about the night of the murder. She had little to say – *surprise!* – apart from maintaining that when it all kicked off she was trying to sleep, in the slaves' quarters. Nobody was with her. She had such an air of oddity and distance, I wondered if the others avoided her.

She said she had heard an upset going on, but she could barely move due to the late stage of her pregnancy. Anyway, she claimed she was too frightened to look out.

I felt myself taking against her. A man might be attracted by the faint suggestion she would resist nothing sexually. I was harder. If she had given me information, I would have assumed it was unreliable. I gave up on her.

★　★　★

88

At the appointed time, I trotted around the corner to see Aviola's executor. I had made sure I looked like an independent free citizen: strands of gold necklace and floret earrings, with deft applications of make-up and perfume. This was to show I was respectable – or in Roman terms, that my associates had money. I always wore a wedding ring, and introduced myself as a widow. Widows are treated with respect in traditional societies. Mind you, I never banked on it.

Sextus Simplicius was at home. He saw me in his private library. He seemed wary, so I made much of my connection with Manlius Faustus. I had to judge that carefully, however. I didn't want Simplicius running off to deal with the aedile direct.

Sometimes being female works in my favour. Some men find it exciting to engage with a woman – so long as they can tell themselves the meeting will arouse no bile in their suspicious wives (I mean, the wives don't have to know about it). If Simplicius had one, he did not invite her to business discussions. In fact, throughout my investigation I was never to meet her.

I spotted scrutiny that made me sit far enough away to prevent any touching. Given a free choice, I would flatten gropers with a lump hammer. But when I need information I have to work around this problem more politely.

This man must be about the same age as Aviola, who had been a close friend. Simplicius told me there was another executor, also a friend, currently away on his country estate. That was fine, unless it made this one too anxious about speaking to me. There was neither opportunity nor time for them to confer and I wanted him to be frank.

Once we were seated I took a good look at him. He was portly, a man who lived well. Their whole circle probably did, because when he produced a plaque with portraits of Aviola and Mucia, Aviola looked the same type. Aviola and Simplicius had strong Roman faces with deep maturity lines and an air of directness, in the style that is labelled 'republican'. That means the subject has an old-fashioned short temper and expects someone else to pick up after him. Society sees such people as harmless, or even decent and approvable. When one is murdered, like Aviola, society is horrified. 'If him, perhaps me next!'

Such bullies will claim to have simple honesty – though they are equally proud of their crookery. Their wives never speak out of turn, yet usually spend what they like and run rings around these men. The men know it, moan about it to their cronies, yet accept it as normal. They tend to have strong mothers, mothers who remain close, mothers who would give them hell if they divorced.

You may think that was a lot to deduce from a formal wedding picture, but Simplicius was there right in front of me, embodying what Aviola must have been like.

Yes, Aviola had had a mother until recently; I asked. Was she a strong influence? Yes, she had been.

Mucia Lucilia was portrayed in the traditional way as a bland, pretty cipher; since my family deals in art, I knew better than to trust this plaque. On it, she had her veil over her head, one hand placed in that of her new husband to show they were married, and a sweet, meek gaze. This may not mean a woman is submissive in real life. Normally all it tells the viewer is that she is really admired for bringing a good dowry to her marriage.

According to Sextus Simplicius, they were a delightful couple. I smiled discreetly. When you need to dig, start slowly.

Despite my request via his steward, he failed to show me the will. However, he answered whatever I asked about it – or so I thought at the time.

It would be a public document so I restrained my immediate annoyance; I could find it eventually – but I itched to scan that scroll myself if it was in the house. Perhaps Sextus Simplicius thought I could not read. Women he knew would all have secretaries. My adoptive mother was highly literate and had expected me to be the same. Once Helena Justina learned her alphabet (which seems to have been when she was about four), she speed-read and speed-wrote anything for herself; that was what she taught me. My father did possess a secretary, but the man spent his time moaning that no one gave him enough to do. The concept of letting a scribe note down your shopping list or recite a poem at you, with intonation *he* chose, was unknown in our house.

The current will was very recent. Aviola made a new one when he married Mucia Lucilia.

'I have been considering this subject,' Simplicius declared, in a self-conscious, pompous way. Every time he shifted in his seat, a faint spearmint miasma wafted my way. Some diligent body slave kept him pleasant for his public. 'His household knew that he was revising the document, so there *may* have been discussion of the contents. I was at the apartment when the lawyer brought the scroll to be signed; we had the usual gathering of witnesses. It was finalised in private, behind closed doors.'

I told him which slaves were under suspicion; Simplicius said none, not even the scribe Melander, was in the room for the will-signing. 'Only witnesses were admitted. Mucia Lucilia was present, though of course she took no part.'

I managed not to growl at that. 'Simplicius, it looks as if Aviola and Mucia were murdered by robbers, but if Aviola's slaves attacked him as the vigiles suggest, I have to consider if the new will caused disgruntlement. There will have been talk about it, as you say.'

'Unfounded rumours can influence staff,' he agreed.

I said, 'I am interested in two aspects. Were there any large bequests, ones that might make someone want Aviola dead in order to cash in? Don't alarm yourself. This is something we always have to consider, when somebody dies in bad circumstances. Also, what does he have to say about his slaves? Who did he intend to liberate, for example?'

'Or *not*!' added Simplicius heavy-handedly, wafting more lotion scents in my direction. I smiled as if I thought him extremely astute.

Yes, I was ashamed of using flattery. But it is undeniably useful.

Valerius Aviola owned several hundred slaves, mostly of the rural type, working as agricultural labourers on his estates. He intended to free a hundred, the most he was allowed.

At this point, Sextus Simplicius finally had someone fetch the scroll and while I sat tantalised by its proximity, the scribe read out the hundred names. Juno, I had to listen to every one, even though most had no relevance because they worked on Aviola's country estates. I chewed the end of my stylus, trying not to let my eyes glaze over.

None of the hundred manumissions were given reasons. A general heading stated briefly that all these slaves would be rewarded with their freedom 'for their hard work and loyalty'. Of those on my list, only Libycus and Daphnus were to be freed.

'Fascinating!' I checked my note tablet. 'I wonder how Aviola made his choices? Amethystus and Diomedes are a couple of old lags and won't be surprised to be excluded. Libycus is an obvious candidate for freedom; he was the personal valet, so they had an intimate relationship. Daphnus not so, however. He's bright, a go-getter, painfully ambitious, and may have caught Aviola's eye as someone who deserved a chance. But he is only eighteen, and only a tray carrier. Sextus Simplicius, you must have been to the house often. Do you know Daphnus?'

Simplicius raised his heavy shoulders and looked shifty. He probably did not even know the names of his own tray carriers. Daphnus would have been a silent presence placing a drink in front of him, worthy of less notice than the drink.

'Others won't like him jumping the queue. Take Nicostratus, the door porter – a responsible position – he was nearly thirty, so may well have been hoping for his freedom soon. He has died of his injuries, so he won't have to know . . .'

Some of Aviola's deserving slaves had been freed in his lifetime, when they became eligible, the steward for one. Polycarpus and a few others were rewarded for past services with minor bequests.

'Polycarpus!' Simplicius recognised his name with enthusiasm. 'He will be looking for a new position now my poor friend has passed on. To be truthful, I was already eyeing up the situation. There was a rumour that Mucia Lucilia wanted to kick him out and have her own steward take charge. Well, one way or the other, I am hoping to snaffle Polycarpus myself!'

There can be a scramble for good employees after a death, and apparently after a marriage, though I had met his own steward who seemed pleasant and efficient. When I asked what would happen to that man, Simplicius said cold-bloodedly that the fellow would have to accept being pushed aside and sold off. He actually joked that if *he*, Simplicius, was then found murdered, I would know who did it.

I replied that this would be most helpful.

I knew that four of the refugee slaves (the second porter Phaedrus, the attendant Amaranta, the musician Olympe and the philosopher Chrysodorus), plus at least one sent to Campania (the steward Onesimus), had belonged to Mucia Lucilia. I asked Simplicius if he knew anything about Mucia's will, since Roman law did grudgingly allow a woman to dispose of her own property. He claimed to have no idea, though I screwed out details of a freedman who had acted as her official guardian before she married.

We moved on to an outline of Aviola's bequests.

In the will as it stood, I was told, there were a number of gifts to close relatives and old friends. There were rewards for the two executors, payments which Simplicius described demurely as 'generous'. Overall, however, no one person would receive a whacking amount. Freedmen and women were provided with pensions but ordered to continue service to the family in various non-controversial ways. Donations were made to temples. The usual perk was earmarked for the emperor, a bribe to dissuade him from seizing more. Domitian's reaction could never be guessed in advance, but Simplicius told me no one, not even the paranoid tyrant who ruled Rome, had a real reason to speed up Aviola's departure to Hades in order to inherit. Their legacies would be welcome yet were not enormous.

As was a wife's right, an allowance was left to Mucia Lucilia. Simplicius and I discussed the legal problems with both that bequest and her dowry; he intended to take advice (I recommended the Camillus brothers). He needed to know whether Mucia died first. I had to tell him that in my judgement she was killed after Aviola. Since this could not currently be proved, and might never be, Simplicius wanted to obtain a legal opinion that would allow him proceed as Aviola's executor on the basis they 'died at the same time', negating bequests to each other. Possibly there was such a rule.

'Does this will say how Aviola's bequest to Mucia Lucilia should be reassigned if she's no longer alive?' I asked.

'Oh yes. Wives can die early . . .' Childbirth (Mucia was young enough), accident, disease . . . 'The amount would be shared out pro rata among the other beneficiaries. They all get more, therefore – but as they are many, the addition cannot be called significant.'

That would depend on how rich you were to start with, I supposed.

'As a matter of interest, Simplicius, what happens now to slaves who are *not* freed in the will?'

'The rural slaves are part and parcel of the farms they work on.'

'And any others?'

'Have to be liquidated.'

I was startled by his casual turn of phrase. 'What?'

'Sold for their cash value. Some may be taken on by the beneficiaries, for a price set against their legacies. A few may be able to buy their own freedom, according to their assessed value. Otherwise, it's the slave market for any bummers, special auction for the best.'

'They would have known this?'

'Standard practice, my dear.'

There was nothing else I wanted to discuss. The conversation had taken me no further, other than suggesting no beneficiary was likely to have helped Aviola on his way. It cast a little light on why some slaves might have held grudges, but nothing dramatic.

Sextus Simplicius escorted me to the door. He seemed anxious. 'I should warn you about Mucia Lucilia's guardian . . . The man can be a menace – he holds some wild theories. Do not believe everything he may say.'

I like wild people. I thanked Simplicius for the advice – then opted to make the guardian my very next interviewee.

13

Hermes was a sixty-five-year-old family freedman. He had a long, narrow head with vase-handle ears. This came with a pinched, unhappy expression, though I bore in mind he had recently lost his patroness, in grim circumstances.

Women have to be assigned a guardian when they have no husband, father or other obvious head of household. Some women are so much under their guardian's control they marry them, others manage to bamboozle their so-called protectors. As I established when I took Faustus to meet my uncles, I would never have wanted one; I was not prepared to have *anybody* sign my contracts, speak for me legally or invest my capital. Mucia Lucilia had known Hermes since childhood. Perhaps, like so many women I would judge as dimwits, she just accepted the situation – or had she married to escape constraints, thinking Aviola would give her more freedom?

Everything may have been amicable. The picture Hermes gave me was that he and Mucia had enjoyed a friendly relationship and that he organised her affairs with a light hand. Certainly she liked him enough to have kept him as her executor, even when she re-wrote her will recently (which she had done on her marriage, like Aviola); at that time, she could easily have dropped Hermes. If she was nervous about dismissing him, she could always have said her husband made her change.

'Would you call Mucia Lucilia a woman who knew her own mind, Hermes?'

'Very much so.'

Not the nervous type then. This was the first I had heard of Mucia being strong-willed. 'Was she domineering?'

'Oh no. There was never unpleasantness. Mucia Lucilia got her way very diplomatically . . . But she had firm opinions and was quick to act when the mood took her.'

'With Aviola?'

'With anyone. But being contentious was rare; it was just not her way.'

I insisted on being sure; this was important. 'Nobody thought of her as tyrannical? She was well liked?'

'Very much so,' said Hermes again. I would have left it – had he not added, ' – by most people.'

I pricked up my ears. 'Who disliked her?' Apparently Hermes failed to hear the question.

Pretending to change the subject I asked what might seem an innocuous question: 'This probably has no bearing, but if their plans had worked out better, the two victims would never have been at the apartment when the thieves broke in . . . Do you happen to know why they could not leave for Campania straight after their wedding?' The freedman leaned back on his stool and said nothing. His silence screamed at me to persist. 'Hermes, they wanted to go the day before. What stopped them?'

'*Who*, you mean,' Hermes said. He pursed his lips, then gave up the answer. 'Valerius Aviola had been letting someone use his villa. The guest failed to vacate the house when requested – that was why he sent so many slaves on ahead. I believe they had orders to assist with the guest's packing – by force if necessary. Mucia Lucilia was not prepared to share the accommodation.'

'Ah!' So Mucia was firmly putting her foot down – only one day into her marriage. 'Who was this unwanted guest? And why were they being difficult?'

'On *why,* I cannot comment,' returned the freedman primly, indicating the reason was not favourable to the sticking limpet. 'I can certainly tell you *who* she is.'

She? The discovery that Mucia Lucilia refused to share the villa with another woman was intriguing. Had Valerius Aviola kept some long-term mistress secreted away in the country? . . . I guessed Hermes was about to reveal his wild theory, the one Sextus Simplicius had not wished me to hear, in case I believed it. Normally I have no time for other people's crazy thoughts. I like to invent any mad theories for myself – and then discount them.

Hermes flushed red with real anger: 'She was digging her heels in, refusing to go. She was malicious, it was unacceptable, my mistress was adamant and nobody blames her. Flavia Albia, the household slaves had nothing to do with what happened. I can tell you exactly who wanted Aviola and my dear young mistress dead. They thwarted her and she wouldn't take it. She wanted Aviola's villa and to get it, she arranged to have them murdered.'

This must be an amazing villa. 'But, Hermes, who is she?'

'The most jealous, manipulative, evil, scheming woman you will ever meet – his wife!'

14

*D*iana Aventina!
     That blew everything apart. All previous theories had
to be reassessed.

Disappointingly, it turned out that Aviola had not been a
bigamist. He had been previously married but divorced.

Hermes erupted into an outburst where he claimed the
ex-wife was a schemer who had sworn Aviola would not get
away with his remarriage. From the moment it was
announced, she tried to poison him against his new bride.
She was famously vindictive and would stop at nothing,
even murder.

I downplayed all this. Alleged evil scheming needed to be
thought about later, in private. Damaging someone's reputation unfairly carries a high premium in Rome, even if you
are right to defame them. The worse a person is, the more
likely they are to demand compensation and the higher their
claim. I knew my legal uncles would advise restraint.

Cautiously, I prised out the facts. Galla Simplicia had
married Valerius Aviola in their youth, a marriage that lasted
long enough to produce three children. They divorced way
back, yet remained in contact because of those children.
Young at the time of the split, they were brought up by their
mother; she received money for their maintenance and had

grown rather too used to this income. She had property of her own but particularly liked Aviola's handsome and comfortable Campanian villa, where until now she had been allowed to visit, using the excuse that she was taking the children to their family's holiday home.

'How old are they now?'

'All in their twenties.'

'So maintenance payments to their mother ought to have stopped anyway!' I bet the new wife had pointed that out to Aviola.

Hermes said there had never been any question that, as Galla Simplicia now claimed, Aviola had gifted the villa to her. It was well known in their circle that it was his own favourite house. He went down there every summer, and it was natural he would want to take a new wife soon after their wedding. Hermes told me (as Sextus Simplicius had not) that this villa specifically formed part of the bequest from Aviola to Mucia Lucilia in his new will. If he died, he intended that the second wife should have it.

I wondered what his previous will had said. Clearly Galla Simplicia would have angled for it. But possibly the villa had been assigned to the children – and probably they would acquire it now.

I could see exactly why Mucia Lucilia had refused to share the place with Galla Simplicia. I would have done the same. Mucia needed to take charge.

I guessed how sourly Mucia must have viewed the heavily entrenched ex-wife, together with Aviola's now grown-up children. Anyone could guess how much those children must be under their mother's influence.

But there was a reverse slant. Aviola's new marriage, after so many years of easy coexistence, would have destabilised the ex-wife's position. Since they divorced so long before, this change may have surprised her, caught her out. An extreme reaction might have occurred, just as Hermes claimed – yet was it likely?

'She and Aviola had a screaming row. She tried to bully him, using her children.' Hermes flushed scarlet with indignation again, even to his outstanding ears.

'What are the children like?' Spoiled brats, or I was losing my touch.

'Ghastly,' he snapped back. As I thought. 'Expecting to sponge off their father for life.'

'Boys? Girls?'

'Useless boy, two insipid girls. Galla was terrified their father would lose interest, especially if Mucia Lucilia were to bear children who might supplant hers.'

A reasonable fear. Many an older father prefers the fresh little infants of his still-warm second marriage to the ruder, more demanding children of a troubled first union. Galla's three were old enough to have gone through their charmless adolescence, which can leave permanent bad feeling; in any case, Aviola may never have known his children well. Babies lie in their cradles blowing bubbles like helpless darlings who won't cost any money, or cause family quarrels, or ever stop loving their besotted papa . . . Meanwhile the determined second wives are right on the scene, constantly reinforcing the new brood's claims.

'Galla Simplicia is a shrewd woman?'

'Brutally,' snarled Hermes.

'Even so, to want two people dead seems extraordinary, let alone make it happen in such a terrible way. Are you certain Galla would do that?'

'Absolutely!' he assured me.

Without enthusiasm, I mused aloud that I would now have to trek to Campania, in order to interview this woman. Hermes barked with harsh laughter. According to him, Galla Simplicia would have heard that Aviola was dead, and was bound to be hot-footing it to Rome to make a claim on the estate.

'Sit tight and you will soon meet her, whirling in to cause trouble!'

I could hardly wait.

15

I returned to Sextus Simplicius' house, with angry words in mind, but he was 'not at home'. I bet he had gone out on purpose, in case I came racing back to roar at him for withholding information. Alternatively, he was in, but not to me – hiding behind a door until I went away. I hoped he got cramp.

It was the steward who spoke to me. It would be wrong for me to inform him he might be displaced by Polycarpus, but he seemed shrewd. I suspected he knew his job was threatened. I felt sorry for him, and I wondered if an unhappy man might open up.

I sighed, genuinely weary. 'Oh dear. I am running around in circles over this Aviola business. I just learned about his ex-wife, Galla Simplicia, and I desperately need to ask your master for more details. There is a rumour she is troublesome, and on her way to Rome.' The steward, Gratus, smiled slightly. 'I need some background, Gratus, before I have to run up against her . . . Still, I won't ask you questions that you shouldn't answer.' Of course I planned to do just that.

Gratus, who was slim and rather elegant, opened his hands in an ironic gesture. 'Flavia Albia, I cannot possibly give an opinion of the lady . . . and I warn you, my master won't spill secrets.'

'Oh? Are they on friendly terms? I suppose while she was

married to Valerius Aviola she was part of the same circle, and may still be . . .' I made it sound as if I was musing to myself.

'She will stay with us,' Gratus murmured, as if he too were talking aloud to himself. 'I have the bed made up already . . .' Then he enjoyed telling me: 'Galla Simplicia and my master are first cousins.'

I offered my hand formally and shook his. It was acknowledgement for this help, while indicating I could not possibly offend him with anything so uncouth as a bribe.

Gratus definitely knew Polycarpus was about to steal his job. He was still a slave; there would be nothing he could do about it. I wished I knew someone in need of a good household steward to whom I could recommend him.

I had had a busy day. Returning to the Aviola apartment, I felt in no mood to prepare detailed notes for Manlius Faustus, but Dromo was hanging about expectantly, wanting to take my report.

First I found my oil flask and went out to some nearby baths, taking Dromo too. There was just time for me to have a quick wash and scrape in the women's hour, then when the bell rang to announce men's time I waited in a colonnade, scrawling brief notes for the aedile, while the messenger washed. I had promised him a cake, and was true to my word.

Dromo still smelt – of more than chopped nuts and custard.

'How many tunics do you have, Dromo?'

'One.'

I added a postscript to my notes: *kindly supply your stinky boy with a spare garment! Please treat as urgent and make sure it has been laundered. Do this for me, most admirable Tiberius, so I can apply myself with a clear mind to the monster ex-wife. Should be good value. You know you want details.*

I had no idea whether Faustus enjoyed gossip. If not, I could teach him. All you need is curiosity and a sense of humour. He had those.

Dromo sauntered off with my report, slavering over his pastry and getting custard on the note tablet.

I took a layered date-slice back with me to the apartment. Why should a slave have all the treats?

On the way I bought a hot pie too. This is not good nourishment, but the informers' creed says the demands of our work compel us to live off unsuitable street food and large amounts of drink. Our life is hard. Some really like to suffer, so they attend experimental harp concerts or dangerous political readings, but after a day's serious investigating, you risk falling asleep and wasting the ticket price.

I bought a flagon of cheap wine. You have to keep up the image.

Later, I was glad I stayed in or I would have missed a visitor. Galla Simplicia had rushed to Rome, where the minute she had dumped her travelling hat in her cousin's spare room, she came straight here to view the scene of the crime.

If the murder of Aviola and Mucia was *her* crime, as Hermes believed, this stupidly drew attention to herself. Still, any woman who does arrange to have her ex-husband violently taken out by professional robbers must have a touch of the brash.

I guessed who she was, though she looked a perfectly ordinary woman. That's evil schemers for you. If all those who plotted had talons and Medusa snake hair, identifying them would be too easy.

I had heard voices; I emerged from my room unnoticed. I stood quiet in the colonnade and watched.

Myla must have let her in. They were now on the opposite side of the courtyard with their backs to me. Myla was waiting while the visitor squared up and went into the bedroom where the couple had been killed. I read in Myla's slumped stance that she was unhappy about the situation, but of course she made no objection. Myla was too lethargic. For her part, Galla Simplicia had an air of determined authority, even viewed from behind.

Some women neglect their back view, but this one was pert, cinched and ringletted. Her coiffure must have taken half a day. I wondered if she had it done specially to come to Rome legacy-hunting.

It struck me that if Myla had been in this household for a long time, then Galla Simplicia had once been her mistress, giving her orders – and possibly even forming a sympathetic bond.

I stepped forward to stand between the columns, so as soon as Galla re-emerged she saw me. Myla immediately took herself off; it was the first time I had seen her walking, which she did with a languorous sway. Galla shot a tetchy glance after her (so I could see no residual friendship), then came towards me across the courtyard as if she belonged here and meant to send me packing.

I got in first. 'Excuse me! Can I help you?' I called out, implying *who let you in without permission, and what do you think you are doing?* 'My name is Flavia Albia; I am working for the aedile Manlius Faustus. This is a crime scene, if you don't know. We are not permitting ghoulish viewings. I will have to ask you to leave.'

Galla Simplicia braved it out well. She pulled her stole over her head, modestly burying her face in the material as if genuinely horrified by the hideous events. I could see her assessing me as she peeked out. 'I meant no offence. I wanted to see where my husband died.' For someone supposedly vindictive, her voice was surprisingly weak. A high, decently-spoken but thin voice: I took against it.

Now we stood closer, I saw she had a smooth face with fine, light-coloured hair. She peered slightly, as if she was short-sighted. Hermes' angry denunciations had implied a hard-faced hag, a woman who would look worn by a hard life – or simply a hard nature. But Simplicia looked almost young for her age.

'Valerius Aviola's wife was Mucia Lucilia, who died with him,' I pointed out severely. 'You will be Galla Simplicia. Why don't you sit here –' I indicated the chairs I had put out when I interviewed Polycarpus. Myla had never removed them, of course. 'You can recover from any emotional upset, while I fetch my writing equipment. Since you are here, let's run through some questions I need to ask you.'

'Should I have somebody with me?' I thought her alarm was put on.

'This is not a court.' I steered her to the less comfortable seat. She ended up with an old folding x-stool; I wondered if she remembered it from her marriage. 'I want to establish a few facts. Woman to woman,' I cooed falsely. If she really had been involved in foul play, the last thing she wanted was an intimate exchange.

It took no time to gather up a note tablet and stylus in my room, but when I went back Galla Simplicia was already on her feet again, thinking to escape. She had dithered too long. I raised my eyebrows, as if failure to cooperate would count against her. She dropped back into her seat.

I took the more comfortable wicker chair. 'Shall I ask Myla to bring refreshments?'

'I don't think so!' I spotted an underlying dryness in Simplicia's tone.

'You're right; she verges on useless. It beats me why people keep such girls, but I suppose when they have been in a house for a long time they are tolerated by default.'

My companion said nothing, though the ends of her mouth tightened.

On further inspection, Galla Simplicia must be forty, or closing fast. She was a type, proved by her wearing strappy sandals that just fell short of those beloved by the easy girls under the arches of the Circus Maximus. She indulged in time-consuming manicures, facials and hair-procedures. As well as too many finger-rings, she wore a complex gold necklace with a pendant of big Indian pearls, the kind that women with little-girl voices can extract from weak-willed men. She liked the good things in life; she knew where and how to obtain them. She continued to squeeze money from Aviola after he divorced her, but his marrying Mucia would finally have put a stop to it.

Galla would have hated that.

I began coolly: 'You and Valerius Aviola split up long ago, so you are not a fragile widow around whom I must tiptoe gently. I realise what happened is a shock, but I have to be blunt. The situation has become an embarrassment for the Temple of Ceres, so they want answers quickly.'

'The Temple? . . .' Galla quavered, though I presumed her cousin had explained the situation to her.

I myself discussed the slaves taking refuge. 'They will take the blame and be executed, for not saving their master and mistress – that's unless it can be shown who really murdered them.'

'Do you think you can find out?'

I looked Galla Simplicia in the eye. Was she saying *do you know it was me?* 'That is the intention.' I paused for a beat, then said, 'I was surprised to be told that you yourself wanted the couple out of the way.'

'I deny it!' Of course she did. 'We were perfectly friendly.' Of course they were not.

'Well, I expected you to deny it,' I replied, as if that was enough. A wise woman would understand that I hadn't even started.

'It is a terrible thing to say – and it's a lie!'

'It could be misinformation from people with vested interests –' That sounded fair. I did not want her to be able to allege I was prejudiced against her. 'But much weight is given to informants these days, you know. Our emperor encourages people to speak out against their associates. Please use this opportunity to clarify everything, will you? Accusations are being bandied about that you were afraid for your children's future – so let's talk about the children first.'

We established the family tree. Valerius, Valeria and Simplicia were twenty-five, twenty-one and nineteen. Valerius still lived with his mother. I could imagine what that signified. Both daughters were married, Valeria about to produce her first child; I wondered if the prospect of becoming a grandfather had spurred Aviola to remarry.

'He wanted to prove his virility,' sneered Galla, of her own accord. 'Don't they all? It's so pathetic.'

'You reckon he would have produced a second family?'

'She –' That was Mucia Lucilia. '– had no children. Yet! She wouldn't refuse. Of course he would be thrilled – then he would have died on them while they were still helpless infants. Just *so* selfish!'

'You have a bleak view of men.'

'Don't you?' Galla demanded, staring at me bitterly. It was true I had seen the worst men do. But I felt no sense of sisterhood. Not that this woman wanted my friendship.

Even so, I pretended we were speaking freely. 'So, Galla Simplicia, you were understandably anxious about your children? Perhaps you were afraid of them losing their father's affection? Is it right you would have done anything to safeguard their position?'

'I am a mother, I defend my brood. I have brought them up myself—'

'With financial help, surely?'

'Left to himself, my husband would have begrudged every copper. It was a constant battle to point out what was right. We wrangled for years. Of course the children have no idea what I had to go through; I managed to protect them from seeing the strife.'

'Did their father not love them?'

'Oh *yes!*' Galla made an extravagant gesture. 'But *love* does not pay for somewhere to live, for clothes, schooling, treats to give them a happy childhood – does it?'

Not if luxury is what you expect in life, I thought. If you grow up with nothing, then love – if you ever acquire it – is a huge luxury.

'Were you really afraid Aviola would turn against them?'

'Of course I was! That fear was perfectly justified, believe me. It does not mean, Flavia Albia, that I felt driven to send murderers here – even if I knew how one goes about finding such people. A woman like me . . . Or are you suggesting I came here secretly myself, and beat the victims to death with my own hands?'

I toughened up. 'I see the grisly details have been kept from you, Simplicia. Only the door porter was beaten up. Aviola and Mucia were strangled.'

Galla blinked, then looked subdued. 'Horrible. Would they suffer? Is it,' she whispered with what seemed genuine pity, 'a swift death?'

'It can be.' She must know I was watching her closely. 'They both struggled. As the scene has been described, my interpretation is that Aviola was killed first, which implies he was perhaps taken unawares—' I paused for effect. 'Mucia Lucilia would have seen Aviola being killed, so she knew what was coming for her. Her terror must have been extreme.'

'Unbearable,' agreed Galla briefly.

She did not say it as if she rejoiced in her rival's torment – but who would? Even if Galla Simplicia was involved, I judged her too good an actress to betray herself.

16

Mother's Boy had been dragged from Campania to Rome with Mother. Did she want to be able to produce him as the wronged heir, like a tame dove from a conjurer's sweaty armpit? I made arrangements with Galla to interview her darling the next morning, but graciously allowed them time to wake up first, after their journey. Mummy's Precious was bound to be master of the long lie-in.

Tingling at this unexpected swing in the case, I myself rose early.

'You are causing me a lot of trouble!' Dromo whined.

'How come?'

'He made me go to some baths *again*! Two times the same day. He hauled me there himself and got a horrible attendant to torture me.' He, being Faustus, had then equipped Dromo with an old tunic of his own. I had seen Faustus wearing the faded garment, when he was acting as a man of the streets, incognito. It gave me an odd feeling.

The restless slave continued to brood on the unfair treatment inflicted by this cruel master. 'I'm not going every day! . . . Oh, don't make me do that, Albia.'

'Get a grip, Dromo.'

'Can I have another cake for being washed twice?'

'No. Eat this.'

I had made us breakfast rolls, fresh from a local bakery and filled with cold sliced beef; I went out for the ingredients myself. 'Do you want a pickled gherkin with it?'

'I don't like them.' Refusing pickles, Dromo was like a big five-year-old.

'Good. I can eat both.'

'I could *try* one.' Make that a three-year-old.

'Too late, lad.'

I still had time to spare before interviewing Aviola and Galla's son. Since Polycarpus had not appeared that morning, I took the chance to go upstairs and investigate where he lived. Secundus and Myrinus, the North African leather-workers who were Libycus' friends, were opening the shutters on their shop and they pointed me to the right stairs.

It was a long hike up, almost to the top of the building. In this it was typical of Rome, and no worse than my own office at Fountain Court. Stone steps led directly from the street; they were cleaner, with more light than I was used to in my building. I guessed housewives swept and tidied them, not a lazy general cleaner. So there were no lost toys to trip over and hardly any smells. Well, I noticed *some* smells, though not bad enough to make me want to hold my breath until I reached the next level.

As I reached the door I heard a dog start excitedly barking. When I knocked, a woman called out to know who it was; this was followed by exasperated orders to the dog. After a period of paw-scrabbling, a door slammed inside. A short, breathless woman with joined Eastern eyebrows and dark moles, though not unattractive, opened up. She looked out as if she feared I would be nagging her to buy worm-eaten sponges from a tray. I repeated who I was. She cannot have heard properly, while struggling to control the dog.

'I suppose you should come in. He's out.'

'Thank you. I don't need to see Polycarpus himself; you can probably help me.'

She looked worried by that. Was she unused to speaking for herself – or, rather, speaking for him? Many an ex-slave who has had to obey orders all his life behaves very strictly with his own household once he acquires one.

I even wondered if Polycarpus beat his wife, though I saw no bruises, nor was she cowed.

The apartment was only three rooms, as far as I could see. She led me to their main room. I was not invited to inspect the rest. She had just introduced herself as Graecina when the dog began barking again. She stepped out, closing the door behind her, and I heard her tell someone to walk the creature.

'There; that should give us some peace. The lad has taken him out.'

I never saw the dog, though I would have liked to. He sounded like a savage guard-dog, but I suspected he was barking above his weight. I never saw the lad either, their son presumably; Polycarpus had mentioned children. I had no interest in a boy. I had enough ridiculousness with Dromo.

The home was neat, spotless, furnished rather heavily as tends to happen with first-generation citizens. There was one couch, padded to a hard finish, on the edge of which Graecina and I both perched.

We exchanged light chit-chat about how long they had been there. I was surprised to learn that Graecina did *not* come from the Aviola household, as I expected. I wondered if she had been a bar girl, though if so she had learned to disguise it. She had turned her back on the filthy aspects of the refreshment trade. To gain this better life, she had to sleep with Polycarpus, but not with every sweat-stained randy Titus who had a drink then wanted to take her upstairs for a cheap thrash.

Every side-table in her apartment was crowned with a doily, while a set of matched glass tipple-tots was on proud display, probably never used.

I asked first about the night of the robbery. Graecina confirmed what Polycarpus had said about him returning downstairs on a whim, and then discovering the robbery. If he had coached his wife in this story, I could spot no signs of collusion – though a good steward knows how to get a tale told right.

This apartment was similar in layout to that rented by Lusius and Fauna on the other side, which I had already visited. It had the same small high windows, letting in light but not made for looking out. According to Graecina, no noises from the courtyard had risen up here that night. She denied Fauna's complaint of increased disturbance around the wedding; still, if Graecina and Polycarpus loyally declared that Aviola's household were as quiet as mice, that was only their duty.

Actually mice can make a hell of a racket, knocking about a building and gnawing like maniacs in the middle of the night. The mice in Fountain Court were hideously loud, as well as fearless.

While witnesses are true as steel, of course.

Maybe.

★　　★　　★

'So was there anything else you wanted, Flavia Albia?' Graecina seemed uneasy, and anxious to be rid of me.

'Well, the reason I came up was to ask Polycarpus for his private opinion of Galla Simplicia, Aviola's divorced wife. Have you met her, Graecina?'

'No, I've only seen her from a distance.' Graecina hesitated over whether to speak about the ex-wife of her husband's master – but she decided to enjoy the chance. 'My husband never had much good to say about her, though at least she's better than the new one.'

'What did Polycarpus have against Mucia Lucilia? Reorganising the household?' I asked, playing innocent. His main beef may have been that Mucia planned to let him go, in favour of her own steward, Onesimus.

Graecina conceded the point. 'Yes, she wants – wanted – her own people around her. Personally, I don't think you can blame her.' She shrugged. 'It was all going to sort itself out.'

I decided to test ideas on her. 'Am I right, that Mucia's steward Onesimus was sent to Campania to be in charge through the summer, while your husband was to be left here? Onesimus will be back empty-handed now, of course . . . Mind you, hasn't any conflict between the stewards resolved itself? I heard Polycarpus might be offered an opening elsewhere?'

'Well, you keep your ear to the ground!' cried Graecina admiringly.

'Just doing my job.' I slipped in a question about the ex-wife: 'I'm surprised you spoke well of the ex. I heard Galla Simplicia is the kind of woman who would resort to violence? If Aviola brought in a rival, wouldn't she do her utmost to remove the rival?'

'What are you asking, Albia?' Graecina was stalling.

'Would Galla go so far as to hire killers – as has been suggested?'

Graecina looked truly shocked. 'That would be terrible!' I wondered. Did Polycarpus' wife have to feel grateful to Sextus Simplicius for offering Polycarpus a new place? Did that mean she couldn't risk blackening the name of the new master's female relative? 'Oh, Albia, how could she do it? How would a woman find people to do such a thing?'

'Well, she herself might have no idea – however, there is someone here with excellent local contacts . . . I have to ask you: Graecina, did Galla ever try to get your husband to do something bad?'

'He wouldn't!'

Maybe Galla asked him, but Polycarpus hadn't mentioned it to his wife. I always assume men do *not* tell their wives anything those wives might disapprove of.

Think about it. If Galla Simplicia restored friendly relations with Polycarpus by persuading her cousin to offer him a job, then Polycarpus, the all-knowing, wheeling, dealing facilitator, might have been able to tell Galla who the criminals were around the Clivus Suburanus. If he didn't know to start with, people Polycarpus knew could tell him.

I had seen him operating. *He* could work out how to make contact. Adept at dropping the right word in the right ear, he could fix a secret meet. I bet the neighbourhood's chief gangster either knew who Polycarpus was, or had sidekicks willing to vouch for him. After which, employment is always welcome to businessmen, including gangsters. It would be short work for them to tender for the job, agree a price, claim a deposit, programme the work, receive the necessary victim-profile and a sketch plan of the apartment, then do the deed.

Polycarpus would have been able to arrange for someone to open the door. Maybe the timescale of his trip downstairs 'on a whim' was all wrong, and he came for this purpose.

Maybe he unlocked the door himself.

On the other hand, maybe Polycarpus was exactly as he made out: an honest, hardworking, loyal long-term servant of a master who might yet have resisted the beseeching of his misguided new wife. Aviola might never have replaced Polycarpus with Onesimus as Mucia wanted. Sextus Simplicius could have got this wrong. Or Onesimus might make a hash of the work in Campania and lose his chance.

Even if Aviola was ready to dump Polycarpus, maybe Polycarpus remembered too much about Galla from the old days. He might not want to work for her cousin.

Even if he did, surely Polycarpus still had more sense than to assist Galla Simplicia with a crime that carried a death sentence?

Ideas were jumping up like sand-flies. But I concealed them from Graecina, who had concerns of her own. A young child started mithering in another room, so I took my leave.

17

I went for my planned interview with Galla's son.
Marcus Valerius Simplicianus was twenty-five, an age
when ambitious young Roman men can be awarded political
positions. But this waste of space would not be standing for
office. The only thing he would work hard at – *very* hard
– was avoiding work.

His mother thought he was wonderful. Everyone else saw
through it, but that did not impinge on Valerius, who himself
happily believed the myth.

I thought it was extremely unfair that the gods had given
this ning-nong-ninnying noodle such beautiful eyelashes.

He had lashes like an unweaned prize calf. Most women I
knew would drool with envy. One or two would drool all
over him, because of his eye decorations, though I myself
was repulsed. I like effective men.

The remaining parts of Valerius are not worth noting. I
could see only slight resemblance to his mother, a pleasant-
looking woman, nor did he share any facial features with
the ceramic plaque of his republican-style father. So much
for art.

He had an annoying voice. His nasal whine was even more
trying because he could not pronounce his 'r's. Either he could
not manage it because of a real defect, or he simply could

not be bothered to speak properly. I thought it an affectation.

Of course I was not prejudiced against him, which would be unprofessional. He was a witness, possibly a suspect. I therefore remained entirely neutral about the idle, no-good, exasperating, spoiled brat.

'You look as if you don't like me!' So he was not entirely an idiot.

We had a short, brisk interview. I asked bluntly if he had wanted to kill his father; he looked amused at the suggestion and denied it. Believing in himself so much, Valerius Simplicianus was unable to imagine his papa ever doing him down – which meant he really did lack motive. His line was, 'The old man could be annoying, but when all was said and done, we got on fine.'

In other words, since Aviola could not possibly take against such a perfect heir, the heir had no reason to murder his father. Did he?

Weight was against him. His skinny wrists would never manage the steady force needed to strangle someone.

So I asked about his mother and how people were saying she harboured murderous thoughts. To that, Valerius replied in the same languorous, unconcerned tone: 'Well, the old lady goes off into a world of her own sometimes, but she wouldn't harm a fly. She's horribly distressed about what happened – and really you ought not to hound her.'

I said I was sorry if his mother felt hounded. All anybody wanted was to discover the truth about this terrible crime. 'Me too!' answered the wonderboy, speaking very earnestly. He had put on his serious face. He leaned towards me and seemed to think he had cleverly deflected my enquiries.

His mother came into the room at that point. There was no point tying to dissect the son while Mama was supervising.

Since the executor, Simplicius, had been keeping quiet about the ex-wife and children when I spoke to him, he had of course misled me on Aviola's will. I now ascertained from Galla Simplicia that when Simplicius vaguely spoke of 'a number of bequests to close relatives and old friends' this included recognition of his three children. Being an effete wastrel, Valerius knew in full what he was due. (They have to. How else will they live? Besides, legacy-hunting is a very Roman occupation.)

He seemed oblivious to the implications of admitting he had known he would come into money when his father died, though I could tell from his mother's narrow expression that she was well aware it made him a suspect.

I took my leave.

I still had an open mind about Galla Simplicia. I needed evidence. If she had plotted, then let her think she had escaped, while I dug deeper.

I doubted that she killed the couple herself. Strangulation can be a woman's method, but not when it involves more than one person at a time – well, except when a deranged mother kills all her infant children. Aviola and Mucia together could have driven her off. More importantly, Galla Simplicia did not have the physical strength to have beaten the door porter, Nicostratus. More than one attacker must have taken part, and whoever did it really knew how to inflict fatal damage.

That presumably indicated robbers – though it might not. I was supposed to be investigating the slaves, and if they really were guilty, I must start wondering whether any robbers had been involved at all that night. Or was the story a cover-up?

I wanted to pursue that. Manlius Faustus had insisted that my commission was not to include contact with criminals. That wouldn't stop me if it was needed.

However, so long as there are alternatives I am not foolish. I had not yet tried consulting the vigiles. Perhaps they had wise words to offer on this case (feel free to guffaw). Then, if I did decide to go behind my employer's back, at least the vigiles could tell me first which ghastly local gangsters might have been involved. But I presumed they had questioned the usual suspects.

I had to steel myself to visit the Second Cohort. For a woman, even talking to the vigiles means a trial of courage and personality, especially in a strange district. I needed to get this over with before I lost my nerve.

18

'I'm glad to know I haven't lost my touch!'

Uncle Quintus, the handsome, likeable one of my Camillus uncles, surprised me by arriving at the Aviola apartment. I was just slinking out, with a stole wrapped around me to look like a respectable matron. He claimed he had guessed what I would be up to. I kept mum and glared.

'You are going to tangle with the vigiles – then you'll want to go after the robbers, don't deny it, Albia. I checked progress with your client this morning and it's obvious. Manlius Faustus is an idiot if he trusts you to obey orders.'

'He's not an idiot – but he is wrong, and so are you, to try and tie me down.'

Quintus tipped his head on one side. He had rather fine brown eyes which he deployed – perhaps unconsciously, though I thought not – to inveigle women who knew better to fall in with his wiles. Don't ask me what wiles. I preferred not to know. 'So what's the story there?' he asked.

'Where?'

'Devious Niece, you and the plebeian aedile?'

'There is no story. Nosy Uncle, why don't you trot into the apartment and inspect the scene of crime, while I nip out for an onion? There's a slave called Myla who has been waiting all her life to be bewitched by you. Leave me alone and ask her some questions.'

'Ooh, will she make wild relevations?'

'You will doubtless get further with her than I did.'

'She can wait,' decided Quintus annoyingly. 'I'll plan my assault on the winsome Myla while I am escorting you.'

I gave in. To be honest I was glad. He must have come straight from the Curia, so was still togaed up. It never does any harm to take a senator, with his full purple banding, when you venture into the offices of armed men who despise women. Besides, despite his snooty rank and mild demeanour, my uncle kept in shape; he always made handy back-up.

He had a couple of bodyguards following him about discreetly too. Because of the case, I took more notice of them than usual. They were his usual lost lambs – ex-legionaries who had been invalided out of the army, one with a paralysed arm, one who hadn't actually lost an eye but might as well have done, he was so short-sighted – and he really did have an ear torn off, probably not in battle. This was typical of Uncle Quintus. His career posting as a military tribune had left him feeling responsibility towards the Empire's damaged soldiers. He had felt sorry for my late husband in the same way.

Would these two squaddies, with not a whole set of limbs between them, be good enough protection today? Quintus probably had innocent faith in them, but I would avoid anywhere we might be mugged.

I was not accompanied by Dromo. He had been asleep with his mouth wide open and I had tiptoed past him.

Good work – until I ran into my uncle.

As we set off walking, I admitted that 'winsome' Myla was a lazy, lactating lump on whom Uncle Quintus would not want to waste his skills.

I also admitted I was going to see Titianus. My uncle declared the Second Cohort were donkey dung (which I told him was normal for the vigiles), and corrupt (which we agreed we also expected), and even more undermanned than the other cohorts – which last point showed Quintus Camillus Justinus in his true light. He had carried out useful research before he turned up.

Of course he was good. My father trained him.

The station house of the Second Cohort had been built down the highway from the Esquiline Gate. It was most fragrantly situated between the large Pallantian Garden, created by a freedman of the Emperor Claudius, and the even more elaborate, statue-crammed, water-featured, gazeboed and porticoed Gardens of Lamia and Maiana, with the Gardens of Maecenas adjacent, containing a fancy auditorium where my father in a misguided moment once held a public poetry reading. This area was a topiary seller's dream. Lopsided sea monsters and one-winged phoenixes, clipped in laurel and box, watched your every move. In June you couldn't breathe for poplar fluff. The vigiles were beset by elegant recreational facilities – which I bet they never even noticed. More importantly for their work as firefighters, they had easy access to aqueducts.

On a good day, Titianus would have been off duty. I would have pressed his disloyal colleagues to give their opinion of his half-baked Aviola inquiry, and they might have dished dirt. It was not a good day. Instead of working at night, like any conscientious investigator who goes out on foot with the troops, this swine liked to take his ease on the day shift, playing with paperwork by himself. He was available in his snug.

I could see why the Second Cohort had made Titianus their inquiry officer. He would never meld in anywhere else. The average firefighter is built like a stone sarcophagus, with short wide legs and no neck: a wide-loom tunic man. They like ripping those tunics off in public, to amaze onlookers with their physique.

Sadly for him, Titianus had hair of an indiscriminate colour, pouchy eyes and a desolate expression, while his physique was far from fantastic. He did wear a tunic that was wider than it was long, but it hung off him in folds. It looked like the skin of an obese patient whose doctor has starved him into losing two hundred pounds, the week before he collapses and dies of malnutrition. ('At least he was *healthy* when he passed away.' 'Well, thank you, doctor!')

Unlike normal inquiry officers, we found Titianus sitting up straight at his desk. Evidently he had not been shown how to put up his boots on the table while he cleaned out his ear-wax. What was wrong with the Second Cohort's training manual? Finding him *not* belching over a packet of cold bar snacks, Uncle Quintus looked disappointed. He is always hungry and was expecting to pinch nibbles.

After introductions, Quintus left me to it; he wandered back outside to the exercise yard, the hub of any vigiles barracks, where men on call were tidying equipment. I knew he would start asking questions about firefighting kit, then while he endeared himself to the troops by treating them as human, he would fish for any facts that Titianus might prefer to keep from us.

In the office, I started by asking the dolorous-eyed Titianus about the night of the robbery. There were no surprises. That in itself was no surprise.

'Yes, it all fits!' He probably thought my remark was a

commendation. 'One thing you can tell me, Titianus, is what the killers used to strangle the victims. Rope has been mentioned. Is it correct you took it away as evidence?'

This time Titianus squirmed unhappily. 'There was a rope, left around the dead woman's neck. That steward, Poly-wotsit, took it off her – act of respect to the dead. I didn't collect it from the scene immediately as I was too busy, and later it had vanished. Thrown out when they tidied up? It wasn't important.'

'It might be. An aggressive lawyer may call this careless-ness,' I warned him frankly.

'Bull's balls. Let him. I don't see it. What point is some nasty twine? We confiscate knives – to be honest, we find our own uses for those. But we haven't enough space to store endless crates of rubbish, just because perps have used them as murder weapons. We'd be cluttered up with rusty pruning hooks and broken planks off building sites. We can't do it.'

'Not even in cases you haven't solved yet, where these may turn out to be clues?'

'Oh, face it, Flavia Albia – nobody's ever going to solve this case!'

I was tempted to declare that *I* would solve it, but I was starting to agree with him. I made much of needing to file a report for the aedile: 'He's going to ask about the robbers, Titianus. What story can we give him there?' Saying 'we' was deliberate. Even a vigiles inquiry officer who stayed in the office to play about with bureaucracy, or whatever Titianus played with, would avoid having his work checked by a magistrate.

'I don't reckon there were any robbers,' Titianus claimed, his attitude now defensive. 'It's staring you in the face, woman: the slaves killed their masters, then they snaffled the silver and made up a story about the house being broken into, using that as cover.'

'They didn't fool you then . . . Still, I assume you do have villains around here who occasionally climb into apartments and remove important property?'

'Plenty.'

'Care to suggest names? I like to supply detail. Then my employer thinks I have been thorough.' Actually, I like to be thorough in fact, so any details I supply to a client are correct.

Titianus listed some Esquiline ne'er-do-wells, each time asserting that these were small-fry no-hopers who would not touch serious bullion even if they came across it hanging on a washing line, let alone would they go out deliberately targeting fine drinksware. Nobody here wanted to steal anything that would be recognisable. According to Titianus, this was because the crafty vigiles would come calling while the thieves were still in possession of the goods.

According to me, that was cobnuts.

'Somebody is in possession of the pierced silver wine strainers and the dinky goat-legged coaster set!' Titianus looked puzzled that I could itemise the stolen goods. I almost expected him to start writing down what I said; I felt pretty sure he had never made a list himself. 'So who is the big octopus on the Esquiline rocks?' He shrugged. 'Come on, Titianus, share your expertise. Which gangster has the fattest file of case notes in the scroll cupboard, yet no arrests are made – or if they ever do go to the praetor and onwards to court, somehow no prosecutions stick?' Titianus remained boot-faced. 'Who are all the other villains afraid of, Titianus? Who dares brazenly kill, in the process of another crime?'

'Could be the Rabirii.' He answered straightaway, now I spelled it out for him. He could have told me in the first place.

'So have you pulled the Rabirii in for questioning?'

'Of course not,' snarled Titianus. 'They would only deny it. Then their barristers would take my tribune for a drink and suddenly I would lose my job. The Rabirii would visit my old mother and make her cry. If they were particularly annoyed, they'd write foul messages about my sexual habits on a Forum wall.'

I smiled at him gently. 'I understand. But I expect your ma would give them a seeing to . . . Mothers tend to be tough. So,' I nagged, refusing to give up, 'Titianus, if I want to have a word with the deadly Rabirii, where shall I find these exciting master crooks?'

Titianus spent the next few minutes telling me I was out of my mind, with colourful details of what led to his diagnosis. 'Are you so bored with life you want to be found in pieces on a rubbish dump?' Uncle Quintus put his head back around the door, looking interested.

Once the officer simmered down in senatorial company, Quintus spoke sympathetically. 'It's very good of you to care so much about Flavia Albia's welfare, Titianus . . . Tell me, if you very sensibly wouldn't go anywhere near these muckers, does the Second Cohort have a man who does? Someone who has annoyed your tribune so much the poor fellow has been deployed as your organised crime liaison officer? I know it's usual to assign specialist oversight.'

'That will be a new concept for the Second Cohort!' I scoffed.

In his clean upper-class accent, Camillus Justinus tutted

mild reproof at me, then greased up Titianus who turned out to be a sucker for charm, and soon had us in an office further down the barracks portico where a different vigiles layabout, with a hunted expression and his boots held together with string, told us it was too dangerous for us to know his name.

His name was Juventus. He had scratched it on his metal mess tin. Without actually winking, my uncle subtly let me know he could see it too.

The anonymous one sucked his teeth and confirmed that the Rabirii were the chief local professionals. If anything major happened, they would be behind it; no other gang would dare to invade their territory.

'They are a family firm, long line of descent from other career criminals – bloody born to it. Embedded in the Esquiline. They rule by fear. It's nothing to them to batter someone senseless. A lad of ours had his eye put out when he arrested one of their runners for nicking purses – he didn't know it was a Rabirius associate. Old man Rabirius said he ought to make it his business to know, though in fairness the old bugger did give us a big donation afterwards for the widows and orphans fund.'

'I expect your lad was happy with that,' said Justinus, the sly beast. The half-blinded vigilis would have received no compensation, in fact. Widows and orphans were scarcely looked after either, well, not unless the widow was pretty. 'So would this gang carry out violent house-breaking?'

'Meat and drink to them. They always know who owns antiques or gilt goblets, who bought a new Greek statue last week, who gave an emerald necklace to his mistress who is careless about locking doors.'

'Ever killed a householder before?'

'Certainly not, legate. Why would they need to? Anyone

who has heard about the jeweller being poked up the arse with a red hot fire-iron because he tried to stop them grabbing his oriental pearls, just quivers in a corner and lets them walk away with whatever they want. People who think they are about to be a target make sure they go out to dinner and stay away until dawn.'

'Wouldn't they go out to dinner and put their valuables in a safe place?' asked my uncle.

'No, if you're targeted it's better to give in and hand them over. I heard about one man who actually packed up his stuff all ready for them, with helpful labels, and left them a donkey to carry it. Including a driver!'

Justinus whistled quietly. 'And what strategy are you using to tackle this gang?'

'Strategy?' asked Juventus.

'Operation Bandit King. What's your action plan?'

The so-called special liaison officer still looked blank.

I thought about my other uncle, Lucius Petronius of the Fourth Cohort, who spent decades trying to bring the hated Balbinus-Florius gang to justice; he had to give up on them, exhausted, when he retired. But he knew what an action plan was. He nagged tribune after tribune to commit funds for such initiatives. A Rome-wide crime-busting scheme, Operation Bandit King had been first set up by Uncle Petro.

Fortunately for Juventus, Camillus Justinus could hide his disapproval of incompetence. I myself pretended to believe Juventus must be diligently monitoring the Rabirius gang so I asked if he could advise us how to make contact.

He was not prepared to come along and introduce us, but in line with vigiles practice, he released one minimum fact: he gave us the name of a bar.

19

'Hmm!' Quintus sized up the place we had been sent to. 'Pretty moulded acanthus on their lintel, but let's not be fooled by leaves. This is the kind of thermopolium your colourful father would nickname the Itchy Bum.'

'He's never so rude.'

'Think so? You surprise me!'

We had come straight here from the station house. Otherwise we would have been expected. Inevitably, Titianus, Juventus or some other member of the Second Cohort would have tipped off the gang as a favour. We wanted to do this on our own terms – so we had to get here first.

Justinus might be my mother's favourite brother, but Helena Justina would thwack him with excoriating rhetoric if she knew he had let me come on this mission. Neither he nor I mentioned that, but it made us both nervous.

The Galatea (its proper name) stood in a quiet side street. You probably think thieves lurk down a dangerous alley, something with a sinister atmosphere; in fact they are just like the rest of us and prefer to drink at a respectable bar with nice tubs of laurels that actually get watered. Calling it the Galatea didn't mean the owners were interested in myths about statues coming to life, it was an excuse for a sign showing a nude woman.

She was rather pale and skinny, but the painter had given meticulous attention to her bosom. Sign artists are so predictable.

What did single out the Galatea as a rats' nest was that it was large enough to contain an interior courtyard where illegal transactions could take place out of sight of the public and the authorities. Justinus and I sauntered up to one of the counters like innocent tourists just off the boat from Tarentum. This was clearly not the case, since he still had his toga. It was scrunched up and carried over one arm, but anyone could see what it was and with his tunic broadly banded in purple even the dumbest waiter had to twig he was a senator.

Leaving the two bodyguards streetside at the counter, Quintus and I went in and pretended to study the wall sign with a list of drinks. With expressions of delight we 'discovered' the inner garden. We sat down there at a wooden table and spent time trying to decide whether to have fried anchovies or stick with olives. We didn't make a lot of noise, nothing too obvious.

No doubt some bars that act as gangs' headquarters show unfriendliness to casuals but at the Galatea they were more relaxed. The waiter ambled up and took our order without blinking. He even recommended the anchovies, though he did not push it. A man at the other table gave us a friendly nod in greeting. The waiter took his time coming back – but only as much time as hopeless waiters anywhere. He was gossiping with a local at a counter, not sending a message to tell some clan chief in the crime community that we were here.

So far, if we hadn't been told this was a dangerous place, we would not have realised.

'Must be his first day,' said Justinus to the other man, winking after the waiter. The otherwise pleasant customer had enormous biceps and a broken nose. But if he was a villain, he was one who had work to go back to. He mopped his chin daintily with a napkin, called for the reckoning, left coppers for the waiter, nodded a goodbye like a man whose mother had taught him manners, and left.

Apart from us, there was now no one else here. Our order came. True to family policy on refreshments, we decided we might as well eat up, not just leave empty-handed.

As soon as we relaxed with our bowls and beakers, a man who looked like an imperial invoice clerk turned up. Half bald, clean tunic, just short of swaggering. The kind who serves forty years in the same position, always at the beck and call of superiors, but knowing his eventual leaving-present will buy him a villa. One with solid silver plumbing fitments.

He came straight to the other table in the garden, clearly familiar with his surroundings. Within seconds the waiter had moved in, swept the board clean of crumbs, placed a bread basket with new rolls and set a beaker ready for the small flask of house wine and the water jug he swiftly brought without the customer needing to specify what he wanted.

Justinus kicked my ankle under the table.

The new man had made sure he was sitting so he could see who else entered. He even moved the heavy bench. Who moves a tavern bench?

Although he ignored our offered smiles, he then gave us a hard once-over. While the waiter brought appetiser bowls (several more than we had received), the man muttered to him and the waiter glanced over at us. He said something, perhaps defensively.

However much this customer looked like a docket-diddler, diddling dockets was not what he did.

A typical late lunch proceeded. It was early afternoon. Anyone in a bar around now had time to spare: those who did not need to work and those whose work involved leisured negotiating. Shippers, retail middlemen, investment advisers, publishers of epic poems – and cut-throat gangsters.

At a point when the waiter was alone at a counter, I got up and walked over to him, carrying a bowl as if I wanted a refill. I asked about the man who was not really a clerk. The waiter supplied the answer I expected. Juventus had named him for us. It was Gallo, a trusted agent of the Rabirii, whom the waiter called 'local businessmen'. He seemed unfazed at being asked.

I left the bowl on the counter. I walked across to the businessmen's trusty, sat down at the opposite side of his table, and folded my hands neatly. From our table, Justinus let his gaze follow me, though he went on eating and drinking quietly. He was close enough to hear what was said. The casual way he chucked up olives into his mouth showed that he saw nothing unusual in me approaching a stranger to ask questions. How a highly placed gangster would react remained to be seen.

'Please excuse me. You are eating and I won't mess about. I believe your name is Gallo and you can put me in touch with the Rabirii.' I made sure I spoke with heavy respect. Like my uncle, Gallo continued with his meal, no more concerned than if a wasp had landed on the table. But one wrong buzz and he would swat me. He did not appear to be armed, but I never rely on appearances.

I tried again. 'My name is Flavia Albia. I am assisting an

aedile with his investigation into the recent murders of Valerius Aviola and his wife on the Clivus Suburanus.' At that, Gallo did flex his eyebrows. Whether it was a comment on the crime, a disparaging sneer at women in general, or at women who said they worked with magistrates, I could not tell.

He wanted to know what I wanted. Until he found out, he would not pose a threat. Afterwards, I would need to be extremely careful.

'Bullion was taken. The Rabirius organisation is highly regarded for dealing in quality goods of the type that were liberated from the Aviola property. Mind you, if interlopers came onto your ground and carried out a robbery, unsanctioned by you, I imagine the Rabirii are extremely unhappy about it.'

Gallo gazed at me. Though his features were so unremarkable, he had very cold eyes.

I myself would not like to invade this gang's territory. If another gang had carried out the Aviola theft, and the Rabirii knew, there would be blood on the cobbles. I almost wished there was, because the absence of local warfare suggested the Rabirii were not annoyed with anybody else. If they did the job themselves, it was scary invading their bar.

'I'll be frank – if you took the silver, I cannot prove it. As a woman, I may not initiate prosecutions anyway. There will be no repercussions. My interest goes beyond the theft. I am following up the murders – and I don't believe the Rabirii were responsible. These killings were pointless, drawing attention in a way that your well-run organisation must deplore.'

I had nothing to offer, but I pushed it as brazenly as possible. 'Surely the Rabirii want this cleared up? It must be offensive to them to have such stupidity happening in their district.'

Gallo tore bread off a loaf segment with his teeth. I don't think he sharpened his incisors into points with a smith's file, but he would have done if he had thought of it.

'All right, just tell me this,' I cajoled. 'Aviola's slaves are being accused of the murders. Perhaps no robbery ever took place and the slaves are bluffing. So was Aviola, or was he not, visited that night by professionals?'

Gallo finished chewing then he answered. 'Go away, little girl.'

You can amend that mentally. 'Go away' was not his chosen verb.

20

'Flavia Albia, you managed that superbly!'

There are times when I can do without a companion who employs a wicked grin. I told Uncle Quintus to go away, using the crude word I had just learned from Gallo. We did not linger in the Galatea.

21

Quintus Camillus and I walked very slowly back to the apartment. We were both thinking, both not talking.

Dromo had woken up, in a fine panic about where I had got to. Faustus must have really given him stern orders to guard me. He glared at my uncle's two bodyguards, jealous of anyone else with responsibilities, even though he himself resented being assigned to me. The bodyguards stalked around Dromo too, equally suspicious. They were like a group of dogs, sizing each other up on first meeting, feinting an attack with fangs bared. But each man had an eye on Quintus and me, knowing we would slap them down if there was trouble.

We left them to their devices, and went to sit in the courtyard. We discussed what we could do next about identifying the thieves, assuming they ever existed.

Quintus' suggestion was predictable: 'We'll have to raise our level of engagement with the vigiles. Titianus is a lightweight and Juventus has absolutely no idea. I propose that Manlius Faustus and I hold a speedy face-to-face with the Second Cohort's tribune. I can send a message now to tell him we are coming. That gives him time to pick his men's brains; it's only polite. The tribune can decide for himself, depending on his personal style of management, whether to have those idiots present, or present for part of the time.'

'You presume "management" is what a vigiles tribune practises,' I chortled. 'So tell me – does the Camillus-Faustus personal style include taking me to the meet?'

My uncle wagged a finger. 'Now you know, Albia sweetheart, if it was up to me . . . '

'Faustus approves of me.'

'That is definitely my impression! But,' said Quintus Camillus, turning into a paternalist Roman bastard, like them all, 'we have to assume the tribune will be traditional. We don't want to antagonise him, do we?'

'I don't mind.'

'Ah, but Albia, we need answers, not moral confrontations.'

'I like to use confrontations to thrash out answers.'

Quintus remained tolerant. 'From what I have seen of your work, you can be devious. You try to avoid upsets. Hercules, Albia, let's face it – you flirt!'

Biting my lip, I made no reply.

After a moment, Quintus added slyly, 'So are you flirting with the aedile?'

'You do keep on plucking on the same old lyre, Uncle.' Quintus was laughing. We had a good relationship and I was honest with him. 'I flirt when it's needed, but I don't flirt with him.'

'Yes, he seems a little tight. Doesn't he like your banter?'

'I wouldn't know.'

I knew all right. Faustus liked it.

Quintus, who was shrewd in the intuitive way of my mother, his elder sister, was still laughing. I reflected privately how glad I was not to be having this conversation with Helena Justina. She could winkle things out of people that they didn't even know they thought and felt.

It made her a wonderful partner for my father. When I

worked with the Camillus brothers, as I did intermittently, we had a similar relationship, but they always tried to take over the investigation. I was better on my own.

I never despaired of finding someone else to share my work in the balanced way my parents tackled commissions together – but I did not expect it to happen.

Quintus borrowed equipment and swiftly wrote letters, one to Faustus which Dromo took, and another to the tribune, carried by one of the bodyguards.

Commenting how quiet it was here (compared to his own lively ménage, with all those children tearing about), my uncle made himself at home. He had a nap, commandeering a bed in one of the good rooms. I sunned myself in the garden.

Polycarpus turned up, mithering about my visit that morning to his wife Graecina. I had half-expected him to check up. The steward was the type who needed to involve himself and be in charge. Now he wanted to satisfy himself first-hand that nothing had been said that he himself would have concealed.

'Routine questions, Polycarpus. I just wondered if you could give me any useful background on Galla Simplicia. You must have had many dealings with her while she and Aviola were married, perhaps even since they divorced. I would value your opinion.'

'Did my wife say something?' he asked narrowly. Justinus had left his toga on the second chair, so the steward had to remain standing; he was a little put out and awkward. Excellent!

'Nothing untoward.' I presumed he had been told that

in my talk with Graecina I had speculated on Polycarpus helping Galla Simplicia.

I tried to be honest with myself. Was I feeling prejudice? Did I want to think he was involved, because I had taken against him? 'Polycarpus, we haven't talked about your master's ex-wife and children. Why didn't you mention them?'

'You didn't ask.'

'I was never told they existed! You could have said. So, come on – share your views.'

Polycarpus pulled a non-committal face, though what he said was pretty clear. 'She looks soft, but she's hard.'

'Why did they divorce?'

'She was a handful. He found it all too much. From little things he said, I think he was relieved to live as a single man again.'

'But not permanently . . . Did he miss having a companion in bed?'

'There are ways around that.'

'Do you know what ways Aviola found? Assuming he did?'

'I couldn't say.'

He must know, but Polycarpus would not say it to *me*. I presumed this was the usual nonsense of men ganging up.

I changed tactics. 'What about the suggestion that Galla Simplicia was so aggravated by Aviola remarrying, and the possibility he might have more children, that she arranged his murder?' The steward looked startled – or at least made a good show of it. 'Do you believe it?'

'No,' he said.

'You never found her vindictive?'

'I never found her violent. Or that stupid,' he added. He was shifting from foot to foot, though he appeared to be talking straight. 'She likes to play the innocent in formal matters, business matters, yet Galla Simplicia is very intelligent.'

'She used to twist Aviola to her will?'

'Yes – and I thought,' Polycarpus confided, 'she reckoned she could continue to get around him even after he remarried.'

I said that, having met her, I too thought that very likely. Of course continuing to obtain whatever she wanted meant Galla Simplicia had no motive to kill.

I probed Polycarpus on the subject of her cousin, the executor. 'Is it true you hope to be offered a position by Sextus Simplicius?' Apparently the offer had now been made. Polycarpus said that since he was still so shaken by his old master's death, he had kindly been given time to consider. This was not so generous to the existing steward, Gratus, on whose side I found myself. 'Does your past experience of Galla Simplicia make you at all wary of working for her family?'

'Maybe!' the Aviola steward agreed with a wry smile, as if to tell me that was why he had asked for a moratorium. He was unwilling to speak further. I ended the conversation and let him go.

Shortly afterwards a message came that the tribune would make time for my uncle and the aedile. Clearly Quintus knew how to pen a graceful request for an interview. I admit, I myself could never have persuaded a tribune to see me on my own initiative. Senators have unfair advantages.

I had the idea of inviting my uncle and Faustus to join me for supper, in order to tell me what they learned. Quintus happily accepted and said, hinting, that he would be sure to bring the aedile with him. I replied coolly that then he could see for himself how there was nothing between us.

'Ah, that's a shame!'

That kind of annoying so-called humour is why I ought to stick with my rule, never work with relatives.

22

While my client and uncle were engaged in masculine business, lucky boys, I was left with time on my hands. I took Dromo out with a shopping basket, bought and prepared us a meal. I could do that. I refused to see this task as demotion. I enjoy supper with friends, especially on a fine June evening. Someone has to check that the shellfish are fresh.

One thing I like about Rome is that women go to dinner along with their men. Aulus Camillus' first wife, Hosidia Meline, who came from Greece, expected to be left at home, and even when there was a party in her own house she tried to hide away. She felt uncomfortable when we encouraged her to join in. My mother had taught me that I must never accept being left out. Only a man who wanted me to be at his side as his equal was worth considering. In my own house, I was always to be the hostess.

This was not my house, but I issued the invitation, so it counted as the same.

When they appeared, Uncle Quintus greeted me with a fond kiss on the cheek, so Manlius Faustus followed his example, more diffidently since he was not a relative; still, it was unforced.

I led them to Aviola and Mucia's summer dining room. There were three formal couches, big cushioned three-seaters, so we spread ourselves and flopped on one each. I had laid out the food and drink on the central serving table. It was a stretch, but we helped ourselves, in the absence of slaves. Dromo had moaned that he had to go to the baths again. Myla could have served us, but she had made herself invisible all afternoon. I wondered if that was what people meant when they said 'Oh, she's just Myla' – she had a faultless instinct for when to keep out of the way?

It must have been in all our minds that this was where the feast took place on the night of the murders. The room was decorated in sea-green and white, a delicate palette, with refined panels of garden scenes, where an occasional painted dove frolicked on a scalloped fountain. The frescos looked new, as if redone for the wedding. I wondered if Mucia Lucilia had instigated that – the new wife, beginning to exert her influence?

Empty buffet shelves would once have held the stolen silver wine set. We had to eat and drink from pottery. But the pottery here was glossy red-glazed ware from northern Italy, with elegant scenes of hares and running antelopes. In this household, even the items left behind when the rest was packed up for Campania were more than decent.

I had folded back the wooden doors, which made the room airy and gave a sense of space. The view of the courtyard needing prettying up; Mucia cannot yet have started on that.

Perhaps on the feast night they hired tubs of topiary and draped the place with garland swags. There would have been lights. By the time of the attack, if witness statements were correct, the lamps had been put out, most probably removed; I had seen them, now routinely stacked in a store room. No doubt as soon as the guests left, someone went around and saved lamp oil. That was the kind of household Polycarpus ran. It could have been done while the debris was being cleared and the table goods washed in the kitchen.

The feast ended at a reasonable hour, then my guess was that the tidying up happened at some speed. The master and mistress had an early start next morning and they were eager for bed. They would have wanted all domestic bustle to be out of the way and the house quiet.

At our own little feast, Manlius Faustus, Camillus Justinus and I had been silent. We all gave proper respect to meals and were rather introspective anyway, each perhaps pondering the day's events.

When the moment arrived to talk, my two companions praised my hospitality. It is always good to have your efforts noted. I let them vie with each other over showing good manners. Neither was a slimy flatterer. They both knew I was not taking it seriously.

Work occasionally had such sociable moments, often over a meal. It made me realise that although I managed well alone, I would like things to be different. Mind you, only in the right circumstances. According to my little sisters, I have impossibly high standards.

Justinus and Faustus took turns at narrating what they had learned from the tribune. Although he had not added much that was new, he coloured in some details about the gang and their influence. The tribal chief was 'old Rabirius', a vindictive degenerate going on eighty, whose habits were as filthy as his attitude was hard-bitten. He was born into crime; he had links with all the traditional organised crime families.

I glanced at Uncle Quintus. 'Yes,' he confirmed quietly.

'His family tree runs inexorably into that of the late un-lamented bugbear, Balbinus Pius – their mothers were sisters.'

Balbinus Pius had been a leading gangster who, after years of violent trafficking, thievery, the sex trade, illegal gambling and intimidation had been tracked down by my father and Uncle Petro. After his death, when his criminal empire was carved up and handed on to willing associates, most was inherited by his son-in-law, a cursed man called Florius. Many years ago and far from Rome, I fell into the clutches of this Florius. I hated him, with good reason. Even the thought of him, or anyone connected to him, agitated me.

Justinus did not explain to the aedile. I never talked about the past but Faustus was shrewd. He had caught the nuance.

My uncle, frowning, chewed an apple and fell silent as he remembered past adventures. Manlius Faustus, looking thoughtful, took up the story.

Like the Balbinus empire, the Rabirii ran lowlife bars, also engaging in stealing and prostitution rackets, much of which took place in those bars. Profits often came from minor theft too – street crime such as snatching purses, even knocking people over and grabbing their small change. Their men raided baths. The women stole from shops, leaning across counters or in through windows. The whole clan took advantage of tipsy crowds at arena festivals or religious processions, though mainly they homed in on markets. Markets provide all kinds of opportunities.

'Petty thefts add up,' Faustus said. 'They also carry out a great deal of house-breaking. They have been doing all this for generations and are experts. Old Rabirius receives a share of whatever his associates obtain, so he is a very wealthy and powerful figure.'

The Rabirii rarely dabbled in white-tunic crimes such as fraud. In a city full of spies and informants, where the emperor welcomed snitches, they kept out of the authorities' sight, never passing on information unless it served their own purpose. They were tight. They dealt with their own quarrels, and did so harshly. They operated according to a tough moral code, a code based on terror, using both extreme mental pressure and physical pain. Like many cruel people, they pretended a high belief in family – though that only meant their own; their creed excluded any respect for the families of their many victims.

If they really had stolen the Aviola silver, it would be documented by accountants who worked on their payroll, slickly disguising their procedures and real income. Needless to say, the income would never be reported as taxable, though in this they hardly differed from many legitimate businesses in Rome. The Rabirii also had access to metal-workers who would melt down illicit goods and to fences who would slide items back into sleazy retail outlets when that would be more profitable. But if the silver here had been stolen to order, that didn't seem to fit their usual methods.

'They work for themselves and avoid contact with "respectable" people.'

'Does that mean,' I asked Faustus, 'they are not for hire – even for murders?'

'No, they hand out plenty of violence, but the tribune thought they would be very unlikely to act as paid killers.'

'And anyway, I suppose even they might feel sentimental about killing a new bride!'

Faustus smiled at me. 'I doubt the Rabirii are ever senti-mental.'

Justinus agreed. 'No, and they initiate their own crimes. It is a matter of pride not to carry out dirty work for others. That they see as menial. They do commit many robberies, and they do kill. However, mostly they go for other members of their own community, as a result of professional or family grudges.'

'I presume they escape justice for that,' I replied bitterly, 'because the authorities simply think one less villain has to be good news.'

'Exactly,' said Faustus. 'Feuds are common. Retaliation is fast. Bad feeling may simmer for decades, though if an act of violence or vengeance is seen as justified, everyone regards it as fair punishment and quickly forgets.'

'So as we thought,' I summed up, 'given their record for house-breaking, the Rabirius gang might carry out the kind of robbery that supposedly took place here – but even so, they are very *un*likely to have killed Valerius Aviola and his wife.'

Both men nodded.

'One other thing though. What about beating up the porter?'

Faustus seemed prepared for my question. 'The tribune felt the Rabirii were quite capable of such violence, but they would never inflict it without a good reason. Unless there is something we don't know, they would have had no social interaction with Aviola, and the porter himself, Nicostratus, would be way below their line of vision.'

'Did the tribune suggest any other villains who might have robbed the house?'

'No, he backed Titianus on that. Even if it was a rival gang, the Rabirii would by now have imposed a punishment – and very publicly, to reassert their supremacy.'

I tested another angle: 'Could they harbour mavericks? Upstarts, who want to challenge the old man?'

'Olympus, you do like to cover every feasible idea, Albia!' Faustus in fact looked impressed. 'It is possible. We were told there is a nephew, Roscius, the youngest of a large brood – brought up a favourite, and now testing his muscle. He specialises in burglary rather than street crime or brothel-mongering. So yes,' Faustus concluded, 'this nephew may be changing the pattern. The vigiles view him as the coming man. The tribune does not want to tackle him yet. His policy at present is to let Roscius run, while keeping him under observation. He won't agree to any premature confrontation.'

'You respect that view?' I demanded.

'I have to. In my role, I must work amicably with other law authorities.'

Justinus was watching us tangle.

'Of course. So you must.' I withdrew my objection grace-fully. Faustus looked slightly alarmed by the ease with which he brought me round. Justinus hid a chuckle.

The men seemed to have convinced themselves that there was no organised crime involvement. Someone possessed the loot, however, so they had persuaded the Second's tribune to order further enquiries at places where such silver might be sold on, putting extra pressure on retailers. Although Faustus had pretended to be satisfied that Titianus and his team had looked for the lost wine set at the apart-ment, he would tomorrow bring men of his own to carry out a discreet new search: a search of this house, plus the adjoining apartments and shops, then extending to the rest of the street if it could be done quietly.

'I'll tell my men not to be heavy-handed. Titianus need

never know we have doubled up on his work. Householders won't go running to him to complain.'

'It's certainly not the normal way of conducting an apartment-to-apartment search!' I commented.

At this point, Uncle Quintus stretched and hauled himself off the couch. He begged to be excused; he wanted to go home in time to see his children put to bed. He was a good father, but even if that had not been the case, Claudia Rufina ruthlessly extracted a certain domesticity as payoff for his slightly untrustworthy past.

Faustus said he wanted to talk to me about the case, so I took Quintus to the front door. I said goodbye and watched him depart. He cut a good figure: taller than average, slim and raffishly good-looking, with his hair still dark as it flopped over his brow, and that ever-easy manner.

His two bodyguards had made themselves friendly with the leatherworkers. Quintus, naturally, strolled up to where they were all sitting on stools outside the shop and introduced himself. He shook hands with Secundus and Myrinus, a nice courtesy. I waited, and sure enough when he set off homewards, with the bodyguards limping behind him, Quintus Camillus Justinus had a tawny leather drawstring bag tucked beneath his arm, a handsome present to placate his wife. I expect he paid for it – but not the normal price.

A cluster of men were leaving a bar; otherwise the street was empty. It was still not late, a warm June night. Rome at its most benign.

23

I emerged from the long corridor and crossed the atrium. Myla had uncharacteristically deigned to appear; she was clattering bowls and scraping leftovers in the dining room. This commotion had driven out Faustus. He was standing in the courtyard, head thrown back, apparently enjoying the night air.

I fetched a light stole and was about to join him when someone began banging on the front door. I could hear it was Dromo, who was shouting at the top of his voice as if he thought he would be left outside all night. I went.

As soon as I opened up, the slave sauntered past me as if nothing had perturbed him, but then he ran into his master. Faustus had followed me; from his look of alarm he must be remembering how the porter was attacked that night when, if the story was correct, Nicostratus mistakenly let the wrong people indoors.

Unexpectedly, Faustus took his slave to task. 'Where in Hades have you been, Dromo? A simple bathe should not take so long. In future, come back promptly. I do not want Flavia Albia having to answer the door to you when it's late and could be dangerous!'

He rarely sounded so sharp. Dromo hung his head, like a child reluctantly playing sorry, but sulking.

'Don't look like that,' Faustus ordered, keeping his voice level. 'You were in the wrong, Dromo.'

The slave improved his expression then slouched off to lie on his mat. We heard him muttering complaints under his breath to some imaginary friend.

Manlius Faustus breathed deeply a few times to recover his calm. We took the two seats that were still outdoors. I selected the x-stool, letting Faustus have the chair.

'I saw Quintus off on his way,' I said, making light conversation while Faustus settled. 'He wasn't making excuses, you know; he really does involve himself in the bedtime ritual. Neither he nor Claudia are strict and it can be hectic persuading six self-willed infants to quieten down. But Uncle Quintus is a soothing presence. Luckily his children like him.'

This produced an interesting reaction from Faustus. 'I gather you and he are on close terms?' The aedile's tone was almost carping, and it was not a hangover from his spat with Dromo.

I assessed him, surprised to find him assessing me. Sometimes he could seem dour. Sometimes he made it plain he thought me flighty.

'Just family,' I answered gently, yet he scowled.

Where did this come from? Had somebody been gossiping? It could be Titus Morellus, from the vigiles Fourth Cohort on the Aventine. Morellus had harassed me a few times officially, a penalty of being an informer; the idiot now believed himself an expert on my history. Faustus knew him. Had Morellus told Faustus that I once had a yen for one of the Camillus brothers?

I decided that if the aedile wanted to know which it was, he would have to ask me.

He chose not to.

I therefore did not tell him it was Aulus who had let me think we were best friends then broke my heart. Nor did I say that I was only seventeen, so of course I got over it years ago.

I had been married since then. The poor lad was killed in an accident. Faustus damn well knew I spoke very fondly of my husband.

If I was cool, he deserved it. 'Aedile, you wanted to review the case?'

'You set me a task, remember.' Now he sounded himself again, humorously feigning anxiety about his orders. 'I was to ask the slaves how they made their escape.'

'What do they say?' *I* was not myself yet, though I don't suppose he noticed.

'Once Titianus was about to accuse them, they waited until dark then made a bolt on foot. You wondered how Nicostratus managed; they put him in a carrying chair that belonged to Mucia Lucilia. The other men took turns on the rails so they could hurry through the streets as fast as possible.'

'Why did they take him? The severity of his wounds exonerated him from not helping his master.'

'Phaedrus, the other porter, claims Nicostratus did not want to be left behind alone. Amaranta and Olympe told me they had not realised how bad his condition was; they imagined they could look after him.'

'And do we know whose idea it was to flee?'

'They were vague. My feeling is the steward put them

up to it.' So Polycarpus really was more loyal to the slaves he supervised than to his master. Interesting!

'Or who suggested the Temple of Ceres?'

'Chrysodorus. The philosopher.' For once Manlius Faustus sounded unsure of himself. 'Is it significant?'

'Probably not.'

'I wish I had pressed the point.'

I made him a reassuring gesture. 'He will probably dodge the question . . . There must have been interesting discussions among those slaves – I wish we could have sight of that playscript!'

Since I had been keeping him up to date with my daily reports, there was little else for us to discuss. My client seemed satisfied I was doing my best, repeating that I should take whatever time I needed.

Faustus then talked to me about his own work. I knew something of his preoccupation with the city's plague of random killers, so he shared the latest developments; he even asked advice. This was a sensitive subject, highly confidential. I was furious to notice Myla as she went from the dining room to the kitchen, slowing up and obviously trying to listen in.

Faustus saw her too. He stopped talking. He was naturally reticent, so when he took me into his confidence – which in fairness to him, he had always done more than I expected – I resented someone else interrupting. Was it another illustration of 'Oh, that's just Myla'? She acted vague, yet habitually eavesdropped?

If so, whether she exploited what she heard or was just nosy, I would have sold the woman and not put up with it. I bet Mucia Lucilia shared my antipathy.

As she sashayed along a colonnade, swinging her hips,

Myla was giving Faustus an obvious sexual invitation. I might as well not have been present.

Manlius Faustus was a rare man; he disliked unsought attention of that kind. He even picked up his chair and moved it around, so his back was turned on the colonnade. The action seemed automatic. I was not sure he realised he had done it.

He and I sat in silence for a time, the way you can only do with a friend. I suppose that was when I seriously acknowledged to myself that although I disliked him when we first met, I liked Faustus much more now. How much more I would not contemplate. Best not make the same mistake as Myla.

It was late, clearly time for him to make a move. Unlike my uncle, who anyway lived nearer, he admitted he was so weary after a tedious day of meetings, he felt reluctant to walk. To reach his house, he had to trek all the way up the Aventine and across the heights.

He would never have asked, but I made it easy for him: 'You have no bodyguards with you. You might not keep your wits about you if you're tired. Stay here. Go back in the morning. Who is going to mind?'

I told him where to find a bedroom. It was the one Quintus commandeered that afternoon, though I did not say so. Faustus took himself off gratefully. I sat on outside, merely bidding him a quiet goodnight.

I changed to the more comfortable chair, still warm from his presence. I stayed for a while there in the courtyard, wondering if Faustus would return. He did not. That did not surprise me.

My mischievous uncle may have left us together on

purpose – such a waste of thoughtfulness. Still, Holy Venus. How bad was it to be spurned because a man was *tired*?

I was still there, unintentionally drowsing, when another commotion woke me. People – several this time – were in the street outside, hammering on the door for attention.

Manlius Faustus shot from his room. He pushed me behind him as he unzipped the grille and cautiously looked out. When he demanded to know who was making such a disturbance, we heard it was slaves from the Camillus brothers. Aulus had sent them. They had horrible news.

As Uncle Quintus made his way home that evening, he and his bodyguards were ambushed. His men managed to drag him to their house, but Quintus had been hurt.

Oh dear gods. It was Nicostratus all over again. My imagination filled with the terrible image of the door porter's corpse, covered with blood from those many gruesome wounds, those injuries from which he never recovered consciousness. The injuries that killed him.

24

'Is he alive?'

The slaves knew nothing.

I realised what had happened. Those men I saw earlier departing from that bar opposite were not innocent drinkers, but criminals. Watching the house. Waiting for someone to leave, with specific orders to look for a senator. The Rabirii sent them after us. The men tailed Justinus until he reached a suitable spot, then brutally set about him.

It was no random act. It was a warning. We had taken too much interest.

'Tiberius, I have to go!'

'Stay here, where you are safe.'

'Was Nicostratus safe? Aviola and Mucia Lucilia?'

'Albia, do as I say, please.'

'Don't give me orders.'

'Only advice.' Well, aedile, that is always irritating.

We were standing in the street by then. The damned man was so stubborn with me, he might as well have been one of my family. I was trying to break away and he was trying to shepherd me back into the house. I wanted to kick him, but I was wearing only house slippers. Besides, I would never have aimed right, as I havered in panic over whether to pelt straight off to the Camillus house or first rush indoors for shoes I could run in.

People were looking out of windows and doorways. The disturbance brought Polycarpus' wife down.

'Dromo – come. With your cudgel, fool!' Faustus finally went along with me. I calmed down. Better he decided to help me than I rushed off by myself. I knew from experience he made a good ally.

Polycarpus must be out but, assuming responsibility on his behalf, Graecina produced a carrying chair. It must be Mucia's, sent back by the Temple of Ceres after the slaves ran off. It had been kept in a lock-up while attempts were made to clean Nicostratus' blood off the seat. Not very successfully, I noticed.

The steward's wife also gave us a lantern-carrier, a callow lad who worked for her, and a cloak of her own – I was shaking – which Manlius Faustus bundled around me, a practical man, ignoring how angry I had been with him. He noticed I was on the verge of tears and murmured, 'Don't go jittery. This is not your fault.'

'I don't jitter. Let me go. I need to go.'

'I am coming with you. Get in – *go, go!*' He was shouting not at me, but the Camillus slaves who would be carrying the chair containing me.

Thank the gods it was downhill to the Capena Gate. It felt as if we were travelling across half Rome, a rough journey at the speed they ran, and I was so keyed up I soon felt sick. We had to scramble from the Fourth district, past the Fifth, across the Second and into the Twelfth. At least it was not as far as the Aventine.

It was a quiet evening by Rome's standards. The streets were negotiable. The Rabirius gang had done their worst for one night. Nobody attacked us.

When we arrived, the men took the chair right into the house and I fell out of it in the atrium, almost before they were stationary. Someone gestured to a room. Quintus, stripped and sporting livid marks, was lying on a couch.

Aulus was attending to his brother. He had rejected the family doctor, a freedman they kept for dosing the children, who had tried to use lambswool for cleaning the wounds, only to be ordered away in case fibres killed Quintus with an infection. The doctor was still maundering on about this, while Aulus explained his reasons through gritted teeth, apparently not for the first time.

Aulus used a sponge. He must have already spent some time cleaning Quintus up. Several bloody bowls of water stood on the floor around the couch. Even so, I could see no sword or knife wounds, only bruises and scrages where dark blood welled but only to the surface. The damage was extensive. He would hardly be able to move tomorrow. But he would safely have a tomorrow.

Aulus had knocked Quintus out with a strong dose of poppy juice, judging by a beaker I sniffed and by the patient's smiling, unspeaking acceptance of everything that was happening. Quintus knew people were there. He had no idea who we were or what was up with him. Tomorrow would be soon enough – too soon – to grapple with his pain.

Six entirely silent children held hands in a row on the opposite side of the couch from where Aulus was perched. Children here were generally sheltered, but not excluded when they wanted to know what was going on in a crisis. They were a bright, pushy bunch.

Aulus looked up and nodded to us without speaking, since at that point he was suturing a cut on his brother's elbow, the kind people get when they go down heavily on one arm.

You had to know Aulus very well to understand how nervous he felt. Some of the little boys on guard beside their father were critically watching every move their uncle made. When he tied off the thread, he puffed out his cheeks, suddenly sweating.

'He'll live.' Now he was calmer, bandaging with a slow rhythm. 'No broken bones, just this cheese-grated skin, which was full of grit from the roadway. I hope his internal organs are intact. The worst is bruising. He's already feeling that.'

'Weapons?' murmured Faustus, standing behind me.

'No. Fists. And boots. But they must have been big buggers.'

I wondered what had happened to the bodyguards. I assumed they were similarly beaten. Faustus murmured to me that this looked different from the attack on Nicostratus. Was that bad or good?

I made soothing noises to reassure the children. They viewed me as a peculiar aunt, but my being from Britain explained most of it. A row of dark brown eyes stared back at me with the sketchiest politeness, then they concentrated again on their father. Their mother came in; Claudia hugged me, as if consoling other people helped her cope. A couple of the youngest children set up pathetic cries, wanting her attention.

'Silence in the ranks!' commanded Aulus, no lover of the young.

Although Claudia Rufina often seemed distracted, in emergencies she grimly took it upon herself to be the one person who stayed strong. While everyone else was weeping over a broken vase, Claudia would sweep up the shards and move the other antiques along the shelf so the gap was less noticeable. In any crisis, while disorganised Romans were colourfully panicking, Claudia Rufina came along, tutting under her breath, to show practical Baetican womanhood in action.

I was surprised she had let Aulus tend her husband. However, Quintus was her weakness. Claudia stayed with him out of love; yes, he was the father of her children, which limited her freedom to leave, but they had been together for ten years through many personal upsets. It was a testament to what people can do when they make their minds up. In other words, it was like many marriages.

I guessed Claudia could not bear to watch painful medical processes being inflicted on Quintus. She would have gone off to see to the bodyguards.

She had been followed back here by a maid bearing a big jug of hot mulsum and enough tots to serve everyone with this sweet, soothing beverage, relieving shock. Aulus certainly needed it; he tossed his beaker back in a single movement. The maid came round of her own accord pouring refills. This left the tender mother free to see that each child kissed Quintus and whispered private endearments to him, before being carried away to bed. That done, Claudia organised Faustus and me.

'Albia, I have put you in little Aelia's room. If she wakes in the night she can creep into your bed for comfort, if you don't mind. You have always been so good with children . . . Aedile, you must naturally stay with us. It is too late for you to go up to the Aventine, unless many guards were to be sent with you. I want our people all under our roof; you will understand. You will be most comfortable in a room at my brother-in-law's house; I have spoken to my sister-in-law, who has everything ready.'

Faustus opened his mouth, then subsided in the face of the Baetican whirlwind. I secretly wondered whether dear Claudia, a high-minded woman, was making sure no sly creeping along corridors occurred between Faustus and me.

'Your sister-in-law is still *in situ*! Aulus still not divorced?' I asked dryly. I rather enjoyed the notion of his wife having to give hospitality to a friend of mine – the third wife who had given up on Aulus (and who could blame her . . .). And that grouch Aulus would hate having to offer a nightcap and smalltalk to a fellow they must all think was having an affair with me . . . A fellow of such fabulous reserve I could trust him to give no clue as to whether it was true.

Hades, Faustus never even gave much of a clue to me.

Claudia pulled a face and rattled her bangles with disapproval. 'The poor woman is still waiting for Aulus to make arrangements. I suppose he will bestir himself in his own time. They share the house but lead separate lives.'

'Didn't they always? . . . And where is ridiculous Aulus, incidentally?' I noticed he was missing. He must have slipped out of the room during the hot drinks.

'Gone to the vigiles. He insisted on escorting the prisoner personally.'

'What prisoner?'

That was when Faustus and I were informed that as Uncle Quintus went down under a hail of blows, he shouted to his bodyguards, 'Never mind me – just take one of the bastards alive!'

Being devoted to Camillus Justinus, as all his stray lambs were, that is what the two ex-soldiers snapped to and did.

This capture could be vital. Whoever ordered the ambush had made a mistake. They could be traced. The vigiles would fully interrogate this prisoner, where 'fully' meant using a torturer. He would name the Rabirii if they were his masters. If his orders had been from the rising young blood Roscius, Roscius' easy times were over. The prisoner himself was as good as dead, though the bloodied relics of him would sing like a caged finch before he was executed. Execution was inevitable. He beat up a senator.

The gang had forced the vigiles' hand. It could escalate. Questions were bound to be asked in the Senate about the dangerous condition of the city if mobsters dared to attack one of its noble members.

Aulus Camillus Aelianus would be on his feet in the Curia, for one. This was his younger brother; he would be expected to make much of it. A Roman has to represent his family when they suffer an outrage.

I imagined Aulus already scripting a speech about Justinus innocently going home to his own house, after a civilised dinner with a widowed niece (an equestrian's daughter) and with a serving magistrate . . . Such details would be received as touching and significant.

Normally Aulus needed to be wound up on a ratchet, but he was trained by Minas of Karystos, the eminent Greek practitioner. Once the noble Aelianus let rip, he could hold an audience. (Aulus once spoke for almost half an hour on whether it was permissible to clean up the copious shit deposited by the augurs' chickens on the Capitol – who conceivably shat holy guano – and hardly anybody left the chamber. A Vestal had slipped over on the poultry excrement. There was a lot of interest in my uncle's declamation, with some people not even sniggering.)

If the Rabirii were very unlucky indeed, our emperor would jump on the idea of a moral campaign to eliminate the criminal element in Rome.

'Of course,' announced Claudia, who had her peculiar moments, 'there will be more questions asked, and even perhaps useful action taken, if my darling Quintus dies from this.'

That doesn't mean she was hopeful he would. Claudia Rufina merely wanted to emphasise how stupid it was for anyone to attack a senator.

Slaves were waiting to lead Faustus and me to our separate quarters. He would have extremely smooth sheets and neatly aligned pillows. I would be on a pull-out bed, spending the night cuddling Aelia, the only daughter of the house, four years old, her father's pet (and didn't the sweet little piece of mischief know it).

As I glanced back, Claudia had taken over as nurse. I saw her stationed at her husband's side, patient, brave, disposing herself to the will of the gods, not allowing herself to cry because that would be no help to anyone.

Uncle Quintus lay with his eyes closed. He showed few signs of being in our world. But I noticed that he moved his right hand and covered one of Claudia's. She shed tears then, though silently and without moving a muscle, so as not to disturb him.

25

Claudia was clearly wrong to worry. I would not go wandering corridors that night, looking for the aedile.

I was a free woman. I was twenty-nine years old, so people had no obligation to tell my mother what I got up to. But in the homes of close relatives, you are never truly independent. If I was seen chasing a man around my uncles' two houses at midnight, not only would *both* my parents hear about it (and my sisters, and my young brother), but the story would be retold to innumerable other relatives every Saturnalia for the next four decades . . .

I was twenty-nine, which is old enough to know when to follow their rules for a quiet life.

26

Well, all right, I did go. But not immediately.

My niece took an age going to sleep. After that night's upset, the house took what seemed like hours to fall still and silent. Even then, to be frank, I spent more time than you may think in deciding that looking for the aedile was what I wanted to do, plus even more while I plucked up courage.

I only went because I was worried that if he came looking for me, he would waken little Aelia.

He too had decided we should liaise. His timing matched mine too. We met one another half way. It is true we had exchanged a glance when Claudia packed us off to our rooms, but there was no pre-arrangement. And we certainly made no bedroom assignation. Barefoot and each carrying a tiny lamp, Manlius Faustus and I came face to face in a colonnade beside a small garden, just this side of the link between the Camillus brothers' two houses. Neither of us remarked on the other being there. No explanation was needed. He steered me to a bench beneath some fancy wickerwork, where we sat with our heads close, whispering.

Forget intrigue. For heaven's sake. If he was weary before, the man was completely past it now. I was drained by tension myself. We were not seeking thrills like adolescents on holiday. We just both needed to talk about what had happened.

'What do you think?'

'This was to warn us off, Tiberius.'

'Arising from our enquiries of the vigiles – and you tackling that man, Gallo.'

'If Gallo took offence at the bar, it could have been me who ended up being hammered.'

'And it could have been me, if the Rabirii know that Justinus and I visited the tribune together—'

'They are bound to have that information. Vigiles barracks leak information like worn-out gourds.'

'The question is, Albia – did the gang act because they *were* guilty of the theft and they don't want us finding out?'

'Or do they just want to frighten us?'

'To avoid attention? – If so, they have attracted even more.'

'Yes, but they thought they were in control. They won't have planned on having a man arrested.'

'Right. Now if we can prove he has a connection to them, they are in trouble. Their best choice was no action at all . . .' The aedile sounded urgent. 'I am worried about tomorrow, Albia. Aelianus has arranged to visit the Fourth Cohort's tribune.' Because my uncle had been attacked almost on his own doorstep, the crime came under the jurisdiction of our local vigiles. 'He couldn't get to see the man tonight, but he's anxious to liaise directly, first thing. He has asked me to be there.'

'You saw Aulus when he came home?'

'Briefly.'

That was him; never a great one for chat. 'Tiberius, why

so worried? You can handle a tribune. In the Fourth it's Cassius Scaurus. You know him; he's just a bully and an imbecile. But he won't bully you.'

For once Faustus coughed with amusement. 'It's when he tries to stop looking like an imbecile that I find him scary – such a terrible actor . . . No, I'm really cursing over the search for the missing Aviola silver. If I am over here, supporting Aelianus, I cannot be there to supervise.'

'Stick with him. I can be at the Esquiline in time. Let me exercise a watching brief.' Always a useful phrase. State officials use 'watching brief' to imply they will be observing an activity, yet will not interfere. That leaves them free to interfere like energetic billygoats.

Faustus fell for it. That is how I knew he was exhausted. Otherwise he would have seen through my innocent-sounding offer.

There was a noise, a small thump somewhere, behind or near to an open second-floor window in a room above the garden. It could just be a pigeon shifting in a gutter, or an eavesdropper.

In a house like this there would be slaves everywhere. Some might be close by in the very shadows here, tucked up behind the battered fountain or curled on a mat under the jasmine on the trellis. Possibly they were sleeping, perhaps they were listening to us. There was no moon and the sky must be full of haze because only a few faint stars could be glimpsed in the open square between the pantiled roofs around the courtyard.

Quintus and Claudia would rely on the slaves' loyalty to them and their immediate family. As visitors, that might not extend to Faustus and me. Slaves were human. And we lived in a poisoned city, where a paranoid emperor had caused often-lethal mistrust.

Caution ruled.

Faustus and I stood up to leave. I felt a light touch of the aedile's hand in the small of my back, guiding me to the colonnade. He had blown out his lamp, risking a stumble over some abandoned mop and bucket but enabling him to glide invisibly back to his guest room, assuming he could remember the way. He whispered goodnight and I did the same. At the end of the corridor I glanced back, but it was too dark to see him. I had no idea whether those grey eyes were surveying me. All he would have seen if he looked was a shadow and a faint pinpoint of light from my tiny oil lamp.

The discussion was worth having. It had eased my mind. Back in my room, I fell asleep in moments.

27

I was up very early, though had already missed Faustus
and Aelianus. They went to see Cassius Scaurus at very
first light. The vigiles do most of their work at night, while
they are fire-watching, so the best time to catch any of them
is at the end of the watch. Scaurus rarely went out with the
foot patrols but he would have to be in his office when the
men returned to base with prisoners and reports. He gathered in the human trash not only from his headquarters
team, but the lads at the out-station up on the Aventine,
which was my local.

As I poked around trying in vain to find someone to give
me breakfast, I envisaged the scene at the station house this
morning. Among the usual bunch of feckless householders
who had left braziers burning unsafely and needed a
pompous lecture on responsibility, Scaurus would be thrilled
to find a hardened criminal who had been caught in the
act. This signalled fun. He might not welcome a *Daily Gazette*
report on the mugging of a senator in the Twelfth District,
but he would love holding a villain from the Second Cohort's
patch. Scaurus could annoy the Second by retaining him
for as long as he wanted, then when he grew bored with
this simple entertainment he could shunt the fellow back to
his opposite number, leaving his counterpart stuck with any
tricky decisions and all the tiresome form-filling.

There was time before I was needed at the Esquiline. I decided I had to see it.

I could not find Dromo. None of the Camillus slaves would agree to wake up and take me, especially after all the excitement yesterday. Luckily it was early enough to hope no one dangerous was out on the streets. Never mind safety precautions, I could move faster on my own.

First I dropped in to check on Uncle Quintus. He seemed to be drowsing, though the poppy juice had worn off so there were fitful movements and groans. Claudia must have gone to bed; she would want to be rested to cope with today. One of their sons had crept downstairs and lay curled up beside his father.

'Looking after him?' The child – I think it was the one called Constans – nodded. He was afraid I was going to send him back to his own room, but I ruffled his hair and left him. He looked about seven, worried and tear-stained. Uncle Quintus would not want this young soul sent off on his own in a state of such anxiety. 'Good boy. Try not to worry; he's getting better. I have to go out. Will you tell your mother I went to see Uncle Aulus?'

After another nod, Constans said suddenly, 'That boy left.'

'Who?' Surely not Dromo?

'The lamp boy who came with you. He went home to see his dog.'

'Right. I hope he can find the way all by himself . . .'

'I don't like him.'

I paused, on my way out. 'The lantern holder? Why not, Constans?' He shrugged. 'He's just a slave. Did he do something to you?' A headshake.

My nephew lost interest. He put his thin arm around his father and buried his face against Quintus' side. I went over and gently placed a light rug over both of them before I slipped away.

I can be a sickroom attendant. I just had no time to hang about right then.

The streets were quiet, apart from stallholders unrolling their awnings and setting out their stock. At one bar someone was doling out hot broth to market workers, but most places still had their shutters closed. Occasionally I passed a sleepy public slave sweeping up the sad remains of last night's parties, which were best not examined closely. The air felt thin and chilly as if the city had not yet properly opened its lungs. Overhead was cloudless, though washed out, in the waiting period before the sun burned the mist off the river and turned the sky to its hot summer blue.

The Fourth Cohort's station house stood at low level on the lesser of the Aventine's two heights, beside the Clivus Triarius. The troops at the end of a long shift should have been too tired to call indecent suggestions after me but, well done those boys, they bravely managed it. I looked straight ahead and kept going. The catcalls had nothing to do with me being unchaperoned. Dromo would have been no help.

The Fourth Cohort had held the prisoner in special custody all night. By the time I arrived, inevitably he had talked. I did not ask what persuaded him to speak. I had lived long enough around investigators to be sure I preferred not to know. I never saw him, nor even knew his name.

The aedile and my uncle were in the tribune's office, looking tight-lipped, while Scaurus, a loud-voiced, long-in-the-tooth ex-centurion, bragged about what his men's brilliant interrogation had achieved. As Faustus muttered under his breath to me, there was no guarantee anything their now blood-spattered prisoner had told them was true. I agreed, but pulling limbs out of sockets and cutting off fingers is what makes the vigiles feel comfortably professional. Scaurus was a caring commander, who liked to think his men were happy in their work.

Fairly early on in what the vigiles shyly called 'processing', the prisoner had claimed that to his certain knowledge nobody from the Rabirius gang (to whom he had admitted he belonged) had broken into the Aviola house. No one of theirs took the silver. No one murdered the householders. That was all Faustus and I wanted to know, though for Aulus and the tribune there were bigger questions.

The man had agreed – wisely, given the circumstances of his capture – that he took part in battering Camillus Justinus but he would not name who gave him orders. Whoever despatched him must be more frightening than the vigiles. Cassius Scaurus said dolefully, 'My lads could put more pressure on – but the pathetic lump would only go and die on us. I'm not going to tolerate do-gooders asking how a prisoner came to expire in custody before the praetor even knew we had him, when I can wait for the parts we toasted to heal over, then have him nicely executed as a treat for the public – well, am I?'

No, we answered.

The praetor, holding a post second only to consul, was Rome's chief law officer. His role was to examine suspects that the vigiles said should be sent for trial. In public order cases, outside their remit of imposing set fines for basic misdemeanours, this gave their victims a tier of appeal – not that most praetors troubled to look closely at pleas of innocence. Well, not without strong inducements of a kind I won't mention.

This prisoner expected to avoid seeing the praetor. He thought he would be rescued. It seemed he was right. Just then the man I talked to at the Galatea, Gallo, paid the Fourth Cohort a visitation, full of swagger and hung about with an expensive-looking legal team: a couple of shiny lawyers wearing togas with a fancy nap. They must have earned a lot of fees to pay for those outsize signet rings. The entire party was belching after what must have been a good breakfast.

Gallo was so blunt and straightforward he could have just come from reading a tract on republican values. What happened to criminal deviousness? The direct furrow he ploughed here from the Esquiline would have impressed Romulus. Why muck about? He came to pick up their man. When Gallo arrived at a vigiles barracks, his aim was to walk away with what he wanted, plus a sack of compensation money. His lawyers were mouthing that dire speech about 'loss of reputation' and 'mental distress'. They hadn't even seen the physical damage yet. As soon as they did, they would be charging double for consulting their lexicon of indignant adjectives.

Aelianus, Faustus and I stood back in silence to watch how Scaurus dealt with this. Doubts must have been running through all our minds. I was sure the useless slob of a tribune would either cave in just to save himself bother, or he would be influenced by gain. When Gallo asked 'How much?' that seemed to be the clincher.

But Gallo was about to be caught out by a technicality. The Rabirii did not extend their criminal reach to the Aventine, so they had never bought off Cassius Scaurus, tribune of the Fourth. As a result, he could pretend to a high-mindedness that was, for those of us who knew him, a revolting spectacle.

'Gallo, when I want to have a sweetener slipped into the contingency fund, I can get it from my own despicable crooks – if I let them. The Second may like you all cosied up under one blanket, but the Second are stupid bastards and I don't run their kind of show. Shove off, Gallo!'

This was the way Rome kept a degree of control over chaos, with no single group of villains able to take over the whole city. Each criminal gang would have to buy off not only its own local cohort, but six others. It would be too expensive and not worth the bother.

The fancy lawyers spoke up again, earning their keep in front of Gallo. I could not bear to listen. I knew Scaurus would happily let them bleat all day without him getting a sweat on. Camillus Aelianus, being a lawyer himself, stubbornly wanted an argument, so I tipped the wink to the aedile to stay with him and ensure my uncle did not resort to libel, or even to thumping the opposition. Aulus was chunky, more muscular than his brother, and what happened to Quintus had made him genuinely angry.

I took myself across to the Esquiline to oversee the local search.

Manlius Faustus had told me the orders he intended giving. He provided a mix of men, as many as he could muster in a hurry. He must have sent out notes last night to organise this. Aulus' wife would have had to provide stationery and messengers; it is a usual courtesy for a guest who needs to contact his associates, be they friends, aunts-in-law, or hapless farm managers. She must have been relieved that Manlius Faustus was not a man penning endless letters so one day he could publish his collected correspondence. Imagine the nightmare of having Cicero or that tacky show-off Pliny to stay.

With a normal law and order search, doors are shoved in with their latches broken before people have time to come and open up. There is much noise, damage and aggression – a supposed aid to public order. Property is smashed on purpose, other property is later found to have gone missing. Women are routinely felt up; dogs are kicked in the ribs; scared children are bawled at until they scream their heads off. From time to time wise men, or men who think they are, have explained to me why this approach is regarded as efficient. I once told Uncle Petro it was bull's bollocks. He just grinned.

Some of the men were from the aediles' office, others seemed to be Faustus' own staff or at least his uncle's. They were all so careful they never had to shake off protesting housewives and never became nervously hysterical themselves. Everything went smoothly. That was so like Manlius Faustus.

No complaints arose. No stolen silver drinks vessels turned up either. A couple of householders were cautioned about other items, mainly unused materials that had obviously walked off building sites, plus five wine amphorae of unknown provenance that were found hidden under hay. No arrests were made. We wanted people to be on our side, and stressed our willingness to listen to anyone who might have witnessed something useful – where 'listening' meant giving modest payment for information.

Towards the end it became clear there was one horrible place left to inspect. All the men put a copper into a bowl, then sticks were cut and they drew lots. The lucky winner of the sweep had to lift off the wooden seat then go down the hole to empty Aviola's kitchen lavatory.

Nobody in Rome uses a household latrine if there is any alternative. They are disgusting. The man was given a bucket and a scoop to remove the contents; we sieved the sordid products of his labour. I helped. I don't hang back. I learned more than I ever wanted to know about the household's eating habits, until I feared I would never manage dinner myself again. What we produced was the usual: apart from fish and meat bones, vegetable husks and nut shells, horrible pot and bowl scrapings, dead rats, and enough human pooh for an army cohort, there was lost jewellery, oil lamps that had fallen in at night, fresco painters' leavings that ought to have been taken off site, odd shoes, snapped styluses, tablets that could have been fascinating love letters or significant lists of property but which were too indecipherable now to be clues for me, and a big group of broken potsherds that must be the end result of the quarrels between slaves that I had heard about.

There was no silver. Still, it could not be called a waste of time. I had nothing else to do that afternoon. At least we would be leaving the apartment with a spotless, free-running home facility.

Manlius Faustus had sent a docket that his foreman brought me to sign on completion. I was able to certify that the search had been thorough. This must be a bluff on the aedile's part. I could not decide whether he genuinely believed it would make the men more diligent if I was watching them – or if he thought ticking off the job on a waxed tablet would give me a laugh.

28

Failing to find that silver left me downhearted. It had to be key to the mystery. While it might yet turn up a few pieces at a time in some dodgy backstreet homeware shop, the longer those goblets stayed missing, the less chance we had of finding them and we were missing the big clue as to who came into the apartment and carried out the murders.

If the Rabirius gang never took the loot, I had to accept that the vigiles investigator Titianus had been right all along: this must be an inside job. I badly wanted to best Titianus. But suppose he was right and the slaves were guilty: what had they done with the items they stole? Those who fled surely did not rush through the dark streets to the Temple of Ceres carrying a sack full of rattling bullion.

Well, it was just possible. We would look really silly if the lost property had been hidden there in plain sight all along. I would ask Faustus, the next time he was in the Temple, to double-check the display cases of gifts to the goddess. People deposited treasure to win themselves divine favour (or at least the glutinous thanks of the priests).

No, I do not care for priests. My father taught me to distrust them, whether they are members of the public holding office to further their ambition, or devious professionals with filthy morals and an eye for behind-the-cult-statue liaisons.

Yes, some priest must have upset my papa badly. Though Didius Falco can take against members of other professions just because they have a wart or are wearing pea green. Actually I agree with him over green.

Enough of this rambling – another thing my father taught me. You are supposed to witter on about nothing important, while the answer to your problem pops into your mind.

Look, even a brilliant informer can believe in crackpot routines. Father had them. I had them. You do your work your own lousy way, legate, and leave us to solve our cases in ours.

I admit, I had hit the low point here: that moment in an inquiry when frustration and even boredom threatens to make you abandon it. I had to remind myself that I was hired to report to Manlius Faustus that the slaves at the temple could be proven innocent. The truth threatened to be that I could not prove it – and maybe they were not.

It seemed impossible to say that any of the refugee slaves, except the deceased porter Nicostratus, were certainly *not* involved in strangling their master and mistress. Even Nicostratus could have been part of a conspiracy to steal the silver.

I kept returning to him. Even allowing a scenario where Aviola and Mucia were killed by their slaves for one of the normal reasons slaves turn against masters, I was unable to explain the first attack that night. However I looked at it, what happened to Nicostratus was an anomaly. Who killed him? Who beat him up so violently he died of his injuries – and why?

I supposed it was feasible that the other slaves conspired against Aviola and Mucia, but Nicostratus remained loyal to the couple and refused to join in. So the others may have turned on him. Perhaps they carried him away with them because if he regained consciousness he could tell the vigiles what the rest had done? But that was no surety because he could still have told the temple authorities.

If the other slaves had murdered Aviola and Mucia, they cannot have been tender-hearted. Why in that case did they not finish off Nicostratus straightaway?

Another curious aspect: why was Libycus, Aviola's body-slave, out of the house? If he was part of a conspiracy, what was the point of him being off-scene when the killing took place? Had he too objected to killing Aviola, whom he had served so intimately for so many years? Did somebody suggest he go and see his friends in the shop, to get him out of the way?

Supposing Libycus refused to contemplate killing Aviola, how did Amaranta feel about disposing of Mucia Lucilia? Of course male cynics will tell you women are more blood-thirsty. But she seemed a perfectly decent young woman to me.

You may think I am bound to say that. Not me. I am ready to believe the worst of anyone. I judge by feel and instinct, the informer's precious tools. My gut said Amaranta was hoping to be freed in the near future, which gave her no motive for murder. Far from it. Her mistress' sudden death had removed all her hopes. I could not imagine that sharp girl, with the fancy hair plaits and plenty of men hankering, would jeopardise her prospects.

I thought back to the day I interviewed the slaves. When I saw them at the aediles' office there had been no sign of tensions between them. Even though I had now been told there were ructions in this household, the small group had sat together quietly, dull-eyed and anxious over their fate, but as far as I could tell they were bonded, a single entity. Some – Amaranta, Phaedrus the other porter, Chrysodorus the philosopher, Olympe the girl musician – came from Mucia Lucilia's previous house; the rest had a long-term service with Aviola. Some had general duties in the house or garden; others carried out more personal services. Some – Amethystus and Diomedes – seemed reconciled to a life of slavery; others were hankering for freedom and perhaps very close to obtaining it. Had they not told me, I would have been unable to distinguish.

Did this mean they were indeed bonded – through joint involvement in the crime?

After mulling until my brain was in turmoil, I left the apartment. I had no wish to stay there that particular night, especially since I had mislaid Dromo. Last night's violence against Quintus Camillus had made me jumpy.

I ventured out of doors nervously. To my relief, as I scanned the street for anyone from the Rabirius gang, I spotted the foreman Faustus had sent for the search. He was finishing snacks at a bar with his men, so I asked to join them as they made for home. Escorting me to where the Camillus brothers lived hardly took them out of their way to the Aventine.

At the Capena Gate I found that Uncle Quintus was awake, up to a point. He had chosen to dull his pain with a large goblet of Chian red wine. This, he claimed, was a more natural and cheering painkiller than medicine – and anyway the Chian was ready to drink. Lying on multiple pillows, with offspring sprawled around him telling him stories and playing quiet games among themselves, he smelt curiously of turpentine balms when I leaned in to kiss him. He was not making much sense, though seemed easy in himself.

I found Claudia Rufina in a salon with Aulus' first wife, Hosidia Meline. These two well-dressed women from ancient civilised provinces, Spain and Greece, regarded me as a wild barbarian since I came from Britain. Meline had a habit of teasingly calling me a druid. The Romans had invited, cajoled and coerced most gods of the Mediterranean into their city, no doubt to cover themselves in case the Olympic pantheon were not truly the tops. At no point had they brought the druids. Nor would they.

The elegant ones told me Aulus had gone out. On occasions he surprised us with brief bursts of social manoeuvring; today he wanted to move among his peers, canvassing support for the speech he intended to make about gangland criminals.

'I hope I was not expected to invite that aedile to lunch!' Claudia said, at which Meline shook her head. In cahoots, these two senatorial wives openly shunned Faustus for his plebeian status, even though he belonged to a family that had been established and wealthy for years, and was himself the holder of a high office. 'I know he is your client, Albia . . .'

'And a friend!' I snapped, letting my aunt see what I thought of her bad manners towards Faustus. It made me change my intention of staying here another night.

I asked to borrow escort slaves. I would have reclaimed Mucia's carrying chair, but Claudia informed me it had already been collected, by Polycarpus. He had told her that it was a valuable asset which he needed to keep carefully for the executors.

'I am appalled that you were put into a vehicle with dried blood on the seat, Flavia Albia. Whoever was murdered there? I was glad to see the back of the thing. My children kept playing in it . . . Your own boy is still here, if you need an escort.'

I managed to find Dromo, who had stayed at the Capena Gate because nobody instructed him to do anything else. I dragged him with me up to the Aventine. First we went to the aediles' office, but Faustus was absent. If he had been denied lunch by Claudia, he probably needed an early dinner. I knew where he lived, but was leery of visiting him at home.

Instead I went to Fountain Court. 'Cor, this is a dump!' Dromo informed me, in case I had not noticed. I told him to doss downstairs with the porter.

I took myself to the haven of my own apartment. This was indeed a dump, but I felt overdue for a night in my own bed. I had been away from home for five days; after that time any woman needs to refresh herself with a change of earrings.

29

Since I was up on the Aventine, next morning I walked over to the aediles' office beside the Temple of Ceres. First I went into the temple, to check for myself whether the Aviola silver was there among the donated treasure. No luck.

I would have liked a catch-up with my client, and perhaps a sociable breakfast, but Faustus was still absent. He might have been at a meeting, though realistically no magistrate works every day. The point is to hold the office so it goes on your record of honours. Faustus seemed more conscientious than most aediles, but no one expected him to flog himself carrying out public duties. He was a rich boy. His uncle ran the family business, owned the house where they lived, let Faustus draw money as he wanted. He had never been in the army, so this would be the first time in his life (at thirty-six) that any demands were made on him.

What a shock that must have been.

I was feeling bitter.

I took another look at the fugitive slaves, not with much sympathy. I warned them this could be their last chance to tell me anything that might prove their innocence. The Temple was unlikely to allow them sanctuary much longer, whatever tradition dictated. The attitude in Rome was that somebody had to be punished for the deaths of their master and their mistress. I had failed to identify anyone else, so they were still chief suspects.

Most listened with little reaction. One or two looked shifty, especially Amaranta and the girl Olympe, but I had no leads for further questioning and I was not in a mood to listen to frightened sobbing.

'So we are running out of options,' said Chrysodorus, the philosopher who had to look after the lapdog. Puff wheezed out a languid bark. Chrysodorus glared vitriol at Puff. 'Bad girl! Albia, all I ask is make it quick. I can accept that life is merely a stroll to the cremation pyre, but please spare me hooks and ropes and naked flames.'

'Torture, Chrysodorus?'

Chrysodorus explained his gloom: a specialist contractor had been to the office, wanting to tender for squeezing information from the slaves if the temple kicked them out. Hearing Chrysodorus telling me about it made them all more agitated. Daphnus, the ambitious tray carrier, reckoned that had Manlius Faustus been at the office that day he might have accepted the contractor's blandishments and handed everyone over.

I assured them Faustus was a benign wimp who didn't believe inflicting pain made people tell the truth.

That was guesswork, though I had seen him be devout when organising a religious festival and he had told me he refused to see slaves as polluted by their condition. I thought it unlikely he would suddenly lose interest and end my commission; he had to answer to the temple, for one thing. Still, I never entirely trusted clients. Just in case my work was about to be cancelled, I asked the contractor's address and went to have a proactive chat with him.

He was called Fundanus. His premises were down in the valley, on the nearest side of the Circus Maximus, below the Temple of Mercury. His primary business was that of a funeral director. The area was notoriously frequented by whores. Fornicating with their backs against the wall below his signboard, the night moths may have found that gave their tired trade a special frisson. I expect he buried the ashes of plenty of those sad women.

As I reached his yard, where carts, biers and headstones were arrayed, a mixed group of men, wearing matching red tunics, hurried out past me. I had seen this uniform on running men in Rome before, though never knew what it meant. Sometimes one of them was banging a bell.

Fundanus explained cheerily. 'My men, fetching in a body – see the hauling hooks? The bell is to let people know we are coming. They want to jump out of the way quick, to avoid a corpse that's contaminated by slavery. A bed-maker in Cyclops Street hanged herself this morning.'

'When a slave dies, the corpse has to be removed in two hours?' Faustus had told me this.

'Only one hour if the silly bastard pulls the rope trick,' Fundanus corrected. 'Well, twisted sheet in this case, to be strictly accurate. My fellows should make the deadline, but we're pushing it. People are so thoughtless. They arse about after they discover a body, discussing what has happened – when it's obvious – and all the while, precious time is flying. I could lose my licence if I miss the deadline.'

'Why did she do away with herself?'

'Couldn't endure any more from the master.'

'You mean sex?'

'Fucking morning, noon and night.'

'He was not married?'

'Where have you been? Of course he was. The wife said the bint had to put up with it, since it kept him happy.' Presumably, that saved the wife from having to endure the pervert herself. Confirming my dire view of this family, Fundanus said, 'He likes to beat the wife as hard as the slaves if she crosses him. So she lets him do whatever he wants – provided he's doing it to someone else.'

He led me into the cabin where he normally seated the bereaved when they came to make arrangements. We took stools, not quite touching knees. He apologised for being unable to offer me mint tea, but said the serving boy had gone off as one of the red tunics. Feeling fastidious in this environment, I assured him that was fine.

He had a face like a root vegetable at the end of a hard winter. His humanity was just as shrivelled. The man was a plebeian, no doubt of it. That meant he came from the same rootstock as my father or Manlius Faustus. Their ancestors used their wits to build up businesses – warehouses and auctioneering. These were businesses where they could keep their hands fairly clean while generating filthy lucre from the uppercrust who sneered at them for being in trade – all of whom, it is fair to say, were themselves as bent as a discarded nail.

Fundanus had stuck at the filthy end of society, in a profession where *everybody* hated what he did. He had a stroppy attitude, and clearly enjoyed being awkward.

It is perfectly possible even Fundanus thought his job was a boil on the world's bum. Still, he put up with it, never thinking of retraining in some more pleasant area – say, as a tunic-maker, a poet, or in the pastry trade. The man was overweight, under-endowed with muscle or brains, and outclassed by every sewer-rat who ever poked his nose out of a drain.

I noticed that his warts looked as if they had been infected with putrefaction from a long-time dead body. I told myself not to be squeamish, then told him my connection with the Aviola slaves.

Fundanus explained his own interest, a man who liked to hold forth. Yes, he was a funeral director, but he had a lucrative sideline in punishing and executing slaves.

'This is for private customers?' I asked.

'Can be. Someone has a slave who needs keeping in order, kindly chastisement, we can supply the necessary.'

'What would that be?'

'Posts, chains, ropes. Floggers too – my operatives can work with the cross or the fork.' I did not need to ask; the slave victims would be either nailed to a wooden cross or hung on a very ancient device called the fork. Then they would be flogged to as near death as their owner chose – or actually until they died. They were property. An owner could dispose of his slave; killing them was frowned upon nowadays, but theoretically it could still happen. 'We make one charge, applies across the board – four sesterces each man, whether for a fork operative, a flogger, or an executioner.'

'That's fair.'

'I don't muck about,' claimed Fundanus smugly. 'Of course on a public contract, different rates apply. A magistrate gives the orders, we supply crosses as standard, plus free nails, pitch, wax, tapers, anything else required. All covered by our retainer. Copy of the rules hung in the premises.' He gestured to it.

I admired his certificate and said I was glad to see a public role being properly administered. 'This is not an area where sloppiness can be tolerated.'

'Right, young lady!' Oblivious to my satire, Fundanus decided to set me straight about my own commission. 'I expect this will come as news to you. Those slaves, that whingeing bunch who've got themselves bed and board at the temple's expense, ought to have gone to their master's aid. Me, I support extending blame to all the little shits under one roof. We have to fight the enemy, both within and without.'

'Might they not have been loyal servants who were unable to do anything?'

Fundanus gave me a pitying look. 'I can tell what sort of home you were brought up in!' My parents would have been proud to hear that, especially as he clearly meant 'among dangerous philosophers, who think all beings born on earth have value'.

'I try to see both sides,' I murmured, feeling my mother's influence.

'That was what I meant!'

'I am sorry,' I apologised meekly, mentally writing a curse tablet against this man.

'Let me tell you a few things about the world, my girl. We cannot let these people get the upper hand. Slaves have to be forced to protect their masters by the threat of their own death if they don't. They ought to come running without thought for themselves whatever's going on – including throttling, strangling, being thrown over a cliff, or struck with any stick, missile, blade or other weapon.'

He must have seen this list in an edict somewhere. I wondered if the weapons would include fireships or military catapults. I merely said, 'Seems comprehensive.'

'Oh, it's not ideal. It doesn't cover poisoning – because the argument goes, how would they know? Pathetic! Or once the effects of a poison become obvious, it's too late and what could they do? With a master's suicide, the sentence only applies if the slaves are on the spot at the time and could prevent the attempt.'

'Understandable.'

'What,' asked the funeral director, lowering his voice as some mark of respect, 'happened to the victims in the tragic circumstance under review?'

'Strangled. With a piece of rope.'

He nodded, with grim satisfaction. 'That would be covered.'

'I know.'

'As I said. Your bastard clients should have gone to help.'

I didn't bother to contradict him that Faustus was my client, not the slaves. 'They all say they didn't hear anything. No cries for help.'

'Mule-dung. I'd clean out the lying snots' earwax with a lighted taper . . . Anything useful been done to them so far? What has been tried?'

'Just intense questioning.'

'You are having a laugh!'

I admitted I was serious, but promised that when the time came to use proper methods, he would be the chosen operator.

'You can put a word in?' From the way he sized me up, he was wondering who I slept with.

I assured him I had contacts, not mentioning names. Before things became tricky, I made my excuses and left.

As I walked back to the Esquiline I felt demoralised. The Fundanus world-view was depressing enough, but I was having my own crisis. Earlier I had wanted my commission to continue, because I hate being thwarted and still hoped to find the truth. With time to review the situation as I walked, I decided I had now done everything possible. Some informers would drag things out for the daily retainer, but I faced up to the fact my inquiry should be wound up, even though it had proved a failure.

I never get sentimental about cases. If they are dead in the water, it is always best to admit that. Save yourself time and effort; keep your integrity. Your clients may even be so fair-minded they appreciate honesty.

Well, I had one once who claimed she did. She thought it meant she could get away with not paying me for work done. I soon explained how that was a misapprehension, so then she decided that I was a cheating bitch she should never have hired. I had to send a debt-collector. She coughed up when she saw Rodan. She didn't even try to buy him off with the promise of her body – restraint in which she showed both morality and taste. Such rare qualities.

The same woman even tried to hire me a second time. She seemed surprised when I refused, even though I was lying on a sunbed at the time so she could see I was not busy.

This case was over. Faustus would pay me for what I had done, and I would accept the fee.

He might never commission me again, although if he was a just man he would see that we had simply run out of evidence. It can happen. I still had doubts whether the slaves were guilty. But now we would be forced to follow the law and damn them, if and when the temple authorities chose to terminate their asylum.

Then something happened, as it sometimes does. The whole inquiry had to be reopened, just as I was on the verge of writing the report that would tell Manlius Faustus we had to close it. Someone else in the Aviola household died.

30

I continued back to the Esquiline, considering how I could formally explain the position to Faustus. I thought he would probably accept it, causing me less of a headache than I got from my own bad mood. I cannot deal well with failure.

Dromo was dodging about behind me, looking at stalls and shops. I needed to keep an eye out all the time, in case I lost him. Faustus had taught him one route to and from the Aventine but our path from the undertaker's was new, while Dromo's grasp of the Roman map was limited. If we separated, I did not trust him to find his own way to the apartment. Besides, he was supposed to guard me.

The weather had warmed up. It was a long hot walk. I should have paid for a chair, but I chose not to sting the aedile with a hefty fare at the moment when I was dropping his case. If I did, as soon as the carriers set off, Dromo was bound to be left behind. How often have you seen women leaning out of chairs and helplessly calling slaves' names, shouting themselves hoarse while their difficult entourage pretends not to hear?

I needed Dromo; I was going to the apartment to collect my personal belongings and Faustus' property, so Dromo would have to transport it all on his handcart. While I could rely on Polycarpus to return these things eventually, he had no incentive to be prompt and it was foolish to suppose every item would reappear. Even a good steward could not prevent messengers picking out choice goodies for themselves.

As it turned out, asking Polycarpus to organise it was not an option.

Close to heat exhaustion, we passed the Market of Livia but I did not go in. If I was leaving the apartment, I had no further need for provisions. I could not face the crowds, nor the barracking shopkeepers. You have to be feeling confident to cope in a Roman market. I was too demoralised.

When I reached the part of the Clivus Suburanus where Aviola had lived, I looked around carefully from the shelter of a doorway, telling Dromo to stand close and not draw attention to himself. He knew what had happened to Camillus Justinus, so was prepared to follow orders temporarily. But the butterfly-brain would not keep still for long.

I carefully checked for gangsters, though identified none.

Everyone appeared to be going about their normal business. It was just a street. Elderly women muttering abuse after young men who had barged into them; young men staring at young women as if they had never seen anything female before; one girl and her mother brushed mud off their skirt hems where they had accidentally stepped in a gutter puddle. Overhead, someone invisible inside an apartment pulled a cross-street washing-line hand over hand as they hung wet clothes out. A clean tunic fell off into the same puddle, followed by a magnificently inventive torrent of screaming curses. A door slammed. A couple of pigeons lifted themselves laboriously from a sill, flew in a half-hearted circle and landed in fluffed lumps, to continue their midday drowsing.

A dopey-looking boy stood outside the leather shop, which was closed for lunch. A couple of feet away from him sat a very hairy black dog. It had fleas. I could tell from here, by the intent way it was scratching among its long matted fur. It was loose, so could have belonged to anyone or no one, but kept looking at the boy as if it half hoped for a titbit and half feared a kick.

'Cosmus,' said Dromo, catching the direction of my gaze.

'Who is he?'

'Their lamp boy yesterday. And Panther.'

'His dog?' Constans had told me that the boy went home to see his dog.

'Right. You're good at this,' Dromo declared, mock-admiring. 'Have you thought about making guessing-games your career?'

'No. I'm too busy thinking, when shall I get around to beating you for cheek?'

The last thing I wanted today was careers advice.

Panther might be the beast I had heard barking when I called at Polycarpus' apartment. His wife, Graecina, had said 'the boy' took the dog out for a walk, so at the time I assumed she meant their son. Cosmus must be about fourteen, quite a lot older than the child I had heard wailing when I visited. Graecina must have meant 'boy' in the other sense. As a freedman, Polycarpus was entitled to possess slaves. Mind you, someone who had been a slave himself ought to know how to buy better. It's one thing for an adolescent son to loaf about the streets looking for trouble but a slave ought to be kept better occupied. This one looked impervious to training.

Graecina came down from their apartment. She spoke to Cosmus, though I could not hear what was said. He hunched up and stayed put by the leather shop, looking lethargic. Graecina waited a moment, then she walked to one of the other retail outlets. It was where Polycarpus had pulled open a shutter to produce Mucia's chair for me yesterday.

The shutter was obviously not locked but now it refused to move freely. As best she could, Graecina hauled on it then said something, as if someone – Polycarpus presumably – was inside. It looked like a routine exchange between a wife and her husband. He might be continuing the process of cleaning up the seat cushion, and she might be calling him upstairs for lunch.

I was intending to exchange greetings as I went into the apartment. As I came closer, Graecina spoke again, more impatiently. Seeming on the clumsy side with physical mechanics, she failed to apply her weight properly so could not heave the heavy folding door any further open. I went forwards to help. Giving up, Graecina squeezed through anyway, muttering. It was a tight fit. She was a fleshy woman. She would have acquired bruises.

I reached the shutter; I was standing on the threshold when, within the dim interior, the steward's wife let out a shriek.

31

The scream sounded more like surprise than anguish, but sometimes you recognise trouble. With a great struggle, I pressed myself through the narrow gap, following Graecina inside. Through the gloom, I saw why the shutter was so hard to open. Polycarpus was lying against it, in a partly bent position with his shoulders and upper body pressed against the inside of the wooden leaf, his weight jamming it.

I joined his wife as she knelt beside him. He was warm, though lifeless. Graecina was breathing fast, but she held herself together, a loyal wife and mother, refusing to give way to hysteria while there might be something necessary to do.

No chance. No pulse. No breath. No life left. I said nothing, but the wife knew too.

Together we lifted Polycarpus away from the shutter, so I could pull it open properly. We hauled him out and laid him on his back in the street. I checked again, but it was pointless. Light and air failed to revive him or alter my verdict.

I sent for a doctor anyway. A widow needs to be sure. Graecina provided an address and I told Dromo to go; I reckoned Cosmus would be unreliable.

Having brought back the cloak Graecina lent me the day

before yesterday, I folded it and placed it beneath the steward's head. It was too soon to cover over the body, not while his wife was still reluctant to accept he was dead.

Though the corpse was recognisably Polycarpus, with the same build and desert-dweller's chin stubble, all the spry bonhomie had vanished. To me, it was no longer him.

Graecina and I sat side by side on the kerb; I held her hand. I had taken to her on first acquaintance and, unbeknown to her, we shared this hard experience. I too had once had my husband abruptly despatched, in the middle of what had seemed an ordinary, bright and sunny day. So, as the world went about its business unaware of her tragedy, I knew all too painfully what Graecina was going through.

She stayed silent. Some people immediately become stupefied. Others of us clench up and fall into deep thoughts, planning ahead, already readjusting because we need to be ready, we need to be strong.

She would be thinking about her children – how to tell them, how to console them, how then to provide for them, on her own, in whatever difficult future lay ahead. I had not had that worry, but on the other hand, when my husband died suddenly, he left me to a life alone. That's hard, even if you call yourself tough. As far as I knew, her children were still young, and so Graecina would at least have someone to talk to, cry with, even snap at when everything became too difficult. The infants would grow up. They would grow up fairly well, I thought, from the little I had seen of her. She would have her family.

The hairy dog came over and licked Polycarpus gently. His manner was sad and respectful, as if he realised he was saying farewell. This is why I like dogs.

He sat down beside the body, a couple of feet from Graecina and me, sharing our vigil. Occasionally he had to scratch at a flea, but he did so unobtrusively. He seemed to understand our sadness, and wanted to be part of the scenario.

The dog's behaviour contrasted with that of the slave Cosmus, who had mooched to a new spot outside a cutler's shop. He was staring at the goods on show, as if he had not seen us bring his master's body out. I worry about young boys who gawp at knives – though many of them do it, some never actually reaching the stage of owning one.

When Dromo brought the doctor, he said Polycarpus had died of heart failure. The man needed to see an oculist.

It must be true that the steward's heart had failed at some point. He had told me he had been freed for five years, making him in his mid to late thirties, young for this to happen unexpectedly. There had been no sign that his heart was diseased, no warning that his body was liable to fail him. He had never lived foolishly. Yet plenty of people leave the world at his age or younger.

Stress could have caused a heart attack. If he had been in an argument prior to his death, it was not with Graecina; I myself saw her arrive on the scene. Watching her discover the body, I had witnessed true shock.

Her grief was real too. 'Why?' she asked, fixatedly. People do ask that, and generally there is nothing you can say in reply.

I knew that heart failure alone did not kill the steward. The doctor saw nothing amiss, but I had noticed immediately: Polycarpus had been attacked.

It was probably quick and simple. There were no self-defence bruises, no rope around the steward's neck and no rope burns. But I could see tell-tale fingermarks.

I answered the wife's question. She had the right to know. 'Look at his throat here, Graecina. Somebody strangled him.'

32

I decided to involve the vigiles. I had no doubt Polycarpus' death was related to the murders of his master and mistress. If I failed to notify the Second Cohort, it might cause problems. This was a high profile case.

Again, I sent Dromo. He had not evolved by magic into someone helpful; we had had no lunch and it would not happen in the near future. He would soon start to nag me. To pre-empt the misery, I gave him a few coppers, with orders to go to the station house with my message first, then buy himself a cake on the way back. He skipped off eagerly.

Covered with crumbs, he returned with Titianus. Even the vigilis appeared to be chewing. I was stuck with him; he would probably fail to investigate properly all over again. Sighing internally, I sent off Dromo for an undertaker, ignoring his pleading looks for more tuck money.

Titianus took the line that I was trouble. Nevertheless, he did not exclude me from his thoughts, which were as hidebound as ever. He immediately swore this was a second murder by the same parties. He had hardly looked at the corpse or considered the circumstances.

I pointed out quietly that the original group of slaves had certainly not carried out this killing, because not only were they under guard at the aediles' office on the Aventine, as Titianus well knew, but I had actually seen them that morning and could give them all alibis. This confirmed his bitter theory that I was a menace, intent on ruining his life. Still, he settled down to do his job, while I tried to make his efforts fit with mine.

Polycarpus must have been murdered during my walk back to the Esquiline. I mentioned that the body had been warm when I first touched it. Titianus borrowed a stylus from me and wrote that down on a waxed tablet, asking how to spell 'temperature'. He got lost in the middle of the word and had to ask twice.

At least he paid attention to the time-of-death issue, though he only wanted to know because the closer death occurred to the discovery of the corpse, the shorter the time period Titianus would need to cover in his enquiries. I already knew he was a minimalist. But there was no hope he would give up and leave things to me.

He went over to the nearest bar and asked if anyone had witnessed the killer entering the shop while Polycarpus was inside. Of course not. People spend their time at bar counters staring out at the street, but nobody ever really sees anything that happens. Zeus could descend in a shower of gold and rape that fat woman at the bread counter, the one with the daughter-in-law who ran off with a sailor, but the divine apparition would pass unnoticed.

The same drinkers now stayed on, to gawp at the dead body.

Anyone else walking down the street at the crucial moment was long gone. People slip in and out of shops all the time, even when they are empty or closed. This is daily life. No one ever takes it in. If there had been a noisy altercation, nobody had heard it. If they had, they would have walked on faster.

After a while, Secundus and Myrinus came sauntering back to their shop. They had been taking lunch with Secundus' aged mother; she could vouch for them. Titianus sniffed; I saw he would have liked to pin the crime on the leatherworkers, because they were foreign. They must have known it too.

Titianus had to treat them politely, especially with me watching. They equally politely told him what little they knew. They had seen Polycarpus go into the empty premises. They exchanged greetings while he was opening up the shutter, but he was still in there on his own when the two North Africans left. He had pulled the shutter closed after him, except for a space of about a foot – which I thought was odd, because whatever he wanted to do there, the place would surely have been too dark.

'Graecina, did you know why your husband came down here?'

Something about the carrying chair, but Graecina did not know what. I went and had a look at it. The soiled seat, a padded drop-in rectangle on a wooden frame, had been lifted out. If there had been a bucket of water and a sponge, that would have answered the question for certain, but there were no cleaning materials.

Apart from being bloodstained, I could see nothing odd about the cushion. I swung open the chair's half door and inspected inside. There was a compartment underneath the seat. It was empty.

As I emerged, Titianus spotted Cosmus loitering and remembered him from the Aviola incident. Apparently it was Cosmus Polycarpus sent that night to the station house.

'Come here, you!'

Cosmus looked around as if he thought Titianus meant someone else, then loped across. He was a sturdy lad, just growing his first moustache. The vigilis muttered under his breath to me, which at least meant I was now a colleague he could grumble with.

Titianus questioned the slave with the air of a man who had wasted effort on the hopeless many times. He had an impatient, bullying approach which only drew out answers he clearly expected. Cosmus was the kind of slave who drifted about the neighbourhood, yet never heard or saw anything.

Cosmus said he had been sent downstairs by Polycarpus that morning to carry water to the apartment, so he was either away at the fountain (out of sight further down the street) or indoors out of earshot at the time when someone must have visited Polycarpus in the lock-up. Just before I arrived and saw him by the leather shop, Cosmus had been inside the house talking to Myla.

He was useless as a witness. Titianus could only roll his eyes and let Cosmus go.

I told him, 'See if Graecina wants you to do anything. Then stay with her. She needs support.'

To make sure, I myself led him over to Graecina who was talking to the undertaker. She confirmed the story about Polycarpus sending Cosmus to fetch water, as he did every day.

Titianus and I went indoors to question Myla. She was in the kitchen nursing her baby. She made sure Titianus had an eyeful. He was more tolerant with her than I would have been, perhaps because he was riveted by the breast-feeding. Typical.

I told Myla Polycarpus was dead. She responded quite aggressively. 'I hope you're not saying I had anything to do with that!'

'Well, did you?' asked Titianus, unmoved.

'How could I, when I'm in here all day with the little one and with all the jobs I have to do?'

I managed not to snort.

'So is it right, you were here talking to that half-baked boy Cosmus?' Titianus persisted.

'Cosmus is all right.'

'He behaves like a spook, who doesn't know who he's supposed to be haunting. Answer the question, Myla.'

'We were here, I suppose. I don't know. I don't know when it was, do I?'

'An hour ago, or less,' I said, joining in, hoping to speed up the agony.

'Well, Cosmus came in for a bite of lunch.'

'Does he not get fed at home?'

'Yes, but he comes down to see me sometimes. When he wants to chat.'

'What do you chat about?'

'Anything.'

'Such as?'

'He says what he wants to. He's a sad boy.'

'Why is he sad?'

'He doesn't know how to be happy.'

That was a conversation-stopper.

I started to rustle up lunch for myself, inviting Titianus to share. A true vigilis, he asked if I had anything to drink and when I said no, he went off to buy something from the bar. By the time he returned, carrying two full beakers on a rocky take-out tray, I had laid a portable table with snacks in the courtyard. The two chairs were still there.

He apologised if he had been a long time. 'That place opposite serves sewer silt. I had to walk down to the other one. I met an old codger who wanted to talk about Polycarpus. Nothing pertaining to the death, but the old fellow would go on. Apparently the steward was very friendly.'

'His modus,' I said. 'He kept in with everyone around here. I can imagine he would generously share some listening time with a maundering grandfather – though when he had had enough, I bet Polycarpus also knew how to go on his way without causing offence.'

'I never seem to manage that,' Titianus confided. He spoke with an innocence that reminded me of my late husband.

'It's a knack.' I let myself reply consolingly, even though I thought it was a knack anyone who joined the vigiles ought to have mastered by their third day. 'Did you find out anything from the old man?'

'Polycarpus had had a moan about Aviola intending to give his job to someone else.'

'Bad feeling against his master?'

'Well, the old 'un said Polycarpus wasn't exactly pleased. You can't blame him.'

'Polycarpus lined up something else for himself as soon as Aviola died.' I said. 'He had a good reputation. He was always going to find a place.'

We ate. Titianus drank. I merely sipped. I would enjoy the wine more on my own in peace, after he had gone. I could have a melancholy reminisce about Lentullus, my husband. I did that occasionally, often when a case was proving troublesome. You have to share with someone. At least the dead don't argue with you about it.

Not that Lentullus ever argued much with me. The dear lad thought anything I said was wonderful.

It was ten years since the gods took him, though it felt like only as many days. Poor Graecina had no idea yet what she would have to go through.

As he mellowed with a drink, curiosity got the better of Titianus. He had to ask me about the man captured in the attack on Camillus Justinus two days ago. Of course he knew that my uncle had been to see his tribune before that. I caught a hint of grumpiness; Titianus evidently thought Justinus and Faustus went over his head. As of course they did.

'I hope you don't resent them,' I said, aiming to win him over with frankness. At least I was able to assure Titianus that the male-only meeting when they saw his tribune was nothing to do with me.

'They made themselves marked men when they interfered. Old Rabirius is bound to have heard about it. You must be glad not to be identified as their associate, Albia.'

I did not tell Titianus that it was me who had spoken to Gallo. Titianus clearly didn't know that. He certainly would not approve. He was not as stubbornly 'traditional' as, say, that funeral director I saw this morning, Fundanus, but anyone who works with the vigiles hates women joining in their games.

'So you think it's obvious the attack on Camillus was set up by this gang?' I pretended to ask for an expert opinion.

'Seems likely.' Titianus preened himself. This might have been easier if he ever bothered to have a good lotion on his awful hair. 'I heard that their henchman, Gallo, went strutting to the Fourth's barracks, asking for the captured man to be released.'

'No – really?' I cooed.

'Gallo must have thought they were bound to hand him over.' Titianus sounded as though he had supposed the same. 'Apparently their tribune uses a different protocol. He refused outright.' Titianus whistled, either in astonishment or admiration, it was hard to tell.

'I am amazed as you are, Titianus. What did Gallo do?'

'He abandoned the man, apparently. Just scowled, walked off, and left him to his fate.'

'Did the fellow talk?' I had no need to ask. Of course he did. The Fourth can do their job.

'I believe the screams were terrible,' Titianus told me salaciously.

'What will be done with him? The usual?'

'Correct. He'll never resurface on the streets. He'll be among the criminals labelled "tunic-thief" and "sheep-abuser" in the morning arena show.'

I kept playing my part, looking innocent. 'When the slashing is fast and routine, while nobody in the audience is paying too much attention to the pieces of meat getting killed? Do you think the Rabirius gang will go to watch?'

'Bound to. They will show proper respect to their own,' Titianus surmised. 'After that, we may have some crap to deal with. Maybe the fellow's mother will start harbouring horrible bitterness because Gallo abandoned him. One of their family feuds may blow up. Blood at the barber's. Some senior Rabirius stiffed over his lobster stew at lunch, while gang members look the other way and hope they won't be next.'

'A lot of plotting at funerals,' I agreed.

'Even the great Gallo may wind up thrown into a stinking alley with a knife between his shoulder-blades – for dumping the fellow.'

'All very colourful, Titianus.'

We sat in silence for a while. Then I pointed out that – thinking of gangsters – in order to be absolutely thorough, we ought to investigate whether it was the Rabirii who had now strangled the steward.

'We' being Titianus and me. And 'investigate' requiring a visit to the gang.

33

Lunch is a wonderful mechanism. Some chunks of bread, a few scraps of ham, a bowl of cherries. Washed down with mediocre bar-room wine, this was enough to woo Titianus. It probably helped that he rarely shared investigations with anybody. He may have had a deputy he didn't trust, or a low-level bunch of door-knockers who took orders from him if he could think of any orders to give, but normally he worked on his own. Now he believed I was his friend. If I suggested a jape, he had to fall in with it.

He was too nervous to approach the grandee, Rabirius, in person. Instead, I managed to persuade him to tackle young Roscius. Titianus would have to find out the nephew's haunts, which he would do that afternoon. He went back to the barracks, planning to oil up Juventus, the gangster liaison officer. Titianus believed he could squeeze him without arousing suspicion. According to him, Juventus was not very bright.

I sympathised with him, for having to deal with idiots at work.

We agreed to meet up early next morning when Titianus said Roscius would be out and about and accessible, collecting cash for the old man. I spent the rest of the afternoon double-checking the neighbourhood for people who could have seen anything in connection with the steward's death. No luck, needless to say. Although Polycarpus had made himself friendly with everyone, no one would cause inconvenience to themselves by coming forward as a witness.

I wrote a report for Faustus. I first outlined the reasons why the case had seemed to be dying on us. After that, much of my news concerned Polycarpus, but I did slide in a mention that Titianus had agreed to make further contact with the gang. I did not say I was going with him. I sent Dromo off, then spent a quiet evening by myself before an early night.

I should have realised Faustus would guess what I was up to. So next morning who should come breezing into the apartment but my client. He was dressed not in his aedile's purple stripes, but the street clothes he wore for going undercover.

He did not trouble to chastise me. He acted as if his presence was a lucky coincidence. But he stuck there until Titianus turned up, then he came out with us. *I* acted as if I was perfectly happy to have Manlius Faustus do that. No choice really.

Titianus looked wary. Annoyed, I saw that he thought I had deliberately sent for Faustus who, in his eyes, was tainted by visiting the tribune. Even with the aedile disguised as an unshaven lout in a shabby brown tunic, Titianus was never going to like him. This busted up his and my relationship as cronies, jeopardising Titianus' willingness to be frank. Well, thank you, aedile!

Faustus, who noticed a lot, gave no sign that he had noticed any of this, but I knew he would have done.

Titianus led us first back to the Galatea. The sour fixer Gallo was not there; maybe he only turned up for his free

214

lunch. Instead, as we scrutinised the bar from across the street, Titianus said he could see Roscius. He was laughing and joking with two other men, gang members our guide recognised. We had agreed the ideal was to corner Roscius by himself, when he might be easier to work on. So we stayed put outside, watching.

When I say 'we' agreed a plan, Titianus and I did that while Faustus, in one of his introverted moods, merely listened and made no objection. I was trying to rebuild the investigator's trust, so I was pally with him and ignored the aedile. If Faustus felt left out, it was his fault for interfering. I did not need a nursemaid if I was staking out a suspect with a vigiles expert. In my opinion, I did not need a minder ever.

Titianus pointed out Roscius. He was about twenty-five, short-legged but good looking in a way that would not last past thirty. He thought himself a wonderful beast, with a ripped-neck tunic worn one-armed, in order to show off his well-oiled pectorals. Inevitably, a medallion of dubious metal with twinkly red glass inserts nestled among his curly chest hair. This jewel probably cost a packet (assuming he'd bought it, not stolen it); the deal must have made some lying, cheating jeweller extremely happy.

After a time, Roscius left the Galatea with one of the men he had been talking to. The underling was a fish-faced bag-carrier. We split up to follow them, which is supposed to make you less noticeable. We all played the game of shifting positions, now me at the back, then Faustus, criss-crossing the street with Titianus. Tragic. It fools no one.

The gangsters behaved as all of them do. They sauntered about, making their presence known. Money was picked up at a couple of places for certain. Banter was exchanged. It all looked friendly. That is the evil side of such people. They come around smiling, but their position in the neighbourhood is entirely based on threat.

Roscius picked out an apple at a fruit stall. He paid nothing for it. The stallholder made no attempt to ask him. Roscius strolled on, munching, then threw most of the apple in the gutter. He was just enjoying his power.

I had his measure. That familiar mix of boorish self-belief and ingrained bad manners. From the way he walked – knees apart, arms loose like a bad wrestler – I could see why the vigiles thought he might be aiming high, or was ready to split off by himself if the gang chiefs let him. I bet when he sat in a bar he had a hand in his lap and constantly jiggled his privates, not knowing he was doing it.

I wondered how he got on with Gallo. Gallo looked as if he had been around a long time. His backing could make Roscius a leader, but if he despised the young upstart, Gallo could be the one to thwart him. The fixer's choice might depend how much talent Roscius really had. To me, he did not look too clever. Not that stupidity holds back career criminals (as my father would say glumly), any more than it hampers promotion in the vigiles, election to the Senate, making a rich marriage, bringing too many children into the world, or being an amateur who buys an 'ancient Greek' statue and then sells it on for a fifty per cent profit, despite that new label from a workshop in Capua stuck on the base . . .

I wondered whether old Rabirius saw his nephew as an asset or a liability.

Then I wondered how healthy Rabirius was. What if he passed away? Could the Esquiline be facing an underworld power struggle? Would Gallo, the hard-man fixer, expect to inherit the business to which he had presumably contributed much? Would he be strong enough to dispose of any challenge from young Roscius, or would the old man nominate family to take over, and disappoint Gallo?

Titianus was gesticulating. Faustus and I caught up with him. 'They've gone in the Dilly-Dally.'

It was the kind of bar that thinks it's a brothel, or a brothel that pretends to be a bar. There was only a sketchy pavement presence. Moth-eaten curtaining hid the interior. They did not bother to have tie-backs. Whatever went on at the Dilly-Dally went on in hidden indoor places where the night sweeper always missed corners and the same dead mouse had been stiff on a shelf for three weeks.

We parked ourselves outside. After a long time the other man came out on his own, the fish-face. He waved an arm to Titianus mockingly. Faustus looked at us, then strode across to the bar on his own and went in. Moments later he reappeared, head shaking. Roscius was not there.

34

Titianus may have felt surprised that Faustus made no attempt to blame him. The aedile barely reacted; he merely asked what next?

Titianus had details of one last location supplied by Juventus. He led us to a street on the Cispian ridge, one of those happy havens that are lined throughout with eating places. Mostly you find these on seaside quays, where the restaurant owners all keep little boats and go out fishing. You eat fish, unless you are crazy. That day's catch will be varied and though never as fresh as they tell you, much fresher than any other item scrawled on the menu board. Never, ever opt for the beef hotpot in a harbourside fish restaurant.

Roscius might choose any bar for lunch; Juventus had said it varied. We sat down to wait midway, at a place that had outside tables. Manlius Faustus imposed his punishment on the vigilis for what happened earlier. Faustus elected that now he and I would be the close cronies, with Titianus being made to feel left out, so he told Titianus to go inside to order drinks – not giving him any money.

'A working threesome!' exclaimed my client when the tired-eyed vigilis wandered back. 'This reminds me of happy times, with you, me and Morellus, Flavia Albia.' Faustus leaned back in his seat, in a relaxed pose with his hands linked behind his head. It sounded sociable, but Titianus looked unhappy, realising that the balance in our trio had shifted.

Titianus had been too easily conned by Roscius, so I allied myself with Faustus. 'Dear Tiberius, I have not seen Morellus recently. Is he working on a case – or working on a love affair?'

'Dice,' announced Faustus, impressively deadpan as he invented. 'There's a three-day league at a dive called the Sweaty Armpit – you would love it; I must take you there some time – Morellus is in knots because gambling for money is illegal; he thinks I'll pop along and close the place, then he'll be blamed by the whole district. Of course it's never going to happen; they paid the usual sweetener as soon as I told them to.'

I could not help laughing. Faustus chuckled with me. Titianus knew Faustus and I were playing him up.

In fact Titus Morellus, Titianus' counterpart in the Fourth Cohort, was stuck at home, recovering from a near-fatal attack by a serial killer. Morellus was a miserable character, but he had been brave. I knew Faustus visited the invalid from time to time, probably taking baskets of plums and toys for Morellus' children. I could even envisage him slipping cash to Morellus' wife Pullia; supporting someone who had suffered in a public role would be natural philanthropy for Manlius Faustus, a good citizen's duty. Probably the kind of behaviour that had won him votes when he stood as aedile.

'Where's your waiter?' Faustus asked. Titianus' request for service had not worked. It was one of those bars. All frantic bustle, where strangers can never get a drink.

We were still waiting for any refreshment to appear when

Titianus decided to give up. He claimed he had to be back at the station house; it was probably the end of his shift. He lingered, as if he thought Faustus and I should come too, but we stayed put on observation, waving airy goodbyes at him and insincerely promising to let him know what happened.

'Don't worry,' murmured Faustus in a lazy tone. 'I can look after Flavia Albia.'

Titianus could only amble off, while Faustus watched him go, rather narrow-eyed. When the aedile turned back to me, I thought he was going to be critical of me cosying up with someone else, but he merely looked delighted we had got rid of the man.

Faustus caught a server's eye immediately. Titianus was still near enough to see how easily the aedile managed it.

We two had positioned ourselves side by side on a bench, both looking out at the street so we could watch for Roscius in two directions. The area was busy. I had a stole, which I pulled up over my hair; this was partly a professional move, so I looked different from when I was following Roscius. I rarely veiled up from modesty, but sometimes I liked the subtle extra level of privacy.

Faustus could sense a mood. 'Feeling down?'

'Polycarpus.' I sipped my drink.

He nodded, then touched his cup against mine and slowly swallowed wine himself. The other tables were too close and crowded for us to talk about the case. At first we talked about nothing. We must have looked like a man and woman who knew each other, easy together as we enjoyed a small flagon of house wine (with a lot of water) in the warm sunlight.

Sometimes we exchanged a glance, confirming that some character in the street who had looked like our subject was not him. Once I acknowledged how much the latest murder had depressed me, my mind cleared, so I slipped more happily into sharing our task. We had a good working relationship and Tiberius seemed content to be here. 'Could be worse,' he commented.

I agreed quietly, 'One of those times when you wish it wasn't work.'

He smiled, raising his cup in a mild salute to me again.

Almost at once I saw him stiffen. He gestured slightly with one forefinger.

'He's coming! – Shit, we'll lose him again, he'll see us . . .' It had to be presumed that when Roscius spotted Titianus tailing him earlier, he had noticed us as well.

As Tiberius nodded down the street, I moved. I swung round in front of him like a girl who cared nothing about her reputation. With a shameless lunge, I came in close and hid my companion from where Roscius must be. Tiberius gave a nervous start, then he went with the act, playing a tipsy opportunist as he grabbed hold of me. My stole began to slide off my hair, but he noticed and pegged it. His flattened palm felt strong against my head.

We held the pose, so close our breaths intermingled. I watched his grey eyes following the suspect. There was absolutely no need to embellish our charade, but suddenly he leaned in and kissed me.

As he did it, he was watching. Roscius must have gone in somewhere, but Tiberius continued. He was an unexpectedly good kisser. I liked his faint disconcertion because *he* was enjoying it more than he had been ready for . . . Classic male surprise.

When he released me, he flashed a quick gleam, all the recognition he would give or I would want; after all, we were play-acting for work. 'He's in the Three-tailed Dog.'

'Looks a dump!' I slid back into my seat, feeling warm. I could act suave, however. 'We know him now. He'll buy a drink, gulp it quickly, leave half in the beaker then go for a pee out the back. He'll shunt down the alley and saunter out through one of the other bars.'

'You're good.'

'You too!' I remarked ambiguously.

I was watching as many bars opposite as I could. Tiberius spent a moment watching me, then he too reapplied himself to surveillance.

I glanced back at him. He steadily scrutinised the exit from the Victorious Soldier and the public counters of the Moon and Stars. I resumed my careful watch on the Ship, the Castor and Pollux, the Cow and the Dead Man's Fingers.

Roscius emerged through the food counters of the Diana, a workaday thermopolium that seemed to be full of brick-layers. He had somebody with him, a bald man who looked Cappadocian, possibly the subordinate we had earlier seen him leave behind at the Galatea. They strolled together down from the Cispian Hill, with us gently following. We did not bother with the dodging technique, but merely paced ourselves to remain a good distance behind, where we might not be noticed.

They reached the Clivus Suburanus at the Porticus of Livia. They stayed together on the main road as far as the

Esquiline Gate, where Roscius waved off the other man. He went on alone through the arch and into the Gardens of Maecenas.

Faustus gripped my elbow, then we quickened our pace and caught up with him.

35

'Going somewhere? Mind if we tag along?' Manlius Faustus must have learned this ghastly old line when he pulled in persons of interest for questioning. How many shopkeepers who encroached on pubic pavements had he arrested with that cliché? Perhaps he had first heard Morellus use it.

At least the familiar script made Roscius feel at ease. However, he lost his confidence when Faustus then took us into the Auditorium of Maecenas for our conversation.

We had walked on through the gardens, with the aedile and I either side of the young criminal, until this beautiful place appeared and Faustus moved swiftly to have a word with the curator. I saw money being passed over. Then we were let in.

'I thought so!' exclaimed Faustus, grinning at the crook. 'Nice and big. No one else here. Nobody will overhear us.'

That may not have given Roscius any sense of security.

I knew the building. The Gardens of Maecenas had been built over an ancient graveyard, reclaiming an area that for years had been a famously unhealthy necropolis, full of burial pits of the poor.

My mother once read me a poem about witches haunting this sinister spot under a lonely moon, a terrifying piece of work where cruel hags murdered a young boy: Horace, in spooky mode; he did it gruesomely. I was going through a mystic period at the time, a teen myself, in love with the supernatural without seeing its true menace. Now I despised horrors. Forget plague-ridden burial grounds with bones sticking out of broken old pots. All I wanted were these tranquil and elegant new gardens that had finally resulted from a land-grab by entrepreneurs. The first time I went for a walk in a grand public space after Helena and Falco brought me to Rome, I was astounded. There was nothing like any of these public gardens in Londinium.

All right. There is nothing fancy at all in Londinium.

Some garden-creators were freedmen of the imperial court, those high-rollers with moneybags for eyes, who always know how to fix themselves up with gorgeous property. Maecenas had been different, born a fabulously rich Etruscan, friend of Augustus and great patron of the arts; he made his garden particularly fine, with libraries and pavilions. This became his retirement home, a setting so elegant that the Emperor Tiberius had lived there for a time.

To enter Maecenas' Auditorium, as it was called, we passed down a long ramp with a herringbone floor. The monument was built substantially below ground, perhaps as a sunken dining room; when they turned on the water, the inner hall was cooled by a cascade that tumbled down at one end, where deep, white marble steps lined a semi-circular apse. Though never a great socialite, I had been here to a couple of events. The body of the hall can take dining couches, but generally it hosts stand-up soirées with drama, music or readings for well-dressed cultural snobs. Very small appetisers are handed round by blank-faced servers from Gaul in identical uniforms. Flute music nobody listens to wavers over the loud hum of pretentious chatter and rattling jewellery. The ticket price makes you wince.

Though originally a private building, the Auditorium could nowadays be hired, and my father once recklessly shared an evening there with a senator he knew slightly, who wrote epic poetry. Their joint recital was even graced briefly by Domitian, in the happy days when he was only Vespasian's spare heir; back then he had big dreams but no real expectations of becoming emperor.

Do not ask for a critique of Falco's writing. I am a loving, loyal daughter.

Today we had it to ourselves, a rather over-elaborate interrogation room. The well-proportioned interior was lined with large wall niches that were beautifully painted with garden scenes and landscapes, all exquisitely done in that endearing Roman style where indoor frescos mimic living plants that you can see simultaneously outside. One end of the hall opened onto a terrace with lovely views towards the Alban Hills. Unfortunately, once Alba became the infamous location of our emperor's citadel villa, nobody could gaze eastwards without the warped image of Domitian brooding in his fortress, planning ways he could make our lives miserable.

This was an unusually sophisticated venue for an interview with a gangster, but none of Roscius' violent associates would come looking for him here. If he was overawed by the grand setting, it might work in our favour. He looked around, no doubt hoping to identify statues he could steal, though this was strictly a performance space and no art gallery.

Faustus seemed at home. Did he have an unknown life as an arts connoisseur?

For me, it made a welcome change from barracks and bars. But it would not be my natural choice. The place was too busy making its gorgeous presence felt. I prefer a neutral background for grilling suspects.

'I am not saying anything!' Roscius began, predictably.

Faustus pointed out that we had not asked anything yet. 'You don't want to get on the wrong side of me, Rabirius Roscius. I am more ruthless than you can possibly imagine. You don't even know the meaning of "vindictive bastard" yet.'

If true, to me it was an unfamiliar side of Manlius Faustus. I knew he could be tough, even unpleasant when someone annoyed him, but otherwise I saw him as a man of steadfast noble virtues, including restraint. Restraint in particular. Unfortunately.

Roscius told Faustus to push off.

Faustus told Roscius he was not going to do that.

I stepped in as a sweet female ameliorator. 'Roscius, trust me, I advise against upsetting this aedile. There are stall-holders all along the Vicus Armilustrium who shit diarrhoea when he goes on a walkabout, even if their special counterfeit corn-measures have been left at home that day. I'm nice. Why don't you talk to me?'

'Oh, not "good bastard, bad bastard"!' snorted Roscius like an experienced hardnut.

'I have no idea what you mean . . . But I do know that whoever arranged that attack on a senator three nights ago has knocked over a hive of extremely angry bees. It may not have been announced in the *Daily Gazette* yet, but there

227

are strident calls for a Senate inquiry, with possible intervention by the emperor himself. Everyone in your position can expect a very heavy crackdown. The scrutineers are being urged to go for all the old crime families. Be wise, man! Anyone who cooperates first in the aedile's investigation may avoid having his door kicked down.'

'Don't be so generous, Flavia Albia,' Faustus joined in, making himself sound scratchy. 'Why should one gangster escape justice, when we have an opportunity to round them all up? I am just waiting for the formal order, then I shall be scarifying my patch. Every felon on the Aventine is really going to feel this. No scum unturned.'

'I have heard,' I said gravely, 'Rabirius Roscius has more political know-how than some.'

'Ha! How's that?'

'Well, dear Tiberius, this man will surely see that you and I are intent on solving the Aviola case, so for us, the senator-bashing is a separate issue.' Neither of us had mentioned to Roscius that the bashed senator was my uncle. I guessed Roscius had not yet joined up all the dots in the sketch. Did he know Camillus Justinus had visited Gallo with me? Did he even realise Justinus went to the Second's tribune with Faustus?

'If we did solve the Aviola case, Roscius, your name could be omitted from the senator-bashing inquest,' Faustus returned thoughtfully. He sounded as if he meant it.

'I presume that would be a relief to the Rabirii,' I offered to Roscius. 'They won't want this commission to take a piercing look at what happened to Aviola. It is very high profile, the victims were well-to-do and the circumstances – such violence, and so soon after a wedding – have attracted the wrong kind of public attention. That's even without the slaves fleeing to the Temple of Ceres. For Romans, a religious connection makes it so much more sensitive.'

'And it's messy!' quipped Faustus with some glee, as if he revelled in slurry.

Showing signs of alarm, Roscius piped up suddenly, 'We never done Valerius Aviola. Nor his precious bride neither.'

I refrained from correcting his grammar. He would have been too busy learning how to operate a jemmy to attend a decent school of rhetoric.

Faustus leaned towards him, sounding more reasonable. 'That so? Do you want to tell me what really happened?'

'No, I bloody don't!' Roscius fell back on the criminal's professional motto: 'If you had any evidence, you wouldn't be asking.'

'*Evidence?*' laughed Faustus.

'Oh, Roscius,' I suggested gently, 'you are forgetting this is Manlius Faustus, the infamous plebeian magistrate – and vindictive bastard.'

Roscius was standing with his arms folded, a defensive stance, though his bravado was dwindling. I could see in his eyes he was making wrong decisions almost every time the conversation took a turn. We had been right to approach the junior. Old Rabirius must still be dealing with the gang's business himself, supported by Gallo. He had not yet exposed Roscius much – not enough for the young man to be able to handle this competently. One day he would know better. He would stand firm and keep denying everything. He would be laughing at us then.

Now he was under too much pressure. We had a few more exchanges on the same lines, until he gave way. He agreed to discuss the night when Aviola and Mucia were killed – though he made one last feeble attempt at a stand:

'Why are you asking me about it anyway? This is victimisation, totally unfair. You have nothing to link me or my boys to it.'

'You are the robbery expert,' Faustus flattered him. 'The word is, if a big break-in occurs, you are the only one capable. So did you know Valerius Aviola owned a cache of special silver?'

'Do dogs shit in the gutter? You bet I knew. Wine set, plenty of items, all very pretty. Kept it in his dining room.'

'Summer or winter?' I asked, making a show of testing him.

'What?'

'Summer or winter dining room!' Faustus spelled out, sounding irritable.

'On shelves or display table?' I asked.

'If table, three-legged or monopod?' rapped Faustus.

'If monopod, marble or fancy wood? Then citron or cedar wood?'

Faustus and I were enjoying the word games, while Roscius clearly felt nervous. Trying to follow our banter made him breathless. 'Lay off! You're confusing me . . .'

'Oh, forget citron and cedar. Stone beats wood every time for me.' Faustus kept rambling. 'Give me Euboean onion-skin marble for setting off silver any day. Lovely green base, good wavy lines . . .'

'Stop joshing around,' I chided. 'You heard what he said – we are confusing him. Roscius, just tell me, did you know that the family were leaving for Campania?'

'Yes, I did.' He answered the simple question with relief.

'So did you go to the house that night to lift the silver while you could?'

'We went.'

'And you took it?'

'No.'

'Why not? You got inside?'

'Of course. Sweet as a nut.'

'So why not take the stuff?'

'None there. Not a piece of it. We found the dining room all right, but the shelves were standing there all empty.'

Roscius looked awkward and unhappy. In telling this odd story, he seemed unable to decide whether he was embarrassed by failure or defiant because he was innocent of theft. Faustus shot a glance at me, then he took up the questioning. 'Something happened?' he asked in a quieter voice than formerly. 'Get it off your chest, why not?'

Roscius nodded, though he still failed to speak.

Faustus went back to the beginning. In his work as aedile, he must be used to questioning wrongdoers. He was calm, courteous, almost sympathetic. 'So, let's start with getting into the house. Is it right that you burst in past the porter?'

Roscius bridled indignantly. 'No chance! Am I good or not?'

'Of course; you're tops. So tell me.'

'I got us in. My usual method. Did it sweet and quiet. Got past the lock with my special magic.'

'A pick in the keyhole?'

'Not saying. Trade secret. Anyway, no one knew we was in their house.'

I stiffened, realising just how much the scenario I had worked on before was wrong. Faustus showed no reaction.

Roscius was suddenly flying. He could not tell his story fast enough: 'We got in, there was nobody around, we found the room, the shelves were empty, we started searching. Having made it in, we wasn't leaving empty-handed. Unprofessional!

Well, that was what I thought until we knew what had gone down. I was the one that discovered them. Just opened a bedroom door, quiet like, not knowing what might be inside, who I could be facing up to if I was unlucky. There the two of them was. Stark naked and flung out in agony, horribly staring up at me.'

'Aviola and his wife?' insisted Faustus. 'Dead?'

Roscius nodded.

Being so sure of the details previously, I jumped in: 'But hadn't you already come across the door porter? Nicostratus? Beaten insensible and lying in his blood, in the long passage from the front entrance?'

Roscius blinked. 'Never saw him. Never saw nobody.'

'What?'

'This is the true juice.' Roscius was determined for us to believe him. Though he prided himself on being hard, remembering the deathbed scene had moved him. 'I let out some yelp, I can tell you.'

'All right.' Faustus knew how to imply he believed the story.

'Flying phalluses, tribune, your honour, that was terrible. Who did it? I see you looking at me, but me and the boys, we don't do nothing like that. Why would we? My boys came up and had a gawp as well – they wouldn't have believed it if I didn't let them have a look to see – then we legged it like runners racing up a stadium. Got out the way we had got in. Went for a bloody big drink, I can tell you.' He shook his head in disbelief, appalled. 'The couple must have been going at it and never heard anybody come in the room. What a way to go. The old man had made an effort. He was half off the bed, part way under her. It looked as if she had wanted to save him, threw herself over

232

him, trying to protect him – probably hampered him, getting in his way. She must have been pleading to the one who did it. But they put that bit of rope around her throat and did her too, poor naked cow. Gods in Olympus, it was really terrible.'

36

We were all silent.

When we first arrived here, the helpful curator had folded back the big doors onto the terrace. Now we moved outside slowly, as if needing fresh air in our lungs. The walk across gave us time to adjust to this new story. None of us looked at the view.

Faustus glanced at me, saw I was full of questions, then made a small open-palmed gesture like an orator giving way to a new speaker.

I began tentatively. 'Roscius, I want to be clear – the way you tell this, it sounds as if you arrived to an apparently empty house. Is that right?'

He nodded. 'We didn't see anybody the whole time – except the dead two.'

'There were supposed to be slaves all over the place, sleeping off drink, or just normally asleep . . .?'

Roscius shrugged. 'Can't help you.'

I pressed him and he told us he and his companions, of whom there had been two, turned left on arrival, went around to the dining rooms.

'Did you know in advance where to go?'

'Obviously. I could tell you the layout of most of the big houses – been inside a lot of them.'

I made no comment. 'So once you realised the silver was not where you had expected?'

'We split up to search separately. The lads kept going in the same direction, looked in more rooms in case there was any more dining places. I crossed the courtyard on my own. I thought the stuff might have been in the kitchen. It looked as though they had had a party, so they might have used it.'

'Friendly neighbourhood thieves don't generally go to kitchens?'

Roscius looked surprised. 'Oh yes, we often have a bite while we are working. You can get good scran on a job. But I popped into the master bedroom first, and that was enough for me.'

'And you still saw nobody? There were supposed to be women asleep in one bedroom at the front, others in the slaves' own quarters at the back, two drunks paralytic in the courtyard; those two would be right by where your accomplices were searching . . . Didn't any of you see any of them?'

'Sorry. Cannot help you.'

'How did you know the room you went into was the chief bedroom?'

'Garlands hung around the doors.'

'Probably been there since the wedding night . . .' I mused.

Faustus chipped in: 'Was the house in darkness?'

'That doesn't bother us.'

'No, but was it?'

'We like it dark.'

'I'm sure you do, but please answer my question.'

'Mostly. The dead pair must have been screwing by

lamplight before they was interrupted. They had a little pottery lamp on their bedside table, still flickering away.'

'That all?'

'There may have been candelabras in the big place next to where I found the bodies. I never got in there.'

Faustus checked with me. I said, 'The Corinthian oecus, the fancy saloon. It could have been dressed up, so it could be shown off to the guests that evening. But I can't imagine why it would still be lit once the feast was over and the guests had gone. Not unless someone forgot about it when they doused all the other lamps.' I thought Roscius must have been mistaken, and after listening to my comments he did not insist.

Now that he had unburdened himself, Roscius quickly rallied as a gangland heavy. While Faustus and I were considering, he was perfecting his mindless stare. One day it would actually intimidate people.

I asked, 'Did either you or your companions touch the bodies, Roscius?'

The supposed tough leapt back, gurning in disgust at the thought.

'Settle down! I just wondered if you could tell me whether those corpses were still warm.'

'You are joking! None of us went near them.'

'Assuming you did meet someone in one of the porticos, what would you have done?' asked Faustus.

'Put them down. Swift tap,' explained Roscius, miming one very hard knock on the head.

'Not set about them with a weapon? Something like a plank, say?'

'Too messy, tribune. Aedile,' the crook corrected himself, wanting to sound like an accurate witness.

'Not your style?'

'No way.'

'And excuse me for asking – I have to cover everything – do you ever take rope with you on your excursions?'

'I don't have nothing to do with rope, tribune. I have enough to carry, with lock-wagglers and carry-home sacks – assuming I was the kind of fellow to have such stuff in the line of business.'

'Well, you may as well admit you do,' Faustus reminded him. 'You have confessed you went on this burglary, and that you are a practised house-breaker.'

'I'm saying nothing!' Roscius sounded panicky.

'You have told us you were in a house where two murders of citizens and the third of a slave took place.'

'I was given immunity!' The crook's eyes swivelled to me, hoping I would support this claim.

'You were given no assurances,' said Faustus heavily. 'The only thing you can rely on is this: if I can identify the real killers as a result of your evidence, any assistance will be taken into account. You volunteered the information – which will count more in your favour than if it was extracted from you by any other means. Keep calm, place your faith in justice, and if you have nothing else to tell us, you can go.'

Roscius turned to me. 'He's a cool one!' he adjudged.

'Sits in a bath of snow for pleasure,' I answered. 'Bunk off quick, while he's given you the chance.'

Rabirius Roscius rushed to an access door at the end of the terrace. We heard him stride up the ramp as he left the building.

In silence, Faustus and I walked slowly back inside through the folding doors to the main hall.

The curator appeared while we were staring at one another in astonishment and bafflement at what we had heard. This keeper, a grimy old man in a long tunic, went and turned on the cascade. It was a ploy to get money. Faustus tossed him a coin without comment, then the man slunk away again. After a few hiccups, the nymphaeum display surged into life. Sheets of water, slightly brackish at first, sluiced over the steps and vanished away through secret exit channels.

'Do we believe him?' Faustus asked, frowning slightly at the unsought entertainment. I felt cooler already, standing near the moving water, though I pulled in my skirts in case of splashes.

'I think so. It's a weird tale to invent. Roscius had no need to admit ever being in the house, not unless his story is genuine. Oh, and Tiberius, he seemed truly horrified by what he says he saw. I definitely accept his depiction of the crime scene.' Faustus nodded, in one of his silent moods. He liked to absorb information at his own pace.

More used to making quick assessments, I blew out air, then ticked off questions that surged into my mind:

Where were the slaves while the robbers were poking about the apartment?

If it was not the robbers, then who had stolen the silver, where had they hidden it, where was it now?

If not the robbers, who did kill Valerius Aviola and Mucia Lucilia?

Why was Nicostratus not at his post in the corridor? When was Nicostratus attacked, if not before the theft and killings? Who attacked him? Why – and why later?

I tested some possible answers, but weakly.

'The other door porter, Phaedrus, told me he was having

238

supper in the kitchen. Maybe they were all there? Would they have had a chance to eat earlier, while the feast was going on? Maybe not. Maybe the slaves could not eat until after the party was over . . . Would there be enough room in the kitchen for all of them? I don't think so. It's too full of cupboards and cooking benches. There were ten, plus the hugely pregnant Myla. I think Myla told me she was dossing down in the slaves' quarters at the time of the attack, but like all their claims, that now comes into question.'

'We need to reflect,' Faustus decided.

'Speak for yourself, aedile! I need to jump on this straight-away or it will drive me crazy.' He smiled a little. I rushed on: 'I shall have to re-interview those deceitful beggars urgently. This afternoon I'll look over my notes from their first examinations, then I shall come up to the office for a showdown.'

'Want my help when you speak to them?' asked Faustus, seeming keen to be involved.

'No, thanks. I took the initial statements; I prefer to do the follow up myself.' He was the client. It was my commission.

He agreed to leave it to me. Perhaps he looked put out. I could not tell if he knew I was blaming myself for previously believing lies. He must concede I did have a sense of trouble earlier. I had told him then that I felt the slaves were holding something back; something was not right.

The aedile and I stayed briefly in the Auditorium, each considering the implications, though independently and without further discussion, while finely judged torrents of cool water splashed elegantly over beautiful white marble in the background.

37

Eventually we emerged, into a Rome full of glaring warmth and light. We picked up Dromo, who had stayed kicking his heels outside. All today he had been following us around at a distance, barely noticed by his master or me; that was the normal life of a slave. Faustus had whistled to him a couple of times when we were about to change venues. I hoped Dromo had not seen that moment of theatre between Faustus and me at the bar, but he gave no sign of it.

Faustus set off alone on the long haul back to the Aventine. I walked to the Aviola apartment. The streets were quiet, towards the end of lunchtime. The sun was hot, so even though it was not far I went slowly, keeping to the shady side. Dromo plodded along behind me, apparently too tired even to be distracted by pastry stalls. When I took a drink from a fountain, he did. When I set off again, he trudged behind obediently. I had to trust him to keep an eye out for trouble, because I was too deeply preoccupied with what Roscius had said.

At the apartment I flopped in a chair in my room, chin down, fanning myself with the top of my tunic. This only stretches the neck of the garment. It never cools you. I needed to jump in a freezing cold fountain, nude, then come out to high-class attendants fanning ostrich feathers . . .

I had gathered my previous note tablets though felt too drained to begin on them. I was no stranger to starting all over again on a case, but it is dreary. For once, Dromo went to the kitchen and brought me a tray of lunch. It was only because he could see I had no interest in fetching my own; he knew that unless I had something, there would be nothing for him. I accepted the tray and remembered to thank him, at which he found the energy to mime being startled.

Revived, I read up my notes. While I was going over the old interviews, voices disturbed me. Galla Simplicia and Sextus Simplicius – Aviola's ex-wife and his executor – had heard about Polycarpus. She had come with condolences for Graecina; he no doubt accompanied her out of curiosity. I thought I had better be present, though I kept out of sight to begin with.

Galla had sent Myla to fetch down the widow. When Graecina came, Galla embraced her with every sign of affection. Grief had now descended on Graecina. The poor woman occupied her own, newly terrible world. I was impressed by the steady way Galla Simplicia talked to her and consoled her. She asked questions about how Graecina was coping and how she would manage in future; she made suggestions about the funeral, offering help. For once, I saw an extended Roman family operating properly: the mistress (a role Galla had taken up again with alacrity) kindly looking after the wife of one of their freedmen.

I could not fault her. And this was the woman people said had wanted to murder her ex-husband and his bride. Unintentionally, Galla Simplicia did herself some good with me that afternoon.

Her cousin wandered about the courtyard at a loose end. I slipped along a portico, as if by chance, and greeted him. Since he had now lost his intended new steward before Polycarpus even started in the post, I asked whether he would now keep Gratus, but when people once make up their minds to dismiss a staff member, they tend to go through with it. Simplicius insisted Gratus was still to be 'let go' via the slave market.

It struck me Gratus might have had a motive to dispose of his rival Polycarpus. However, since Gratus was to be sent packing whatever happened, and he probably knew that, all he would have gained was revenge. It can bring joy to the bitter or indignant, but Gratus never struck me as that type. His measured attitude had been why I thought him a good steward.

Still, what did I know? I had let a bunch of household slaves fool me with an elaborate fiction whose purpose I had yet to uncover.

Myla was hanging around, taking too much interest in Simplicius just as she had with Faustus the other evening. Galla then called to him and they left.

Galla Simplicia had ignored Myla. She seemed completely involved with Graecina, which was worthy work. But afterwards, I did wonder if she hustled her cousin away on purpose.

I was ready to leave myself. I told Dromo he could stay behind and rest his tired feet. He could take one hour off (this presumed he could work out how long an hour was). Then, he was to see if he could do anything useful for Graecina and if not, I suggested he got together with her slave Cosmus.

'Oh no! I've seen him gawking around the place like a dopey bum. He's just a nipper.'

'He looks almost as old as you. Be boys; pal up with him for a while, will you?'

Dromo stared at me. 'Is this for your work? You telling me to squeeze him for gen?'

'I am saying, get to know him a bit if you can.'

'Have I got to be a spy?' I must be insane. Sending in Dromo was like army engineers setting up a catapult with a wonky wheel on a very steep slope with no ballast.

'Just see what you think.' I had remembered that my uncle's young son had taken against Cosmus, when he was over there. Would Dromo feel the same? Perhaps Cosmus would be different with a fellow slave to how he had behaved with privileged, aristocratic children.

'That dog of his sounds vicious!' Dromo complained, though he did look interested in what I had asked him to do. Well, almost.

For a change, instead of going down towards the Caelian, I walked a northern route to the Aventine – Clivus Suburanus, Clivus Pullius, Clivus Orbius, on to the top end of the Forum, then around the back of the Palatine on the river side, through the meat market to the corn station, and up the hill to the Temple of Ceres from the Trigeminal Gate. I must be growing homesick. I ended up very near my parents' town house although since they were away at the coast I did not drop in. I had no wish to visit their home-sitting slaves. My favourites were Helena's favourites too, and had gone with the family.

Faustus was not at the aediles' office. Nobody had seen him all day. I hoped he was not annoyed that I turned down his offer of assistance with the interviews. More likely, he thought I was getting ideas about him.

Fine by me.

The nine survivors were in the office garden as usual: those two old workshy cronies, Amethystus and Diomedes, had marked out a board in the dust and were playing a game with pebbles for counters, watched in a desultory way by the ambitious young Daphnus and his twin, the dim scribe Melander. In another group, the African Libycus was talking to the women, Amaranta and the girl Olympe. Phaedrus, the tall German litter bearer-cum-porter, was sitting by himself, acting as if he wanted a sculptor to turn him into a Defeated Barbarian. Chrysodorus was on his own too. He was lying on his back on some grass, with his eyes closed and his hands folded on his chest, as if he was waiting for the pains of life to be over. The awful little dog, Puff, had curled up beside the philosopher, oblivious to his loathing.

I marched over to them and called for attention. First, I announced that Polycarpus was dead. Keeping an eye on as many as possible, I told them how he had been killed. I heard subdued muttering, and noticed a few glances from one to the other, but no significant reaction. Few workers are truly sorry when their supervisor comes to a bad end.

I mentioned that this did not affect their position. 'You were here. In fact it happened yesterday morning, while I saw you all, so I can even vouch for you myself.' One or two still looked subdued; after all, they were still indicted for the murders of their master and mistress. The killing of Polycarpus, a freedman, hardly made a difference.

I had thought carefully how to approach my next task. I informed them as a group that 'new information' had been supplied by a witness. Then, assisted by the public slaves who guarded them, I interviewed each slave individually. I did it the same way as before, not letting them return to the others afterwards. As the waiting group decreased, the remnants had an opportunity to discuss among themselves, and perhaps to worry, what I might have been told.

With each, I began by stating angrily that I knew they

had lied. Nicostratus was not attacked by robbers bursting in, because the robbers entered discreetly and they never even saw him. Valerius Aviola and Mucia Lucilia were dead *before* Nicostratus was attacked. The robbers did not find, let alone steal, the silver.

Every slave stuck doggedly to his or her original story. They refused to explain discrepancies. None had any idea, they claimed, why the robbers said they failed to encounter Nicostratus nor could they tell me who removed the silver wine set, if it was not thieves.

Diomedes who, according to the tale, had been lying in the courtyard in a drunken stupor with Amethystus, claimed the searching robbers must have stepped right over them. 'Must have tiptoed like dancers, very light-footed!' he quipped. His impudent implication was that Roscius and his men were lying about what they saw, or did not see.

Only Amaranta and Olympe, together with the young scribe Melander, seemed frightened that this new evidence was casting doubts on their story, though none of them changed it. All the others stuck to their bluff.

Daphnus, the bright tray carrier, fiddled with his amulet and did query why this witness of mine had not come forward before. I said he had not wanted to get involved, which seemed to satisfy Daphnus. Most people think giving evidence about a crime will rebound on them and cause too much trouble.

It was left to Chrysodorus to challenge me outright. 'So,' he proposed, 'you have nine of us saying one thing and one person supplying new evidence – yet you automatically believe the singleton? Numerical probability is against you, Flavia Albia. And who is your surprise witness? Am I to deduce that if he can speak for the robbers, he is a robber himself?'

I had to admit he was. 'Intriguingly, Chrysodorus, you are alone in working that out! How pleasing to find a philosopher with a genuine enquiring mind, and willing to engage in debate. Something to be said for intellectual training.'

'Your informant is a person of such admirable character, Flavia Albia!'

'Now you are speaking like a lawyer, which does not endear you to me. Keep your irony to yourself, please. I'll do the rhetoric, if any is needed.'

'Let me speak in a cruder argot then – if this man avows the robbers did not take the silver, is that not what a criminal is bound to say – especially if he wishes to stop you looking for his loot?'

'A good point – though I believe him. He was undoubtedly honest about seeing the bodies. The scene horrified him. He had the shakes even talking about it. So I do accept he legged it empty-handed, in shock.'

I thought about this. I was certain Roscius had taken part in violence before. Even killing might not be new to him, though perhaps serious damage to others was mainly inflicted by the enforcer, Gallo. Even if Roscius was present during fights, I bet he normally left any victim behind, on the street or in a bar, possibly with a lot of spilled blood, yet either still alive and crawling, or else abandoned merely unconscious: the way it was meant to happen in that street attack on Uncle Quintus.

Roscius could distance himself from that. What affected him with Aviola and Mucia was their nakedness and their agonised faces. The memory of their dead faces would stay in his mind for a long time.

I had not even seen them, yet his horror affected me.

★   ★   ★

I sat writing up a report to leave here at the office for Manlius Faustus.

While I was doing it, the slaves must have held an urgent conference. I did hear raised voices, reaching me in waves. I wrote more slowly, allowing them time.

At length, a guard knocked on the door and told me a deputation wanted to see me.

38

There were three of them: Amaranta, Libycus and Phaedrus.

I was not surprised to see Amaranta as a ringleader. She was a quicksilver hopeful, with years to enjoy ahead of her if she escaped this unscathed – and she had organising skills. Libycus, the other body slave, made a natural partner to her now. Phaedrus, who had not budged on his original story when I talked to him again, was unexpected.

Of those who did *not* come, the hard-drinking gardener and the man of all work – Diomedes and Amethystus – were bound to keep well out of anything tricky. Olympe was too young; Amaranta, being motherly, might even have told her to hang back. I would have expected Daphnus, so I wondered if there was unknown coolness between him and Phaedrus.

Chrysodorus surprised me by his absence, given that he was the only one to tackle me beforehand over the new evidence. Still, although philosophers reckon to address the issues of all mankind, most are loners and many are awkward socially. He may have upset the rest and been rejected as a co-commissioner. Or he may have pulled out in a huff.

I was still working in the office that Faustus used. I stayed where I was, on a reading couch. They stood. Of course they did. Making use of furniture is the sign of superiority in Rome. Men of power all sit their podgy posteriors on thrones and ceremonial stools. The mistress of any house has her armchair. Even an informer gets to recline when addressing a hangdog trio of slaves. The only unusual thing here was that I bothered to think about it.

I waited for them to speak. Amaranta had been chosen as their spokeswoman. 'Flavia Albia, we have not been entirely straight with you.'

I raised my eyebrows. Informers should always take the trouble to keep their brows plucked. So much easier to express genteel scepticism, if you have neat arches for the uplift.

Since Amaranta had fallen awkwardly silent, I said, 'Why am I not surprised to hear that, Amaranta? So, what secrets are you about to give up to me?'

'We think we ought to explain about what the robber has told you.'

'Indeed, I think the same. You should.'

'We need to say why he never saw any of us.'

'That's right. You do.'

'We were all there really. In the apartment.'

'Yes, you must have been.'

'We were having our supper.'

'All together?'

'Yes, Albia.'

'And where was this meal taking place?'

'In the oecus. There wasn't room to squash in anywhere else.'

I swung my legs around, turning to sit up, with my feet on the floor. It gave me a view of them straight on. Bangles chinked as I leaned on the end of the couch, one-elbowed. I tugged at an earring thoughtfully, easing its hook.

As excuses go, this was not bad. They had no way of knowing (for I had mentioned it to none of them) that Roscius told Faustus he remembered lamplight in the Corinthian oecus. Amaranta had just unwittingly confirmed that.

I discussed what they were now saying, drawing out a portrait of a house that went to sleep with the master and mistress, only to reawaken once they were settled; a house that lived a second life – a life where the slaves held sway. In many homes this happens, so it was a credible tale. Sometimes it is perfectly harmless, because staff are permitted some form of private existence and their nocturnal sociability causes no disturbance. Sometimes riot occurs. That was not what Amaranta wanted me to believe.

According to her, the loaned kitchen staff departed. Polycarpus went home too.

'He did not eat with you?'

'No, never.' It would have been his private relaxation time, in his own apartment, with Graecina and their children. His escape. A luxury only a freedman could have. 'We quite liked him living somewhere else,' Amaranta admitted. I did not blame them. Every evening the steward's departure must have given them an hour or so of something close to freedom.

'Who made your food?' I slipped in.

Amaranta must have thought quickly – though not fast enough. 'Myla.'

I laughed out loud. 'Oh, come off it! Not only was she squeezing out another baby, foisted on her by who knows who, but the idea of *Myla* providing a meal for ten people is ludicrous. When I am there, I can barely get her to bring me a cup of water.'

The trio were silent.

I refused to accept their version. 'No, Myla could not have produced your dinner.'

Libycus piped up. 'It was not cooked food, just bits. We collected a few comports from the kitchen. The leftovers. Myla had scraped it together for us on serving dishes, that's what Amaranta meant.'

'Ah, a cold collage to mix and match . . .' My favourite meal.

'The master had never minded his slaves taking unwanted food,' Libycus stressed, looking anxious.

'I suppose, Libycus,' I said encouragingly, 'that was why you personally came home, after you went out and saw your two friends?' He was eager to embrace the suggestion – and he was faking when he did so. Myrinus and Secundus had told me he was afraid to stay out longer, in case his master wanted something.

I was still thinking about how a group of slaves could take over the best space in the house and enjoy themselves there. How they did it, apparently, while terrible events happened right next door . . .

'We were not doing any harm,' Amaranta assured me, pleadingly. 'The same thing used to happen in our old house, before Mucia Lucilia was married. She knew what went on. At our house, Onesimus used to arrange it, then he would be with us.' I knew that Mucia's steward was still a slave. 'Just a meal, Albia. People have to eat.'

'So you want me to accept that this nightly gathering was habitual?' I was not intending to cave in too easily.

'Well, some of us had only been at that apartment for two days.'

'Yes, some of you came when Mucia Lucilia was married . . . So this kind of meal after hours was not yet a ritual for the conjoined households, but could have become one? You wait until your master and mistress retire for the night. Then you collect somewhere. Eat, drink a little too, if Amethystus can liberate a flagon from the household supplies. I imagine you would only be able to talk very quietly; no laughter, no music, no noisy tiffs.' So very unlike dinner in most Roman families! 'Passing bowls around in virtual silence. Not letting spoons knock on pottery. Putting things away and washing up afterwards extremely gently – but making sure you do it, so the mistress doesn't take exception in the morning. Then you all went creeping off to bed, as if the house had never had its second life.'

I was embellishing because it made no difference. It all sounded so normal – yet even if this had been a ritual in the making, surely it never happened on the night the couple were killed, not while they were already lying dead on their bed.

Roscius was not my only source. Their description failed to fit what I had been told by that other witness: Fauna, who lived upstairs. She had told me of commotion, alarm, voices shouting, people running around with lamps. At what point did that happen? The slaves would not know about Fauna and her husband, standing on stools to look down at the courtyard.

'So what is the sequence of events?' I asked, suddenly addressing Phaedrus.

He jumped, but managed not to look shifty. 'We had our meal and that is when the robbers must have come. We found the silver missing and the dead bodies afterwards. When we came out and went to tidy up quietly, like you said.'

I surveyed him, unimpressed. 'According to you, the

252

robbers never knew you were all in the oecus, and by the time you emerged, they had been and gone?'

'Must have done.'

'So what happened to the silver and who killed Aviola and Mucia?'

'The robbers did both. Took the goods and murdered our master.'

'Your word against theirs, Phaedrus.'

'They are criminals and we are loyal slaves of a good master.'

I let Phaedrus think I had swallowed it. 'So when they deny it, the robbers are lying? As Chrysodorus said to me earlier, "that is what professional criminals are bound to do"?' All three slaves nodded hard. 'Well then. You were invisible in the oecus, a place where nobody would ever expect slaves to be, so the robbers missed you. They must have crept around so surreptitiously, *you* never heard *them*. But Phaedrus, according to your version, there is one big flaw.' The tall blond porter realised what I was going to say while I was still speaking; I saw it in his eyes. 'What happened to your colleague, Nicostratus? When do you say he was attacked?'

Quick-witted Amaranta moved into the conversation smoothly. 'He was not with us. We had saved some food for him. Phaedrus was going to relieve him after he had finished, then Nicostratus would come across for his bowl.'

Libycus took this up: 'The robbers bashed him when they came in, exactly as we have always said. We all thought he was on duty at the front, and if he made any noise when the thieves got in, we never heard a sound.'

'Just like you never heard a squeak from Aviola and Mucia – even while they were murdered right next door? One wall between you and that horrific crime – I shall have to check how substantial and soundproof it is! . . . Are you still saying, Phaedrus, that you found Nicostratus lying in the corridor, so that was when you discovered the crimes and raised the alarm?'

'That's right.' No; according to what Roscius told Faustus and me, that was wrong.

'So, Libycus –' I turned suddenly to Aviola's body slave, '– *you* must have come home before the thieves struck? Nicostratus let you in before anything happened? Yes?'

Libycus had a wild-eyed moment, but nodded.

I was terse. 'Frankly, that fails to fit the timing I had from your two friends. You are supposed to have seen Aviola to bed – helped him out of his party clothes and so forth, blew his precious nose nicely – then you went out. Secundus and Myrinus told me you spent a lot of time with them, and it was very late when you left.'

He had no answer, merely muttered that I must have misunderstood what his friends said.

We were going around in circles. I could not see what these slaves hoped to achieve here. All they seemed to want to say was that the thieves had been unaware of them because they were closeted in the oecus. It was a good-sized hall, and I could accept that their presence went unnoticed if they were behaving very quietly. But they failed to shake my belief in what Faustus and I had been told by Roscius.

The slaves still maintained the robbers carried out the crimes. For that to be true, Roscius must be a robber, a killer and a blatant liar. He was a habitual denier of his gang's guilt, yet I still felt he had told the truth about that night.

39

I returned to the apartment, to find cypress bushes either side of the front doors and a corpse in the atrium: Polycarpus. Although he lived upstairs, the Aviola executors must have allowed him to be presented to mourners here. He was lying on a simple bier on the marble table, which at least meant that table had a function sometimes. He had been dressed in a plain white toga, and placed with his feet towards the door.

There was a strong smell of incense but I was glad to learn from Dromo that the funeral was to be tonight. According to strict tradition, it should take place on the eighth day after death – but tradition tends to be ignored at the height of summer. Don't start complaining about the decline in religious observance. You try living for a week with a dead body lying in your house, in the middle of June in Rome.

I love the potential of a funeral. I had missed seeing Aviola and his bride going to the gods, but when their steward was cremated, I made sure I was right there. For an informer it can be vital. While people have to stand for hours watching a corpse burning, something in the insidious scent of the oils – and their boredom – is apt to loosen tongues. Even if they say nothing, the way people behave can be revealing.

I went upstairs and spoke to Graecina, who was getting ready. I helped arrange her veil, and since someone had to pay for this funeral, I asked how she was placed for money; she told me the family had savings tucked away. She and Polycarpus had been careful to provide for the future. (I noticed she said they had made financial plans together.) They had been an up-and-coming family, but were mindful how easily they and their children could be ruined by fate. It was clear, however, the widow and children would not face immediate hardship after their loss.

What they did need was social support. That was being provided by Galla Simplicia. She had even suggested Graecina might like to work for one her daughters. I did not mention that Polycarpus had told me the daughters were spoiled. Graecina was a free woman and had the right to quit if she found she hated the position.

Since tonight's event was private, she also had control over who came to her husband's funeral. Myself, I would have liked the slaves to be brought from the aediles' office. I wanted to observe reactions. I offered to make overtures to Manlius Faustus, who could certainly have arranged it had there still been time. Graecina refused, I think because they were so closely associated with the deaths of Polycarpus' master and mistress. She understood that there could be no accusation of them being involved in killing her husband, yet she was obviously prejudiced. If, as I suspected, Graecina started life working in a bar, her own background would be regarded as shameful; it was interesting that she chose to look down on slaves. Everyone needs someone to despise.

Graecina seemed to have made most of the funeral arrangements herself. She was organised. I wondered whether she had learned from Polycarpus, or whether that was always her character and he had liked it in her.

I managed to get some rest before the formalities started. I could have done with more. Informers have to be tireless, and work is unpredictable. You sometimes find nothing to do with yourself for a week, then you have a day that never seems to end. This was to be one of those.

Graecina wanted a ceremony with 'nice people', so she did invite Galla Simplicia, plus Galla's cousin and all three of her children. The pregnant Valeria did not stay to the end, but both she and her husband thought it right to show their faces at the start. Mother's Boy and the younger sister did stay. They were pleasant; even he behaved to the widow with good manners. Though Galla Simplicia had complained about the difficulties of bringing up children single-handed, she seemed to have done a good job.

Graecina was accompanied by her own young children, of whom there were two, a shy little boy and a girl who whimpered ceaselessly, though who could blame her? Both were only infants; they would never see their father again and must be terrified of the change that would devastate their once-settled lives. They found the walk to the necropolis too long and standing for several hours at the tomb tired them even more.

Present when we left the house was a large number of neighbourhood associates of Polycarpus, people in trade whom he had known and dealt with in the course of his work. They may not have fitted Graecina's definition of 'nice people', but they all spoke of her husband with respect. I was there, shadowed by Dromo. Of the Aviola household, there was no time for anyone to return from Campania, so we were only graced by Myla, who attached herself to the procession as it was leaving, possibly unasked. She walked at the back, beside Graecina's slave, Cosmus.

As we made our way, under cover of the racket from a couple of hired musicians, I took the opportunity to ask Dromo how he had managed when I told him to make friends with Cosmus.

'No use. He wouldn't have anything to do with me. He's peculiar.'

I scoffed that that could be said about many people.

'Who? You mean me?' demanded Dromo, his field of vision as always confined to his own world.

'No, the sun does not revolve around you, Dromo. I meant generally, there are a lot of odd people.'

I refrained from saying that rebuffing Dromo could be seen as sensible. Even so, Dromo gave me a sideways glance, as if by now he reckoned he could work out what I was thinking.

When he believed I was looking the other way, he turned around and made a rude gesture at Cosmus. Cosmus gave back as good as he got. Myla aimed a smack at Cosmus; I would have done the same to Dromo, but he had sidled out of reach. There were about two years between those boys, but otherwise I could see little difference.

No, that was wrong. I noticed, with interest, my attitude had altered. In an insidious way, through my dealings with Dromo he had become 'mine'. Both young slaves behaved equally badly, but I felt more lenient towards him. I didn't even own him.

This must have been how the idea developed that slaves should be considered part of a family.

★　★　★

The chosen necropolis was the nearest to the Esquiline Gate, but since the city boundary had shifted with time, we had to go out, cross the Fifth Region, and pass onto the Via Praenestina. As the bier passed the Second Cohort's station house, Titianus and a group of his men marched out and joined us, looking sombre. It was neatly choreographed. They must have had a watchman looking out for the procession. The vigiles like going to funerals. It's a day out. Titianus was not the type to come in the hope of spotting something useful.

I was constantly looking for clues, of course. However, I never noticed any, or none I could interpret. At least I knew I tried.

We sent Polycarpus in a haze of myrrh to whatever gods he had honoured. He may have had none at all, but everyone has gods imposed on them at their funeral. This is the divinities' revenge for lack of belief.

When at last the flames died down, the ashes were gathered by none other than Marcus Valerius Simplicianus. Initially surprised, I realised it was proper. Aviola's long-lashed son and heir had assumed the position of head of household; that made him patron to his father's steward, and under his mother's eagle eye, he carried out the necessary formal duties. He did it with due care. He conducted a sacrifice on a portable funeral altar. He made a polite speech, perhaps written by Sextus Simplicius for him, judging by the anxiety with which the cousin listened to its delivery.

I thought Sextus Simplicius was itching to take over. But this was Rome. A man of twenty-five inherited the paternal role even if he was a swine or an idiot. Valerius did tell a story of Polycarpus carrying him around on his shoulder when Valerius was a child and Polycarpus not yet a freedman;

it made a touching anecdote, which the young man recalled with apparent sincerity. I started to have more feeling for these people as a long-established family, a family crushed by the tragedy of having three members murdered.

In theory it was four members, but I knew I was the only person here who gave a thought to the battered door porter.

There were grand tombs in this necropolis, though we had gathered by a simpler brick and tile tomb. The ashes were deposited in an urn in a multiple columbarium where the remains of Aviola and his bride already stood in a cubbyhole, among flowers that had only half withered since they were placed there as offerings. At one point, I noticed that Valerius Simplicianus stood alone in front of the larger, more expensive urn that contained his father's ashes; he raised his hands, praying quietly. If he had been away in Campania with his mother, he must have missed his father's funeral. I was pleased to see that even an effete playboy could honour his father. His mother noticed too; Galla turned away, hiding her face in her stole, as if even she was surprised and moved to tears.

Graecina announced she had ordered a large inscription for Polycarpus. She insisted on reciting everything it would say (it was currently with the stone-cutter) and describing alternative wordings that she had considered. She was losing her grip on her emotions. As she laboured, Galla Simplicia went up and hugged her, to rescue the situation. Unable to continue, the widow broke down in floods of tears. Galla's younger daughter and I distracted the two little children; they came to us willingly then simply clung to our skirts in misery.

While we all waited, I gazed around the wider scene. Bodies cannot be buried inside the city boundary, so you always have that contrast between the tragic intimacy of the funeral and normal life as it continues nearby. The Via Praenestina was a busy road. As we gathered, many travellers passed on the highway, some on foot, some riding mules or donkeys. Some gawped, yet others seemed quite unaware of what we were doing. Commercial carts were already starting to gather, waiting to be let into Rome when the wheeled vehicle curfew lifted that evening. Occasionally, drivers jumped down to stretch their legs, staring at us curiously. One even relieved himself in full view during the oration.

The necropolis was as mixed as they always are, with grandiose monuments for millionaire families lining the main road, but humbler tombs packed in among them. And because people liked to live in the countryside, yet as close as possible to the city for convenience, there were the usual villas backing up against the tombs, built so close they were almost part of the cemetery. They were handsome, spacious places, some no doubt owned by imperial freedmen and women, or simply homes to people who wanted a pleasant rural situation, with guaranteed quiet neighbours.

I knew that when the Gardens of Maecenas were first created, bodies from the old graveyard had been dug up and reburied here. Broken into higgledy-piggledy pieces by inconsiderate workmen, those long dead bones would have worried me if I lived here. But people can overlook a lot, to gain covetable property.

Eventually Graecina stopped weeping, exhausted. Her considerate patroness released her, mopped her up, then invited us all to light refreshments back at the apartment.

40

The two chairs in the garden courtyard had been joined by more. I was starting to feel obsessed by whether anyone would ever put any of this seating away again. With Polycarpus gone, who was there to insist on it?

In a room off one of the porticos stood tables with a buffet. It was informal; if Graecina followed tradition (if she could afford to), there would be a proper feast on the ninth day. Tonight, people took up their own bowls then servers helped them to their choice from grand platters. Light, fragrant food was provided, substantial enough for anyone who was hungry after several hours at the cremation (me, for instance) but not too heavy for mourners who were suffering emotionally. When you grieve, it is so easy to get heartburn.

It was all organised by Sextus Simplicius' steward, the competent Gratus. Nobody seemed to realise the irony that Polycarpus had been on the verge of losing his own position to the absent Onesimus, and of supplanting this same pleasant Gratus.

His presence as supervisor, bringing staff from the Simplicius home, made me ponder. When the mourners had been served and he could relax, I approached and asked quietly, 'Gratus, tell me: was it your staff that Aviola and Mucia borrowed for their dinner on the night they died?'

He confirmed it – and he had been on the premises with them, just as he was here today. Even though Polycarpus was in overall charge, Gratus never let their slaves go out to another house without being in attendance too. 'Just in case.'

I drew him aside, to another portico. No one could overhear. I had a bowl in one hand and kept nibbling, so it looked as if our conversation was casual. 'I wish I had asked you before. Will you tell me anything you remember about that evening?'

Gratus kept an eye on his staff, but he was nevertheless accommodating to me. He was taller and more refined in looks than Polycarpus, with a tanned Italian face: deep cheek creases, eyebrows that crooked in an upturned 'v', and a small gap between his front teeth. The slaves were in the usual plain material and neutral colours, but he wore a finer white tunic, with narrow over-the-shoulder braid in red.

He told me it had been a normal early supper. His master Simplicius had attended, together with the other man Aviola had chosen as an executor.

'Galla would not have been invited,' I speculated. 'Even when couples have been divorced on what they claim are "amicable terms", that's fake. It is a rare second marriage where the new bride plays hostess to her predecessor – well, not unless the new one wants to gloat that she is already expecting triplets and has really superb wedding presents to show off . . . Galla was in Campania anyway, tightening her grip on that splendid villa.'

I was watching Galla's daughter, Simplicia. She had been indoors and found a box of old toys, with which she was amusing Graecina's children, kneeling down on the ground with them like a friendly aunt. I heard her say they could play with all the toys now, and choose one thing each to keep. This worked magically. Each child grabbed its favourite at once, though the boy looked as if he might risk trying for two.

Gratus saw me looking. 'Nice girl. The best of the family.'

'Close to her father?' After her brother had prayed at the tomb, I had seen this one touch the urn surreptitiously, as if she could not bear it but wanted to show Aviola her remembrance.

'More than the other two. She was only a toddler at the time of the divorce; he seemed to want to make up to her, and always favoured her a little.'

'Gratus, I have the impression Aviola's children stayed in Campania with their mother. Were they not invited to their father's wedding?'

'I believe they were invited, but Galla was difficult. Aviola wanted her out of the villa, so she punished him by withholding his son. Valerius did not come. Aviola kept grumbling about it bitterly. Even the day he died he was still upset. Mucia Lucilia was trying to look understanding, but it had made her twitchy.'

I scoffed. 'If Galla really was anxious about Aviola changing towards the children, this was surely a bad move on her part. What about the girls?'

'The daughters, being married women, were in Rome. They did come to the wedding ceremony, bringing their husbands, and also attended the feast immediately afterwards. The farewell party on the second night was a meal for special friends.'

'Aviola's friends? What about Mucia's?'

'In fact they had most of their friends in common. They were both part of a circle of people who had known each other and socialised for a long time.'

'I'm guessing Mucia did not invite her own executor, the freedman Hermes?'

'Oh no.'

'*Because* he was a freedman?' I asked. Gratus gazed at me with unspoken reproach, as if it were bad-mannered of me to raise such an issue of class. 'Well, Mucia Lucilia must have been close to him,' I insisted. 'To put him in charge of her will.'

'She did not expect to die,' replied Gratus, a succinct correction.

'You think she would have changed it later?'

He nodded. I waited. 'Flavia Albia, there were things going on here, I mean actions being planned, that nobody wanted to speak about openly.'

'Were you aware of tensions?'

'Sometimes.'

'Tell me.'

'Well, even the absence of Galla Simplicia – who was a forceful member of their group – left a gap and made all the guests wonder how things would be in future. Would Galla never be invited now? Had the marriage busted up their group? Talking about friendships,' Gratus said, 'you should be aware that Galla Simplicia had for many years been a close friend of Mucia Lucilia.'

'That is certainly not the impression she gives now!' I commented.

'The wedding came as a shock to her,' Gratus confided.

'That was why she took it badly? To the point that people accused her of wanting Aviola dead?'

'Telling Galla Simplicia about the marriage was handled badly. Aviola and Mucia were embarrassed to broach the subject, so Galla only found out by accident.'

I pulled a face. 'I suppose for Galla, having the news kept secret like that increased her anxiety, and her bad reaction?'

'I imagine so,' answered Gratus with the good steward's long-matured knack of seeming non-committal.

'And are you saying there were other issues in the household?'

'I gained that impression.'

Screwing information out of this upright domestic was hard work but this might be my only chance; I was determined to pick his brains as much as I could. 'So, Gratus, what was causing tension? And who was involved?' He looked wary. I pleaded, 'Oh, come on! This is a murder case. Sextus Simplicius is selling you on, despite your immaculate service and loyalty, so you have nothing to lose – why hang back?'

I saw his loyalty fade out at last. Reminded of the unfairness of his situation, Gratus finally overcame his reluctance and let rip. 'Well, for a start, Polycarpus was grumpy, because his master was going off to be flattered by his rival Onesimus; he was distant with me too, because it was already in the wind that my master had an eye on him for my post. He may have thought I did not know – or if I did, he was afraid how I would treat him. So he was being funny with me. Then some of the slaves were on edge for their own reasons.'

'The slaves who are now fugitives?'

'I noticed it all,' confirmed Gratus, 'because every time any of them went off into a corner muttering, it left more work for my own people.'

'What were they muttering about?'

'Oh . . .' Gratus had not quite lost his reticence, though he did not hesitate long. 'Daphnus was in a right bate. He had his eye on Amaranta, and someone had told him she had been up to no good with Onesimus. Apparently there

266

had been bad feeling before, and even fights. Property was broken. That was partly why Onesimus had been sent away early, after a serious row with the master and mistress. Daphnus thought if Amaranta went down to Campania, anything could happen between her and Onesimus in the fresh country air . . . He was nagging her and she was giving him the elbow.'

'This is good – anything else, Gratus?'

'Plenty! The two porters had never got on—'

'Phaedrus told me they were best pals!' I exclaimed.

'Phaedrus lied through his teeth then. He and Nicostratus couldn't stand one another. They were exchanging insults all night. I heard Aviola wanted to split them up; he had said he would sell them both unless they patched up their differences. I suspect Phaedrus was actually having it away with Amaranta – he's hefty, good-looking and blond, and from little signs between them that night, I am pretty sure he had struck lucky.' So much for Amaranta being a girl who kept aloof. Onesimus, Daphnus, Phaedrus – and Gratus had more on that topic: '*Amethystus*, the horrid old has-been, kept eyeing up Amaranta as well, though she can't stand him; he cornered her in a mop cupboard on the wedding day, and she gave him a black eye.'

'With a mop?' I was laughing.

'I believe so,' Gratus replied gravely. 'You may think Amethystus was giving himself airs, but he was *verna,* house-born, so he believed that gave him precedence over Daphnus and Phaedrus who came from the slave market.'

'Even though he's hideous, while they are both younger and more presentable, they ought to queue up behind him for Amaranta's favours?' I chortled. 'Does this kind of rumpus go on at your house?'

'It does not,' stated Gratus coldly. 'I see to that!' He let go a little. 'In my house it is understood the steward has first pickings.' I was supposed to see this as a joke.

'Go on – you are not promiscuous!'

'No, I'm too busy.'

I pulled myself together. 'What else?'

'Olympe had tried to run away, but her own people brought her back, frightened they would be arrested for harbouring her. She was supposed to trill a few rounds in the dining room, but after a couple of off-tune flute melodies, Mucia Lucilia reprimanded her, so she burst into tears, threw her instrument at the wall, then ran off weeping. Even the lapdog—'

'The adorable Puff?'

'So lovely! During the party, Puff was attacked by that other hound, the rough one from Polycarpus' house.'

'Panther.'

'You seem very familiar with the pets here, Albia.'

'I think I like the pets more than the people . . . Don't say Panther was shagging Puff, or making an attempt?'

'No, he seemed bad-tempered because Puff had nadgered him.'

'Well, if Puff came up and sniffed his rear too intimately, Panther would growl a warning, which Puff would not hear because Puff is stone deaf . . .'

'Cue dogfight.' Gratus sighed wearily. 'Luckily I had spied out the fire-buckets. There were lamps everywhere. I don't know what dangerous fool had decorated the place. If the master and mistress had been discovered in bed burnt to a smoking cinder, that would have been more likely than what really happened – not to speak disrespectfully . . . Anyway,

I flung open the well in the courtyard, cast a bucket of water over the fighting pooches, then they sat down together, all bedraggled and licking up the puddles.'

'What was Panther doing down here?'

'That boy had him. The boy was supposed to help wash up. He was useless.'

'I could have guessed. Why wasn't Chrysodorus looking after Puff, as he is meant to?'

'He sloped off when the dogfight started.'

'All right. Anyone else sniff someone a little too closely?'

'No, that is all I noticed. It was quite enough.'

'Yes, poor you!'

Once Gratus set off rolling, he was good value and enjoyed himself. One vital thing he now told me was that apart from Amaranta and Libycus who had intimate duties that nobody else was trusted with, several slaves kept in Rome believed they were about to be sent to the slave market for their past behaviour. The household was to be rationalised as Aviola and Mucia merged their staffs. Trouble-makers were for it. So far, no one had named the ones to go, which caused more uncertainty and stroppiness. But it was known that when the transport for Campania came next morning, Polycarpus had orders to keep some here and send them off to a big sale later this week.

'He made no mention of that to me,' I said.

'He didn't like having to do it,' replied Gratus. 'Polycarpus had a lot of loyalty to his staff. He would never show any annoyance with his master, but I know he thought it was his job to knock them into better shape and he ought to have been given a chance to do it.'

'Do you agree with that?'

'Yes. Yes, I do.'

'So was there bad feeling between Polycarpus and his master?'

'I wouldn't go that far.'

'But he was siding with the disgruntled slaves?'

'It was his own fault they were disgruntled. He should never have let them find out in advance that some were to go,' said Gratus. 'He needed them that evening. He thought he was being kind and honest, giving them a warning.'

'But it made no sense to have them all stirred up?'

'No.' Gratus shook his head. 'You can imagine the rumours. The ones who thought themselves safe were gloating, and others were very distressed.'

Unnoticed by us at first, Gratus and I were being closely observed by another difficult slave. Myla had been hovering near us, in that nosy way of hers. As soon as she saw me looking at her, she edged away.

To my surprise, she then suddenly marched across the courtyard. I had never seen her move with so much determination. She went straight to where Galla Simplicia, her cousin and son were talking in a small group, interrupting them in such a rude way that Gratus sucked his breath sharply through his teeth. 'That's not acceptable!'

Myla addressed Sextus Simplicius. 'Am I to be sent to that sale next week?' she demanded loudly.

Simplicius looked flustered but he answered coolly, 'It will be sooner than next week. As Valerius Aviola's executor I can say that all the slaves whose freedom has not been specifically given in his will by their kind master will be going to market, yes indeed.'

Myla had gone red. Her next target was Aviola's son: 'You

know that's wrong! You know that was not what your father wanted!'

'A decision had been made,' Valerius said quickly, more positive than I had ever seen him.

'I deserve better than this!'

'You have always had good treatment.'

'I was made promises.'

'I think not. You must accept what has to be.'

'Oh, young master, you have a kind heart – save me!'

'No,' said Valerius. Unable to bear her begging, he turned and walked away.

'I have a child! What about the child?' wailed Myla.

'Do not worry about your offspring!' Galla Simplicia blocked Myla from following her son. Her voice, normally so light in timbre, became hard: 'It is not wanted in this household. You shall go together, mother and baby – "Buy one, get one free".'

Beside me, Gratus gulped. I cringed too. 'Galla was winning me over today, but that was a cruel put down!'

Gratus turned to me with an odd look. 'Has anybody told you about her?'

'Galla Simplicia?'

'No, the slave woman.'

I mimicked the regular comment around here: *'Oh, she's just Myla!'*

There was a moment of stillness. I gazed at the steward. He raised his eyebrows expressively, then also shrugged his shoulders in that elegant way he had.

'I see there is a story. Please tell me?'

'I could not possibly comment,' replied Gratus.

'Oh no! You cannot leave it there, Gratus. I know how

things work. There is nothing to single out that slave as special, certainly not diligence at work. Yet normal household management is never applied to her. She herself implies she is untouchable. She does what she likes – normally very little. Polycarpus, though a good steward, use to let her get away with it.'

'So what does that tell you?' Gratus whispered secretively.

'She had a protector. One who cannot protect her any longer.' I gave Gratus a long look, then put a theory to him. 'Try this: was Polycarpus the father of Myla's children?'

41

'Oh, strip me naked and whip me round the Forum of the Romans, Flavia Albia! Where did you get that from?' I was slandering a fellow-steward and Gratus was raring to set me straight. Anyone would think stewards had a guild (not legal, since so many were not free). 'I had reason to dislike the man but I had known him for years and Polycarpus would never have touched that dangerous piece of mischief.'

'The man was too savvy?'

'He had a decent wife and children—'

'That never stops some people, Gratus.'

'Not in his case. He was faithful – more or less – and, give him his due, he had far better taste!'

I let a slow grin creep across my face. 'Well. Settle down, my friend. I was just testing. Part of my job. I saw Polycarpus' attitude towards Myla for myself. He looked irritated by her, and annoyed at having to put up with her in his well-run establishment. I thought little of it at the time.'

Gratus reluctantly came down from his agitation. He would not demean himself by asking who I really thought Myla's lover was, though I believed he wanted me to know.

I put him out of his misery. 'Once you think about it, it's obvious. She has been here for years. She has borne several children. Nobody ever enquires who their father is. Simplicius views her with distaste. Galla and Valerius Junior are vicious to her. Valerius will not hear Myla's pleas; he absolutely wants her gone. Anyone but Myla herself would know it was stupid to ask him. Can there be any doubt, Gratus – Myla sees herself as special because she was singled out by the one person nobody else could question? It was Valerius Aviola who slept with her.'

'Flavia Albia, I bow to your powers of conjecture!' replied Gratus. He was pretending he had known nothing about it. But that was only because he was a very good steward, and very good stewards are impervious to gossip.

42

After seeing that those who held power over her had now all ganged up against her, Myla stomped off, heading towards the kitchen.

Gratus left me, needing to be among his staff. I waited a moment, gathering my thoughts, then I followed Myla.

I would have liked to corner her alone, but Galla's younger daughter was there ahead of me – Simplicia, a thin young woman in decorous dark funeral clothes. Her mother's daughter, she also had several pieces of gold jewellery and such immaculate face colours I wondered where she had her makeup done. She was probably painted by a slave at home, so I did not bother to ask.

When I came in, she had only just arrived and was addressing Myla. 'I heard a baby crying.'

'He's watching her,' replied Myla gruffly, nodding at the youth Cosmus who was with her. 'Supposed to be.' He was peering into food stores like any ravenous young boy. Unlike the sharp knives in my family, he had no notion of stopping and looking innocent on the approach of adults.

Simplicia was indignant, though not because the baby had been left to cry. She pointed to the child, who was no longer lying in the basket I had seen before, but in an elderly wooden cradle. Despite its age, it was well-made, perhaps by the family's estate carpenter. 'I have been searching for

275

that!' Simplicia exclaimed indignantly. 'It was ours – we all had it, my sister and brother and me. It is now wanted for my sister's baby. You have no right to it; please remove your child at once.'

A married woman even though still young, she spoke forcefully and with obvious annoyance, but Galla had brought her up to treat slaves politely. Simplicia clearly knew Myla, and made no threat of punishment.

Truculent but mute, Myla lifted the child, then took her out of the kitchen.

'You can go!' snapped Simplicia at Cosmus. She seemed to know him too. From her tone, she may have been afraid he would refuse her instructions.

He ambled off, but that was because I added sharply, 'Get lost, Cosmus!'

Simplicia dropped onto a stool and momentarily covered her face with her hands as if things were all too much.

I sat down with her. 'Do you mind if we talk?'

Simplicia raised her head, rocking the cradle absent-mindedly with one narrow foot, perhaps unconsciously reclaiming the heirloom. I said what I wanted to ask was delicate and I particularly hoped to spare her mother. That gave the daughter an excuse to speak frankly, if she needed one.

'Can you tell me about your father's relationship with Myla?'

Her mouth tightened and she gazed fixedly at a pot on the hearth. 'She was there, she was available, he slept with her.' Her voice was tight; it obviously rankled. I waited. 'There was never anything to it, other than he was the master and she was his slave.'

I reassured her quietly. 'This happens everywhere.' As the

young woman remained frowning and silent, I went on, 'I am not condoning it, but men who own slaves, and women too, presume that is what the slaves are there for. A condition of slavery is to be used for sexual purposes. Masters have the right to do it. Slaves have no right to say no.'

Simplicia relaxed, heaving a large sigh. 'She accepted it. My father was head of the household so she thought it made her better than the rest.'

'He only slept with Myla?'

'He was a man of habit.'

'Excuse me if this is painful, but did it have any bearing on why your parents divorced all those years ago?'

'None at all. My mother would not have stood for it, but that is irrelevant, Flavia Albia. It happened later.'

I nodded. I could see the situation. Aviola liked things easy. Set up a routine, so he did not have to think about it: answered his correspondence, ate his supper, had intercourse with his usual slave. All matter-of-fact, because he was the master and he owned the slave to provide whatever he needed: offer a napkin, hand him ripe fruit, lie down on her back – or her front, or stand up, or kneel for him. He did not even bother to go out and buy someone beautiful or skilled in exotic practices. He used the house girl.

It was more than possible his father had used Myla's mother the same way.

So, when he wanted relief, Valerius Aviola called Myla in, screwed her, then dismissed her. He wouldn't have made conversation. He would dislike her offering endearments. If she was moody because of her period, he could give her a slap if he wanted. When she was too pregnant, he could go out and have himself professionally serviced, then he could openly complain about the cost.

It makes you wonder why anybody gets married. The man never had to remember her birthday or listen to her endlessly dissecting what some inane friend of hers said yesterday.

To spare Simplicia, I myself established basic facts: Aviola and Galla were divorced for many years. After they split, he started to sleep with Myla. It was a regular occurrence and she bore him children. He did not formally acknowledge the children. They were sold elsewhere while young. Myla had said she had borne 'several' and they were now 'gone'. Then one day Aviola chose to remarry. It had no implications for him, but was bound to affect her. Superfluous, she lost her special position. She was supposed to return to being a bowl-bringer and pot-watcher.

I decided not to offend Simplicia by trying to probe what kind of person her father was. Hardly the worst sexual predator. People he knew spoke of Mucia and him as a likeable couple. He must have possessed some charm. Mucia wanted the full joys of marriage with him.

I reckoned that his ex-wife and children knew what went on but were able to ignore it. Whenever the children saw him, he may have been discreet. But it was his right. They too had to put up with it. From his point of view it was perfectly acceptable, much better than, say, adultery with someone they knew socially. Sex with a slave did not count.

For Myla it did count but who cared about that?

'Inevitably your father's new marriage meant change. You said your mother would not have permitted a liaison – nor would Mucia Lucilia, I imagine. Your mother and Mucia had been friends; I imagine they were women of a like mind. We can say, when your father married, Myla had no further use and was a menace to his new wife?'

'Exactly!'

'But Myla would not accept her demotion?'

'She was being very difficult.' That would be the problem a wife had to address. She could not have a slave undermining her position. A slave who made demands or harboured expectations. Mucia Lucilia may have been surreptitious with her redecoration plans in the apartment, but for her Myla had to go. Hermes, Mucia's freedman, claimed she was always diplomatic, but I wondered.

'Mucia Lucilia saw what had been going on.' I wondered if Galla even warned her about it. 'Mucia was no meek young bride, but a woman who knew she had to pre-empt trouble. She insisted that Myla be sold? I am guessing your father agreed, yet found it hard to tell Myla? I expect he wanted Polycarpus to break the bad news.'

'No.' Simplicia was quiet. 'He told her. My father had made it plain to Myla what was to happen.'

You could see that as decent honesty – or a cold attitude.

'Did Myla believe him?'

'Not really. The woman is impossible . . . Yes, Flavia Albia, she was upset. We all knew that, and we are not vicious; we understood. She was *verna,* born to a slave of ours long ago; she had never been anywhere else and was terrified. I do not blame her feelings, yet she should have seen the position, her own position, my father's, my new stepmother's. If she had behaved modestly, shown she was willing to carry out her duties as a general maid, it might have been feasible to keep her in one of our houses. Instead, she was rude, she was belligerent—'

'And she was carrying another child,' I said. 'Did your father, more than reasonably some would say, agree nothing should happen until this baby was born?'

'He was a decent man.' His daughter fought a sudden rush of tears.

She was a decent girl – even though she had just evicted her baby half-sister from the family cradle for having the bad fortune to be born to a slave.

43

A change in the activity out in the courtyard signalled that people were leaving. Simplicia stood up and went to rejoin her relatives. She said no farewell to me, simply inclined her head and walked out. In a way, this chit of nineteen treated me with less respect than she gave her father's slave.

It was a familiar experience. I might be a free citizen, a widow and ten years her senior, but I worked. For many people that put me down at the level of bar staff and public entertainers. To girls like Simplicia, I was practically illegal.

I, too, returned to the courtyard. Most people had gone and the last stragglers were disappearing. Gratus had everything swept up, put away, taken out to a mule in no time. His staff carried off food hampers and baskets of tableware. He came and said goodbye to me.

'These were here – shall I leave them out or put them indoors?'

He meant the two chairs. I said he could leave them. I had lost any sense of responsibility towards this apartment and its contents. 'You are very observant, Gratus. The ungrateful Simplicii don't deserve you. If I can think of anyone I know who needs a good steward, I shall put in a word on your behalf.'

I could try leaning on my parents; they collected waifs,

though they probably had enough already. Another possibility might be Manlius Faustus, though his uncle, who ran their household, was a slightly unknown quantity. Uncle Tullius had bought Dromo, for one thing.

I shook hands with the steward and on Graecina's behalf thanked him for his attention to everything today.

The last person to leave was Sextus Simplicius. He told me he would like to know as soon as the investigation was closed. He was eager to close up the apartment, sell the contents and terminate its lease. That was more urgent now Polycarpus was not around, though Simplicius had asked Graecina to keep an eye out, temporarily. She must have seen how her husband ran things. I made a mental note to suggest to her becoming a concierge as a way of earning. Another good deed for the unfortunates I had met in the course of the case.

'I gather,' I said to him, 'you are ready to sell off the slaves?'

'Any who survive your enquiries without being executed!' Sextus Simplicius agreed. 'Not to mention you-know-who.'

Indeed, he did not mention Myla by name but I noticed she was lurking in a colonnade again and heard him.

Since funerals are night-time events, it was now very late. Dromo was pointedly 'asleep' on his mat. Fake snores made it clear he was not intending to take a report to Faustus now – not that I would have sent him out on his own in the dark.

Despite the time, as soon as Simplicius left I called out to Myla. She would have been able to tell from my tone there was no point in playing deaf. So she shuffled up at her own slow pace, complaining rudely, 'I was going to bed!'

'So am I in a minute,' I retorted, not letting her see how she vexed me. 'This cannot wait. I want a serious chat with you.'

Analysing how I felt towards Myla, I could not decide whether I was sorry for her plight or simply felt too much distaste – not distaste for what she had done with Aviola, where she had no choice, but for the attitude she adopted in consequence. I had noticed her looking hopefully at other men who might take her on. I despise women who rely on men entirely for their own existence. I like men, never think otherwise. Today, seemingly hours ago, I had kissed one with memorable pleasure. But a woman should keep her self-respect – because if she does not, men will all too easily lose their respect for her.

I had had a few moments to think through my new information.

'I have been hearing about how things were here, Myla. I know this household looked good on the surface but there were all kinds of jealousies and bad feeling. It is the same in many houses in Rome; some are far worse. But here a master and his bride were murdered.'

I saw Myla's face set. As faces go, hers would have been acceptable but it was ruined by her constant surly expression. Perhaps she kept a better one for Aviola.

Perhaps he was not interested in her face.

If I wanted to be generous, I could say it was possible the very way he had made use of her over the years accounted for her graceless manner. She may not always have been so miserable with the world.

'I am intrigued,' I told her. 'All those slaves who went to the Temple of Ceres, the slaves who are accused of the murders, had little reason to have turned on their master. Whereas you, Myla, have managed to be excluded from the investigation even though you had a big motive.'

Myla still said nothing, though she had been vocal enough when she argued with the Simplicii. She stared at me truculently, and I knew why. There was nothing she could do about me. She ogled men who came here, presumably hoping to gain their protection in the limited way at her disposal. I was a woman. I was an enemy over whom she had no power.

'You know you are shortly going to the slave market. You were already listed for sale, before your master died. This may be your last chance, Myla. If your master had led you to believe something different, now is the time to tell me.'

When she yelled at Valerius Junior, Myla was bursting with grievances. Even though he was a young man with limited experience, Valerius saw trouble coming and immediately walked away. I would listen to her grudges, but I think she knew I would not respond in the way she wanted.

'I was promised my freedom,' Myla declared.

'Did he say that exactly?'

'It was understood.'

'Ah, that tricky situation! Almost certainly not understood by Aviola . . . I hope you were not expecting him to honour unspoken promises, Myla?' She seemed silly enough.

'Yes I was! I was going to be a freedwoman and then he would have married me. He was just waiting for the right time.'

'Oh, Myla! And while he was waiting for this mythic moment, he happens to have married someone else?' I did not believe Valerius Aviola ever made such a promise to Myla, or even hinted. I knew too much about the kind of women he chose as his wives; this slave was not what he wanted. Possibly Myla raised the issue and he avoided answering. Perhaps he answered bluntly but she would not listen. 'Don't be ridiculous. After so many years of you being a convenience, why had he never changed things before? Myla, you were fooling yourself.'

'No! He said this baby would be born free.'

'Did he really say that, or was it just what you wanted? I think you convinced yourself of something he never intended. If he had, he left the formalities dangerously late.'

A child follows the condition of its mother; when Myla gave birth as a slave, her daughter was a slave too. Many people take a lax attitude to this rule, but it is asking for legal problems in future. Of course many lawyers earn a good living from that. Informers too, frankly.

'That was the wife, stopping him,' Myla claimed. 'The wife thought she had got rid of me, but she was wrong. I never would have gone away.'

'I'm sorry, Myla, I think you would have done – but in any case you will be sold now.'

'I won't go!'

She was deluded. They had intended to sell her, and they would. If she refused to comply, force would be used. She would be dragged out, hysterical and screaming. Originally it was supposed to happen once Aviola and Mucia were safely travelling. Polycarpus would have organised her removal from the apartment, then a vicious slave-master at the market would have taught her the realities with a knotted whip.

'How old are you, Myla?'

I could tell by her face that she was uncertain, but she said crisply, 'Almost thirty.'

This was my own age; I had a year to go. The slaves who would soon be entitled to be given or to buy their freedom were at the same stage of life as me. I liked the ones who were determined to achieve something better, using their talents. Not this one.

All this woman had to show for her life was a string of children she could never see again and a man who, she really must know, had cared nothing for her. Myla might have been groomed to do his bidding when she was barely into puberty; she could have carried ten pregnancies by now, only to be dumped with a child at the breast.

I could not let that influence me. 'Yours is a tragic story, but I cannot exonerate you simply because you are unhappy. I need to know if you attacked your master, Myla. You had the most reason to lash out and kill Aviola – and his wife too.' Particularly the wife, if Mucia instigated the plan to sell Myla.

'Not me!' Myla answered in a drab yet defiant voice.

'Listen! You need to understand that you are under suspicion of murder.' I was warning her formally.

'I don't care what you say.'

I saw exactly why the family all thought the best way to deal with her was to shed her. A slave needs to be obliging. Having to ingratiate herself even though she thought she had rights was the curse of Myla's slavery, yet the only way she would survive was to accept the position. Stupidly, she kept railing. 'I was at full term. I couldn't move. Anyway, he was my only hope of a future, anyone who thinks I hurt him is mad. It was the last thing I wanted. I wanted him left alone. I was lost once he was dead. Whatever you think, I needed him alive.'

Her argument had some logic.

44

I had had a long hard day: tailing Roscius, re-interviewing the slaves, Polycarpus' funeral and its aftermath. It was best not to press Myla any further. I needed sleep. She too looked drawn. It might even do her good to spend time reflecting on her position.

I warned her we were not finished. Looking back now, all I meant was that we would resume first thing in the morning. My manner was not threatening, not by my standards. No murder suspect can expect smiles and sesame cakes.

Myla humphed and took herself off.

I fell into bed and must have dropped off immediately. I slept long and deep. When I woke next morning, everywhere was quiet, though my body clock said it was not especially late.

Dromo was missing. I went out alone to fetch fresh bread and food for breakfast. I felt stiff, the kind of sluggishness I hate, especially when I am facing important work. This was a morning when I would have liked to go to the Stargazer, not just for food, but to consult with Manlius Faustus if he happened by. Mind you, the last time I did that I ended up with this bothersome commission . . .

I had taken a clean tunic and managed to persuade a local bath house manager to let me in. The water was nearly cold, of course, last night's leavings, and they would not fire up the furnace again until this afternoon.

What I needed was a lengthy hot soak and steam; that would have given me time to decide, before I spoke to Myla, whether I really thought she was implicated in any of the murders. She had a strong motive for attacking Aviola and Mucia, though she was lumbering in the last stages of pregnancy at the time. As for Polycarpus, I supposed she may have argued with him about the plan to sell her but I knew of no other grievance. Stewards get blamed for everything, even when they are only carrying out their masters' orders. Polycarpus had been Aviola's point of interaction with staff when there was any difficult issue. It was feasible that Myla made him into a hate figure. If so, I had seen no sign of it.

I gave myself a quick scrape, basic ablutions, no relaxation. Deep thought was impossible. I had almost made up my mind that Myla would not be a serious suspect. I had to re-examine her, but her words yesterday weighed with me. It was in her interests to have had Aviola alive.

Shivering but clean, I emerged from the bath house which was a deadbeat place with half-blocked drains and mean towels. Even slowing to twitch my tunic where it clung to my damp body, it was a rapid walk to the apartment. I stopped only to buy bread, by now feeling peckish.

My meal was not to be. As I drew near the apartment, I could see figures engaging in agitated behaviour outside. Instinctively, I speeded up.

Fauna, the woman I had met from the apartment upstairs, was excitedly talking to Myrinus. 'You've missed all the excitement!' she exclaimed to me as soon as I was near enough. She was lapping it up, though the leatherworker looked more sombre.

They told me Graecina had come down that morning, carrying out routine checks the way Polycarpus used to do. After exchanging a few words with Myrinus and Secundus as they opened up their shutter, she went into the apartment. A short while later, the two men heard her having a furious argument with Myla. Much of it was audible through the back of their shop. They did not hear how the commotion started, but when they ran to listen, they could tell Myla's imminent sale was the subject. Graecina was insisting it had to happen – so replacing Polycarpus as the agent of Myla's doom.

'Graecina made the mistake of saying, "Don't expect me to be as soft as he was." She went for her!' Fauna was almost jumping up and down in her excitement.

'What? Myla? Went for Graecina?'

'You're right – who knew she had that much energy? Except between the sheets . . .' muttered Fauna cattily. 'No, Albia, it was horrible. She ran into the kitchen and brought a big pan of hot water from the hearth. She threw it over Graecina. Her screams were awful; that was when I came running down.' Fauna must have been on her stool looking, while the argument took place. She caught my eye, then added guiltily, 'To see if there was anything that I could do.'

Myrinus said Graecina rushed out of the building, badly scalded. In terrible pain, she was tended by the two men from the shop, and had now been taken by another neighbour to an apothecary for treatment.

'So where is Myla?'

'That's the thing!' cried Fauna.

'She burst outside,' Myrinus explained. 'She saw me and

Secundus – we were standing here, wondering what to do. We were nervous of approaching her.' It was noticeable that no one thought to send for the vigiles. Neighbourhood problems are not resolved that way.

'I'd hardly ever seen her out in the street,' said Fauna. 'I was here with poor Graecina when Myla came out. She gave a shriek, then shouted something, and ran down the road.'

'What did she shout?' I had a bad feeling.

'She said, "Tell them I did it then! Tell Albia she can blame me!" then she belted off down the Clivus like a mad thing.'

'Oh, Juno! Did she have the baby with her?'

'In her arms.' Myrinus knew this boded ill. 'I told Secundus to run right after her and try to catch her. He's nippier than me. He took your lad, Dromo.'

'Dromo? Where had he been holed up?' I asked crossly. Myrinus nodded to the bar opposite, where Dromo was allowed to have his breakfast. 'Fine. Never mind him. This is bad news, Myrinus. You thought she meant something?'

'I know she did,' Myrinus confirmed. 'She screamed it at us, Albia: "I killed them all! – and now I'm going to kill myself!"'

I delayed only long enough to slip indoors and haul on walking shoes. Then accompanied by Myrinus, a man of conscience, and Fauna, a woman of curiosity, I hurried down the Clivus Suburanus in the direction Myla was last seen taking.

If anyone went far enough that way, it led them to the river.

45

It was a long walk if you were desperate, or even for concerned parties like us, hastening, fraught, wanting to prevent tragedy. It was one straight road after another, all the time having to shove through meandering crowds, dodge pavement obstacles, stand out of the way for soldiers, litter-bearers and hot pie-sellers with enormous trays. Clivus Suburanus, Clivus Pullius, Clivus Orbius, the push across the top of the Forum and the curve round by the Theatre of Marcellus . . . the same route I took yesterday at a much more sedate pace, on my way to re-interview the fugitives.

If someone was in despair and suicidal, who knows? With their mind in turmoil, this distance might fly by. Or it might be the longest walk of their life – which for Myla it surely was in every sense. In life, she hardly went outside. Seeking death, she crossed most of Rome. It seemed she knew where people went for the purpose. It was the Pons Aemilius, from which so many have fatally cast themselves into the brown Tiber waters.

We were too late.

As we approached, we could make out the body. Boatmen or wharfingers must have dragged her out, so she was now lying under the celebratory arch erected by Augustus. Up above, the inscription proclaiming how that emperor had devotedly rebuilt this ancient bridge; below, the dripping corpse of a non-citizen. Nobody bothers to read the plaque. Nobody bothered with the corpse. People were walking past on their way to the meat market or Tiber Island, barely noticing the scene. Secundus and Dromo were there. Hardly anybody else stopped to look. It was just a dead slave.

I knew better than to blame myself, though I cursed my failure last night to see her desperation. I knew she was angry and bitter and probably afraid. I could not see her despair. Perhaps I failed to look for it. I should have done.

Myla must have been so used to showing impassivity, she could hide her feelings even when she was asked to explain them. Thank goodness, I did give her an opportunity. *This may be your last chance . . . now is the time to tell me . . .*

No use.

Secundus, who had wept with frustration at his failure to stop the tragedy, rushed up to Myrinus, gripping his friend's shoulders, talking rapidly in a harsh foreign language: Punic. I recognised it from the Mythembals, neighbours of mine at Fountain Court. Myrinus let him talk, but translated scraps for me. 'They only caught up here . . . She was on the parapet . . . They could not prevent her . . .'

I thought of the baby. Had the child been bowled away in the current, unseen by rescuers? Then I saw: Dromo was holding her. He stood white-faced, speechless, with the little bundle grasped between the spread fingers of both hands. He looked terrified of dropping her.

'He got it,' Secundus said, changing into Latin as he saw me look. 'He got it off the mother. He saved its life.' I made a small gesture, offering to take her, in case Dromo wanted to be relieved. He was as yet unable to relinquish his responsibility.

Then the child upset him by beginning to cry, that forceful, endless, new baby wailing. She was less than two weeks old. She had so little hope of survival without a mother, most people would say it would have been better if the baby had died as well. Not me. I shall never have the luxury of condemning an abandoned child. I was one once myself.

Had her mother even given her a name? Someone else would do that. Even if Myla had chosen one, none of us knew it.

We did not have to wait there long. Authority swept into action. Tragedies happened regularly at the Aemilian Bridge. Arrangements to remove the corpse were swift. Without us being aware anyone had sent for them, men in red tunics, ringing a bell, scampered up like a troop of dwarves in a theatre. Synchronised and determined, they dragged off the body, using their traditional ropes and hooks. It was the same as the removal of dead gladiators in an arena. It is not meant to be respectful. Such carcases are taken away like dead animals. I could not look. Pedestrians merely stepped aside to let them through, then carried on walking along the Marble Embankment.

Well, that man Fundanus had told me: the funeral director. A slave suicide must be removed from the city within one hour. You have to prevent pollution by contact with those who are less than human.

At least Myla would be spared the use of cruel implements to make her tell the so-called truth. For what it was worth, she had 'confessed' already. I felt doubtful. Confessing to a crime whilst under the burden of unbearable despair had about as much validity as confessing under torture, surely? It was some sort of cry of pain – but not one I trusted. Still, in theory, my case was solved. Myla killed those people. She had said so.

She had left me with few ways to test her claim. Was this what she intended? I was certain of one thing; if Myla did not kill them herself, then she damn well knew who did.

46

Dromo squatted on the kerb, still clutching the baby. I crouched down by him.

'*Aargh – she's done something!*'

'They do . . . hand her to me, Dromo.'

He could not give her over fast enough now. I sat the baby on my knees, holding her fragile torso, surveying her. She seemed so surprised, she stopped crying. She wore a tiny tunic that seemed to be made from a floorcloth, and a fibre bracelet that looked like a pulled thread from a different garment.

'Oh, little one! You may grow up to be a beauty, and let us hope you do, but at this moment you are all milky pooh and snot – and far from pretty. I am your sister in misfortune and I tell you, sweetheart, this is where you start out on your own. The good thing is that every day you live through, every gain you ever make, will be better than the absolute nothing you possess today.'

I saw Dromo looking at me in wonder.

'You want to know what I am talking about, Dromo? Well, my dear, this is a sad story, but I will tell you. You must decide for yourself if it had a happy ending . . . When I was a baby myself, in faraway Britannia, the native tribes had a terrible grievance so they rose up in rebellion. They burned Roman cities and massacred their inhabitants. I was found all alone, not much bigger than this child, screaming in the ashes of a half-built town called Londinium.'

'Where were your parents?'

'Dead, for certain.'

'Killed by the barbarians? Did they just leave you behind or had they dropped you by accident?'

'Those who found me always said I had been hidden carefully.'

'What happened to you after?'

'People took me in, because finding a live baby when all around had been destroyed and burnt seemed like a miracle.'

'How did you come here?'

'The first people were no good in the end. Better, more generous people one day became my Roman family.'

'So whose baby were you?'

'No idea.'

'Don't you want to know?'

'There is no way I shall ever find out.'

'Are you going to have her?' Dromo then demanded gruffly, indicating Myla's baby. I could tell he really thought I would. I suppose to him it seemed obvious.

'I never take in strays.'

Even a puppy would be too much for me, and I like dogs. Plenty had given me entreating eyes, even dogs of obvious character. But I was realistic. Tied to a baby I stood no chance.

When I was much younger I might have taken this poor tot home to Mother, but I now realised what a burden that would be. Helena Justina would do it if I pleaded; she would do it out of love for me. That didn't mean it was right to ask her.

'Understand, Dromo, the baby is not mine to adopt. She

is an orphan, yet she is a slave – which makes her someone else's property. Taking her would be theft.'

The innocent boy really wanted to believe he had saved the child for a decent life. 'If she is worth money, they will look after her?'

'I dare say.' I had already heard this babe being discussed by her owners, so I had doubts. She was Aviola's daughter: posthumous, and damned by his legitimate heirs.

We clambered to our feet, with Secundus, Myrinus and Fauna, preparing to leave.

'I never saw somebody die, right in front of me,' Dromo announced. He was white-faced, needing to share his shock.

I answered him quietly. 'If you want to talk about it later, we can do that. Here is my advice, don't brood. Right now, it is better for you to keep busy. I have a little job for you. While we are so near, please go up the Aventine and tell Manlius Faustus what has been happening. You can find your way. Over the market – don't slip in the blood. There's the Trigeminal Gate waiting for you, then straight up to Ceres.'

'You have to write it all down, what you want to tell him. The messages I take are written.'

'Get a grip, Dromo. You can describe what you saw this morning. You were there and I was not.'

Dromo remained agitated. 'No, he likes it written by you; he has a laugh, the way you put things.'

'Well, none of this is hilarious, so you can go and tell your master for me.'

Dromo still gnawed away. 'I've seen him read your tablets, having a good chuckle—'

'Not today. Go, Dromo.' I had nothing to spare for the slave boy; I wanted Faustus to see his distress and take over.

Faustus ought to comfort him. The boy belonged to him, so he must do it. I had my own sadness to deal with.

I watched Dromo set off, stumbling over his feet in his unhappiness. Then the rest of us began to trudge homewards with the orphaned baby.

Behind us, ships plied upon the river, people went to the cattle market, the vegetable and flower markets, the Temple of Fortune and the Temple of Portunus, while the hot June sun beat down upon the bridge, where the pavement was already drying.

47

Galla Simplicia, to whom rumours flew like messenger pigeons, was waiting for us on the apartment doorstep. A carrying chair stood nearby, with two carefully matched bearers; a couple of maids were flittering about in attendance. She had the full parade. Galla seemed to grow in importance daily, as she reclaimed her position as the matron who mattered.

She said she had come to see Graecina, after being told she was scalded. From what Graecina had told me about Galla, this closeness was new, though useful to the freedman's widow. I saw it as one way Galla was reasserting herself in the family from which she had once been divorced.

Just as we arrived, Graecina returned from having treatment for her blisters. Full of concern, Galla took her into the ground floor apartment, along with Myla's baby, whom she took from me as her property. Fauna tagged along indoors too. The inquisitive neighbour did not intend to miss a moment.

I stopped behind for a moment to talk to Myrinus and Secundus. I had a point I wanted to take up with them.

'Right, my boys! You need to explain yourselves . . .'

They plumped down on stools in their shop, heavy-hearted. Men are so easily deflated by a bad experience. I stayed on my feet, arms folded, anxious to knock their knowledge out of them while they were emotionally low. As I had said to Dromo, it helps to stay occupied. I was not drained in the same way as them; after what happened to Myla, I felt bitterly businesslike.

'Don't think I missed this. Earlier today, Myrinus, you let slip something significant. When Graecina and Myla had their fight indoors this morning, you said you heard it from the back of your premises. So you *can* hear anything noisy that goes on in the Aviola apartment?'

They looked shamefaced. On an earlier occasion they had said it was impossible. I told them if they answered honestly now there were unlikely to be consequences. They must have heard that kind of lie before, but they could see there was no escape. 'It's me or the vigiles – and the vigiles will not ask you nicely!'

They came clean. Their mezzanine sleeping ledge was in a half-way, half-height nook at the back, which they went into via a short ladder; through a poorly-built wall Secundus and Myrinus could hear quarrels, fights, dogs barking and music – any loud or sharp noises. They were not bothered by events in daily life. Normal sounds went on like all the background hum of Rome: the cries, creaks, bells, barks, crowing, mooing, whistling, laughter, singing, hammering, barracks trumpets, mystical incantation and sexual moans that we all lived with on a daily and nightly basis. But they would take note of any real excitement from inside the apartment.

'I have been told there was quite a lot of that!' I commented. I felt sour. I liked this pair and was sorry they misled me earlier.

On the night of Aviola and Mucia's dinner party, after the guests left, Secundus and Myrinus had sat in their shop with their friend Libycus. He was saying goodbye. He knew he was either going to Campania the next day with his master – or else he was listed to be sold at the slave market.

'He thought that was a possibility?' The two leatherworkers nodded. 'Really? I thought Libycus had been with his master for years, worked intimately with him, and was so much trusted he is due to be freed under Aviola's will?'

Secundus and Myrinus said that was true, yet it could never be relied on. Neither of the personal attendants felt safe. Mucia Lucilia had been afraid Amaranta was so pert and attractive it was dangerous to keep her, in case Aviola was tempted. He in turn, the two friends confided with sweetly coy expressions, was none too keen on having a handsome black man in the house. I assumed this was because of North Africans' reputation for sexual prowess, which was not mentioned to me by these polite men, though naturally I had heard of it. Who hasn't?

Mucia and Aviola were thought by Libycus to have struck a bargain: 'I'll sell mine, if you sell yours.' He suspected they would both ruthlessly get rid of their body slaves, and buy new, unthreatening ones. Slaves are supposed to be loyal to their masters; masters have no moral requirement to be loyal back.

With this unjust threat of sale hanging over him, his friends said Libycus had been glum that night. As they all had a drink, he sank into deep thought. In the absence of conversation, even from the shop it had been perfectly possible to hear terrible shouting start up in the apartment. Whoever it was sounded crazily angry.

'Out of control?'

'Screaming mad at somebody.'

'Just one person?'

'Apparently.'

'Was it a woman?'

They were not sure.

'You heard Myla sounding off today – make the comparison, please: was it her that night?'

Secundus and Myrinus thought not. They were more inclined to think the voice was male.

'Aviola?'

No. He had a much stronger, deeper voice. It was not him.

Whatever was taking place, it spelled trouble. Libycus shot off back home at once. He was afraid he was about to be found out and punished. Secundus and Myrinus did what they usually did when there was a row in the apartment. Thinking it no worse than normal and supposing the commotion would soon die down, they went over to the bar for a quiet drink.

Later that night, they came home to silence. Libycus could not return to their shop then, but the next morning he burst in, very upset. He told them about the killings, said the vigiles had been asking questions and that Titianus was obviously intending to accuse the slaves. They all knew that meant execution. He told his two friends that he and the others had decided they had to flee to the temple for sanctuary. It was their only hope of appealing for justice and making anybody listen.

'And they were all innocent?'

'That's what he said.'

I mused for a moment. 'Did Libycus say whether Aviola and Mucia were already dead when he got back to the apartment?'

'Yes.'

'His exact words?'

'He said he ran indoors and they were dead.'

So this gave a new picture: there was a sudden burst of disturbing shouts, from one person, who seemed to be male, then the couple died in the next few moments. The speed of it explained why they could not escape, even perhaps explained why nobody reacted and came to their aid.

'If you were in the street going to the bar, did you see Libycus go indoors?'

'Yes.'

'Who let him in?'

'Nicostratus.'

'You saw him?'

'Yes.'

'Did anyone come out?'

'No,' said Secundus.

'That boy,' said Myrinus before he could stop himself. It turned out he meant Cosmus, being sent to fetch the vigiles, afterwards. They reckoned by then they had been on their third drink in the bar.

'While we were having our first, we saw Polycarpus come down and let himself in.'

'On his own?'

'Yes.'

That confirmed Polycarpus was not there when the deaths took place. Not that he needed an alibi, now he was dead himself. But it placed him.

'Did you at any point see three burglars? Going in either direction?'

'No, never.'

'How many drinks at the bar did you have?'

'Five or six, then the barkeeper stopped serving us and

threw us out,' admitted Secundus. 'We had had a drop at our house earlier and might have been a bit merry. He called us a menace.'

'Again!' chortled Myrinus.

'I hope you were not so very drunk that I cannot rely on you as witnesses . . .' They smiled sweetly and played innocent. I kept it light. 'How fast do you drink?'

Fast, they said. With sheepish grins.

Not very sheepish. They were men. They were proud of it.

I left it there. Back in the Aviola apartment I found the usual two seats left out in the courtyard had been paired up with two more. Galla, Graecina and Fauna were ensconced in a group, clearly waiting for me; they urged me to join them. They had all made friends and looked set in for the day.

I had seen Galla's carrying chair go off down the street while I was talking to the leatherworkers. I learned it contained the baby and Graecina's children, who were to be looked after today at Galla's cousin's apartment. She would hand over the baby to a wet-nurse she had lined up for her daughter's child – 'Bit of advance practice for her!'

When Valeria gave birth and claimed the nurse for her own child, the slave baby would be found a place, probably deposited on a country estate, where she could vanish into obscurity. Sitting here in the city, we all assumed the countryside was laden with resplendent big-breasted farm women, who could generously provide milk for the motherless while hardly noticing an extra mouth attached. If they were not busy, they probably suckled orphaned kid goats.

I assumed 'going to the country' was the way Myla's previous offspring were removed. Some fathers do not mind their slave-born by-blows skipping around the house; others

304

prefer to shed them. Aviola must have taken that view – or else he had it taken for him by his insensitive, unwelcoming, 'legitimate' family.

Country farms must be stuffed from oil-press to pigpen with inconvenient characters who have been dumped out of the way in infancy. No wonder they grow up believing they have been robbed of glittering inheritances by devious townies, so they start angrily cutting off each other's legs with scythes and running over rivals with muddy onion carts (look up any legal textbook and you will find copious agricultural casework).

My late husband grew up on a farm, and assured me this is a true picture. My father has a whole cohort of peculiar country relatives whose lives are one unbelievable feud after another.

Graecina's little boy and girl had gone with Galla's maids temporarily, while their mother recovered from her fright. Graecina herself seemed not as badly hurt as had been at first thought, though she was shaken. Her resilience was at a low ebb because she was already grieving.

The attack could have been much worse. The water hurled at her had not been dangerously hot. Myla was a reluctant domestic and she was always letting the fire die down or pots go off the boil. So most of Graecina's skin damage appeared to be on the surface, swelling and redness rather than deep blisters. The apothecary had applied a soothing lotion; he told her to keep the affected area in the air if possible and to rest for three days. No mother of infants can do that, which was why Galla Simplicia had insisted Graecina was relieved of the children at least for the rest of today.

Graecina was agitated because the apothecary removed her wedding ring in case it stuck. She was fretting in case she lost it. Clucking kindly, Fauna untied a hair ribbon, looping it through the precious object and hanging it around Graecina's neck. The invalid's anxiety subsided enough for her to sit with us quietly. Much of the time she hardly spoke. I wondered if she had been given a drug to dull the pain. But even when she seemed ready to nod off, she listened. I thought she was anxious about something.

We all slumped, relaxing: four women from very different backgrounds, drawn together by a series of tragedies. None of us wanted to sit in an atrium weaving. None of us felt like tidying our jewellery boxes or writing overdue letters to our aunts. Instead, Galla Simplicia made a declaration that would give traditional Roman men a fit, though it was very pleasing to us, brazen women all:

'Well, girls, I don't know how the rest of you are feeling – but I need a drink!'

48

I was starting to like her.

It was not even late morning, but each of us could see what the other poor dears needed, so selflessly volunteered to ease their troubles. A triumph of generous sisterhood.

Galla took upon herself the rights of the mistress of the house; she marched to seek out the necessaries. Without Myla, there would be no one to serve us, but we were unswayed by that sad irony. Fauna sat with Graecina, while I helped Galla. We speedily collected portable tables, beakers, a water jug, spices, honey and the best wine we could find. Galla knew where the cellar with the good stuff was and, more importantly, where Aviola hid its key. The store still contained amphorae.

Quite unexpectedly, somehow we four women gelled: sitting together unattended, while we talked over the recent crises, unburdened ourselves of dark feelings and drank – daintily yet deliberately.

Most of the time I work alone, but the concept of a feminine gathering is familiar to me. I can hold my own when the gossip is flying amidst the heady mix of giggles and bared fangs. I do have two sisters and a beloved mother, a matron who we say needs taking out of herself. That is not hard to achieve. Helena Justina can easily be persuaded to jolly up for us: she looks restrained but this is deceptive, just as it was with Grandmama. Mother knows how to measure out a bowl of extremely strong liquor, call it a libation, hand it round with a dish of almond fingers and see it happily poured down throats. Or in a crisis, not to bother with the almond fingers but to send out for a large cauldron of belly pork and pease-mould for soakup purposes.

At one point that morning I remembered Horace's witches: Medusa-haired Canidia and Sagana, ganging up to cruise graveyards as they dripped blood into trenches, searched for children to murder for their marrow bones, and rattled their own false teeth. To escape this ludicrous fancy, I grabbed the flagon and poured us all another round.

It was such good wine we did not spoil it with the honey and spices.

'Did she do it? I have an aedile breathing down my neck—' (That could be nice, I thought madly). 'I need to work out the truth now.'

'Did she buggery!' That was Fauna who, when under the influence of carefully aged but ready-to-drink Caecuban wine, did not mince words. 'This is tasty – is it supposed to be white or red?'

I knew. I had family who would rave on for hours about classic wines, though often while quaffing some liver-dissolving rotgut that even the most lacklustre caupona would refuse to serve. 'It comes as white, but you have to keep it in store for many years, during which time it turns fiery-coloured. Most attractive, as you see. I've never had a chance to become an expert, but I would say this is just about right!'

Since we were not a literary circle, I kept to myself the delicious coincidence that Caecuban was Horace's tipple of choice. Perhaps his scary witches came into being after he had swigged a chalice. Or several.

'Absolutely ready to drink,' Galla agreed, quaffing as if it were a religious duty. Apparently, when new, the wine had been a wedding present from her father-in-law. Maybe he read poetry. She admitted a quiet feeling of satisfaction that she was doing Valerius Aviola out of his cherished, laid-up treasure, when he had thought that by divorcing her he kept it from her. Fauna took that as a good reason to have more. Even Graecina smiled.

'So did Myla do it?' I wondered again.

'No, Albia. She did not.' Fauna seemed to have appointed herself the judge in our case. She was well able to hand out opinions while pouring at the same time. Hardly a wobble. Well, hardly any spilled. 'That night the robbers came, she was three days from giving birth. I know there are plenty of people, men that is, who will say that pregnant women can get wild and out of control, but poor old Myla always swelled up as big as you can get so she was helpless. By the time she could have manoeuvred herself into position to strangle anybody—'

'Two people at that,' I reminded her.

'Yes, and if there was a tussle, the row would have brought other people running and she would have been dragged off.'

'You are right, my dear.' I thought Fauna's reasoning was good, though I wished she would calm down a little. Listening to her was a strain. I was preoccupied, trying to work out what I thought myself. (This was a reason why I did work alone; other people's ideas were generally a pointless hindrance.) 'I really doubt she attacked Aviola and Mucia – not even if she knew they were in bed making love, which had been her role. Nor can I see her picking up a plank of wood and battering the door porter.'

'I've never seen the lazy slug pick up anything,' scoffed Galla.

'Quite. Polycarpus, poor man, is harder to rule out, because she had given birth by then, so she would have been more active physically. She may also have had a motive, if she blamed him for sending her to the slave market.'

Graecina roused herself. 'He had no choice; the master ordered him.'

'Was that the cause of your spat with Myla today?' I asked, bringing her into the discussion now she seemed willing.

'I knew she was difficult, so I wanted to avoid the subject. But she jumped out at me, demanding answers, because someone had at last convinced her she was now going to be sold.'

'That was me last night,' I admitted. 'I started a conversation – one I never finished – to test whether she was involved. I thought I was giving her plenty of leeway to justify herself. I doubted she was a killer. But the house is to be closed and the slaves moved on, so it was time she faced up to her situation.'

'I don't suppose you were unkind. Myla never faced up to anything,' Galla Simplicia reassured me. She nursed her beaker, as she began to reminisce. 'My children used to come home to me after seeing their father and tell me all the latest. Every time one of her own youngsters was taken away, it was the same old story. Myla would refuse to believe it was going to happen, even though she was warned. Every time, right until the last minute she kept saying the master would intervene and stop it – which he never did, because every time he saw her Myla was too attached to them already.'

'He wasn't daft; he could see if a brat of hers stayed, she would make it a source of trouble in future.' Fauna seemed to know.

'Aviola could be a soft fool,' his ex-wife agreed. 'But he always had a keen instinct for self-preservation. He never intended to get stung, not for a slave's brat. Still she created whenever one was sent away. Every time, a mighty scene.'

'And no doubt each poor child had to endure screaming and a tug-of-war . . .' I stretched my legs out in front of me, waggling my toes. An old informer's trick; it helps you think – or so I am told by untrustworthy old informers. 'When I talked to Myla last night, she had convinced herself the latest baby could have a free life. She was clearly desperate for manumission herself. She had blotted out any other possibility.'

Galla nodded. 'Inflated ideas. But never going to happen. Aviola wasn't one of those ludicrous childless men who fall for a girl's smooth talk because the silly brute is desperate for an heir. He had his family, thanks to me. That didn't stop Myla. My son Valerius came to me in tears once, when he was about ten years old, because Myla had been telling him one of her spawn was his little brother and would be sharing our life.'

'You had a row over it, did you?' Fauna demanded, eyes bright.

'One of many.' Galla's slurred voice said she was becoming tipsy, though she remained in control as she repeated it in dreary reminiscence. 'One of very many . . . Still, for all our disagreements, I would not have wished Aviola dead, and certainly not in that way. Juno, our life together was not all bad and he is my children's father. They are devastated by the way he died.'

'Myla was not guilty of murder.' I won't say wine makes me belligerent, though I had become decisive. 'But I cannot exonerate the other slaves. The master and mistress of the house were killed while a bunch of them did nothing – nothing to intervene, nothing to try to save their owners.'

'That's what I can't understand!' declared Fauna, waving an arm so her cheap bangles jingled, a tintinnabulation of glass-eyed Cleopatra snakes and faux silver charms. 'It's natural to go and help. Surely anybody would?'

'I suspect there was simply no time to react.' Even awash with honeyed and fiery Caecuban, I could still try to be fair. 'I learned just now that from the moment the shouting began to when the couple were discovered dead was a very short period.'

'Fair enough then!' Fauna liked rapid judgements.

'I disagree. Even if they couldn't stop it happening, they ought to have rallied to capture the killer afterwards.' Galla could be thoughtful. Perhaps that explained why people had previously accused her of murderous schemes: they believed she had worked out a thoughtful plan to remove the couple . . .

I jumped and shifted restlessly. 'So afterwards, what did happen to the killer? Wouldn't they try to make a getaway? But how? Nicostratus was by the front doors, and there is no other way in and out. I know Nicostratus was there, because he let Libycus back in. Nobody was seen leaving. Polycarpus came down, which was just after the deaths, and *he* was spotted. There was a fixed number, smaller than usual, in the apartment. This says to me that all along the killer was one of those slaves.'

'Well, that's depressing!' Galla was acerbic – and a pragmatist. 'If my darling ex-husband had taken a grip instead of shilly-shallying, if he had sent them all to be sold at the right time, none of them would have been present to do him and Mucia in!'

'I thought you didn't like her,' Fauna murmured.

'Known her for years. She was a nice woman.'

I suggested, 'Plenty of people have told me your late ex was a nice man.'

'He had his good points.'

'Many do.'

'If you can overlook them farting in bed all night.' Fauna spoke with such deep feeling we could tell it was from experience.

As Galla and I tried to keep straight faces, I said I had no need to ascertain whether Valerius Aviola suffered from night-time wind. The fact was, or seemed to be, that by staying in an apartment staffed by disaffected slaves, he had put himself in the classic position of 'wrong place, wrong time'. That did not excuse what one of them did to him. Even though his policy of shying away from telling his slaves their fates outright may have caused the tragedy, neither he nor his bride deserved such violent, frightening deaths.

What were the slaves so worked up about anyway?

In Rome, standing naked on a plinth in the slave market could be a gruesome experience, but there were degrees of indignity. Amaranta, who was attractive, and Olympe, who would undoubtedly be advertised as an exotic virgin, must feel trepidation, but the rest were house-trained, well-kept, healthy specimens, and Chrysodorus was educated. A decent trader would emphasise their qualities. He would treat them well, make them look smart and obedient, so they appealed to discerning buyers who wanted useful assets. For most of those slaves, the chance of ending up in a worse home was balanced equally by that of ending up somewhere better.

'No more uncertain and dangerous than getting yourself married!' as Galla put it. We were all rather silly by that point.

Not too silly for me to wonder, 'Did the killer of Aviola and Mucia then kill Nicostratus? The story goes he was attacked first, by the robbers as they burst in. That depends on robbers being here, and on them committing the murders. Suppose this: suppose everything was, as the vigilis Titianus always said, an inside job. The stranglings came first. *Then* came the plank attack on the porter. Perhaps the killer tried to leave and Nicostratus got in the way – on purpose even, since no one has ever suggested he was incompetent. The rope had been left behind around Mucia Lucilia's neck, so another weapon was needed.' I thought of a quibble. 'Mind you, in any apartment that had been used for a wedding yesterday and was decorated up for a dinner party tonight, why would a plank of wood be lying around?'

'Oh, some homes are *very* untidy!' sniffed Galla Simplicia, eagerly disparaging this one that had ceased to be hers.

'Not with my husband in charge!' Graecina corrected her. She spoke with the tight, demure manner of a woman who had been resolutely drinking even more than the rest of us. I blamed the pain from her scalds for that.

We all sat silent for a time, in deference to the late Polycarpus. We were drunk, but nonetheless capable of good manners.

49

We passed through a period of silence. No one was drinking now. We had speculated ourselves to a standstill, at least temporarily.

We were women completely at ease with each other. We could have been going to the same baths at the same hour for the past twenty years. We could all have been mothers, or more likely grandmothers, watching small children perform in a rustic masque – criticising the costumes other women had made and making lewd cracks about the musicians. *That hand drum player is fit. Hair too long, but a wicked look. He can patter me up and down any day he likes . . .*

We might even be members of that awful cult that the devotee matrons ran at the Temple of Ceres, where they fussed around with ritual vessels and showed off to the public in fake 'Greek rites' at festivals . . . Laia bloody Gratiana. She would *not* fit in with us.

It was significant that we were women not girls; we had all lived. Graecina and I were the youngest, yet married and widowed, both familiar with work. Galla and Fauna might like to pretend, but they were both around ten years older. Fauna, for one, had had a hard life.

From what I had heard, I thought Mucia Lucilia would have made an easy fifth in our gathering.

I thought about the dead woman, as we sat in this bare

courtyard that she can hardly have started to call 'hers'. Her fresco improvements to the summer dining room implied she would have made this space better too. Out with the deadbeat gardener first (goodbye, Diomedes; anyone can see why you are doomed to sale!). Tie up and water the bedraggled climber. Better still, since it was only ivy, slash it down, dig up the roots and dump it. In with some big lily pots and oleanders, or at least lavender. Surround the yard with box hedges. Have roses. Position a fountain and water channels. Haul in proper, permanent benches so this garden area could be like all those other wonderful sitting places in Rome houses, where people met, rested, talked, ate and enjoyed a real social life.

The pockmarked pillars could have been mended, then if necessary rendered, maybe painted as mock-wood or mock-marble. If she could have winkled enough cash out of Aviola, or even used money of her own, the wall space between rooms could have had horticultural painting too: plants, birds and butterflies, with theatrical masks and musical windchimes dangling among them.

This was a woman embarking on a new life: new husband, new home – and if it made life easier, new staff. Old friends, though. She still valued those, and dined with a group of them before leaving town. That last dinner together had been important.

Mucia Lucilia was not rushing into change for change's sake. Not ripping out everything all at once, but nurturing a project. A woman in her prime, still full of energy and lively ideas, she had brought something of value to her new husband. Aviola, who had been divorced for nearly twenty years, would have gained not only willing sex but conversation and companionship. Perhaps before they married, he had been lonely. I guessed she had.

Mucia chose marriage, as far as I could tell. Nobody shunted her into it for their own social or political gain. It may even have been her idea. It was too easy to assume Valerius Aviola proposed it. Friends could have made sly suggestions in order to ease the process, yet Mucia may not have needed even that. She knew her mind. I could imagine her broaching the subject with Aviola. Delicately no doubt but yet, even though they had never previously been lovers, making him feel a marriage would be useful and comfortable for them both.

I knew a little of what she looked like, from that plaque Sextus Simplicius had shown me when I first visited him. Of course the artwork was heavily stylised, but thinking about it again, I had some sense of Mucia as a warm and living creature. How she must have been before her thread was snapped off, not at its due date by the Fates but by some corrupted human in a few moments of rage.

As I mused, I had to remember that I was investigating the unlawful deaths of real people. They had rights and deserts. My commission had given me a duty to them.

The terrible acts that happened here that night deserved solving. The legal aspects might intrigue my uncles and the practical outcome at the temple bothered Faustus, but at its heart was genuine tragedy. It mattered that I should name whoever burst into Mucia Lucilia's bedroom, killed her man and put that rope around her throat. It mattered, too, that if people should have helped her, I should identify them too.

50

Galla was also thinking about the apartment. 'This is where Aviola came when we were divorced. I never lived here. But when the children used to visit their father, it was a happy home.'

'Will you sell up?' asked Graecina.

'Not for me to say. My cousin reckons that will be easiest for the probate. In any case, my son could never live here, not now. None of us can bear the place.'

We all understood that.

Fauna went indoors for a comfort visit. She took the jug but came back saying there was no fresh water left in the kitchen. 'Have to drink that wine neat!'

'Shocking!' said Galla, apparently not shocked at all.

Sighing, Graecina apologised that no water had been brought in, which was a constant source of aggravation. Myla had never bothered, even though all she had had to do was mention to Polycarpus that the water carrier was needed again.

I asked what was wrong with the well. Polycarpus had told me when I first arrived that it was unusable.

'It has bad water,' said Fauna, letting Galla pour her a refill of wine (Galla's excuse for having more herself). 'The family who were here before all died of dysentery. About five of them. The landlord keeps saying it was good before that, so he refuses to fill it in, but he never bothers to clean it out either. So there it sits.'

We all stared over at it. Yes, there it sat. Boarded over at ground level, with an urn stood on the boards.

I myself popped indoors for the usual reasons. When I came out I went over to the well, walking with more sway than customary. I had a look, and came back to sit down. Sitting was a relief, frankly.

I could still talk. Any slurring of the tongue would be allowed to pass politely unnoticed among these wise, tolerant women.

I asked Fauna to go over again with me what she claimed to have heard on the night of the violence. 'Fauna, around the time when Aviola and Mucia were killed, there was shouting by one person, probably male, then a silence. I am wondering how this fits in with you hearing more voices and seeing people running to and fro with lamps.'

'I'm glad you asked me that, Albia darling!'

'Why so?'

'Since you came up to ours to talk to me, I have picked it over quite a few times with my handsome husband.'

'Don't forget, some of us have seen your husband!' Graecina chuckled. 'He wheels a veg cart at the Market of Livia,' she informed Galla. 'He looks more like a carrot than the carrots on his cart.'

'*Long, yellow and twisted!*' Fauna was the first to agree. 'Don't ask why I did it. Too many years ago to remember. There must have seemed to be a good reason at the time. Anyway . . . we worked it all out, Albia. The first voice, which sounded very disturbing, was what lured Lusius out of bed.

By the time he got himself on the stool and looked out, the shouts had stopped and nothing else was happening. So the lummock comes grumbling back to bed, and since we are awake he wants to start some marital push-and-shove around the blankets. That must have taken some time, though not as long as old Lusius tells himself he can keep going . . .'

Galla, Graecina and I all looked at one another in a way that said we knew exactly what Fauna was saying but were too refined to let on. Mouths pulled down and raised brows.

'So there were more noises later?' I asked.

'Oh yes. Toing and froing, whacking and thumping, cries, footsteps running, abuse, lights moving about, panic, who knows.'

'This stopped eventually?'

'Must've. We got bored edging each other off that stool to peer out. Lusius said if this was going to be their permanent way of life downstairs, he would demand Aviola buys us a second stool. Or better still a ladder.'

'How long would you say the silence lasted, in between the noises, Fauna?'

'Couldn't tell you. In the quiet part we fell back to sleep.'

'And the second burst of noise, how long did that last?'

'Seemed ages, but may not have been. Not long enough for my twisted carrot to pull up his roots and go downstairs to complain.'

Fauna had no more to say. Perhaps because she had been talking about her husband, who gave them to her, she began to rearrange the armoury of tacky bangles that were lined up along her forearm. It was a ritual, twisting them and spacing them until the effect was to her liking.

Galla Simplicia was watching me. 'What's on your mind, Albia?'

I was thinking that I now understood a lot more about what must have happened. The first shouts, the loud agitated ones, ended in the murder. A silence followed, as the horrified slaves saw what had happened to their master and mistress and tried to decide what to do. I reckoned they all went into the oecus to talk, possibly because lamps were already lit there. They had told me the truth about having their supper. I accepted that most of them were there while Aviola and Mucia met their fates.

According to what Secundus and Myrinus said, by the time the slaves were discussing what to do, Polycarpus was in the apartment with them. As their supervisor, he may have taken the lead. I did not want to say this in front of Graecina, but her late husband must have been party to a hasty cover-up. Though the slaves were particularly vulnerable, what had happened could also reflect badly on him.

Graecina was now sitting with her eyes closed, frowning slightly so her dark eyebrows came even closer together than usual. It looked as if she was in pain. Was that physical pain from the scalding, or mental anguish? Had she herself known before now about what happened? Had Polycarpus shared the full story when he returned to his own apartment? Did he tell her or did Graecina guess parts of it?

Why didn't Polycarpus and the slaves simply bring in the vigiles and wait for justice to be done? Because slaves know the rules. These slaves were bound to be accused. By the time Titianus told his tribune next day that he thought the crimes here had been an inside job, the ten slaves were ready to run for it to the Temple of Ceres the moment he pronounced them guilty – or better still, before he came to arrest them.

I now thought Polycarpus must have been right in there,

helping them to get away. With his position under threat, bonds to his master were loosening, yet he still felt close to the slaves he supervised. His plight, if Aviola decided to have a new steward, was little different from theirs in being sold.

It was too soon for me to confront Graecina with what Polycarpus might have done. Luckily, or for me not so luckily, at this point we were interrupted. Just as we reached the most dishevelled point of our morning, we heard banging. Fauna was the first to gather her wits, so she went to see who it was while the rest of us made feeble motions of tidying our drinks tables and straightening ourselves up.

Fauna returned looking apologetic, followed by two visitors. With coy glances at me, Galla and Graecina immediately rose to their feet, Graecina exercising a lurch that nearly toppled her, until Galla caught her and they tottered in each other's arms. Winks occurred. I took no part in that, for I was the object of my companions' sniggers.

'Albia's boyfriend!'

'Client!' I corrected.

Standing this side of the atrium, with one fatherly hand on the shoulder of his pale slave Dromo, was the aedile Manlius Faustus. Both he and Dromo looked amazed at the scene they had interrupted.

51

In general, I prefer not to let my clients learn of any unusual measures I am forced to adopt in order to pursue facts.

Fortunately Tiberius Manlius Faustus already considered me wild and irresponsible, a barbarian beyond saving. There was no chance of me sinking any lower in his estimation.

Nevertheless, I wished old grey eyes had not walked in.

The aedile announced pointedly that a carrying chair was waiting outside.

Galla jumped to. Graecina suddenly became extremely tearful, so Galla insisted she go home with her so they could have a weep together. Fauna whispered a hurried goodbye and scurried off out there as if she had remembered a pot that might boil over. That left me on my own with the situation.

We could have been a bunch of carousing teenagers who had just heard someone's mother come back into the house unexpectedly.

Cobnuts. I was a grown woman. I could do what I liked. It wasn't as if we had set fire to a scroll box of Virgil's *Aeneid* in order to fry a Lucanian sausage.

I did not try to tell him that. When the others had gone, Tiberius looked me up and down with his chilling stare and said I ought to sleep it off. He would take Dromo out for some lunch then they would come back when I was 'more myself', by which he meant sobered up. He made me hand over my door key, in case I was too comatose to let them back into the apartment.

'You need to drink plenty of water.'

'The house has run out.'

'Then Dromo will go to the fountain and fetch more. Dromo, arm yourself with buckets from the kitchen. Better bring an extra one for Flavia Albia, in case we are due for an up-chuck.'

'Not me.'

'Shall we take bets?' growled Faustus, at his most disparaging. 'Just don't heave your heart out on me, will you?'

I maintained that I would not dream of vomiting on him since the tunic he was wearing was bound to be his favourite, one woven by his grandmother with her own hands. (He was in his aedile's white and purple, so I knew the tunic was not old. On the other hand, it was expensive and must require high-price laundering.)

The brute snorted.

Although my head was spinning, I refused offers of help to reach my room. I must have had the kind of exaggerated dignity that tells people you are on the verge of losing all your grace and elegance, but I summoned up enough willpower to stalk indoors. That may have confirmed to the aedile that I had been drunk in the morning on other occasions.

I heard them leave. I felt desperate to collapse upon the bed. However, that would have meant crushing the loaf I bought all that time earlier for the breakfast I had never eaten. Stale crumbs are painful to lie on.

I knew what to do. I tore it into its segments and ate the loaf now. All eight pieces. I chewed carefully to lessen the chance of what Tiberius had called up-chuck.

There was an experiment that I had to try. I could ask the aedile and Dromo to help, but I didn't want to look foolish if my suspicions were wrong. If I was right, I wanted the heaviest possible impact. When dealing with theories, I follow the good informer's rule: mull it over; test it for yourself; be certain of the answer; *then* bedazzle your client.

Action.

When I walked back out into the courtyard, I groaned. It was now midday, with the sun right overhead. I covered my eyes against the fierce glare of warm light in that bare space. I stood for a while, swaying gently.

Forcing myself to move, I walked over to the well in the corner. It had been boarded over with a set of wide planks, butted up against one another. Someone did a neat job. I pulled up one of the edge planks, which were smaller, trying not to get splinters as I held the end, then turned it as I heaved it over away from me. The top must have been scrubbed. The underside no one had bothered to clean. There the wood was covered with dark, rust-coloured stains, which I knew must be dried human blood.

'As I thought! Well done, Albia.'

The planks must have been taken up before. I was sure the boarding on this well was lifted when Manlius Faustus sent his men to search. They looked down inside. I knew they found nothing. The extremely neat re-covering for safety had been their work. Very soon afterwards, unless I was mistaken, Polycarpus must have had some of the boards up again briefly for his own purposes.

Even if they noticed these stains, Faustus' men would have thought nothing of them on old wood. They had been ordered to look for stolen silver – not to search, as I was doing, for a murder weapon. I had found it: this was the plank deployed in the attack on Nicostratus.

I had not finished exploring. Next, I hauled aside the featureless stone urn that always stood on the boards to deter access. This took me some time. I could have ruined my back. Since my father runs an auction house, I had been told how to prevent injury when moving very heavy objects. The best way is, get large men to do it. Otherwise, I was too tipsy to remember how to apply myself and too eager to stop now. I dug in my heels, grasped the top lip and eventually pulled the thing right over. I jumped back, quick, to save my toes. Then I rolled it in a big curve along the ground. This was not an approved method, and it damaged the urn, but I was trying to work fast.

Sweating, I rested for a moment. One by one I pulled, pushed or edged out the remaining boards. They were not excessively heavy, though the large ones were awkward for a drunk who did not want dirt on her tunic. Eventually, I had the well opened up completely. I won't say it was no work for a woman, because we do what we have to do, but inebriation did not help. Even so, stubbornly I shifted the whole lot.

I knelt on the edge and peered down. People in my family have the horrors about holes underground, especially wells. I tried that trick everyone does, gently tossing a small pebble down. It was not deep. A splash soon came from the dark water below.

The sides were straight and smooth. If this had been a source of water in regular use, someone would have built a top frame, with a winding handle. As it was, I saw a big iron hook at the top of the side wall. Attached to the hook was a rope, going right down into the water.

I had to lie on the ground to take hold of the rope safely. I was still wobbly. Standing, I could easily have tumbled in head first. Ropes are heavier than you expect and this one felt as if it held a lead bucket. Drawing it up was so difficult, I dropped it once, but it was still safely tied to the hook so I started again, keeping a more careful hold of the rope. In the end I managed to extract the bucket, along with its not-unexpected contents. It was wooden, but it contained a sack, which was what had been heavy. I hauled the sodden bucket and sack onto land, collapsing in a warm heap beside them. At least there was plenty of cold water trickling off, which I could smear over my face and neck to cool myself down.

Stiff wet twine tied the neck of the sack, then also tied the sack to the bucket to prevent it falling out. This posed a challenge for my tired fingers. But again, I was not defeated. I brought out the contents, drained them of well water, then set about arranging them like a diligent housewife.

When Manlius Faustus and the boy strolled back into the courtyard, I had cleared away the debris of our drinking bout. I was sitting in one of the chairs, half asleep. I opened my bleary eyes just in time to see them take in the glittering spread I had organised to welcome them.

Covering the tops of two small portable tables, their metal shining as they dried in the sunlight, were jugs, drinking cups, coasters, strainers and even spoons: a distinctive array of high quality decorative silverware. The 'stolen' silver that Roscius had said he could not find. The silver that was supposedly the cause of all that happened to Valerius Aviola and his bride, their door porter and probably their steward too.

52

The aedile strode across the courtyard, stood and looked down the well. 'I've seen you do some things, Flavia Albia, but this beats everything for stupidity!'

'It worked. Look what I found.' I waved an arm over the silver. 'So much for praising my brilliant perspicacity.'

Faustus came back and sat down with me. 'Stop it!' I thought he was talking to me, then realised he was admonishing himself. He turned to me, appealingly. 'Albiola, you terrify me. I could have come back and found you drowned in that well.'

'You love to accuse me of behaving badly!'

'Don't do it then.'

To look reasonable, I made a sketchy apology. 'I ought to have waited. Still – congratulations?'

'I might go that far.' He sounded sombre, but that was better than his punishing mode.

Dromo stood at his shoulder, jaw dropping at the beauty I had laid out. I raised one of the fancy goblets, into which I had poured the last quarter-inch of Galla's fine Caecuban wine. There must have been well-water still lurking in the cup; it tasted less fine now. Nevertheless, I drained it and told Faustus how good the Caecuban had been, though sadly for him it was finished.

'You have drunk enough for both of us.' Faustus was impervious. He fumbled at his belt and produced a small packet. 'This came for you.'

'From whom?'

'Your aunt, Claudia Rufina, with a tart message saying she was very surprised you had not gone along to enquire how Justinus is doing.'

'Someone would tell me if he died.' Faustus scowled. He ought to know I was not that hard-hearted. 'Oh Claudia was simply too mean to send a messenger all this way. I'll be charitable, and say maybe she thought a messenger would more easily find the aediles' office.'

'She said she did not know where you were working.'

'Nuts. She should have asked Uncle Quintus.'

'Right.' Faustus reined in a little. 'I sent a deferential note on behalf of both of us, claimed you were caught up and could not reach the Aventine. In case you want to know, I received word your uncle is progressing well.'

'Good.' I too backed off: 'Thank you for excusing me.' He in turn made a graceful gesture. 'So what's this thing she sent, aedile?'

'How should I know?' he answered tetchily. 'It is addressed to you. I was told your aunt took it from one of her children.'

With a grunt, I opened the paper, an old bill. Inside was one of the silver coasters from the Aviola wine set, a small circular stand, with three little curly legs.

'Well, that fills in another part of the puzzle.' As Faustus gave me an enquiring look, I explained. 'My aunt mentioned that her children kept playing in the carrying chair that I was loaned when Justinus was hurt . . . This tells me the silver stayed hidden because it was moved around.'

329

'In the chair?'

'Underneath the seat. When I raced over to Capena Gate that night, I was actually sitting on the stuff!'

Faustus whistled. 'On the night Aviola was killed, the silver was hidden in the chair?'

'Seems so. The chair was either already stored in an empty lock-up shop, or was put there that night. When Titianus and his men arrived at the crime scene, they searched, but only the apartment.'

Faustus sucked his teeth. 'They would say, believing the silver was long gone with thieves, they had no reason to look elsewhere.'

'Lazy bums! So in the lock-up it stayed for days, until Graecina offered me use of the chair. I guess she had no idea what was hidden in it. When she told Polycarpus she had lent me the chair he must have been beside himself. I thought it was odd that a busy steward went in person to reclaim the chair, and went so soon too. He must have been shitting bricks – sorry, very perturbed – because he remembered the silver was inside. Presumably, Polycarpus thought the loot might be discovered, so he chased off to retrieve it. One of my dear little inquisitive nephews had been playing in the conveyance. But the little boy failed to tell his mama, when she caught him with the coaster, that he had seen a whole load of other things under the removable seat.'

'Well, don't snitch on him.'

'I don't grass up naughty boys, Tiberius.'

'That's a relief to all of us!'

'Why, what have you done?' Dromo demanded of the aedile, who gave him no answer. He just sat there, as he did, with that pleasant face giving nothing away like some fisherman on a wharf waiting for a bite on his line, knowing it would eventually happen.

I said, 'I am sure your master was speaking hypothetically.'

'What?'

'A joke, Dromo!' I squared up and continued. 'It could have been a girl, by the way. My little sweetheart niece Aelia finds things she is not supposed to . . .'

'Some girls are into everything,' remarked Faustus obliquely.

I sniffed. 'Polycarpus could well have fetched back the chair too soon, because you, super-efficient Tiberius Manlius, had arranged for a much more detailed search to take place here.'

'Yes, and you certified my search was thorough! So the silver was not found because? . . .'

'It was still at my uncle's house while the search was going on. Polycarpus was on his mission to fetch it. I bet when he brought the chair back, he was horrified to hear you had searched again. The day he died, he had been moving the silver to the well, a safer hiding-place.'

'You think his killer discovered him doing it?'

'It seems likely. I wonder if they had a quarrel over this silver? The one thing I can say is this,' I told Faustus. 'On the night of the attack, Polycarpus and the others organised a spectacular cover-up. It involved the steward and slaves disguising the crime as a burglary.'

Faustus held up a hand. 'Did they know real thieves had made an attempt? Roscius?'

'Maybe they knew, though I think it was an extraordinary coincidence. Aviola and Mucia had been killed – for whatever reason and by whomever; we don't know yet. The slaves went into the oecus to decide what to do. They may have known that if they stayed outside in the courtyard people like Fauna and Lusius, the neighbours upstairs, could hear what was going on. While they were indoors, Roscius broke in. He never saw the slaves, but perhaps they saw him. They all kept quiet. Once the burglars fled, some quick-witted slave – or Polycarpus – worked out that this was their deliverance. They could blame these robbers for everything – murders included.'

'So that was when, and why, the slaves first concealed the silver?'

'Yes, I bet it had been in the kitchen. Roscius never went in there. Polycarpus had the wine set washed by his own people, after the slaves who came with Gratus had all gone home. Everything was probably upside-down on a draining board, drying.'

Faustus sat quiet for a while. 'It was a good try. But with the cover-up, the slaves have only made things worse.'

'That will be your problem,' I told him, sympathetically. 'I shall show what happened; you must advise the authorities at the Temple of Ceres how to respond. My uncles may provide a legal steer.'

'Thanks for landing me in it!' Faustus growled, yet sounded lenient.

'Nothing has changed since we started; it's the slaves who have caused your problems.'

'Do you have any idea who committed any of the murders?'

'I have a few thoughts.'

'Was it Myla?'

'I doubt it. I want to have one last attempt to urge the fugitives into a confession. One tell-tale would be enough. Is there any chance you could offer an amnesty, if I make someone sing out the real song?'

Faustus frowned. 'I disapprove, but it has been talked about in official circles.'

332

'It would be in the style of our beloved emperor,' I reminded him. 'Buying evidence. Making prosecutions look good. Ensuring the outcome of trials . . .'

'So modern! Give out a big reward and set the informant free.'

'Is that what I can offer?'

'I suppose so.' He sighed.

'Right. I'll see what I can do with them.'

'Make it tomorrow morning. You need to be sober.'

That was what I had intended. I looked sullen.

'Sorry!' said Manlius Faustus, rather unexpectedly.

He was learning to read me.

Faustus sat leaning his chin on one clenched fist. Looking over his knuckles, his eyes went to Dromo, still standing with us unnoticed.

'Sit, Dromo. Sit and join the family.'

Dromo looked as startled as I was. But why not? A man's slaves formed his *familia*, his wider household. You may wonder why would Manlius Faustus choose to extend the privilege to an idiot, but how many people have real blood relations who are idiots or far worse?

Dromo did not seek inclusion, nor expect it, but he only needed to be asked once. He sat down.

Faustus and I both surveyed him. It seemed to me the boy was different. He had that subtle alteration that happens with a teenager, marking their shift from child to adulthood. One day you look at them and see a new person. I glanced at Faustus; I reckoned he saw what I thought.

'I gather this young man did something brave today; he saved a baby,' Faustus told me. 'I know he found the event upsetting. I brought him to see if you could help him come

333

to terms.' Dromo must have told him what I said, that old story from Britain.

'Why did she want to take the baby with her?' Dromo had no sense of timing. When he wanted to ask something, he burst straight out with it. Inexperience. Lack of observation. I doubted he would ever improve.

I had sent him to Faustus because Faustus ought to look after him. Why was I now lumbered? But both Faustus and Dromo were waiting for me.

I sighed. 'Dromo, as far as I understand it, some desperate parents who are contemplating suicide feel they cannot leave their children behind to suffer.' I did not tell him that others, especially in bitter divorces, think *if I can't have them, he or she won't have them either* . . . I had been involved in cases like that. The law said a child belonged to its father; in practice, many infants went with their divorced mothers – Aviola's three (well, his legitimate three) were typical. Once in a while, a couple could not reconcile themselves to either solution. I would try to mediate, though I was normally hired by one side to find dirt in order to prevent their antagonist having custody.

'Will that baby know what her mother did?' asked Dromo, very subdued.

'Who can say? By the time she is old enough to understand, people around her may have forgotten. In any case, the people she grows up with may not know – I believe she is to be sent to a happier life on a farm in the country.'

'*The country?*' Dromo was disgusted. 'I think I did the wrong thing.'

'No, Dromo.'

'I bet you blame your mother for leaving you.'

I felt myself grow tense. 'I may have done from time to time, but no longer.'

'Why not?'

'I came to realise my parents must have loved me. I was not abandoned from choice. They may have known they would be killed. If they did survive the rebellion, they may have tried desperately to find me afterwards . . . I grew up an extremely unhappy person, but I am not now.'

'What changed you?'

'Something I saw many years later.'

'What?'

'Dromo, don't pry any more,' murmured Tiberius. In my view, it was high time he intervened.

Dromo was still glaring at me, wanting answers.

I sighed again, then gave in again. 'Dromo, have you heard about the huge volcanic explosion in Campania? Have you heard about the great fire in Rome later that same year?'

He had. Everyone knew about Vesuvius, and though an infant at the time, Dromo had been in Rome during the fire, safe up on the Aventine, which escaped the inferno. Since I had been drinking, today I lost my usual reserve. I told Dromo what had happened in our family that year, and how it changed me.

My father had a favourite nephew, Larius, a talented fresco painter, who worked at Stabiae on the Bay of Neapolis. He lived there on and off; despite a few wild episodes, he had a local wife and a family. When Mount Vesuvius so catastrophically erupted, he was the kind of fixated artist who would have tried to finish his wall, even though the whole house where he was painting faced violent destruction. As soon as we heard about the eruption, my father went to see if he could find Larius, though he never did. Falco spent weeks there, in anguish as he tried to dig down through twenty feet of mud or ash. He could never find any trace. We decided the whole little family must have tried to escape too late; Larius was killed, along with many other people, most of whom were never found.

Shortly afterwards, a huge fire in Rome destroyed many monuments, including the Saepta Julia, a gorgeous two-storey gallery where we had a family antiques business. Father worked there with another nephew, Gaius, who had always seemed a tricky, fly-by-night character, though the ragamuffin had a heart of gold. When the fire came tearing through the district, Gaius became a hero; he refused to run and save himself but stayed to help other people. The roof collapsed while he was still in there. The firefighters never recovered his body.

'So we lost both brothers, but that did not mean nobody cared. Dromo, when I saw how desperately my father struggled to find Larius, how he raged over his helplessness, how long he kept up the search, and then when I saw how distraught everyone was over losing Gaius, I found some faith. I was able to believe that when I was a lost baby, I had that same degree of love. I no longer hated my parents for abandoning me; I stopped feeling bitter. I saw I was fortunate to have been saved, and eventually to be rescued a second time by the fine people who are my family in Rome.'

'Will Myla's baby think she is fortunate?'

Dear gods, I doubted that. 'I hope so, but who knows?'

Faustus, who had listened in silence to my story, leaned forwards to his boy. 'You must thank Flavia Albia for telling you this . . . The point is, Dromo, only Fortune can know what will happen to any of us, including that baby you saved. *You* cannot tell. What matters for you is that when you had to choose, you did what your conscience told you was right. You gave Myla's baby a chance.'

'You have to answer to yourself, Dromo,' I added, seconding his master. 'You saved her because your own human kindness required it.'

Dromo had started to squirm now. He looked self-conscious about sitting in the chair. His eyes glazed a little; he was losing interest in talking. Personally, I was amazed he had managed to last this long.

'So that's it, isn't it?' He looked from Faustus to me then back to his master. 'In that work you do, you and Albia. On the night in this apartment when those people were murdered, the slaves here ought to have tried to help them. Because even slaves like us ought to have human kindness. And they didn't, did they? None of them?'

Yes, said Faustus. That was it.

53

I cannot claim to have achieved much else that day.

The aedile was leaving to return to the Aventine. Faustus stood and gazed at me. 'I ought to be more respectful. I do admire your expertise –' Thank you, aedile; that is what I like from a client. '– especially with a splitting hangover!'

I had not reached even the real beginning of the hangover, but his teasing praise worked better than the usual Roman cure of parsley. For one thing, you were supposed to eat the parsley before you started drinking, which I had failed to do. I read in an encyclopaedia that topping a canary and deep-frying it in olive oil for breakfast does the trick – if you want a crunchy, fat-filled methodology. It probably worked because you had to jump around so much while you were trying to catch the birdie . . .

I could not decide how serious Faustus was, so I replied stiffly. 'I have been edging towards answers for a while.'

I probably had been, though you never sit around thinking, *Oh, I am edging towards answers here, using my admirable expertise* . . . I had been lucky. On the other hand, controlling your luck is part of an informer's professional toolbag. Had I been unlucky, I would have soon faded from the scene.

'Who were those women, incidentally?' Faustus asked. 'Friends of yours?'

'My drinking pals? Witnesses and suspects.'

'Suspects?'

'Not high on the list. Having a little nip together helped me rule them out.'

Faustus managed not to humph.

He left. Since he was an aedile, I trusted him to take the silver away with him. On his way down the Clivus Suburanus, he would return it to Sextus Simplicius, to be reabsorbed into the Aviola estate. Dromo went with him as escort. An aedile may be sacrosanct, but it was crazy to hope he could carry a large sack, obviously full of bullion, down a public street yet not have it snatched from his sacrosanct grasp by irreligious criminals. And then have his skull kicked in by them, for taking a stupid risk.

As soon as Dromo came back and I had let him in, I went to bed. Clearly this was never going to happen with Manlius Faustus. Had I been sober, that thought would not even have occurred to me. Perhaps.

For some reason, as I lay awake, I thought back to the bar where we kissed. He was just play-acting. Just as well. If I had an affair with a magistrate, what trouble that would cause! I had no idea how I would ever confess to my father, whose views on the elite were firm and frequently stated. Still, I believed Faustus would not kiss and tell, and if there is one thing loving daughters learn early, it is how to keep secrets . . .

Not relevant, Flavia Albia.

Next day I prepared to finish my case.

Out of bed early. Stand-up wash, in cold water. There was not even the lukewarm pan that Myla used to tend in her desultory way. Dromo complained. I explained to him that now she was gone, somebody else had to do her work. He could have stirred up embers and put pots on trivets. I, however, could not because I felt queasy and should have been looked after by those whose duty was to tend to me.

'You mean my master?'

'Crazy caryatids! – *You*, Dromo!'

'I thought so!' he muttered, in my hearing, though as if to himself or the imaginary companion who shared his thoughts when he was unhappy. ' *"Being nice to Dromo"* was never going to last!'

I took him to breakfast with me, at the good bar. I even gave him most of mine, since I felt no desire for food.

They had a canary in a cage on the counter. I refrained from ordering fried bird. It was bound to be some child's pet. Besides, the thought of anything in oil risked what the aedile called an up-chuck.

I could not even fantasise these days without that man worming his way in. Time for a new case, with a new client.

From now on they would be ugly seventy-year-olds with brown eyes – and women at that.

I took Dromo back to the Aviola apartment, telling him we would load all our things onto his handcart and take everything away with us.

'Have you solved the case then, Albia?'

'Not quite, but this is as far as I can go.'

'Has my master said you have to finish?'

'No. I set my deadlines for myself. I have to know what is realistic.'

I left him to start packing up, while I went to say goodbye to Graecina. At my approach to their apartment, the rough dog kicked up his normal racket though when she let me in he calmed down, walking off to gnaw at a table leg.

'Where is Cosmus?' Graecina lifted an eyebrow to query why I asked. I indicated the dog.

'Oh, Panther is ours. He belonged to my husband, really. Polycarpus fed him; he used to bring unwanted scraps from the master's kitchen. Panther knew who to love.'

'I thought he belonged to Cosmus.' From things he said, Cosmus either thought that too, or he pretended. A lot of slaves have pets. The poorly-treated like to have something of their own to beat. 'Apart from barking, which a guard dog is supposed to do, he seems obedient.'

'He's a good boy, aren't you, Panther?' asked Graecina in that exaggerated voice some people use for their animals. Panther wagged his tail, even though he was sitting on it. 'He's wonderful with children.' I bet he gave them wonderful fleas too.

I was working up a theory. 'I noticed that when Panther is out in the street, you don't have him on a lead.'

'He trots back if he's called. He had a bit of old cord for a long time—' Graecina stopped, as she saw where I was heading. She was an intelligent woman. She looked at me in a mixture of wonder and horror. 'Oh no.'

A true sense of surprise was missing. Yesterday, while we were drinking and talking in the courtyard, Graecina spent a lot of time lost in her own world. She must have had doubts even then. Thinking about Panther's lost lead confirmed her pre-existing fears. She had half-expected me to ask the question.

She made no attempt to put me off. She went to the back of a door where a hook was nailed. It held a hat and a cloth bag for shopping, nothing else. 'The dog's lead used to be

341

kept here. It was not much more than a length of raggy twine. He doesn't have a collar; we just looped it around his neck . . .' Graecina swallowed and I felt my own mouth go dry. 'They lost it.'

'They?'

'Cosmus, my husband . . . one of them.'

'Which?'

'I don't know.' I felt she did not want to say it was Polycarpus who disposed of the lead.

Graecina sat down. She folded her hands neatly in her lap, but she was breathing too fast. This was a woman who recently lost her husband and who was scalded with hot water yesterday. One of her bare arms was so red raw it must be hurting badly. She had two small children to worry about, as well as her own grief; I could hear the son and daughter playing in the next door room. And now she had to cope with . . . what?

I sat down too. At that point it was a toss of the coin whether I would end up having to tell her the answer, or she would tell me.

'At one time, Graecina, I wondered if Aviola and Mucia had been killed by Polycarpus.' At that, she let out a small squeak of misery. 'No,' I reassured her at once. 'For a freedman to do that to the master who gave him his liberty is patricide – he has killed the man who gave him life, his second life, his life as a free man. And the penalty for patricide in Rome is as cruel as the crime.'

I did not enlighten Graecina, if she did not know. A patricide is sewn into a sack, with a serpent, a cockerel, a monkey and a dog, then the sack is thrown into the sea. Do not ask me the symbolism. That's Rome, all over.

Whether or not Graecina knew the punishment, I wanted

this woman to feel anxious. I needed to pressurise her so she told the truth.

'Your husband was just protecting someone, wasn't he?' I asked her quietly again: 'Graecina, where is Cosmus?' Her eyes were wide. I guessed some duty to stay silent had been laid upon her by Polycarpus. 'It is too late, Graecina. The charade is over. Now you have to tell the truth.'

'Cosmus ran away. He does that from time to time; he comes home when he is hungry.'

'He is an unhappy boy.' As Myla once said to me.

'He is. He always was, Albia, though he has been much worse lately. I never wanted him here in the first place, as Cosmus must have realised, but my husband took pity on him when the boy was younger.'

'He came from the Aviola household?'

'Yes. I had just had my first child and needed help domestically. Cosmus was to be sold and he hated the idea. Polycarpus felt very sorry for his situation, and I think saw something of himself in the lad.'

'So Polycarpus bought him from Aviola?'

'Yes. He came to us and was nothing but a nuisance. I do not want him in the house any longer.' Graecina rushed on, 'I have asked Galla Simplicia for help with getting rid of him, because I am so afraid he will be difficult about it.'

She stopped, so I repeated it more simply: 'You are altogether afraid of him.'

She behaved as if she had not heard. 'Galla Simplicia's cousin was going to have Cosmus picked up for me, and sent away for sale. I had said nothing about it, but I think Cosmus may have guessed the plan.'

'It seems unlikely he will come home this time!' I returned dryly. 'And that's good, because you don't want him in your house with young children here; you must feel unsafe yourself. I have to report him as a runaway, you understand why. The vigiles must set up an urgent search.'

'Yes. Yes, I understand,' Graecina agreed miserably. There were tears in her eyes. She was a strong woman but she felt extremely anxious. I did not blame her. Her little household had fallen to pieces. Until the slave was found, there were also grave dangers.

I gave my verdict: 'I believe your slave Cosmus killed Valerius Aviola and Mucia Lucilia.' Graecina let out another tiny whimper. She knew it was true. 'He must have strangled them with the dog lead that has disappeared.' I knew Polycarpus removed it from around Mucia's neck – 'an act of respect for the dead,' according to Titianus. Trust him to misinterpret. It was 'respect' that allowed Polycarpus quietly to remove this murder weapon from the scene, so it would not be identified. Later, he destroyed it or lost it altogether.

As Graecina's hand flew to her mouth to smother her horror, I had to say, 'I have no time now to ask, but I find it hard to see why Polycarpus was shielding the boy.'

'Just kind-heartedness, Albia!'

'Well, it rebounded. When you and I went into that lockup, you must have realised straightaway what the boy had done to Polycarpus. Cosmus showed no gratitude for your husband's protection of him. Cosmus went into the shop downstairs and had an argument. Then Cosmus murdered your husband, strangling his kind master with his bare hands.'

'I know why,' admitted Graecina. 'My husband had a great sense of fellow-feeling for all the slaves in the household, but he knew he now had to stop shielding Cosmus. He refused to keep him any longer after what the boy did to the master and mistress. He said we would sell Cosmus.

344

Polycarpus had to think about me and the children. Cosmus became very angry. He swore he would run away for good. He demanded some of that silver to take with him.'

'That must have been the quarrel in the lock-up,' I reckoned. 'Polycarpus had already hidden the silver elsewhere. He may have refused to say where it was, and he refused to give Cosmus anything.'

I would have liked to ask more questions, about how and why, but Graecina was too upset. Telling her to keep the door bolted, I left her with her sweet little children and her flea-ridden dog.

I had other things to do.

54

I almost ran down several flights of stairs.

At street level, I saw Myrinus so warned him that if he or Secundus saw Cosmus they should only approach him with caution. I had to explain why. Myrinus told me that at one point Secundus taught Cosmus wrestling, but he gave up. The boy was strong, but he had the wrong temperament. Secundus said he wasn't suitable to train in combative sport, he grew too angry.

Strong and angry. That fitted.

I found Dromo.

'I packed all the stuff like you ordered me. My master's belongings that he lent you are all on our handcart, but yours won't fit.' My modest luggage was bundled up neatly enough, but lay apart in the atrium, quarantined. If the commission was over, in Dromo's eyes I ceased to have rights.

'Either mine goes on the cart as well, Dromo, or the bad news is you will have to make two trips. Never mind that now. The good news is, you don't have to do it straightaway because I need you to come with me to see the vigiles.'

Dromo kicked the handcart. 'Well, that's a waste of my time! I didn't need to do all that.'

Working with me had failed to teach him any grasp of logic.

At the Second Cohort's station house, Titianus was about to go off duty. I made him stay to take down details, emphasising that this was not simply a runaway slave, but one who had committed three murders of citizens. Titianus put his head out into the colonnade and shouted a few orders, though I could hear little sound of response.

'You seem to have cleared up the Aviola case!' Titianus groused, making no effort to hide his jealousy. 'So now you want me to do the tiresome bit, put myself out catching him.'

I stayed calm. 'If you can make the arrest, Titianus, you are welcome to the glory. The whole Esquiline community will be delighted the vigiles have acted with such efficiency. Besides, don't you have a particular remit to track down runaway slaves?'

Titianus softened up. 'That's because we run into so many of the buggers while we're doing our rounds. The Second funds its entire Saturnalia drinks budget from the rewards we receive for returning lost slaves to their masters. Last year, one good-looking Syrian acrobat from a senator's entertainment troop covered all our bites for our big do.'

'Very public-spirited. Do you splurge all your perks on entertainment?'

'Officially any thank-yous have to be put towards equipment. We can run with that as well. Any time we need new fire mats, we shake out a few homeless varmints from under bridges, make them squeal about who they belong to, march them home and invoice for our finders' fee.'

'Well, just make sure you catch this raging boy Cosmus.'

'Cosmus? Isn't he that odd boy I spoke to? – Bloody hell!' swore Titianus. 'For the record, why is he raging?'

'Nasty personality . . . I am not certain. I have a theory, but I need to check it.'

'Theories, eh? We don't generally bother with those.'

'It's like a new position in sex, Titianus. Give yourself a treat and try it.'

While he blushed, I asked how long the vigiles might take to complete a search for the missing slave, but Titianus had no idea. According to him, his team was fully stretched because everywhere from the Temple of Minerva Medica to the Viminal Gate was full of wounded and dying criminals, with their savage wives and mothers screaming for vengeance and pulling knives to carve up people. This was ever since I and my cronies made such deeply unnecessary attempts to stir up excitement in the gangster community.

'Gallo's on crutches, for leaving that man in the cells. It's a bloodbath!'

'Just up your street then, hard man.'

Titianus stared at me as if he thought I was being satirical at his expense. He was slow, but like everyone else around me on this case, he was learning.

As he showed me out, he darted off into a side room and came out with an iron collar. 'This will secure him.'

'So much easier if every slave who is liable to wander has an *I-have-run-away* dog-collar riveted on, with a return address!' I said.

There was nothing else I could do about looking for Cosmus, so I walked Dromo back through the Esquiline Gate to pick up our things at the apartment.

There we found Sextus Simplicius, the overweight

executor, dithering in the courtyard. He had brought me a reward for finding the lost silver. I thanked him sweetly for this unexpected bonus, though from the weight of the purse, it was a somewhat small reward.

The mint-scented mooner would have to do better than that, if he wanted his next ploy to succeed. He invited me to take a glass of borage tea at some place he knew, which he said was very close nearby and had an extremely nice vine-covered pergola. Clearly this was one of those moments at the end of a case when a man thinks that now he won't be seeing you again he can risk a seduction scene.

Why do they never realise we women already know the 'nice place nearby' routine?

I declined. In this I was aided by Dromo standing at my side, glaring. I would miss him.

So Dromo and I said goodbye to that tragic apartment, and departed from the Esquiline. I still did not know fully what had gone on there, but by the end of the day I would have found out.

Dromo had the handcart, moaning repeatedly that it was overtaxing him. I heaved my own luggage in one awkward bundle over my shoulder, never complaining. An informer ought to travel light, certainly with no more than she can manage herself; she can be sure nobody will help. We cleanse society of undesirables, yet we receive few thanks. Small change and horrible overtures; no real gratitude.

We went slowly, not taking the route that led to the Aemilian Bridge with its miseries of yesterday, but walking down parallel with the Servian Walls, to the open monumental area between the Flavian Amphitheatre and the Temple of the Divine Claudius. This was near the Capena Gate. I called in to see

349

Uncle Quintus, which was one way to a free lunch.

He was fine. We talked about work. He told me Aulus had sent a written judgement to the Temple of Ceres. After careful historical research, Aulus had advised that the temple's reputation as a place of sanctuary derived from its plebeian past: thumbing noses at the upper class by offering refuge to those who had been arrested by patrician magistrates. 'So Aulus recommends taking a hard line: *one*, the status war should be relegated to the past, as a gesture of new thinking. Bit of a shock for my tight-arsed brother to be a champion of liberal thinking, but he can do it if he closes his eyes and rushes at the idea . . . *Two*, the Aviola slaves should therefore be placed under arrest by Manlius Faustus, then passed to the usual authorities.'

'To be charged with not assisting their master and mistress?'

'I realise you are now saying only one slave is guilty of murder.'

'Different household, Uncle Quintus. He also killed his own master, a freedman. When Cosmus is caught, he goes down, no question: execution.'

'And the other slaves, Albia? Faustus commissioned you to exonerate them, but do you say it can't be done?'

I nodded. 'They are certainly guilty of conspiracy. I am off to a final reckoning with them, after which I suspect I can in fact show they are guilty of something worse than non-intervention. You know I am not sentimental and neither is the aedile. If Aulus rules that the slaves have no right to sanctuary, I shall give Faustus very good reasons to arrest them.'

'Oho! Then your devoted aedile will be even more keen on you.'

'I told you before; he's not mine!'

I mimed a lute-plucking gesture. It did no good. Uncle Quintus would keep harping.

I munched a bite but did not dally. Still leading a tired Dromo, I skirted around the southern side of the Palatine, capped with its summit-top burden of marble palaces. We trudged past the apsidal end of the Circus Maximus, then kept going on the flat along the long western side, until we were below the part of the Aventine that held the Temple of Ceres. We climbed slowly up the hill, a short ascent but steep, then we crossed to the aediles' office beside the squat old-style temple with its wide-set thick pillars and its air of Greek disdain.

As we completed that last part of our journey, I felt a twinge of homecoming. Why should this be? There were the same dusty tenements and introverted private mansions as on the Esquiline, the same teeming stalls and bars, the same colourful crowds in the street. Yet even the taste and smell of the air seemed different. I found myself coughing mildly, before my lungs became acclimatised. It was still June, so the roses that grew in enclosed gardens and the lilies in sun-baked doorstep pots were zapping out pollen at their top rate. The bakers, fishmongers and greengrocers arranged their loaves, sardines and vegetables in special Aventine patterns. Street cries had a new ring. When Aventine dogs chose rats and litter to bark at, they woofed from shallower lungs. Working on the largest, highest hill in Rome, Aventine mules developed a special wheeze. Some of the people had it too. You could hear it when they cursed, every time they made a bad judgement while crossing a road where the dung was deep.

Home. I was home. I realised that although this case had intrigued me, I had not enjoyed working in what had been somebody else's house, far from my base, a stranger in the neighbourhood. I yearned for my own apartment, containing my own things. However much I derided my own folk, I was longing to be back among them. I wanted the laundry where they still had a tunic and sheet of mine, the bakery and bath house where I had built up customer goodwill, the caupona run by my relatives. Once the rest of them returned from the coast, I wanted to be among my own family in our riverbank town house.

I did not regret working for Manlius Faustus. I would do it again, if ever he asked me. I knew, as a woman, that was a distinct possibility. He had a germ of interest in me that would drag him back. Even so, it would be better if I could somehow turn in this commission with a satisfactory final report.

I was feeling low, as if I had lost my confidence.

I felt truly grim, though I presumed I had the hangover from Hades after that Caecuban wine. Had it gone bad in the ageing process? Was the gorgeous flavour an illusion? Even my stomach seemed to be growling, which could not be from what I had eaten with my uncle just now. Claudia kept a well-run house. She never served slimy salad or covered up the smell of bad meat with strong sauces. You don't risk six small children performing synchronised diarrhoea.

I preferred not even to think about that.

Well, biliousness could be useful when I had stubborn suspects to interrogate. I would like to believe kindness works, but I knew from experience that shouting at people and tetchily suggesting you are going to throw them to the beasts often has a quicker effect and produces more details.

So in that spirit, for the last time I went in to see the slaves.

55

Faustus was not there. He had left me an extremely peevish note (*'should your condition ever allow you to appear'*).

I guessed he was upset that I had not come to carry out interviews this morning according to my promise. But now here I was, bringing the answers he hired me to find: I had identified the killer of the bridal couple. Even better, I had found their missing property, which always carries more weight than mere life. His agent had succeeded. The killer had been identified and would be caught. Meanwhile I, the uncomplaining hireling, would also sort out what to do with these pesky slaves.

The nine culprits – and they were all culprits, I believed – were loafing about in dappled shade in the garden as if they had no cares. I would put a stop to that.

I hauled out Olympe, the fifteen-year-old, a soft target.

I led the little sweetie-cake into the office, taking some comfort from its association with Manlius Faustus. I fussed about, as if preparing myself, adjusting furniture, laying out note tablets.

'Tell me about your family,' I began conversationally, while I pretended to get ready.

Olympe presumed the real interview had not yet started. She had never had any kind of regular employment; she was unfamiliar with being routinely messed about by some supervisor . . .

As she had hinted previously, she grew up a member of a travelling group of Lusitanian musicians, all one big family; like most Iberian entertainers, they used tambourines and castanets, but also other traditional instruments, which they plied with frenzy while they danced and sang, and occasionally sliced one another up with traditional Lusitanian boning knives. Mucia Lucilia had seen them perform once; on one of her whims, she asked for Olympe and was sold her.

Olympe had convinced herself her family were shocked by the money; she innocently believed that they intended to return it.

'You ran away back to them, didn't you?'

'Yes, but my people explained to me we are obligated by a work contract.'

'I have to disappoint you, sweetheart. That was not a contract, but a sale into slavery. Your people knew it too. Trust me, they understood perfectly what they were doing. When you ran away from Mucia Lucilia and came back to them, your relatives must have been terrified they would be accused of harbouring a fugitive slave, which is theft. For foreigners in Rome, that would be serious. No wonder they hauled you back to Mucia. In fact,' I kept my voice grim, 'in running away, you were a thief yourself, Olympe. The law says, you deprived your mistress of her property – I mean, you. Of all the people being held here, yours is the worst position. I may be able to extricate the rest, but a slave who is a known thief is almost impossible to save.'

'I just want to go home!'

'Poppet, you never will. Concentrate on ways to stay alive.'

Olympe quivered nervously, a petite, pretty lyre-player

who had been betrayed by her family and could not accept that the world was so horrid. Now she was all puppy fat and panic. I knew men who would want to wrap their arms around this poor palpitating bundle, kiss her better and set her scurrying free into the world (well, after they had their way with her). Sadly for her, her fate lay in my hands instead.

I set aside my notes. I looked friendly – as friendly as a weasel, though not many of those can ever have strayed into the campfire light of the Lusitanian band. 'Let's have a talk, shall we, Olympe? See what I can do.'

'What do you want to know, Albia?' she replied, full of gratitude. I might have felt bad about cheating her, had I not been feeling seedy.

I shrugged. I was easy. She cheered up. She couldn't see danger. 'Not a lot left,' I told her. 'I do know it was Cosmus who did those awful things that night at the apartment.'

Olympe nodded. If I had realised before how naïve she was, I might have saved a lot of time. You don't allow for anybody else being so completely daft. And this child played the flute and lyre, which demanded a degree of confidence . . .

'So what did you all think,' I asked, 'when Cosmus started shouting?'

'We were having our dinner—'

'That was in the handsome room, the oecus?'

'Yes. Cosmus must have come downstairs, like he often did, and he'd gone to see Myla. She was in the kitchen.'

'Did Nicostratus let him in?'

'Yes, Nicostratus was always getting into trouble with Polycarpus over it. Cosmus was supposed to stay in their apartment, except when he was collecting water, which he did in the mornings.'

'But he kept coming back?'

'He kept coming to see Myla. And of course she let him.'

'That was because . . .' I answered it myself: 'Myla was his mother.'

'Yes,' breathed Olympe in her sweet way. 'I didn't want to say that, Flavia Albia. I wasn't sure if you knew.'

I leaned back in my seat and gazed up at the ceiling. As a magistrate's room, this was decently done. When Manlius Faustus grew bleary-eyed from counting street-cleaning fines, he could look up at a complicated coffered roof, picked out in several rich tints by a master decorator. Judging by her summer dining room, Mucia Lucilia would have liked to see the designer's pattern book, though she might not have been able to afford him.

Cosmus was one of Myla's children.

'So Cosmus is Myla's boy, the only one of her family she was ever able to keep near her. This was achieved through Polycarpus taking pity, when Cosmus was put up for sale. The kind act didn't work too well though, did it? Cosmus kept coming downstairs and hanging about, near his mother. He failed to settle down with Polycarpus and Graecina. Whenever he was unhappy, he came moping to mother. Later, when he heard Myla was to be sold, I suppose Cosmus thought he would lose her altogether . . . Did that make him very upset?'

'Yes, Albia, he was,' said Olympe, solemnly. 'Isn't it awful?'

'Indeed. Myla was in anguish too, of course, trying to blank what was happening to her after all those years living in the same family, everything made worse by her pregnancy, everything made desperate because her master had now married. Cosmus was upset, an angry boy, about to lose

357

the only person with whom he had any close relationship, any relationship at all, perhaps.'

'Nobody would have much to do with him,' Olympe confided, twisting her small child-like hands. 'Nobody liked him or Myla, really.'

'Let me work it out – so it's the last night at the apartment. The last time anyone can appeal to Aviola and Mucia not to sell their slaves, including Myla.'

'She was absolutely top of the list to go,' said Olympe, not vindictively but full of simple excitement at seeing me set all this out.

'Cosmus is down in the apartment, with his mother, both of them tormented and hysterical. He rushes into the main bedroom and starts shouting. Your master and mistress wake up, to find him pleading with them not to sell his mother. Perhaps, because he doesn't have much idea of life, he is even *ordering* them, not to make her go. I guess at first – because they know Cosmus – they simply try to reason with him. That is why nobody heard them call for help. They never did. They were not expecting what happened next. Cosmus may have already said to Myla he intended to do something drastic if they would not change their minds. Myla is hiding in terror of what he will in fact do, dreading it no doubt, because she needs Aviola alive to protect her interests. Cosmus is overcome by his frustration. In his terrible anger, he strangles your master and mistress . . . then what, Olympe?'

'We had heard him shouting, so we went out and saw Cosmus run into the kitchen, crying. Myla was there, sobbing wildly too. They were both in a tremendous state. Amaranta rushed into the bedroom, as soon as she saw the doors open. So she found the bodies.'

Well, it was good to know I had been told one sorry fact correctly.

'Amaranta finds them. So now Cosmus and Myla are both in the kitchen – weeping and clinging to each other? Or did his mother denounce what he had done?'

'Weeping and clinging,' confirmed Olympe, sadly. 'Myla never told him off; she was the only person who never yelled or beat him . . . Then they just went very quiet together.'

'Polycarpus came down from his own house. Why did he? Was it really just a feeling of unease, or had he missed Cosmus at home, so was worried about the troubled boy?'

'He was worried. Scared what Cosmus meant to do.'

'So! Polycarpus sees what has happened; he knows it looks bad for the rest of you. He takes charge. He gathers you in the oecus, to decide what can be done . . . Was that everyone, including Nicostratus?'

'Yes.' Olympe had withdrawn into herself now.

'Myla and Cosmus?'

'No. Myla had run out of the kitchen and into one of our rooms in the back corridor; she was hiding her head under a pillow. Cosmus was made to stay by himself in the kitchen. Polycarpus locked him in. Polycarpus said it was to keep him out of the way while we decided his future.'

'When was he let out?'

'After.'

'After what?'

'After we heard the burglars. Daphnus was on guard by the oecus door, in case Cosmus broke out or anything. He saw the burglars, so he hushed us. I was frightened; I thought those men would come in where we were . . . but they went away. Not long after that, Polycarpus let Cosmus out. When we had a plan.'

'You had a plan, part of which was to inform the vigiles,' I said. 'You had to tell them, of course. Aviola and Mucia were too important and well known for you to hide what had happened to them. Too many people would have missed them and asked questions.'

'It's wonderful how you can work everything out!' exclaimed Olympe; it was genuine praise.

'Long practice. So, Cosmus was sent to the vigiles, to inform them of the crimes he had committed. That puzzles me. Why him?'

'To get him out of the way. Polycarpus didn't trust him.'

'I wouldn't trust a double strangler myself! But he didn't trust him over what?'

'Over us making arrangements. Also, Cosmus was bound to dawdle like always, so we had time to get ready.'

'Ready with the plan you devised? Hiding the silver wine set, so it looked as though it had been stolen? . . . And what else, Olympe?'

Olympe finally played dumb. Even this too-simple, ridiculously innocent young girl had reached the point where she realised she must clam up.

I asked the direct question then: 'Olympe, what happened to the door porter, Nicostratus?'

She would not tell me.

56

Some people might think Nicostratus did not matter. He was a slave. I had never met him. But that man's death had always niggled me.

Cosmus did not kill him. Ironically, in his case Cosmus had been given an alibi. He was sent to report his own crimes to the vigiles, while Nicostratus was still alive. Nicostratus must then have been attacked as part of the 'arrangements'. I wondered whether going so far as to kill him was an accident.

I led Olympe to the door, letting the others see me smiling and looking pleased with her.

'I just want to be happy and play my music!' she burbled as we parted company.

I had her led off separately. I went back into the office, trying to decide which of this shameless crew to interview next. Obviously as part of their plan, the slaves had taken a vow of silence for mutual protection. Olympe had only talked because she thought I already knew all about Cosmus. As soon as I strayed into other subjects, even she grew mute. I had been unable to budge her, whatever promises I floated. Being 'happy' was never a reward I could offer anyone.

I called for Chrysodorus, the sardonic philosopher. He brought the dog in with him, a bunch of scrawny bones on a wretched string. The creature immediately looked for a rug to pee on. Fortunately the floor was mosaic.

Our talk was brief. I told Chrysodorus what I already knew, then asked directly for help. 'Chrysodorus, Fortune favours the commercial. How about you sell me the facts I need, in exchange for your freedom? Manlius Faustus might even throw in a small cash incentive to set you up in a new life. Isn't it a kind of syllogism? – I need your information; you need your life saved; therefore your information is going to save your life.'

'Invalid,' retorted Chrysodorus. 'I cannot rely on you giving the reward. All humans are dishonest. Some informers are human. Therefore some informers are dishonest.'

'Not all. Not me.'

'That's simply an advertising ploy. Paint it on a bar-room wall: "Flavia Albia, the honest informer". Then wait for the public to scrawl scathing graffiti.'

'So no dice?'

'All bets are off.'

'What do you have to gain, Chrysodorus, by remaining silent? Is it not a contradiction of your life spent in philosophy, which is supposed to be the search for happiness through living well?'

'Whoever taught you that?' laughed Chrysodorus in his bitter way.

'Many people. Manlius Faustus mentioned it once, when talking to me about his attitude to duty. The duty that will force him to arrest all of you very shortly.'

'Oh, fabulous aedile!' scoffed Chrysodorus. 'A holder no doubt of the Socratic view: "virtues such as self-control, courage, justice, piety, wisdom and related qualities of mind and soul are crucial if a person is to lead a good and happy life" . . .' Actually, I thought he was exactly right about Faustus. 'This makes no mention of being cursed with slavery, badly fed, beaten and denied freedom to engage in an intellectual life. It certainly does not envisage ending up in charge of a stinking, snuffling spoiled bundle of mange that passes itself off as a dog.'

I agreed that Socrates had not faced looking after Puff.

'I understand your hardship, Chrysodorus. You told me Puff was even sent to you here at the Temple of Ceres, after you all fled for refuge. I suppose Polycarpus despatched the dog to you?' Chrysodorus nodded. As an intelligent man, I could see him wondering what had made me ask. He worked it out. For emphasis, I indicated the piece of unfortunate-looking cord by which Chrysodorus led around the skinny rat-like creature. 'Did Mucia Lucilia's lapdog always go on a lead, philosopher? Or are you hiding in plain sight the rope that the boy Cosmus used to strangle his victims?'

Then Chrysodorus made that classic gesture, beloved of both Greek orators and Roman gangsters: the open palmed shrug that wordlessly says, 'You got me!'

57

As Chrysodorus left the room, two other people solved my dilemma of who to see next. Amaranta and Daphnus sidled in together. They said they wanted to speak to Faustus, but as he was not here could I act for him? I said being an honorary aedile, plebeian or otherwise, was an interesting concept for a female freelance. If they wanted to try me, I would certainly give them advice. Possibly I could intercede.

I did not imply in any way that the aedile might allow me special favours. I doubted he could be swayed on a professional matter.

Nevertheless, I took his gilded stool of office, the stool with heavy curved legs that represented his authority, shifting about on his purple cushion until I squashed it into the best shape for my own posterior. Next time he turned up at the office would he start roaring, *Who has been sitting in my curule seat?* Or maybe one of the public slaves who tidied up would fluff out his cushion before he noticed.

As they came in, Amaranta and Daphnus both glanced over their shoulders as if they were anxious about the others spotting them. I suspected these two had now joined in a partnership that set them apart from the rest. So it proved. They said Manlius Faustus had let it be known he had been given legal advice to make arrests, though in the right circumstances, he might grant an amnesty. They wanted to claim it, then run off together.

'Would this reprieve be for everyone?' Amaranta asked me. I suspected not all the slaves were willing to own up. Chrysodorus, for one, had opted out.

'I doubt it. Faustus has to demonstrate that justice has been done.'

'Could we two make a deal?'

'How blunt! What are you bringing to the table? I don't need to be told that Cosmus killed Aviola and Mucia. He killed Polycarpus too. The vigiles are out looking for him, and once they catch him they will put him to torture. Once they start on him, trust me, Cosmus will confess. He committed the murders but that leaves the rest of you guilty of failing to help your masters. Manlius Faustus may also want to consider that if you had all told the truth, it might have saved the life of Polycarpus, a third Roman citizen senselessly killed.' I dropped my voice, which had been firm and level. 'What did you have against the steward?'

'Nothing,' said Daphnus. 'He was one of us.'

'And I think he cared a lot for all of you . . . Did he work out your action plan?'

Amaranta interrupted. 'Albia, we have nothing to say without a promise.' That interruption reinforced my idea that she had always been a ringleader.

These were two out of nine. I had had enough of this investigation and genuinely thought it would go nowhere else, not on the meagre evidence. I needed them to clarify things. Amaranta was bright; she knew it.

I gazed at her. She had spent a lot of time intricately plaiting her hair. Her nimble fingers would work busily, accurate even without a mirror and without help. I bet she thought things out while she did that. She created her own hairstyle. She lived for herself.

I seriously wondered about her pairing up with Daphnus. She was almost thirty; he was eighteen. Though he had told me cockily that he hankered after her, he was far too young. Love has no barriers, but I was realistic. Whatever he thought was going on here, Amaranta knew different. If she had let him believe he was in luck, it was for calculated reasons. Any bond they had forged while in refuge would last until they obtained the freedom they wanted, maybe a while longer. Eventually, she would drop him. I could even foresee that Onesimus, Mucia's steward who was still in Campania, might reappear and Amaranta would claim him.

'You two devised the details of the cover-up, admit it.' I spoke tersely.

'Is it worse for us?' asked Daphnus. 'If we admit something—'

I knew Rome. 'In this city, under our present emperor, helping a prosecution succeed is highly prized.' I did not say that under Domitian this was prized even if the proffered evidence was invented.

'Well, you do that, don't you, Albia?' Amaranta risked a sideswipe at me. 'You give information. What's the difference?'

None. That was why my profession has a very bad reputation in some quarters . . . I stared her down, showing I knew it and would not be cowed by criticism.

Daphnus kept glancing at Amaranta. He wanted to play the strong male role, but was confirming with her everything he said. She was definitely the leader. Their partnership today held interesting tensions.

Daphnus was tall, which gave him a presence, but since

I first saw him, so brash in his amulet and secondhand shoes, he had lost his lustre. It was about two weeks since the slaves sought refuge, since when they had in effect been prisoners. The layabouts, Diomedes and Amethystus in particular, were taking it well, since they were idle by nature. Daphnus was feeling restless and, I guessed, bored with captivity.

Amaranta, by contrast, kept her self-confidence. She wanted to extract terms, because if she was to live, she must act decisively, act now, and screw whatever she could out of a damning situation. She would be methodical. She would be ruthless if necessary.

Daphnus thought Amaranta would protect him too, but he might learn otherwise.

I addressed her. 'I am writing my final report. I shall write it now, this afternoon; then I shall leave here and play no further part. It is your choice. If you tell me the rest of the story, I promise I will recommend to Manlius Faustus that the two of you have immunity from prosecution, your freedom, and such other rewards as he and the Temple of Ceres see fit.'

I meant it. Faustus had given me authority to offer as much.

'Three of us,' begged Daphnus.

'Three?'

'My brother, Melander.'

I said it was good to see family loyalty. Far be it from me to separate twins in the city of Remus and Romulus; Faustus would make it a triple amnesty.

Yes, I know about Remus being murdered by his twin out of jealousy.

*　　*　　*

367

So they settled down to confess to me. Daphnus started the story, under Amaranta's watchful eye. I knew the beginning, from Cosmus invading the bedroom and exploding, through the other slaves discovering what he had done – 'Too late to stop him, which we would have tried –' then their deciding with Polycarpus that the murders of Aviola and Mucia put them all at risk.

'Did none of you ever think of handing Cosmus over?'

'Nobody blamed Myla nor Cosmus,' said Amaranta. 'None of us cared for either of them much, but we could see that Myla had been treated badly. She didn't have enough imagination to see she was in a good home and things could have been far worse. Cosmus neither. He was really lucky Polycarpus took him. Cosmus never saw it that way. He just grew up hating the fact that his father, the master, never wanted anything to do with him. He was always obsessed by that.'

'He had reached the age when he brooded,' Daphnus put in. He was young enough to remember his own puberty vividly.

'Myla was used, for years,' Amaranta said. 'Of course she was supposed to endure that sort of thing, but it doesn't mean she felt nothing. Whenever she was angry about it, she would pour out her heart to Cosmus, making him even more resentful.'

'They were very close?' I asked, thinking how Myla had tried to take the blame for Cosmus' acts, just before she committed suicide.

Amaranta nodded. 'He convinced himself he killed Aviola and Mucia in defence of his mother, to stop her being sold.'

'Right. Tell me about the robbers, please.'

Daphnus took up the tale. The fleeting visit by Roscius

and his men had given Amaranta the idea to fake a robbery. Some of what the neighbour Fauna had seen from above – people running about with lamps and whispering urgently – happened when the slaves packed up the wine set; they hid it in the chair seat, then hurried the chair out to the unused lock-up. They had to act fast, because they knew they must soon involve the vigiles.

I tried to sound neutral. 'Once you decided to use the silver to make it look like a robbery gone wrong, was it anyone's intention to keep the valuables afterwards?'

Their eyes flickered towards one another, but they both denied it. I could imagine what would have happened; if they had got away with it, escaped any accusation, then some time later – probably too soon to be wise – a cloaked figure would start visiting a pawnshop where no one ever asked too many questions, on each visit taking some new closely wrapped bundle . . . one by one, the wonderful items in the wine set would have been sold. The slaves would gain a tiny fraction of the pieces' real value. But perhaps to them it would seem more.

Daphnus had played his part in what happened next. This was the incident that had always bothered me. Daphnus had suggested how to make the fake robbery look good: they should give Nicostratus a black eye and pretend the home-invaders rushed him. Nicostratus was willing to be tied up and shut in the mop cupboard, but that was not colourful enough. He was less keen on being battered about, but Amaranta and Daphnus persuaded him.

'Who hit him?' I sounded as neutral as possible.

'The first time, I did,' Daphnus admitted. 'I admit I lacked practice, so my punch made no marks. Nicostratus had already had enough of it, though. He said to stop there and we would just have to hope a few bruises came out on him next day.'

'But?'

'Phaedrus came up behind him suddenly, carrying a plank from the well. He swung it and cracked open his head.'

'He never meant to kill him,' Amaranta put in quickly.

'Phaedrus and Nicostratus had never got on?' I checked.

'No, they were sworn enemies.' She went slightly pink.

From what Gratus had told me after Polycarpus' funeral, Phaedrus had had a liaison with Amaranta. I wondered if Nicostratus was another, or wanted to be? That would explain the quarrels between the porters – and why Phaedrus hit him so hard. If so, this pert young woman had much to answer for. She liked to look neat and demure, but she was a free-wheeling heartbreaker.

'I saw the results of the beating on Nicostratus,' I said dourly.

'Phaedrus went mad,' Daphnus told me, sounding subdued. 'He had had a drink earlier. Afterwards he blamed his German heritage. It turned him into a maniac, he said.'

I realised why Amaranta chose to dump Phaedrus. She saw him as too dangerous a partner. Amaranta would never be a woman who teamed up with a man who thrashed her, and then claimed 'he never means it and he's always sorry afterwards'. She flew straight to Daphnus.

'Did you help out?' I asked Daphnus. 'Did you hit him again?'

He shook his head. 'No, but Amethystus and Diomedes did. They were out of their skulls as well. Nicostratus didn't pass out at once, and as he buckled at the knees he yelled so loudly, they rushed to knock him cold to stop him.

Phaedrus joined in again with that plank while we were trying to stop him. What a nightmare . . .'

'How long did this nightmare go on?'

'Not long. A lot happened very quickly.'

'Phaedrus seemed to feel Nicostratus' death sincerely, when I talked to him about it.'

'He would,' Amaranta argued. 'Phaedrus was as shocked as the rest of us, when he sobered up later. He has no idea what came over him, he says. When he saw the damage he was inconsolable.'

Always sorry afterwards . . . I was angry. 'Inconsolable? He hid that well with me! Phaedrus carried out a vicious attack, in which all of you were associates. Whatever jealousy caused his feud with Nicostratus, there is no excuse for him, nor for Amethystus and Diomedes – and there's no excuse for the rest of you. Tell me, when you brought Nicostratus here with you, was that in case he regained consciousness and told tales? Were you hoping to prevail on him to keep quiet?'

'Partly. We really did think we could look after him, to make amends. But –' at this one point Amaranta showed visible pride in her ingenuity – 'we brought him in the chair, where we had hidden the silverware. So nobody would find it.'

Amaranta was a clever young woman. She had not reckoned with that cult busybody, my bugbear Laia Gratiana, tidying the unwanted chair away from her precious sanctum by despatching it back to the apartment as soon as she spied it.

So that was their story. I told the disreputable pair that even though it disgusted me, I would keep my promise about the aedile.

I could not help reflecting ruefully how these slaves had spent more energy and invention on a volatile fellow slave boy, a youth they did not even like, than on protecting their master and mistress or showing them loyalty after their deaths. Loyalty to Nicostratus had been shaky too. Relationships in the household of Aviola and Mucia, two reputedly decent newly-weds, had been corrosive. Under the surface of a happy home had raged divisions that led to fatal results.

Was it the same throughout Rome? Could somebody like Dromo one day turn on Faustus? I thought not. But Valerius Aviola and Mucia Lucilia probably believed they too were safe.

58

The end of an inquiry was often depressing for me. I tended to uncover spite, sexual betrayal, dishonesty or greed; this case had all of them.

Today my heart felt particularly heavy. I wrote my report for the aedile. It came easily, as written work does if you have been thinking about it for a long time. I kept my statement short and factual. I lacked energy for more. Besides, he might not be the only person reading it. Ultimately, this was aimed at the administrators of the Temple of Ceres.

I signed off formally, then found wax and sealed the report. I hoped Faustus recognised my seal: a worn old coin on a finger ring that showed a British tribal king in unkempt dreadlocks who looked as if someone had just told him a rather dirty joke. The wax was such high quality I was tempted to liberate some to take home. I thought better of it. After all I had lived through in a difficult life, it would be senseless to be caught removing stationery from an aedile's office. Besides, if I sent sealed reports to Faustus, he might recognise it.

I wanted to say that if he needed to discuss details we could meet and talk. Better not. He was a magistrate. I was an informer he had favoured with work. That was all. I had done as he asked and he would pay me. Knowing him, he would send the fee without a reminder.

I knew in advance what would happen to those slaves. The temple would accept the legal judgement produced by the Camilli; the authorities would withdraw the right of asylum with no public comment, as if no one had ever believed such a right existed. Amaranta, Daphnus and Melander, discreetly reprieved, would vanish into society. It would not surprise me if in the end Melander did best, since he was quiet and had no expectations. Daphnus and Amaranta thought a lot of themselves but, together or apart, I could see them coming to bad ends.

The other slaves would be dealt with according to their crimes. I was sure Titianus would capture the boy Cosmus, because not even Titianus was a total incompetent. Cosmus, a slave who had murdered, would be executed. The boy was going to the beasts in the arena, his final unhappiness.

Amethystus and Diomedes, those sturdy toughs who had helped set upon Nicostratus, might be sent to the mines as punishment. Phaedrus, the tall good-looking blond, might well find himself gladiating, where he would probably become a heartthrob. With his aggression, he could even survive enough fights to be freed. He had murdered a slave, but who cared about that? Only the slave's master, and he was dead as well. I had few hopes for the philosopher; philosophers were seen as dangerous subversives in Rome. If Chrysodorus was wise, he would will himself into dying – maybe starve himself to death – before the physical cruelty he dreaded could be imposed on him. Libycus? Of them all, I suspected Libycus might escape. Friends like Myrinus and Secundus would help and hide him. He could disappear among the foreigners in the Transtiberina, maybe find his way back to Africa. Or he had skills. He could find a new master, if he went about it right; offer himself to an old centurion, someone fastidious about his person but who didn't care a toss about a servant's past background.

I yearned to believe they would spare Olympe, who only wanted to be happy and play music. But a fifteen-year-old virgin offered too much sport for amphitheatre crowds. And she was pretty. Olympe, who had probably had no real idea what that night at the apartment was all about, stood no chance now.

As for me, when my client failed to show that afternoon, I left.

I could not bear the thought of carrying my luggage. Dromo had gone home, but I asked to have the bundle taken to Fountain Court tomorrow. I seemed to have no strength.

Leaving, I could hardly drag my weary feet along the pavement. I had rarely felt so drained of spirit and energy. Everything seemed to have changed from when I came back from the Esquiline and felt so much at home. People knocked into me, then muttered curses with unnecessary hostility. The Vicus Loretti Minor and Vicus Armilustrium, my streets, were full of hard faces.

When I finally reached the end of our alley and could see my building, I stood still and thought I would never walk any further. What was wrong with me? A case never normally whacked all the vim out of me like this. I had solved it. My client would be pleased with me and happy for his own prospects, because the Temple of Ceres would be pleased with him. I had not left a message saying, see you for breakfast some time – because I knew if I went to the Stargazer tomorrow, Manlius Faustus would happen along. He ate breakfast, and like any good city man he often went out for it.

Suddenly I was very anxious. Fountain Court loomed

ahead, a dismal enough prospect, yet it was my home. I had often cursed the ghastly place, but coming back to the Eagle Building rarely made me feel so groggy, lonely and upset. I forced myself to move, reaching the dank entrance where the porter, Rodan, ought to be snoozing on a stool. He was missing.

There was a climb to my apartment on the second floor. Two flights of steep stone steps among the odours of piss and old meatballs that characterised our tenement daunted me completely.

I had another room, slightly closer. I was the landlord's daughter, so I could live anywhere I wanted here, rent free. On the first floor, at the end of the Mythembal apartment, I kept a bolthole nobody knew about. In my line of work this was useful because it provided a secret access to my real apartment.

My head was splitting as I struggled one floor up. Something odd was happening to me. Mythembal's wife, the dark-skinned woman with several multi-coloured children, was out for once. She would not know I had come home.

It was lucky that she lived in an apartment without sanitation and had those small children, because among her meagre possessions she owned a robust chamberpot. I grabbed it from the corridor as I staggered through the dismal series of rooms she occupied; I fell into my own place. The heavy door closed behind me of its own accord.

Barely was I in my room when, without warning, I disgraced myself with an uncontrollable eruption from every part of me that could erupt.

After that I was helpless. I would not have thought the human body could be so wrung out. After several painful episodes, I managed to strip off my tunic. Then I lay on the floor, curled up and occasionally crying, naked and despairing, lost.

I had a big old couch here, but I could not reach it. There was a door to a walkway over the courtyard, where I could have called for help, but getting there was impossible.

In a moment of lucidity, I knew what caused this. The well. The well with the poisoned water. I had not been so stupid as to drink from it, but I did splash that water all over my hot face; I had drunk from a silver goblet that had been *in* the well water, not washing the cup, as far as I could remember. No, not washing it, because yesterday the apartment had run out of clean water.

For almost a couple of decades, the disease that lurked in the well had been waiting for another victim. Maybe there was unhealthy leakage, a hidden cracked sewer seeping into the groundwater. Then I came along. *The family who were here before all died of dysentery. About five of them . . .*

I was in no doubt what was happening now. I had that and I was dying too.

This was the penalty for owning no slaves. What an irony.

Nobody knew that I was here. Nobody would miss me. I had caught a catastrophic, virulent infection. Alone and unable to move, even to summon help, there was no hope. I was glad in one way. Lying in this soiled room, soiled myself and disgusted, I would hate anyone I knew to see me. There was absolutely nothing that I could do about it. I would end up as one of the inhabitants of this sour building who died unnoticed, only to be found weeks later, reeking, putrefactious or mummified.

★   ★   ★

I lay there all evening and overnight. Throughout that time, I kept being ill. I reached the most dangerous condition; I knew my internal organs were so wrenched with disease they were bleeding.

At times I could hear muffled noises from the Mythembals, but the door to my room was deliberately heavy. They never came in here. That was our bargain; I arranged for her to live almost rent-free; in return, this room at the end of the corridor stayed shut, was mine, was never even acknowledged as existing. We were on pleasant terms if we happened to meet but she spoke little Latin, even though she had been in Rome for years, and I had no Punic. Mythembal was hypothetical; he may have died or gone back overseas. I never saw her entertain other men, but from time to time she would produce another baby, each one different from its siblings.

Either she had not missed her chamberpot or she thought thieves had walked in and stolen it.

I was growing worse. It would not be long now. I had passed through raging fever and violent shivering chills. Racked with spasms and dehydrated, my whole inside was one great ache. I drifted in and out of consciousness, simply waiting for the end.

After a long period of relative quiet, that I took to be night time, I sensed a new day starting. I knew I could not last another. This would be the day when I would die.

Time passed.

More time passed.

There were intermittent sounds sometimes. I thought I heard a man's voice in the Mythembal apartment. I even dreamed I heard heavy footsteps, in a hurry, someone

378

upstairs in my own rooms. An intruder? Once I would have gone up there with a weapon; now I could not and did not even care.

I was slipping away. Although I was a fighter, there was no more I could do here.

And then I heard the door to this room being thrust open.

I let out a sob of intense relief. Of all those it could have been, this was Tiberius. As I looked up at him, somehow his arrival was no surprise.

'Help me.'

The grey-eyed man was already crouching down to me. Oddly, what he said was, 'It's all right. I am here now.'

59

Give that man every honour: I never saw him flinch.
Nobody would want the tasks Tiberius undertook for me. There was probably no one else on earth I would have trusted. He did whatever had to be done. He made no fuss. He worked fast. Called the Mythembal woman to bring him warm water, which luckily she always had. He could have asked her to help, but I know he did not. She stayed outside the door.

'I'm dying, aedile.'

'We'll see. Hold on, hold on for me.'

He stood me up. Cleaned me down. Used the sponge as gently as he could, but thoroughly, absolutely everywhere.

When that was done, he walked me to the reading couch. That was just somewhere to prop me while he stripped off his own tunic. The undertunic came off as well, so for one strange moment we were both stark naked. I knew why, when he dropped the second garment over me; it was much softer material and warm from his body. I was shaking with cold and my skin could hardly bear touching. Any time nowadays that I want to define bliss, I call up that moment, being enveloped in softness, in comfort, in human warmth.

From him, I simply accepted everything. He lifted me over his shoulder, then carried me bodily upstairs to my own apartment. He had never been there with me. Rodan must have shown him today, and opened the door for him. Faustus must have come looking for me when I never appeared at the Stargazer. Who knows how he realised that I must be in trouble?

He put me to bed. Kept me warm. Rehydrated me. Watched all afternoon and all night. I grew worse after dark; for hours I was delirious, soothed only when he cooled me with wet cloths. He slept in a chair by lamplight, when he felt he could risk sleep. The next day while I was sleeping myself, he went down and cleaned the room or arranged for it to be done; maybe he gave Mythembal's wife money. He somehow acquired broth and when I woke, warmed it and spooned it into me. When I was sick again, he cleaned up uncomplainingly.

I told him to leave, to go to his own life. He stayed, as I still hovered between life and death. He dragged, cajoled me, enticed me back to life.

He must have had help. People provided things. A cook with a delicate touch made those broths that appeared each day. Laundry came and went. I thought I heard Rodan's voice, and Dromo's, at the front door. They never crossed the threshold. No one was admitted to my rooms. That was a subtle respect for the privacy that Tiberius knew I guarded closely.

At length I was stable; I saw him relax.

Still he looked after me himself.

'Why?' I asked.

'Friendship.'

Now he was like a visitor, a helpful, easygoing one. He read in silence to himself. He read aloud to me. He hummed around, tidying the place. He washed up. When he was utterly exhausted, he slept on a couch out in my day room.

We never spoke about the case. He had my report. Even though I was sickening when I wrote it, I knew I had done a good job there.

Eventually, although I had told him not to, he wrote to my family to tell them what had happened. I had said, wait until either I am better or I die; do not put them through this anxiety. Faustus had never met my family, but he knew who they were and how close we were to each other. He sent the letter to Quintus Camillus for urgent forwarding, then when it was too late for me to make him recall it, he told me what he had done.

I was not surprised, therefore, when only a day later my mother came to the apartment.

Faustus was reading when she let herself in. I saw him look up as he heard someone enter. I had recognised her footfall so I did not need to look. I kept looking at him.

'You must be Manlius Faustus!' Helena Justina's familiar voice dryly accosted this unknown man in her daughter's bedroom. Even though his occupation (reading aloud a scroll about how to win elections) was not typical of men in women's bedrooms, as a mother she went straight on the offensive: 'A friend of my daughter's – though for some reason none of us have met you . . . Are you lovers?'

'Not yet.' Tiberius answered without a flicker. Then he looked up with a sudden broad smile. 'I'm saving her for best.'

As I covered my face with the bedsheet, I believe it was the first time I ever knew my mother lost for words.

After that, Tiberius seemed to allow that my mother still thought she owned me. She intended to collect me and nurse me herself. I was twenty-nine years old, widowed, working, independent – but when I was in trouble, my family expected me to go home. A woman of tact, Helena Justina avoided saying to Faustus, 'so she can be looked after properly'.

He must know what she thought. Although his own died twenty years ago, I had to hope he knew the ways of mothers.

He might do. I had learned a little about his mother now. Once, during his care of me, I had asked how he became so competent. He said he had a younger sister; his mother had taught him to help bath the baby. This was so he would not be afraid of children if he ever had any – and he would not be shy with girls.

We smiled together over that. Nobody, on either side, who shared what Tiberius Manlius did for me that week could be called shy.

My mother started to pack things for me, calling in bearers who had brought a chair to take me to our town house. Before I knew it, they were lifting me in and arranging rugs. Faustus retreated to the other room. Of course when he informed my people, he must have known someone would come. They would have assumed he wanted to be relieved of the burden. I ought to think so too, though I had doubts.

Our strange interlude was over. We had been so close it was a painful wrench to leave him. I found myself highly emotional, perhaps because I was still so weak. I had come to rely on his daily presence. I would now be among my own people for as long as they could persuade me, probably even be driven to the coast when I was strong enough, for more sun, sand and fishing expeditions, or at least sun, sand and lying on a rug in the dappled shade of the pine trees. Tiberius would be in Rome, leading his own life.

The inquiry I carried out for him already seemed long past. We would work together again, but socially and professionally there were limits.

As we left the apartment my mother thanked Faustus, apologising as if he had been imposed on. Brushing that aside, he asked to be kept informed of my progress, though it sounded a formality. Attendants carried the chair down to Fountain Court, where they waited for Helena while she talked to Rodan. It was always good to witness a hoary ex-gladiator being reduced to slush by a sweet but stern woman. Manlius Faustus also watched with amusement, as he stood with his thumbs hooked into his belt on what passed for a pavement.

Helena had already sized him up. Later, I was to hear her tell my father that Manlius Faustus looked like a man you could ask to take charge of your wood cart as a quick favour, then when you came back, he would have unloaded all the logs for you and stacked them neatly.

In the depths of the chair, I dwelt on what had just happened between us. The Aviola case had given me a portrait of life with many slaves. In such households, the owners are never alone. Their slaves carry out the most intimate tasks for them – physical, financial, sexual. Slaves make excuses for them and form a protective barrier. In one way they ensure privacy, yet their constant presence everywhere means their owners have no privacy at all.

Those few days that I spent being cared for by Tiberius were absolutely private. He could easily have brought in slaves to help him, but I know he never considered it. I would tell no one, not even my mother, the details of how he nursed me; in future, he and I might not even acknowledge it between ourselves. It had been the most intimate intervention, one I would not have tolerated from anybody else. I accepted it from him because of this: Tiberius did everything, not because he was obliged to look after me as a slave would be, but because he wanted to.

Once my mother was ready, he came closer and said goodbye to me. Being so ill made me stupidly tearful. I was unable to speak.

As the chair lurched when the bearers lifted it, I looked back through the window curtains. He was still standing in the roadway. Seeing me looking, he made a sudden gesture of redundancy, sharing my regret. He would not come to our house, though he might send Dromo with enquiries. I could write; he liked my letters. I would lure him into answering.

I realised that, oddly, Tiberius had enjoyed looking after me. I even thought that as I was taken away, he watched me go a little sadly.